CURRENCY

an imprint of Dzanc Books
3629 N. Hoyne
Chicago, IL 60618
www.ovbooks.com
OVBooks@gmail.com

Published 2010 by Other Voices Books, an imprint of Dzanc Books.

Cover design: Melissa C. Lucar,
Fisheye Graphic Services, Inc.
Interior design: Steven Seighman
Cover images: © Lisa Meehan Williams

06 07 08 09 10 11 5 4 3 2 1
First Edition April 2010

ISBN-13: 978-0-9825204-3-7

Printed in the United States of America

CURRENCY

zoe zolbrod

To Bill —
Best of luck
for your own
writing,

Zoe Z[...]

OV
BOOKS

MORGANSTREET
INTERNATIONAL
NOVEL SERIES

To my mother and father, who let me go

And to Mark, Tillio, and Lilli, who are my home

Chapter 1

Part of my job is to read your face, and I think I know what your face says now. You are wondering something about me. Do I guess right? You wonder if I am like all Thai people. You wonder what bad things happen in my life. You wonder if I sell heroin, smoke opium—what it's like to be me. And you wonder what I think about you, right? Sure. There's no movie theater here. One video plays, but I think you see that one already, maybe in Bangkok, maybe in Chiang Mai, maybe in your home. That one plays everywhere. It's making you feel bored. You have time to imagine. So please. Stay. I will tell you, no problem. Opium? Heroin? I'm sorry, no. But I can tell you about the bad thing. Something about danger. Something about love. That's what you want, right? Okay. If you stay, I can tell you some story about me.

When I am small, I'm living in Kanchanaburi Province. My father is not the farmer anymore; he has one position in sugar factory there. Farangs always come to that place. They make American movie about that one, *Bridge Over River Kwai*. That's the reason why farang tourists come. Also, we have Allied War Cemetery and Erawan waterfall that tourists like to see. My family's not poor at this time, and we can go somewhere. When we go somewhere special to us—Erawan, Wat Tham Mongkorn Thong—farangs are always there. They go all over, even the poor ones, stinking, carrying their bags around, one strapped to their back, one strapped to their front. Even the girls do this. Of course, when I'm small in Kanchanaburi I already know about Bruce Willis, about rock music. Of course, somewhere in my mind I know that the poor farangs I see are not truly poor. They're like electric guitars. Tough. Cool. So I'm always interested in farangs. I want to go somewhere. I want to go somewhere special to them, too.

All Thai boys must serve as monk for some time, maybe three months, that's the traditional time, and all Thai men must go to military for two years, exactly that. When I'm twenty years old, I serve as monk for one week. When I'm twenty-one, I go to military. I'm stationed in the jungle near Cambodia. It's not good time for me. Okay. So I forget that. My father wants for me to go to university, to make one good life, bring pride to our family, so my parents struggle too many years to get money for me. Kanchanaburi has no university, so after military I go to Bangkok, to Ramkhamhaeng University, very good one, to study for business.

The first day I live in Bangkok, before university is starting, I go to Banglamphu area to find Khao San Road. That's where farangs go. That's what I want to see. When I'm twenty-three years old, 1992, wow, I love it. This street crowded with tourists. Many, many guesthouses, restaurants, rasta bar. Now it's even more like that. Now it's Soi Ram Buttri, Tanoa Road, and Ram Buttri Road also. I love to see all these farangs. Young, like me, then. Some girls loose under their shirts. Some blond hair. Hairy arms. Stinking. Ugly beautiful, you know. Ugly sexy. Some of these girls are bigger than me. Big there, too. I hate it, but I like it. Maybe I love it—it tickles my brain. At that time I still have short hair. I dress like Thai. Some trousers, black shoes. One button shirt.

I notice on this street, full with farangs—they wear short pants, colored hats, clothes too tight or too loose; people in my village think that looks rude—on this street almost all Thai people sell to farangs. They set up stalls to sell cassette tapes, books, ugly clothing, things like that. And farangs buy. Buy buy. One girl tries on jeans right in the street. It's one small street! Very many stalls! People—tourists and Thai people—bump into this girl while she tries on. You can hear loud dance music from cassette tape seller. Wow. She buys these jeans. I have never seen anything like that.

So I look. I see one Thai, young guy, with big clothes and hoop earring and long hair. He's selling jewelry. Farang girls stand around him; he talks to them in English. I see those girls laugh. I see them buy. When they leave, I talk to him, and after some time I can ask him: What is this thing? How you do this? And he tells me that he got this jewelry in Indonesia. He travels there, brings it back to Bangkok, and sells it for triple, more, the amount he pays. He tells me this is what the farangs like, and he shows me his silver: some dangling earrings, some jumbled bracelets. At that time, I do not think silver is beautiful. In Thailand, we love gold. Everyone wants gold. But this guy, his name is Chitapon, he says to me: These farang buy from me here, then I get enough money to make studio recording with my band and still go again to Indonesia. Very cheap there. Many things there to buy, to sell, to see.

My study of business at Ramkhamhaeng University, some things about it interest me, but I also study English. This is more interesting, and almost every day I go to Khao San to practice speaking. I go to sit in guesthouse restaurant. Maybe I go to Hello Guest House. Big one. Fifty rooms. They play American movie all the time. It's good one for practicing English, not so good for sleeping. Those rooms smell. Very dirty. Dirty sheets. Hello Guest House 57. When I'm there, I order hot coffee. Thai people don't like that, but now I love my hot coffee. Thai people don't like to be alone in restaurant, but now I am, to help my goal. I want to meet some farang friends, and this is no problem. "Excuse me!" I smile at them. "I'm one Thai student. You have some moment to talk with me? I like to learn about your country, speaking English." Sometimes I listen to them talk to each other. If I can help them, I interrupt. I say, "Excuse me. I can tell you how to get to Weekend Market. I can tell you what bus goes to Patpong. You need to take bus number 15 to get to that one." I'm dressing more like one farang, now. I wear Levi's jeans, Bob Marley T-shirt. I wear silver jewelry that Chitapon loans to me: silver bracelet, silver ring. If some farang friend gives me compliment on these, I say, "You like this one, I show you where to get." If Chit makes good sale from that person, he'll give me something. Sure. Because I study, soon I'm speaking English better than him.

Farang girls like to talk to me. Some do. I learn which ones. Not ones who look like Kim Bassinger, but pretty, of course. I could not be with the girl who's not pretty. "Excuse me, miss," I say to the certain kind. I look better than those farangs.

With English language and with my hair grown down, it's easy for me to make something with the farang girl. But I don't want to sleep in Khao San guesthouse like they do. Hello Guest House, Gypsy Guest House, none of them are clean. They have thin walls, like this, you can hear everyone. Wow. And my own clean bed, no, I won't take the girl there. If farang girl want to make something with me, maybe she can rent one nice hotel. Star Hotel is my favorite one. On Larn Luang Road, not Banglamphu. For seven hundred baht you can get clean room with air-con and hot shower.

When I have been in Bangkok two years, money is gone for me to study at Ramkhamhaeng University. I don't tell my parents, because Khao San is free, and I can learn something for my future there—how to make business, how to make something international. At the same time, I can earn some small money for living, to send to my parents. Sure. Why do I need Ramkhamhaeng? Some shop, restaurant, tailor, ganja seller, guesthouse owners know me. At Star Hotel, they know me. They know I'm like one farang, that I have many farang friends. They give me money if I tell my friend, go here, go there, it's good one. They give me one hundred baht, one fifty, maybe more. I don't tell farang to go somewhere bad, so it's good for them, good for me, too. I don't tell my parents their plan for me is happening different than they dream. Good for everybody.

Star Hotel has one lounge—not like guesthouse restaurant, this is nice one, for relaxing. I relax there at nighttime when I'm with one farang friend. I order drinks. She gives me money to pay. Daytime, we don't go in lounge, but maybe we sit in the lobby. I sit in the soft chair, watch the TV, watch the people come in. Some farangs come, sometimes one whole group, but mostly it's Thai people doing business and some African men in the Star Hotel. The Africans have black skin, and I have never talked to anyone like this. In the beginning, I have the stereotype. I think they're athletes, from America or somewhere like that. I think they're some boxers or some basketball players. They're very tall next to Thai people. Big shoulders, big hands. Especially one of these men, the most tall. First time I see him, this big one, I feel fear. He's strong. He's one boxer, not from this country; what if he gets angry? But over many months I take farang guests to Star Hotel, and these men become my friends.

"How's it going, man?" they say to me. "I see you have a new lady friend." They say this softly while my friend is at that entrance desk, copying numbers from her passport. Now I know they are not athletes. They are three businessmen from Africa. One day they walk into lobby wearing the clothing of their country—material hanging down, bright colors. The big man smiles when he sees me. He says, "We're meeting with some new Russians tonight. Do you think they will respond best to this African ensemble or to the clothing of a transnational businessman?"

It's hard to look at my friend's face, because his clothes have too many colors. I smile. "I don't know any Russian people."

"But you know how to dress! You present yourself as the real Thai, and the ladies come to you."

"Excuse me, sir, but in the countryside, along the Burma border, or in the Northeast, maybe some man there will wear the phaakhamaa. That's possible. But me, no. You never see me like that." I smile again.

"But the white ladies think you have the Thai style. That's the important ingredient."

Now I can laugh with this African friend. His name: Abu. "Oh! Excuse me, sir! I didn't know you were asking about the Russian lady."

We laugh together at this joke. The person they meet is Russian man, and they wear their business suits when that time comes.

Sometimes, one farang friend must leave Star Hotel to go back to Switzerland, or Australia, or America, but she still has too much baht left. Maybe she'll give this to me, or maybe she'll pay for me to stay in the Star Hotel one night or two more. Or if Star Hotel is not crowded, maybe the manager, Saisamorn, will allow me to stay for free until I bring another guest there. Why should I rent one room anymore? If I need somewhere to sleep, I can go to Chitapon's room, but most nights I sleep at the Star Hotel. Slowly, I know these African men better—Abu, Yoke, Jomo. I want to know these men, because I think they do international business.

I sit with them in hotel bar when they drink Johnnie Walker Red. I order one Coke from Resit, bartender, but they say, "Come on, man." They put one hand on my back, and they give me one glass, some ice, some Johnnie Walker Red, and I say thank you, not bad, even though to me it's too strong. They ask me about Thai girl, farang lady friend: what are they like, do they have money, do they need money. They ask me how long do they stay before going back to their country. I say two weeks is the shortest before they go back. Two months, sometimes. Sometimes more. I tell them my friend Chitapon has the farang girlfriend who lives in Thailand. Her mother is married to General Sivara, and they have big house in Ladprao suburb. Abu likes to hear this. He lifts his whiskey to my eyes. "To those unions that bring together people of different nationalities," he says. We all touch our glasses.

Then I ask my friends about Kenya, their country. I want to know what's the language there. What's the business there. What's the tourist attraction. I learn that Kenya's language is Swahili, but these men also speak English from the time they are small. They tell me their country is poor, but it has riches.

"They say one lion brings in seven thousand tourist dollars a year," Abu tells me. "So it stands to reason that if that lion is going out, its cost increases greatly. It's worth a great deal." These men, my friends, come to Thailand, Singapore, Malaysia to do business something about that.

One time these friends tell me they want some ganja. I get them ganja, sure, no problem. Abu, whose skin is shiny, hard and bright, not soft like Bob Marley's skin, says, "Thank you, Piv. You're a good man. Are you with a lady friend, tonight? Tell Mr. Saisamorn to get you a room tonight, on our bill." He takes out one thick fold of money and gives me one five hundred baht bill, another five hundred baht bill. These are purple and sharp.

"No," I tell Abu. I push one bill back. "You are my friend. I take only what the ganja costs. I take cost only because at this time I do not have it myself."

"Take it," he says. He looks over his shoulder. The hotel bar is dark, the window facing the street is colored green, the lights outside look like they're underneath deep river water. "Take it. From a friend. Maybe someday we'll do some business. Maybe one of your lady friends, from Australia or from America, could help us with some business."

I feel disappointed when he says this, because this is not what I want to learn. I tell him I'm not in the woman business; farang girls are my friend. It's not my business to sell ganja; I get him one small portion because he's my friend.

"I know, friend. We do not sell drugs, either. We do not sell women. We're businessmen." Next day Abu, Yoke, and Jomo leave Thailand, but Abu tells me he's sure we'll see each other again at the Star Hotel. Way he says that, I look forward to that time.

That's how I meet some Kenya friends and think to do business with them. But when I meet NokRobin in 1996, I don't think of Abu. No. I see her for herself, sure. I'll tell you about me—but with the bad parts, the romantic and dangerous parts, it's also the story of her.

Chapter 2

Robin needed cash. With a gesture long grown familiar, she slid her credit card under the currency exchange's slotted window. In Italy, in Greece, in Turkey, Nepal, on Khao San Road two times previous, she'd done the same. Scooted the card, waited—heart tense but limbs languorous—while machines whirred and printers clicked, then signed thin pink or yellow papers with a heady rush—debt be damned!—and pocketed the currency. But now a clerk with an undershirt showing through his thin oxford was handing the plastic back to her without a slip to sign, without a stack of crisp baht. He murmured something—it took a moment for her to register what: "transaction denied"—then looked beyond her, beyond the street's morning bustle, up to the shuttered balcony doors of the once-white building across the way.

"Wait!" Robin broke into a sweat. She pushed the card back at him, the inside of her arm slippery against her ribcage. "What do you mean denied? Please. Try again."

While he did, she jerked up her T-shirt, unzipped her money belt. She had a platinum Citibank in among her passport and some folded bills, and she plucked it out and shoved it through the slot. "I must have given you the wrong one. Here." Her voice rose. She heard it as if outside herself. Heard the twang creep into the last three words and hated it. She tried to straighten her cadence, tried to be polite. It was probably just a problem with the Capital One's magnetic strip. "Sorry. Take this one. Please. This one will work."

It had better. It will. But what if it doesn't? Robin drew herself up so close to the counter that the Formica pressed into her ribcage, and her bare toes nudged the gummy treat wrappers that had banked along the building's facade. Her few bills added up to eight hundred baht, about twenty U.S. dollars. She had nothing else: no traveler's checks, no airplane ticket. How long could she get by? Her stomach lurched and growled. At least seventy baht a day for food and water. For the guesthouse, about a hundred or so baht daily, plus what she already owed for the last two nights in her shared room. Her mind went blank, couldn't do the math. Citibank Platinum. It'd better work.

But it didn't. The clerk handed it back, then looked over her shoulder again—not up to the balcony but at the person next in line. A man with dishwater blond dreadlocks stepped to the counter, forcing her aside. Humiliation snaked through her panic, and she stepped out of the queue, stumbling. She put up her hand to catch herself, and her palm's sand-and-sun-toughened calluses snagged on the scratchy corner of the Exchange's wall. She couldn't call home. Even if someone there could come up with enough money, it'd only be to buy her a ticket back. And not yet. She wasn't meant to leave here yet. A tuk tuk screamed by, unfurling a thin black tail of diesel fumes. She saw the gas spread, thin out, and move closer. She was falling with only one place to land: Citibank Platinum. Capital One Gold.

She had to call the banks. They'd tell her what had happened, how to get the credit to work. They'd done that for her before—during college, in the years right after. It was a computer glitch. Or they just needed to extend her credit limit. She was pretty sure that was something they could do immediately, over the phone. They must.

She jammed the cards into her money belt but didn't stop to zip it before taking off at a jog-trot between vendors who were hanging bags of chopped pineapple, stacking sandals into pyramids, spreading jewelry over velvet in anticipation of another working day. Remaining in Thailand was imperative. That much was clear to her. She kept her hand pressed over her open belt as if to hold her guts in. By the time she reached the international phones on the second floor of the post office, she was breathing hard.

Two hours later, Robin was sitting on a low curb outside the P.O., her head level with the knees of pedestrians who stepped off the sidewalk and onto the street to avoid her. When a pair of eyes dropped into her line of vision, she flinched, surprised.

"Robin? What are you doing down here?" It was Zella, her roommate, with frizzed ringlets forming a triangle frame around her little nut of a face. The smattering of gray hairs along her part flew up higher than the chestnut rest.

"Resting, I guess." Robin smiled crookedly. I owe her for the room, she thought. At least two or three hundred baht. That leaves me only five hundred.

"Come on. You can't sit here. Let's get you something to eat."

Zella bustled Robin down the street, deposited her in a chair, got up to place their order. The kindness was soothing. Even the fact that they were eating in the Hello Guest House restaurant, where Robin could get comfort food like a banana milkshake and toast, spoke to Zella's solicitude. Robin knew she preferred cozier places with interesting decor or local haunts that didn't pander to Western tastes, that she liked to escape the backpacker throng. And there was no other way to describe the patrons who sat within the three grubby yellow walls here. They all wore more or less faded flaps of colored cotton. Their floppy day packs hung from the backs of chairs, and Lonely Planet guide books and plates of half-eaten pancakes dotted the tables. Everyone's age seemed all wrong. The limbs of men poked out of boys who otherwise looked so young that they gave the place a freshman dorm feel, their pink ankles and wrists like puttied elastic, while impish patchwork caps sat atop faces creased into middle age by years of sun and drugs. This is where I want to stay? Robin thought, seeing the place through Zella's eyes. But even as she tried to scoff, she knew that the tourist flim-flam was a harbinger of better, deeper, richer things.

Zella herself was well out of her twenties, perhaps out of her thirties, but she wore it magnificently. She dressed neither like a hippie kid nor a sightseer on a two-week holiday. Her black Italian sandals were both hearty and elegant. Her thick rings sparkled with well-set chunks of ruby, amber, tourmaline—not stuff you could pick up on any street corner. She was an old Thailand hand, could even speak a little Thai, but she wasn't here for the drugs. She was a buyer for design teams back in the States, picking up unusual jewelry and old silk tapestries from all over Asia. These would be cut and pieced on clothing photographed for the editorial pages of thick fashion glossies, or they would be tacked onto idea boards in design studios to inspire mass-produced knockoffs. Robin had admired Zella as soon as she'd glimpsed her on the beach at Ko Tao. She'd been flattered when Zella struck up conversation on the ferry back to the mainland—couldn't believe she was American and not Dutch or Belgian, couldn't believe she invited Robin to share a room when they got to Bangkok. But to the extent that Zella's attention had gratified her, Robin was ashamed now. She didn't want to admit that she'd been living on credit—not to someone who actually got paid to travel, who had a life. The answer to "What's wrong?" had to be pried out of her.

"I forgot to make minimum payments on both my cards for two months. Have you ever heard anything so stupid?" She pulled the sand-colored tip of her braid over her shoulder and twirled it around her finger.

"A nice clean little credit card snafu?" Zella looked up from the ginger root she was peeling with a bone-handled knife. She smiled. "That's nothing. As long as you're legal, someone can always help you out, right on up to the American embassy."

"I know, but . . ." Her crisis was mundane. Robin's nose dropped toward her milkshake. She felt Zella waiting for more. And not only Zella. She felt Bangkok, the canals and alleys beyond Khao San Road. She felt the great bulk of the countryside north of this city, solid and substantial compared to the thin beachy strip of it she'd spent time on thus far. If she'd known she'd have to leave, she would have forgone the beaches, started instead with Ayuthaya and Sukhothai, the old capitals. "I definitely need it, but I don't want help if it means going home."

"Hey, when I was younger than you are I found myself in Varanasi with fifteen dollars to my name. And they weren't handing out credit cards to kids back then, okay? But it was another year plus before I turned up in the States." Zella snorted. She quit peeling ginger and rested her hands on top of the root and the knife. Her shell pink nails were clean, rounded into Thai points by a local manicurist. "Now *that* was stupid," Zella finally said. She laughed. "But here I am. Lived to tell."

"Tell what?"

She gave a fluttery shake of her head. "Your cards will be reactivated once you make your payments, right? Then you're on your way."

"I have eight hundred baht. Not enough to send a payment to even one card."

"You really want to stay?"

Robin nodded.

"Tell me why. A hundred words or less."

"Well, this might sound . . ."

"You're going to waste words like that?"

Robin paused. At the front of the restaurant, up toward the lattice that topped the cinder block wall, sun hit the business's spirit house. The purple tips of fresh orchids glowed. Blunt pink joss sticks rose from a sand-filled porcelain cup and formed a bouquet, their burned ends like velvet stamens. The scene was picturesque. Quintessential. But the gloss of a tangerine was what made the assemblage perfect. Robin's lungs filled. The orange contrasting with the violet, complementing the fuchsia, and all for a purpose that was by definition spiritual—that was the key. How to explain this without sounding stupid to someone whose job was beauty, who had a real reason for being here?

"When I started traveling half a year ago I was mostly running away from what my life was like at home. But since I've been in Thailand, being gone feels like something positive. Maybe there's something for me here. A career path, a life . . ."

"Okay. Stop." Zella held up her hand. "Let's spare ourselves. You won the essay contest."

The interruption smarted. Robin made her voice flat. "What's the prize? A new Visa?"

Zella ran her finger along the blade of her knife, wiped the ginger pulp onto the edge of her mug. "You win a fairy godmother."

Robin's breath caught. The sting of the insult dissolved. "You'd loan me?" she said. "But you're going to India day after tomorrow." She continued on in a rush. "I'll FedEx you the money. The minute my cards are activated. Just tell me where."

"Slow down. You'd mean to, I'm sure, but let's face it, you're coming into this with a pretty bad track record." Robin reddened. Zella nudged her elbow. "Hey," she said, "no big deal. Why do I do this work if I'm tied to a schedule? I'll change my ticket; we'll hang out in Bangkok until you're sorted; you'll pay me back. Then you go your way, and I'll go mine. How's that?"

Robin smiled with every part of her face. She wanted to tell Zella that she loved her, that she was beautiful, that she was an inspiration—that having a life like hers, that even being helped by someone who had a life like hers . . . she saw doors open, one after another. She'd been standing in front of them for years, waiting, and now all was revealed:

jewel-toned glows reflecting in the marble corridor of her mind; silvery leaves the size of thumbprints rustling overhead; long-tailed birds darting and swooping.

"I've always needed a fairy godmother," she said. She couldn't mean it more sincerely.

Zella gave her a wink. "They say you can find anything on Khao San Road."

Robin smiled until her mouth froze into position. Until it hurt.

Chapter 3

Old Sukhothai has many wats—very old ones, maybe seven hundred years old, something like that—built by the first kings of Thailand. When they build those—wat, chedi, big Buddha, monastery—they cover them with gold color. Today, you see gray brick and stone. Maybe you see some green moss. The burned wax at big Buddha's feet is the only gold color. When I go there, I buy one candle and light some incense and pray at the foot of big Buddha. Then I visit another wat, Wat Trapang Thong, but I don't go inside. I sit near the pool surrounding it. Many lotus grow there. Small insects fly above the flowers, and they fly around my ears. I have one American book with me, *Through a Dark Mirror*, to practice my English, and I read that book while I wait. Something tells me—I'm not superstitious, but something tells me—what I look for will come to me here.

She comes alone. Alone, she pushes her bike up the path to this wat. She's one farang girl, pretty one, sure, I can tell that already. She's not too big, like some farang women. She's narrow, not too wide, and she has light hair. Her bike knocks her ankles—ouch!—but for her it's no problem, she doesn't notice. She looks around, one way at the lotus in the pool, another way at the chedi against the green hills, and she likes to see this; her face gets soft. She carries one small striped backpack on her shoulder, and the bag is heavy, big on her side. I smile at her, one very nice smile, I know. I hold my book open. "*Sa-wat-dee krup*," I say. "*Schwaba dee-ka*," she says. She tries to speak Thai. She holds her bicycle. I think she wonders: Should she lock her bicycle? Will I steal her bicycle or will I guard that one? Her sandals are ugly, with too many straps. She wears silver jewelry made in Thailand, not Indonesia. I think some tuk tuk driver takes her to the silver factory, tells her she gets very good price there, and so she buys; she likes to get the special price. She puts her bicycle down in the grass. The front tire keeps spinning until she stops it with her hand. With one thin chain, made in China, she locks that wheel to the bicycle's body. She smiles at me before she steps onto the bridge that goes to the wat. She stops halfway over the bridge and looks at the pool. Now I know something about this farang: she likes the adventure, but she has fear, too. And most important: she likes pretty things, and she wants to know Thailand.

At this time, Bangkok, Khao San Road, is not exciting to me. For some years I have been living there, and now I don't say wow, look at these farang, look at these Thai people, dressed like farang. Wow, look at this. No. Now, I see many people looking like this. Now, Bangkok is too much noise, too much pollution, smelling bad. Everyone is trying to make some business with some drugs, some false ruby, some bad credit card, something. No one is believing anything—some farangs think maybe I try to cheat them. When that happens, when one person looks at me like that, and then another one does, I leave Banglamphu. I go to see Chit play with Fallow band at the Trombone Club. If my African friends are at Star Hotel, I sit with them there. On the occasion, I leave Bangkok and visit my home.

Or sometimes I leave Bangkok to go with one farang woman somewhere—to Ko Samet, Ayuthaya, Ko Phangan, sure. One month ago, the nurse from Australia takes me to Ko Samui. She's on holiday, and one holiday ends fast—phsst, done. But she leaves me some money, sure, so I can use that to go to another place; not Bangkok, not beach resort, someplace I choose myself, where I can meet different kind of people. I choose Sukhothai, old capital of Thailand, where King Ramkhamhaeng ruled and made the golden period of my country.

So now here I sit and wait in front of Wat Trapang Thong for the farang girl to return over the bridge. No other tourists come during that time, not even to the museum next to the wat. It's very peaceful. When the girl walks out, I smile at her again. She's not stopping now to look at the water. She goes straight to her bicycle, bends over that. She puts one hand on the Chinese lock that she could break with one pull, and she takes out tin key. "Do you like the wats of Sukhothai?" I ask her.

"You speak English?" She's bent over the bicycle, but she looks up at me to smile. Her face is red from bending. Her hair is falling. Her shirt's neck hangs down, dark inside there.

"Of course," I say.

"This is a very nice wat. I like it here very much. It's very peaceful here." She says this slowly. I can hear that she's American.

"I think so, too. While you were inside there, I think exactly that: peaceful. Have you seen Wat Si Chum?" I ask her. "The home of the big Buddha?" She stands up, her lock open now but her bicycle still on the ground. From her bag she takes the paper map and looks at that. I tell her big Buddha is very special to Thai people, and tourists like to see it, too. I tell her since the time I was one monk, I want to see the big Buddha of old Sukhothai. I tell her in Bangkok I have many farang friends, and I show them Bangkok, but here I am the tourist. I laugh when I say this. I stay in Ratanasiri Guest House. Which guesthouse does she stay? I smile and laugh. I tell her this very fast while she picks up her bicycle, because I want her to know that I am one international Thai man, one backpacker like her. She says she stays in Sukhothai Guest House. I tell her that one seems not very peaceful, and I ask her which guesthouse does she prefer in Bangkok. She says she doesn't remember the name, and then she asks me something.

"Is that an English book you're reading?"

I tell her yes, I like to read English books. "I'm always studying English," I say, "but some words I don't understand." I pick up my book from the ground. "Can you tell me the meaning of this?" I am standing now, and I go near her, pointing to some words: *incipient conspiracy*.

"Hmm. Incipient conspiracy." She says this soft, then talks louder. "A conspiracy is a plan to betray, or trick or harm or get away with. You understand?" She looks at my eyes. Her eyes are not brown, not like Thai people. Not blue like the sea at Ko Samui and the eyes of the nurse there. "Or maybe it means the group who tries to do that." She looks away and wrinkles her face. "Let me see the sentence." I stand closer to her, and she stands with her bicycle. My thumb is underneath the sentence, and my hair touches with some of her hairs, the small ones floating away from her pink-brown face. I think I can feel this—I want to—but how can I feel two hairs touching?

She reads to me one sentence from the book: *Standing across the room, she watched Michael lean over Leta, and she sensed an incipient conspiracy.* She wrinkles her face again. "Well, I guess here it means a plan. She thinks these people are going to make a plan against her, maybe. Incipient means, I don't know, maybe something like a new one. I think it means a new one. Something just starting. You understand?" She moves her head. Her hair is gone. I laugh.

"Now I understand. This one is exciting. Inipent conspircy," I say to her. "Do I say this right?"

"In-sip-e-ent con-spir-a-cy," she says. She smiles. Some small lines on her skin are white from wrinkling her face too much in the sun.

"Incipient conspiracy," I say. We're both smiling now, and we say it together, at one time: "Incipient conspiracy." It makes us laugh.

"Thank you, miss, for one English lesson," I say. I put my hands together and wai her, like to one teacher, my lips closed but smiling, like one funny joke. When I rise I tell her that if she likes, we can go together to Wat Si Chum.

We go together to Wat Si Chum, Wat Phra Pai Luang, Wat Sang Khawat. After, we walk on one buffalo path to the river and we talk. Her name is Robin. She tells me Robin is one kind of bird in America.

"Robin is one bird, so in Thailand I call you Nok, Thai nickname for you meaning one bird." She says she likes to have one Thai nickname. I teach her more Thai words. I teach her how to say *beginning one plan* in Thai.

"How long you travel?" I ask her. Near the river it's cool. We sit on the cool ground, under some bamboo.

"Six months. I'm going to run out of credit, I think, if I don't start being more careful. But I wish I could keep traveling forever, just keep going and going."

"Why not? I think it's cheap for you in Thailand."

"Oh, yeah, in Thailand. That's one of the great things about it. But cheap's not enough. Someday you have to earn money, right?" NokRobin picks one flower, looks very hard at this one. It's some weed flower, not beautiful. She sticks her finger in the hair of its white scrub head, pulls it to pieces. Then she turns to me, smiling. Her eyes are something like the river—not brown, not green, but pretty, sure, that's what she wants me to think, and I do. "I want the world to be my oyster. You understand that?" Her eyebrows fly like one small bird, lifting. "The world is my oyster. It's an American expression. Understand?"

Certain kind of farang, certain kind of backpacker, they don't want to go home; they stay away too long and they get afraid. Maybe they don't remember how to work, how to make money. Maybe they don't remember their friends, how to sleep in one clean bed, same one every night, and get up from that to do the same thing every day. I know. I know this is how they're feeling, because now I'm living like one backpacker, and I'm afraid to do something else, I forget how. But I'm not like these farang, because I don't forget how to make money. The reason I'm moving is to remember about that.

"Yes, even when you're moving, it's very important to remember how to make money."

She smiles at me and says making money is not the only important thing, and that's why she doesn't want to go home—that's what she is afraid of, life at home where everyone only cares about making money. She says she was like that when she worked selling cars. She made too much money, but she wasn't happy.

"Believe me, I know money's important," she says. "Before the cars I worked in an art gallery. I was around art all day. Should be great, right? But being broke was no fun at all, which I should have known from when I was a kid. You have to somehow combine it. Money and the thing you love and the kind of person you are." She pulls apart another scrub flower when she says this. Around her legs, on the grass, the pieces from the other one turn brown already. Then she stops pulling. "What do you love?" she asks me. "What are you planning to do?"

Around us, some small wind makes the bamboo start singing. "Shh, listen," I say. "You know what that is?" Maybe someone who never heard bamboo can think that one beautiful waterfall pours in the distance, or many special birds join in long and sad cry, or some ghosts walk above on the magic floor, singing. That sound makes the world seem big and small both. NokRobin looks at me like she's confused. "Bamboo," I tell her. She still looks confused, so I tell her again, "That sound: Bamboo." Now that she knows the sound, I stay quiet so she can hear it.

"NokRobin," I say, when the bamboo stands still again. "You love to travel, you love it in my country, so I think there is way for you to make money here. Sure."

"What's the way?" she asks me. She wants to know this. Then she says the answer her voice tells me she doesn't want: "Oh, you mean teaching English?"

"Teach English? Maybe in Korea, Japan, that's one way to make money, but in Thailand, money for that is small. No. I think for you there's something different, something like the plan I'm making for myself." I nod at her.

"What plan? Tell me."

"I'm always thinking about this," I say. I look at the river. It's not too big now, not too small, because in the cool dry season everything is balanced.

"This woman I was with in Bangkok, she's a buyer for designers back home. They pay all her travel expenses. She just has to go around Asia and buy stuff for them to look at. But that's a dream job. Not something you can just pick up and do. I've met people who import, buy stuff here to sell back home. Is that something like you mean?"

"Let me think some more about this," I say.

NokRobin looks at me. I smile at her, but I say nothing. "What?" she says to me again, but then we sit quiet, without talking. When I start walking, she follows me. I know that some man in my situation—one pretty girl, the feeling is sweet, and already there is possibility—he feels excited, heart is bumping. But for me, what I feel is some very smooth peace. I don't think of Abu, I don't think of Bangkok, of Star Hotel. I don't think of anything. My mind is empty. When we walk on that path, the bamboo sings.

Chapter 4

It had taken the bus four hours to cover the sixty miles of pocked and mountainous road that twined from Chiang Mai to Pai. Shaken, dusty, Robin and Piv blinked as they stepped down into the sun-baked lot that served as a station, and they grinned at each other when they realized that no rushing touts were lying in wait. The bus rumbled off, leaving their ears ringing with quiet. Robin hoisted Piv's rucksack onto her back. He carried hers, because it was heavier. They made their way to Riverside Lodge, which Robin had been told was the cool place to stay. It was run by a Scotswoman and her Flemish husband, and the bungalows on short stilts rented for the equivalent of three dollars a night. By the time Piv and Robin emerged from the one they let, the palmed hills to the west glowed russet, and a misty chill settled in with a familiarity that explained the mildewed smell of the quilts and futon they had found in their lodging. Some lodgers sat around a campfire, and Robin and Piv joined them for a while before leaving to eat at another word-of-mouth hot spot, The Black Canyon Café.

They walked up a slight rise toward the night market, where vendors prepared foods and others lingered to eat under low-watt bare bulbs. The air was smooth and cool as lake water, and Piv took Robin's hand. In Chiang Mai, Robin had been always reaching for his as an extension of the intimacy they were sharing in bed, and her feelings had been hurt when he'd repeatedly shied. Finally, he had told her that Thai people didn't approve of public displays of romantic affection, and Robin tried harder to control her constant itch to touch him. She interpreted his gesture now, still furtive, as a signal to her of some kind, and his dry palm and thin fingers felt special in hers.

The Black Canyon Café was a stablelike building, open-fronted and thatch-roofed, glowing red on the far edge of town. Thai-style, Piv and Robin took their shoes off and padded thick-stockinged to a low table nestled in rough wool carpets and lumpy pillows. They ate their rice soup and wheat noodles alone, cupping their hands around the red glass globe that held a candle, and when they were through, their waiter shyly asked them if they would like to join the only other people present, a handful laughing quietly at a large table where a Thai man stroked a guitar.

The waiter joined the table, too. He was one of the three owner-brothers sitting round, all of them young and smiling and handsome with thick straight hair in identical ponytails and skin creamier than Piv's.

"Welcome," said the brother without the guitar. With the confidence of an eldest son, he poured Mekong whiskey into two glasses and topped them with Coke. "Please. I'm sorry that we have no ice." He introduced the others: a hang glider from France, a Swiss man who was in the country to study copper foundries, and a German woman, beaming celestially, who did relief work in the hill tribe villages to the north.

"That's great!" Robin said to the woman, liking the sound of the assignment, the philanthropic mission made glamorous by the variegated embroidery and silver ornamentation connoted by the words *hill tribe*. "How long have you been doing that? Where do you stay?"

"I stay here, with Yhan." The woman met the eyes of their waiter, whom she sat beside, and the two of them grinned. "I meet Yhan one year and a half ago when I visit my friend then working in Thailand, and we fall in love." Their eyes melted together again. "I have to go back to Germany, but I try and try to return to here. Finally I find this agricultural project. I specialize in minimal impact agriculture at the university. It's hard for me to explain in English, but this is perfect for me in all ways."

"She came back to me!" Yhan drew her closer to him.

"Oh, lucky!" said Piv. "They say they will come again, but most times, never."

"A toast to true love!" the Frenchman said. Everyone clinked glasses.

The drink was lukewarm and syrupy, and the warmth of it spread through Robin. She saw domestic details she had missed before: toothbrushes in a jar near the sink, hand cream and flowered bath towels on shelves, bedrolls propped between the beams of the low slanting ceiling. She tried to imagine living here, rolling out blankets and snuggling in them to drive away the mountain chill, making love silently, in the darkest corners, so the other brothers wouldn't hear, then, in the daytime, working for sustainable agriculture. She took Piv's hand underneath the table.

The musician brother grew more definite in his strumming. He was playing a John Denver song, "Country Roads," and Robin watched as everyone—hang glider, aid worker, copper man, brothers—began singing quietly and certainly, not stumbling on any words. She felt a hard stab of mocking nostalgia. She'd sung "Country Roads" in Girl Scouts; not even Lite FM radio still played it at home.

The Swiss man reached across the table during the second verse and nudged her. "But you must know this song, yes? This is your song." She smiled at him indulgently, but then saw the German woman and Yhan leaning together, swaying, singing, their bright faces the wick of global goodwill, and she joined in the chorus.

Country roads
take me home
to the place
I belong
West Virginia . . .

Robin's voice grew hesitant at the verse, but the others knew the words, and the candles' glow nestled in her chest. Maybe they were all experiencing a Buddhist transcendence here, in this simple place. She'd ask Piv to tell her more about what that might mean. At the next chorus, she made her voice strong. They all did.

. . . to the place
I belong
Pai, Thailand she sang out
mountain momma
Country roads
Take me home

At the end, they broke into applause for one another and raised their drinks in sticky salutes.

A hush fell when the guitar player started fingering the first fervent bars of "Hotel California," but when he reached the verse only Yhan and his girlfriend whisper-sang along.

"Do you get many tourists here?" Piv asked the older brother. "In all seasons, do they come?"

"Sure. So more and more tourist businesses come, too." He shrugged. He said there were days and weeks with little business, but they had always lived in Pai; they liked its quiet life. A commercial group from Bangkok had begun construction on a resort, and rumor had it that their influence was going to get the road improved, get an airstrip put in, but who knew? "Maybe there is enough change already for the people of Pai. Fifteen years ago, it took two days to get to Chiang Mai. You had to go on foot. Our mother went there, walking, only twice each year. But if the airplane comes now," he shrugged again. "Okay, maybe it's good for business."

Robin wondered whether she and Piv could do something here in this little town, start some mellow business. Not just selling hill tribe stuff—Pai's couple of streets were lined with places already doing that, their owners sitting deep in lawn chairs or idly dusting. And not sustainable agriculture; that just wasn't her thing—although maybe she could help out occasionally by organizing a hill tribe craft fair or recruiting volunteers or acting as a liaison between the villages and a connoisseur like Zella . . .

By the time they traded tipsy good-byes with their hosts and left the Black Canyon, the chirping night was downright cold, and Robin huddled appreciatively next to Piv. She felt properly coupled with him now, alive to their long-term potential, and when they turned their bodies toward each other on the pallet of the soft-floored bungalow, she felt the fever-scratch esctacy he'd given her since the night they met deepen into something like nourishment.

That sense of union ebbed and flowed only slightly during the two more weeks that they spent in the North. When Robin realized, sitting on the bed in a Mae Hong Son guesthouse on their twenty-third evening together, that her visa was expiring in a week and that since she had already renewed once, she had to leave the country in order to renew again, she felt more shock than panic. She looked at Piv blank and wide-eyed, the tissuey receipts, dull metallic credit cards, and grime-edged passport from her gutted money belt scattered around her.

"I have enough cash to get us to Bangkok. But then what, Piv? I don't want to leave Thailand, but I have to. At least for a while."

Piv sat on the edge of the other bed in the room. It was their sleeping bed, laid with a black, red, and brown Burmese blanket that Robin had bought when they'd arrived. They called the bed that Robin sat on their business bed, because in lieu of a desk or a table, that's where they counted their money and where Robin counted the days until her credit card payments were due. Piv had wanted to assign the beds separate purposes, because he didn't like how Robin's feet would end up any which way when she was lounging around smoothing bills or studying her purchases. He didn't want to sleep where her toes had touched the pillow. But Robin wasn't surprised when she saw Piv break his own rule and stand up on the sleeping bed. She watched with a sense of déjà vu, of fateful certainty, as he swept the Burmese blanket up with him, held an edge in each hand and spread his arms wide as wings. With one long step he bridged the distance between the beds. His second leg joined the first on the business side of the divide, the springs of the old mattress squeaking, the coins she had stacked sliding clinkily askew. Then he squatted down in front of her and put his arms around her, his rich, rough cloak encasing them both.

"I think we leave my country together," Piv whispered.

A thrill went through Robin. "Yes," she whispered back.

"This is my plan that I have been thinking—for you, for myself. To be happy, to make money. We go to Indonesia for jewelry. You pick the good pieces, like your friend."

"Yes."

"Then we come back here. You have visa, we have jewelry, we sell that, make some profit. Sure. Then we find things here. Better things, more special. And then we can go somewhere else, always together, over the world, and sell them for more."

As he spoke, the flower bloomed: This was it. This was what was supposed to be happening. Finally, her life. "Yes! Yes! What will we find? Where will we go?"

"Right now, silver. Then maybe some small thing carved from jade. Some ruby. We go to Hong Kong, Australia, Germany, North America." He kissed her.

"Borneo, India, New York. With our beautiful things." She kissed him back.

"It's simple for you to leave my country to get more visa. Then, anywhere. New York City. Everywhere."

They kissed again, falling together onto their sides, the money and documents crumbling beneath them, one bill sticking to their blanket as Piv rolled on top. His black waves of hair rushed down toward Robin, met her caramel strands on the bed, and she stretched her arm up luxuriously and ran her fingers through the mingling textures, hers thinner, his thicker, both cool in her hand.

They flew from Mae Hong Son to Chiang Mai—they were in a hurry, so the forty-dollar flight was no contest over the eight-hour bus trip—but more air travel was out of the question. Robin didn't want to press her luck with the credit cards. At the Chiang Mai train station she smoothed out a five hundred baht bill and a one hundred and gave them to Piv, then asked if he needed any money for snacks. He went to get the tickets while she sat with their bags at her feet and the high yellow ceiling arching overhead. Piv had tied up his hair in a low bun, and she could see his T-shirt gently billow from the valley between his shoulder blades as he stood in line. The sight of him pleased her for the dozenth time that day. Air moved loosely through the station. She didn't mind watching her money closely as long as she had some to watch. In fact, counting and budgeting made her feel capable and situated, and she went over the next few days' expenses again in her mind. No problem.

There had been a problem back in New York, where she'd gone after college. It didn't take long before previous months' bills claimed whole paychecks with the current month's already due—when change for laundry, let alone dry-cleaning, was so scarce that perspiring in an overheated building gave her cause to curse; when she contrived every action to wheedle or scam trial-sized packets of designer soap or train fare or an evening's electricity on someone else's utility bill. She'd been working as a gallery assistant for six dollars an hour then—a gig she'd been lucky to get and believed that she needed to keep, even as her nerves screeched like a field mouse's from the pressures of supporting herself on low pay in the proximity of such gorgeous wealth. Most of her friends and her boyfriend from college had similarly low-paying, culturally cool gigs if they were working at all, but they also had allowances or trust funds and they often lived in the extra apartments their parents had lying around like extra pairs of slippers, and this difference isolated Robin from them even as she moved in their pack. She'd spent those two years unable to plan, only able to react, disappearing into the bathroom when it was her turn to buy the next round and growing more and more skittish as she waited in there.

But that being broke made her anxious was no surprise. The strange thing was how she felt after she'd given up that job and hit a stride selling Nissans at a New Jersey dealership owned by a friend's father. She paid for that opportunity in the cool she'd been collecting, but there was cash now, lots of it. Money rushed in and poured out with the thunderous push-pull of the tide, and it unhinged her. There were back bills, expenses she'd been putting off, a car to get, the grungy shared walk-up to get out of, and a whole slew of deferred desires to attend to—and then another huge paycheck, unless it had been a slow month. Instead of stealing someone else's trial sizes, now she could walk away from a department store makeup counter with three hundred dollars in product. She sent some face lotion back home, and the next time she called down there her mom had spoken in an awed, hurt whisper. "Sixty-five dollars just for some night cream, honey?" And Robin had been ashamed of herself, and ashamed that she regularly spent five dollars on a loaf of bread, and ashamed, too, that when she did her stomach still clutched. She felt like she was caught in some white water rapid that moved downstream more violently as the numbers went up. She dated a man who made much more than she did, and he squired her around. He once spent six thousand dollars on a painting at a storefront gallery because she said it was good, but he didn't care if it was; he couldn't even see it, and she grew to loathe him. When she'd finally paid off her credit cards and caught up on her student loan, she didn't even wait to save up more than a couple thousand dollars before she quit the dealership, got her vaccinations, and lit off for a trip around the world, hoping to start fresh.

And now maybe she had found it, she reminded herself: the something possible, the potential fresh. She turned away from the train's window toward Piv, who had taken the aisle seat, and asked him what kind of car he would like, if he could have anything. They were pulling into a rural station, and women and kids ran alongside the slowing train, their knees bent under the weight of aluminum cooling boxes and buckets brimming with chicken satay. Piv smiled and shook his head.

"I don't care about the car. Some Thai people want the new one, from Germany or Japan. It's their dream. But where can one car take me?"

"Come on, just imagine," she said. "What if you had to pick?"

"I pick you, and now you're here. We're going to fly. We don't need the car."

"You're sweet," she said, but she didn't quite believe him. "You're so sweet I want to give you a car. What should I give you?"

"Give me ten baht."

Robin laughed and handed him the coin, and Piv called to one of the hawkers moving down the aisle. A girl, not more than ten, pushed toward him, already pouring a thick green liquid into a clear plastic bag. She stuck a straw into the drink and twirled the bag around its stem, tying the plastic off in a knot. By the time she took Piv's money the train was chugging forward, and she had to run toward the door, hand her thermos to someone on the ground, and jump after it as the engine picked up speed. Robin watched her, worried and pitying, but also admiring. Had Piv lived a life where even dreaming of a car was absurd? She started to ask him—if not that, then something—but at her intake of breath he gently placed the straw into her mouth.

"See?" he murmured. "So sweet."

Chapter 5

We stay at Star Hotel. NokRobin wants to stay on Khao San Road, but I tell her no, Thai people don't like to stay there. She pays for Star Hotel with her Visa and it's fine, no problem. She likes to have one nice room—not like camping, not like the backpacker—with one Western toilet and hot water shower, with television and telephone and air-con. Yes, this is better. Bangkok is cool and clean up here, floor five, room 517. Sheets are clean, and we stay in bed long on the first morning, with NokRobin smelling clean, too. We plan to go to Indonesia—Bali is the good one—to buy some jewelry that farang tourists like. We can sell this in Bangkok for double, more, the value we pay. We have the goal together: first we do this and then we get better jewelry, I think maybe gold, and go to Australia, Germany, America to get triple, four times the value we pay. I ask NokRobin who does she know in America. Some shop owners? Some vendors? She says no, she doesn't know those people. She knows some poor people, who work in factory, restaurant, car garage, in her home. And she knows some rich ones from her university. Some who work in offices; some who don't have to work because they're so rich—they make movies or paintings or write something about that. She doesn't know any shop owners, but I think this is no problem. I think they would like to do business with one Thai person, to buy jewelry from Bali, to buy gold and rubies from Thailand.

But there is one small problem. I go with NokRobin to Khao San Road, to one travel agent there. We want to buy tickets leaving three days later to Jakarta. NokRobin wants to pay with Visa, but travel agent takes the Visa and returns, saying, "Excuse me. This card is not accepting the charge."

NokRobin turns red in her face. She says, "Oh, sorry," and gives her other Visa card. This one, also, travel agent comes back to give apology, to tell NokRobin this card is not, cannot, no. "Would you like to pay in cash?" she asks, but NokRobin is gone already. One bell rings when she pushes open the door.

I smile at the travel agent. Please hold these tickets for us, I say in Thai. We return soon.

I see NokRobin at the guesthouse restaurant on the other side of the street. Honey Guest House, I know this one; it's not good. The small rooms have no windows, and if you store your backpack here, maybe not everything remains when you return.

NokRobin wants one Coke. "I said a Coke," she yells to the young boy working.

I change that. I order in Thai: Younger person, please, I'd like two Cokes.

NokRobin is still red in her face. She's very hot now. "Don't worry," she says. "This has happened before." She takes her shirt out from her trousers and reaches in her money belt. She puts her passport and some small scraps of paper on the table. She's looking at those. "What's today's date?" she asks me very fast.

I ask another farang tourist, "Excuse me, what is the day today?" I speak very polite.

"I don't understand," NokRobin says. "They're not overdue. I have five more days on this billing cycle. I was going to pay them today. You heard me say so."

"Please explain," I say to her. I touch her hand to smile at her, but she moves her hand away.

"For a while I kept forgetting to pay. I know it was stupid!" NokRobin wears one white T-shirt like the boy would wear. Around the neck is dirt.

"I'm sure it's no problem. We're using Visa at Star Hotel. It's no problem. It's misunderstanding." She teaches me that word.

"It *is* a problem, okay? Don't you understand? Once it gets in the computer it can take more than a week to sort it out. I know it was stupid, but I haven't done anything wrong this time!"

"It's only one travel agent. Don't get so upset about that one. We'll go to Thai Farmers bank. I'll talk for you. No problem. It's better anyway to have real money." I talk soft, lean close. I want NokRobin to do this, too.

"I'm telling you, I know, it's not working." She shakes her hands like something sticky, biting, is on them. "Just let me think."

At this time, I want to be in Star Hotel to think quietly. NokRobin picks up her Coke to drink, then slams it down. It makes a sound—

kunk!—and then the tan foam rises. She can't drink that now. She's looking in her money belt again. I don't know why. Everything's already on the table.

"I have to get out of the country. What happens if I can't get out of the country?"

"Shhh," I say to her. "Calm down. We have our plan. We'll leave the country."

"Hello? Piv? How? It's not no problem, okay? It's a *big* problem. Do you understand the difference?" I look away from NokRobin. Of course I understand. I've found the woman who will make something with me, and the problem has come too fast. Maybe my dream won't happen. But we can find the truth by being calm. We shouldn't yell in this guesthouse. The problem only gets big if we do that.

"Piv? I'm sorry. I'm sorry I yelled. Will you come with me to the post office, please, so I can call the credit cards? Maybe it's just a mistake." Her eyebrows squirm like gold worms. Gold worms that turn gray in the rain.

We sit on wood bench in the post office while NokRobin waits to use one international phone. International phones are on the second floor. There's no air-conditioning there, and none on the first floor, either. It's hot, and the air smells from too many people waiting too close. The ceiling fan spins the dust. Also, the floor is dirty. There are three international phones, in red boxes, and many farang tourists wait to use them. I hear one tourist—very young one, younger than me, younger than NokRobin, with braids all over her head—she speaks rude to her mother. "Mom! I'm learning just as much here as I would in college," she says. "I don't care!" She yells this to her mother. "College can wait. It's not going anywhere!"

NokRobin sits so nervous, bouncing her leg, looking at her paper scraps. I don't like this. I want to be in Star Hotel. I see one fat Thai lady, very big for the Thai lady, wearing yellow dress, yellow shoes, high heels, very much gold, and gold glasses, too, and she's dyed and curled her black hair. Looks like those hairs might break. She's sitting on the wood bench. She's with one farang man. Wow! This one is too big! He's standing. If he sits, then everyone else would have to leave that bench, I think so. His big face is wet with sweat. He wipes it with his handkerchief. I look at them and I know: he's married to the Thai lady. I think they live in Germany. Maybe he met her on vacation in Bangkok, long ago. Maybe she was one bar girl then, young one, beautiful. Or maybe she flew to Germany to marry him, they never meet before that time.

NokRobin goes in the phone box. She's in there for twenty minutes, then more. I look at my watch: one half hour. When she comes out her face is not red, it's white. She sits beside me. She touches me on my wrist, but she's looking away. Her hand is slimy from sweating; it's very cold—her fingers are wet stones from some stream.

"You finished?" I say. "Come on, let's go." I don't want to be with NokRobin if she's yelling in the post office about some money troubles. I take her wrist to pull her up. We walk back through Khao San Road. NokRobin doesn't talk, and me neither. On Rachadamnoen Klang Road we still say nothing. Her wrist sweats under my hand. When the road splits around Democracy Monument, other roads coming in to that traffic circle, NokRobin pulls her wrist from me hard. She stops on the sidewalk, with many people and many cars, trucks, motorbikes, everything—with everything going by.

"I'm over my limit," she says. Her face is wrinkled, dirty. The air is bad here. It hurts my throat, and I hold my long hair over my nose to breathe. The smell of shampoo makes the smell of the street more soft. "I'm over my limit on both cards. How did it happen? I didn't even know what the limit was—it just kept going up. It seemed like so much, especially here." People are walking across street, very many of them, and I reach for NokRobin, but she stands still, looking ugly, her face in too many pieces. I think she might cry soon. "They won't give me any more. They say I have a bad record. And now what? How am I going to get out of here?"

"Come on," I say to her. "We won't talk here. Everything will work out for you. Let's go to Star Hotel."

"How are we going to pay for it?"

"Don't worry about that one. I know those people. They let me stay there. That one's no problem." I take her wrist again. She moves with me now, but the traffic is coming. We take two steps then we must wait, try not to breathe. Every time I turn on the TV it says that this air is very bad for breathing, for health. Lead is in this air. They say that pollution is number one problem in Bangkok.

Back in Star Hotel, I tell NokRobin to shower, that it will make her feel better. I sit at the table near the window while the shower water comes down and beats on the wall. I think about this problem: NokRobin has no money at this time. How can I make something with her, then? How can we make our plan together? With no money, it's better if I start again. When I think that, it hurts me, but maybe it's better. Or the other word—necessary. For longer than three weeks I've been with NokRobin getting no money. I mix the money I have already with hers, and we spend it. I have only five hundred baht left that I save for myself. Perhaps it's necessary for me to start again in Bangkok, on Khao San. I need the lady to make my plan with, to travel the world, to go with me. Perhaps it's necessary to meet another special one who will do that.

But this necessary thought makes me sad. NokRobin is here with me—I hear her turn the shower off; the room is quiet, but I know she's here. I feel her, soft. I've moved with her longer than with any other lady, and she wants to make something international with me. Maybe it's taking too much time to find another girl like that. And if I don't have the feeling, can I move with some other farang for even one week? Smell them and taste them? NokRobin knows some things about me: how I like my hot coffee, how I sleep, what I dream, things like that. And she's very nice person, polite most of the time, or she tries to be. She tries to understand Thai ways. She likes being with me. She can be quiet, can be peaceful, but she likes moving; she likes jewelry, clothing, shopping for these things, and I do, too. She's from America, and she knows many rich people there. Maybe some money can come from them. Or she can call her parents. They're not rich—she already told me, they're something like poor—but they'll help her, sure. In America, even almost-poor parents give money to their children. If she calls them, I think they'll send her money for one airplane ticket home to them. Indonesia's very cheap. Maybe we can use that money to buy jewelry.

Or maybe she'll use this money to fly home, to say good-bye. To disappear. Maybe she's too scared now. Maybe she doesn't like me so much when the problems come. I don't know.

When NokRobin steps out from the bathroom, wrapped in pink towels with her skin pink, too, I get up to kiss her forehead. I touch her eyebrows with my finger, make each one smooth. I walk her to bed. I tell her she can rest here, that she should rest here while I go talk to some friends. I unwrap towel from her hair and spread her wet hair on the pillow.

"This is just one small problem," I tell her. "Really it is. *Mae pen rai*. Thai saying meaning it doesn't matter. Can you say that? *Mae pen rai*. You wait here. Maybe I can do some business to get us more money for the immediate days."

My five hundred baht I have to keep for me, for emergency, but I want some other money to buy some thing for NokRobin—food and cold drinks, taxi ride, whatever we need. If I pay for those things it's better; it will make her less scared. First, I talk to Saisamorn, manager of Star Hotel. "*Sa-wat-dee krup*, Khun Saisamorn," I say to him. I wai, then we shake hands. He says that his employee tells him I stay again in Star Hotel. He invites me to sit, to have some tea with him in one small office, behind hotel counter.

I drink my tea and tell him I stay in the Star Hotel, yes, with one lady friend. I tell him I have come from the North, and we speak of the North, although he has never been. He is Southerner, and business is better in the South. Why go up there? After some time I ask him about his business, how it is going.

He says it's going okay, not bad, but peak season ends soon, and not many tour groups have made reservation plans. He says to me that if I tell some friends to stay at Star Hotel it's good for him, and he'll make it good for me.

Thank you, I say. I am always happy to recommend your excellent hotel. But I am wondering, are the friends from Kenya staying here? Abu and those ones?

Abu arrived yesterday, like you, Saisamorn says. You didn't see him? He has plans to stay for one week here.

This is good news for me. This opens possibility. I thank Saisamorn for the tea, and I get some business cards from him. I write my name on the back of them, in English and in Thai.

On Khao San Road, I go to one travel agency. It's smaller than the one I go in with NokRobin, crowded, but with strong air-conditioning, and I sit next to some farangs who are waiting. "Oh," I say. "Wow. Doesn't it feel good to be in some air-conditioning during hot season in Bangkok?"

"Of course it does," the man says to me. They are from Germany or somewhere, I can tell by the way they speak English.

I ask them does their guesthouse have air-conditioning. "It doesn't? Wow! That's too hot!" I tell them about Star Hotel, that it's cool there, every room has TV with very many stations, and I give them the business card. "This is where I stay when I travel to Bangkok," I tell them. "It's more expensive than the guesthouse, but it's very nice. It's worth more than you pay. You get discount if you show this card."

They don't seem excited to get my news. They don't believe me. I don't think they'll come. They stand up and go to the travel agent.

I find the price of ticket to America, and I go to find some tourists who are looking too hot, to tell them about Star Hotel, but I don't feel easy, I don't feel comfortable. I give out twelve cards, but pretty soon I leave to go back to Star Hotel, and I think no one else will follow me.

I don't go back to see NokRobin; I go back to find Abu. I look in the lounge for him and his friends, but they're not there. To wait, I sit in the lobby where it's bright, and I read *Bangkok Post* to practice English. I read about General Motors, one American company, world's biggest company. They start to build large factory outside Rayong. One thousand people can work there. They say it's good for Thai people, but that's not good for me. That's not the business I want. I want to be together with NokRobin, and Abu always tells me that he might have some business for me and for the farang friend, too.

But at this moment, it is better for me to plan alone, so when NokRobin gets off the elevator, I move softly to one corner and stand behind the tall chair. I watch her and she doesn't know it, like the first time I see her in Sukhothai. She has on one clean dress, blue one, covering nicely her small body. I hear her talk to the boy at the check-in counter. She says, "Excuse me. I'm sorry, but is it possible to make a collect international call from the phone in my room?" She tries to be very polite.

The clerk doesn't speak good English. He says nothing, but NokRobin can tell he doesn't understand.

"How can I make a collect call?" she says, and she makes the phone shape with her fingers and speaks like that. I want to help her, to speak in Thai to this boy, but I can't now. I watch her try alone. I watch her give up. If her parents give her ticket, will she give up on me?

NokRobin leaves the Star Hotel, and I sit and I read and I wait for Abu.

Chapter 6

On the panting-hot, cacophonous street, Robin was aware of the flammable nature of her rayon dress. Since meeting Piv she'd seldom walked alone in public, and without him alongside she had so much space to stretch her limbs that they felt lost, and she tingled with need, was giddy with it. She envisioned herself reaching out her arm, palm cupped open, and asking likely strangers, white ones, "Please. I need money. I need a ticket somewhere. Bali. Anywhere. Home. Please." She would use all her private-liberal-arts-college poise: "I'm sorry to bother you, but there's been a mix-up. You know how it is." She'd appeal just like their daughters, but be less demanding; she'd seem more grateful.

She traced the path back to Khao San Road, searching faces as she went, alive to possibility. During their week together, Zella had taken Robin behind and between Bangkok's rushing skyscraper facade to market districts where ginseng dust shimmered in lone streaks of sunlight, silver prawns the size of cigars rose in domed piles, and jade obelisks and gold and sapphire medallions changed hands in tented shops too small for more than three people to stand in at once. Robin would have never seen this on her own despite passing daily right alongside. She wondered what else she wasn't noticing, what option she was missing now. She had visited the sex clubs on Patpong once, as a sightseer—all the tourists did—and she had noticed a Caucasian girl dancing on the stage, numbered and bikinied like the Thai women shimmying blank-faced beside her. "What's up with her?" Robin had asked her companions, a couple she had struck up conversation with the evening before. The boyfriend shrugged. "Maybe she's living out a fantasy." His eyes were jumpy and he bounced his knees. The girlfriend nodded blithely. Robin's hunch was that the dancer hadn't had infinite choices—but maybe that was the option she wasn't seeing now, the way to earn enough money to get out of and back to Thailand with Piv in tow, or to get back home alone. But no, she wasn't that stuck yet. She trudged down the block under the late afternoon sun. At the post office, she sat once again on a bench to wait for a phone. When a booth came free, its wooden door flapping open with a rude clap, Robin took her place inside it.

"Honey! Where are you? Are you okay?"

Her mother was awake, if only just—the panic in her voice mixed with the husk of morning. Robin pictured her sitting at the kitchen table in her pink robe, a coffee mug in front of her, yesterday's paper spread open.

"I'm fine, Mom. I'm in Bangkok, Thailand. I'm traveling with someone." Robin hoped that sounded reassuring. She hadn't considered the jolt of anxiety an early morning phone call would give her mom, who of course would fear the worst when she heard the ring, because that's what unexpected intrusions had most often delivered to her door. "I'm fine," Robin declared again, although really she had called to ask—not for money; she knew her mom didn't have any—but the question: Will I be fine, Mom? Will everything be all right?

"God, I worry about you. But I'm so proud of you, too, honey. Bangkok, Thailand. I'll be. Isn't that where they did *The King and I*?" She pronounced it "keeng and ah," but Robin no longer minded. She wanted to transform all the sweat and blood of herself into particles that could bounce off satellites, settle in the coffee steam over her mom's mug, and be sipped up. She wanted to be both the source and receiver of comfort.

"Yep. You get that postcard I sent you yet, of the Grand Palace? The one with all that gold?"

"I sure did. I just got it last week, Tuesday. I'm saving all your postcards for you. I put 'em in the recipe box, so you can have a record of your trip. And then you can sit with me and tell me in detail about what it was like to see each thing. My Lord, honey, you've been gone so long. How's your money holding out?"

"Well, it's tight. It's getting really tight. But things are a lot cheaper here."

"I still remember when your dad and me went to France for our honeymoon. Oh, we couldn't afford it. It wasn't in grand style, but no matter what happens, it's something you keep with you for the rest of your life." Robin's mother had made a scrapbook of that trip, and Robin had thumbed through its scalloped-edged cardboard pages scores of times since being deemed old enough to sit with ankles crossed and "act like a lady." Her mom's voice now held the same wistful and sweet almost-smugness it had whenever she reminisced about her one brush with romance, but the track had finally been played too many times; the recollection no longer washed away the everyday weariness.

"How are things for you, Mom?"

"Things're fine. I have Tiff every weekend now, during the day. Britt finally got a job at the Citgo garage. It pays good, but it's weekends, and that's the only time he gets Tiff."

"How're things holding up at Sunstream?"

"Oh well, fine. You know. They let some more people go, but they say that's it. 'Course there's always rumors."

Robin put all her own anxiety into this familiar old one. "Why don't you put some word in at Fisher's or something? Didn't you say they're doing good?"

"Oh, don't worry about me, honey. It helps with Britt working. We're all fine. You just take care of you now." It was little enough to ask, Robin thought—to take care of herself, not to worry her mom. "When you thinking about coming home?"

"Well, I'm getting a little homesick. I might see if Dad'll help me with a ticket."

"I'm sure your dad's proud of you, too, hon'. We better say good-bye, though. These calls cost a fortune. I love you. I'm always thinking of you. You take care."

Her father had been asleep.

"Princess. Whoa. It's early. What're you doing up at the stroke of dawn?"

"It's twelve hours difference here, Daddy. It's cocktail hour."

"Well, where are you now, globe-trotter? I was telling my client about you. She's got a daughter at Skidmore doing a year abroad over there right now. Taiwan. You headed there? You could look her up." At another juncture Robin might've played along with this, expressed the blasé endemic to the clubby assumption that all roads lead back to those one knows, and how nice, but she couldn't afford that charade of socioeconomic equality right now, and she resented her father's indulgence in it.

"I'm in Bangkok, Thailand. Where I've been. You get the cards?"

"Sure did. Mount Everest, even. My little girl is seeing the world. You okay? Staying away from that Montezuma's revenge?"

"I'm fine, Dad. How're you? You have a new client? Have you been working?"

"Oh, yeah. Something big's going to come out of this. We're still working on the details. She's got to approve it with someone higher up on the food chain, you know. But they're going to love it, and this would be a long-term gig."

"Well then, Dad. I was wondering if you could maybe float me a loan?"

"What's wrong, Robbie? I thought you said you were fine. What's the problem?"

"I'm having some trouble with my credit cards. It doesn't look like it's going to be fixed up for a while. And I need to leave the country. My visa's almost expired. I think I'm done traveling. I want to come home." Her heart pounded. She could hear it quite clearly because she was sealed inside herself, the door to the phone box closed, her body pressed into a paint-chipped corner, one ear blocked by her hand and one by the phone.

"Well, what kind of trouble, sweetheart? What are we looking at? Because, you know, sometimes you can squeak by. There's a period in there when you can actually still use your card." This was the kind of advice she got? She turned her face from the corner; she looked out at the room.

"I'm past that point, Dad. Could you please charge a ticket for me? Just one-way on whatever's cheap." A mop-headed boy wearing tie-dye dropped the gnawed saffron core of the mango he'd been eating onto the floor. Pick it up! she wanted to bark. You think your mother works here?

"Well, princess, my credit's all tied up. I've needed major upgrades to land this job. I mean, I'm invested in this state-of-the-art printer, animation software . . ." Robin's father chanted a litany of technological stumbling blocks: computer programs and shareware problems and she didn't know what all. She stamped her foot because the senselessness of the words stung her, because the littering kid had disappeared down the stairs. "And you have to understand, I wasn't expecting anything like this from you. I've busted my balls to get you through college, and I've gotten you out of jams before, but I can't keep—"

"Dad, *I* busted my balls to get me through college. I paid for most of it, and I'm still paying."

"Whoa now, honey. Hold on. That scholarship was mostly symbolic. Your taking out loans was part of the deal. But don't tell me I didn't come through with my ten thou a year. I got the gray hair to prove it."

"But you didn't, Dad. Never all of it. I'm not talking about my goddamn student loan bills; I'm talking about me picking up your end with my credit cards."

"One year I couldn't make it, Robin. One year. And you knew that. We talked about that. You could have done one of those semester away deals, gone to Gainsville for a semester where it was cheaper. But no. You didn't want to go. Okay, I wasn't going to make you."

"You never held up your end. You're the one who wanted me to go to a private school, and then you left me with registration holds every year that I had to clear up with my Visas."

"One year I couldn't make it, and one year I was late. They moved the date up on me, and I was late. I just don't have ten thousand dollars lying around like some of those other guys. Hey, I'm in a changing business. In 1990, I didn't gross more than thirty thousand. Thirty grand, and I paid out ten thousand dollars to keep you in that school. I've done my job."

"What job, Dad? Mom's the one who had the job, and she did it with nothing." She heard herself, and she knew she sounded melodramatic, but it was a relief to yell in English to someone who could understand her words.

"You know I'll be there for you if you get in some real trouble, but this isn't it. Quit acting like a hysterical kid, spoiled rotten. Come on, use your brains. Use your wits. Go talk to the credit companies. Or the aid for travelers. Or take a courier or something. You got a hundred thousand dollar education, you should be able to figure something out. It's not like you're busted for drugs, right? Or, Jesus Christ—is there something you're not telling me? Is that what this is about?"

"No, but Dad, just come on. What's another few hundred? It'd be only about five hundred dollars, one way. I really need this. I need to get home." As the possibility of home receded, she felt the truth of her statement; she reached into the twilight sky for the balloon that had escaped her hand, but too late. "I want to come home."

"Look, Robin, don't you understand? I don't have it. I'm in the same position as you, here. My credit's tapped. I'd have to go begging to get that money, to—I don't even know who I'd go to. Talk to the embassy. That's what they're there for. And look nice when you do it. You've got to present yourself."

"Thanks for your help, Dad. I knew I could count on you."

"Don't be a smart-ass," he said to her wearily. "But call me in a couple days and tell me you're okay. You will be, princess. You'll do fine."

Chapter 7

I read about Siam Center art opening in *Bangkok Post*, and I read about some politics in America, and I get tired from reading this thing in English. I wait in the lobby too long, but something tells me to stay there: I have one feeling. And you see, my feeling's right. Abu comes in from the street, and he's glad to see me.

"Mr. Pivlaierd, my friend!" he says to me. His voice is heavy. He wears Kenya-style shirt, not Bali-style batik but something like it, and his big stomach or big muscles push out that shirt so it doesn't touch his trousers. "We meet again in the Star Hotel!"

He sits down next to me on the couch, and I feel the couch move. He's one big man. He tells me he just comes back from his country, short visit to make some business there. I ask does he see his family, how is his family.

"I have a whole village of a family," he says. "It's a lot to take care of."

One time before he tells me he lives in Mombasa, big city, with three daughters and one young son, but I don't ask him why his family lives in the village now. Instead, I want to answer him. He asks about my travels, asks me do I travel with lady friend, where did I meet her, where she's from.

"You have a talent with the ladies," he says to me. Then he looks at his gold watch, very nice one. I wear watch, too, cheap but with style. One farang gave it to me when she said good-bye.

"I have a call to make," Abu says. "But then business is done, for the day. Join us for a drink in the lounge, my friend."

Through the glass door of the lobby I see the light outside grow thick and yellow. Evening's come, and when I go to the dark lounge, it's night already. Abu, Jomo, and Yoke drink Singha beer. I want one Coke, but I drink Singha beer, too. We speak about Kenya—it's mankind's birthplace, the African friends tell me, proud of their country. Nigeria is the biggest, but Kenya has very ancient culture, very important to the world.

"I would like to visit your country," I say. "I like to visit important places. Do I need visa to go there? How long does the visa last?"

"Mmmh!" Abu makes one deep noise. He faces Jomo, not me. "You're sure they're in his possession? Absolutely sure? I don't want a fracas at the border this time."

Yoke says to me, "Every visitor needs a visa, but he can stay for several months if he has the funds. You might have to prove that you have the funds." Yoke leans close to me. He wants to have my eyes so I don't look at Abu, I think so. Yoke's head is smaller than Abu's, too small for his body and neck. "Jomo, if a man comes from Thailand, does he need to show a certain cash reserve to get a Kenyan visa?"

Jomo holds his hand up, open, stopping this question. "I watched them being signed. I delivered them three hours before we left, into his hands."

"I'm not sure, you see," Yoke says to me. "Because of course I never have to get a visa to enter my own country."

"Mmmh!" Abu says again. Every eye is big in the darkness of this lounge, even my eyes, the seeing part of them grows big. "Not to worry. We can speak freely," Abu says to Yoke. He looks at me. "Mr. Pivlaierd, it would be an honor to have you as a guest in our country. Arranging a visa would not be a problem."

"Thank you," I say. I smile to him. "My American friend has that problem now, while she's visiting my country. Her visa runs out before she's ready to leave."

"She needs only to go to the embassy. They'll extend her visa there. I've done this myself."

"She already do that. She's in Thailand three months, and now she must leave, go to Thai embassy in another country, if she wants to spend more time here with me. We want to go together to Indonesia—I can make some business there, I think so. But. Unfortunate my friend has one other problem."

"Ah, the ladies love you. They don't want to leave!"

"Oh! She'll leave me, sure. But her other visa, Visa card, it's not working either. That one runs out, too! She doesn't have money for tickets anywhere, for her or for me." I make one small laugh. "I wish I could help her with this problem, but at this time, I cannot."

The Kenya men finish with Singha. They ask the bartender, please, four more beers. I don't finish mine, but the dark lounge, the dark glass, hides this. I push my bottle to center of the small table to join with the other bottles, and four more come. Abu gives one five hundred baht bill.

"Keep it," he says to the bartender.

Resit asks in Thai how I know these African men, and I tell him they're my friends. I meet them here.

"How many languages do you speak, man?" Jomo asks me.

"I speak only Thai and English. German, maybe, small amount. If I have one German friend, meet the German girl, maybe then I'll learn some more." We laugh together at this one.

"Can your current lady get her visa in Malaysia?" Abu says.

"Of course. For visa it doesn't matter, and maybe there's some business I can do in Malaysia, too, sure. But, this problem with her visa, money Visa, credit card, I don't know how big this is." I put my hands up, to show their size. "One very big problem, then it's better for her, better for me if she goes home, to America." My hands are small, compared to Abu. I shake my head. "But I hope not. She's nice. Very nice person."

"Nicer than the German lady?"

"Oh! I don't know that German one yet. Maybe that one doesn't like me!" And then Abu wants to know many things: how long I know NokRobin, what her family's like, what's her career in United States. For some things, I don't know the answer. I try to say what's best, but I don't always know.

"Well, perhaps we can help you both. Please ask her if she will join us for supper. If you will show us a fine Thai restaurant, you will both be my guests."

The door to room 517 is thick; the key's thick, too—it feels good, solid, not like one bamboo guesthouse door anyone can break. I open that door and see NokRobin sitting on the bed. Her back is curved, one piece of hair falls down, her hands go under her legs, her feet on the floor.

"Piv," she says. First two days we are together, she never said my name. At that time I wonder does she know my name, was I clear when I spoke it. "Any big business deals?" Her face is two faces. One side smiles at me, one side pulls down, and she wants to pull me down; she does that, onto the bed. NokRobin's skin smells like Singha beer. Before she says anything, I know she tried to fix her cards, but that didn't work, so she drank. Not good for the plan we make now.

"Perhaps," I tell her. She doesn't listen. She says my name again, and her face is in my neck. I laugh. I keep my arms loose. I don't want to make something with her now. Over her shoulder I see Buddha statue on the floor. I think when she came back from drinking, she took that from her backpack and left it on the floor near some wrinkled purple cloth. I tell NokRobin before this time: Thai people must put Lord Buddha up high. Floor where you walk is disrespectful to Buddha.

I put her head away from my neck; I hold it between my two hands. It looks very small there, like one small nutria or squirrel, tan color but you can see white underneath, round eyes with moss in them, small bones two hands can break, and sad, scared.

"Shh," I tell her. "Listen. Some friends invite us to eat with them. Don't worry. They pay."

"What friends? I don't want to. Let's just stay here and enjoy our nice clean room." Her hand goes under my shirt. "Our fortunes have changed, Piv. We can't afford this room. Let's just enjoy it one more night together."

I don't want her hand there. It doesn't feel good, so I remove that one. Then she moves her face back to my neck. I roll onto my back to stop this but she rolls, too; she puts one leg over me, heavy. She's like some jellyfish you try to get off but then it stays somewhere new. Clock says 7:25.

"You don't have any money and I don't, Piv." She whispers this to me, hides her face. "We're going to have to part ways. We're just going to have to, so I really want tonight to be just me and you."

When she says this, I feel cold—it makes me wonder something: Maybe NokRobin didn't go today to fix her cards, instead she called her parents for one ticket back to America, and they already send that one. Tomorrow she'll fly away. The farang woman do this sometime, to the Thai man. They want to go somewhere—if it's to one island, maybe they'll take you. Perhaps. Somewhere too far, they never do. I want to move Lord Buddha off the floor.

"I already tell you. For me it's no problem to stay at Star Hotel. But tonight we have one business meeting. If you want to make some business together, make another visa for Thailand, you must come, too." I roll on my side so our faces almost touch, our bodies press together. I pull my face away, body still all touching, so she can see me when I smile. "Do you want to? Okay?"

"Business?"

"Yes, I tell you. You didn't hear me? Some business with Kenya friends."

"What kind of business?" Maybe NokRobin's not drunk. Her arm goes loose around me. She wrinkles her face, her counting look, wide awake.

"You must leave Thailand, right? To get other visa? You want to do this?" I kiss her once before I get up from the bed. I put Buddha on the top of the tall dresser, then, quick, I wai.

"The wanting to isn't the issue," she says. "It's the money. Neither of us has any money to get me anywhere."

"Not at this time. That's why I arrange this business." I go to the table and light one cigarette. NokRobin doesn't like cigarettes. In bungalow, guesthouse, with her I don't smoke. But I measure this now. Maybe her parents send her one ticket. How can I get her to stay with me? If she sees that I'm strong, very adventure, like Marlboro, maybe she'll stay. She won't stay if she thinks I'm weak.

"They're from Kenya? How do you know them?"

"I know these friends maybe . . . two years now. They have some business for us to go to Malaysia."

"To do what?" She sits up in bed. "You know, drugs are punishable by death in Malaysia. I mean, it's serious. It's not drugs, is it? We're not going to be carrying any drugs?"

"Of course not. They're not drug dealers."

"There were some African men staying around Khao San who were drug dealers. At least that's what everyone said. They stayed at that blue guesthouse, what was its name? That one behind the wat. Did you ever see them?"

"These friends are not drug dealers."

"How do you know? It's not like they'd tell you."

"You want some business? Come to see. Then you think it's drugs, go away."

"They really have some legitimate business? Doing what?"

"Really, really," I smile at her and nod. The red numbers on the clock spell 7:40. "We go to dinner, they explain. But get ready now. Take fast shower. We meet them at eight o'clock."

We ride in one meter taxi cab to Suan Malakaw, good restaurant. Five people ride in this taxi and the driver looks at me cold, I think so, but I just tell him where to go, and I turn to the backseat and talk to Abu. NokRobin sits in front with me, but her eyes stay outside the taxi window. Traffic moves forward together, and the lights outside the window pass quickly.

I order food for everyone, many special Thai dishes. There's the feast on our table. On the cart near Abu, one bucket of ice, some Coca-Cola, one bottle Johnnie Walker Red whiskey. Waiter serves this, and the second time he serves I put my hand on my glass. No more. NokRobin doesn't cover her glass. She sits very straight—she wants to seem tall, but she's small at this table, pale. Her skin gets darker in Thailand, sure, but the front of her blue dress slips low, and one finger of white shows there, the place where her bathing suit should cover. I know the places where she's banana white farang, and now everyone can see. In this restaurant, there's only Thai people. No other black man except Abu and his friends. Now these friends don't wear their African shirts; they wear plain button shirts, pressed trousers, like Thai, but still people are looking. They wonder: What's this? They don't like my long hair; they think I'm bad, rude to my parents. What do I do with these farang? Black ones, too—they think I'm disrespecting.

When Abu holds his hand open to offer NokRobin more noodles, his palm is like one flower, blooming pink. He asks NokRobin many questions: where has she traveled, what does she do in USA, things he already asked me about her. Thai people don't ask so much—not the things he's saying now, so many questions all together—but she's polite. She's very nice person, and when she gives answers she tilts her head to one side, to other side like the bird in the tree. She laughs, quick, after each thing she says. Everyone else sits, watches NokRobin, except when Yoke points with his chin to one Thai lady, bar girl, I think so, who comes in with one farang man.

"But what about you?" NokRobin asks Abu. "What business of yours lets you come to Thailand so often?"

"Ah, I have been lucky enough to establish a small import-export trade. I have clients and colleagues throughout Southeast Asia, but I prefer Bangkok, where I can see my friend, Mr. Pivlaierd." He lifts his glass to me, nods his head, then he drinks. "We base ourselves here as much as we can."

"What kind of things do you export?"

"It's a very specialized market," Abu says. His voice is deep, and he speaks English deep, too; his words roll like the sea, not like NokRobin's, high and sharp. "We supply certain Kenyan products to collectors. It sounds incidental, I realize. But a rich man is willing to pay much for a relatively small thing, if his neighbor does not have it. I'm sure you have seen this attitude in the United States, when selling automobiles."

"With cars, it seemed more like people wanted what their neighbors did have." NokRobin laughs again.

"I'm sure you managed to convince them, Miss Miatta, that their neighbor had a very fine car, just the kind you wanted to sell. Perhaps your namesake?"

"I wish. But no, I worked for a Nissan dealership. Do you do a lot of sales?"

"I do the contacting, which takes a certain amount of discretion. And I arrange the paperwork and the transport. Very important. Some of my products require hand delivery. They're too expensive to trust with a delivery service. Too rare."

NokRobin bends to Abu, but for one moment, she shoots her eyes to me. She wants to know exactly what he delivers, how much he pays. She wants to know if I know. She doesn't ask. Maybe she learns this from Thai style, to be quiet, but why's she look at me now? I listen close, but I show glass eyes to NokRobin. I look somewhere else. Bar girl points to menu, translates between the waiter and the farang.

"So you deliver them?"

"Personally? Yes, on occasion. But we often use a courier. The trick is to find someone trustworthy, well spoken, professional. And so, Miss Miatta, here we are. Mr. Pivlaierd has indicated that you and I may be in a position to benefit each other."

"Well, I'm certainly in a position to need benefiting!" NokRobin laughs again, too loud. She looks at me, but I look at other customers. I wish NokRobin would act more sweet and cool.

"I have in my possession a package that must be delivered to a gentleman in Kuala Lumpur. And I'm sure he would appreciate dealing with an attractive American woman instead of this black African man." Abu laughs. Jomo and Yoke laugh, too.

"I'm sure Piv's told you I need to go somewhere to renew my visa. But what exactly would we be carrying?"

"You'll have plenty of time for that. My business won't take much more than an afternoon. You'll just meet briefly with our client at his office. You might need to meet someone a few days later to receive a bag to take back—just some Asian curios for which I might have a Western buyer."

NokRobin wants some message from my eye, but I give none. Her eyes make circles around the table, and she starts to laugh but stops after making one small bedroom sound. Behind me I hear the customer order eel. Someone says yes, they will build new mall in Thonburi district, third new mall to open this year. When my parents live in Bangkok, they work very hard to get money. They save their money to come home, for our house there, for my sister and me. Where they live then, too many fights, some men are drunk all the time. They don't tell me this, but I know. They never come to restaurants like Suan Malakaw when they live in the capital city. But the man eating eel, I hear his voice and I think of my parents, my home. Sometimes I feel tired, always being with farang people, people who don't speak Thai. But I study them, too. I learn something.

"Asian curios? That's right up my alley. What is it, exactly?"

"Nothing outlandish, I assure you. It's best if you don't concern yourself."

"But how can I not? We need to know what risk we're taking." She makes three sounds, trying again to laugh.

"*We* will be putting our trust in *you*, Miss Miatta. You will be carrying expensive artifacts and then a great deal of cash, but we give you the benefit of the doubt, because you are a friend of Mr. Pivlaierd." Abu's body is relaxed. He leans back on chair pushed far from table, elbow resting on top of that one. But his eye on NokRobin is not relaxed.

"Thank you. It's just . . . How do I know . . . ? How will we know?" She stops talking so she can breathe. I hear her. One breath. Two breath.

"Take me at my word when I say I don't want for myself the risks that narcotics bring. As for the rest, we'll give you exact instructions once you're there."

I hear Robin breathe, and I see her breathe—ribs get wide, shoulders lift, ribs fall in, shoulders fall. I feel her grow and shrink beside me. She's deciding.

"There'll be a ticket, right? And . . . what about money?"

"A per diem cost, of course. And a bonus when you get back to us all here. But let's look at this as a trial run. You are in a tight spot, yes? You'd have to be leaving the country anyway? Let's see how this fits and talk some more when you get back. In the meantime, we might be able to set Mr. Piv up to something here while you're gone. Right Piv?" Abu puts his hand on mine and shakes it.

First I think he tricks me. Even though I help him and show him NokRobin, he doesn't help me. He doesn't help me to travel with her, to travel, to leave here. He takes her away. But I bury my feelings inside my cool heart, because many possibilities exist. I lift my chin at him and say *yes, of course*, without one word. Malaysia's very small place. I wait longer, I go farther. Europe or USA or Africa. I don't look at NokRobin when she looks at me—her eyes say too many questions.

"Piv's not coming with me? But Piv, I thought this was for us both."

Now I look at her. Now I smile at her. "This just one short trip, to open up some possibility. In Kuala Lumpur, you get double-entry visa to Thailand. Then, Mr. Abu sends us on the better trip. Something like you call honeymoon." We look together at Abu, and I lift my chin at him again.

Abu smiles at me. "Yes. Of course. If all goes well. You do understand, Miss Miatta, that while I instinctively trust you, and while you come with the finest referral, we are dealing here with delicate situations and, of course, with a lot of money, which can occasionally confuse. And so Piv will stay here—and so will your address book."

"Address book?"

"And, oh, yes. That's a lovely dress you have on, and you look lovely in it. Like that movie star. We always go to see the American movies when we're in Bangkok. What's the new one we saw, Jomo?"

"Miss Miatta looks as lovely as any movie star."

"Yes. But as a traveler, I assume that the clothes you have with you are all somewhat casual."

"Except this dress. I didn't expect to be working."

"Of course. You've been on an extended holiday. But now that is changing." From his pocket Abu takes one black billfold. I want to see inside this canyon; money from all over the world is there, I know it. He gives me, folded, some thousands of baht—I can feel it's that much, of course I don't count it. "You'll need some business clothes. Something conservative for the air travel. Something presentable for Kuala Lumpur." Abu touches his fingers together to show what kind. "Piv will take you shopping tomorrow while we arrange for the tickets."

Not many people are in the restaurant now. At this table, everybody looks at NokRobin, skinny farang. She sits straight. "I got some Thai silk when I visited Jim Thompson's house. Sort of plum. I had planned to get it made into a suit. Does that sound like the right sort of thing?"

Abu spreads open his hand and tips his head to her. "Mr. Pivlaierd, you know a good tailor, I'm sure." It's true. One lady I know, she gives me two hundred baht when I bring in farang who orders the expensive suit. Abu picks up the Johnnie Walker and pours this in every glass. In my glass, too, and I don't want it, but no problem. He raise up his whiskey. "To doing business together," he says. He makes this toast. He taps his glass to mine.

Chapter 8

Getting ready to go to the airport, Robin shaved her legs so close they gleamed; she slipped on hose in addition. She tucked a silk blouse into a trim skirt that matched her jacket. She slicked back her hair and put on full makeup, swiping at palettes she had bought for this purpose at a ten-story shopping complex the day before, recalling gestures that a year ago she had used every day and hadn't used once since leaving the States. Grinning at her reflection, the brittle lines she had painted on herself, the serious prettiness, she turned to Piv and said, "Hello, sir. I understand you're interested in the new Maxima." Fabrics whispered as she walked from the mirror toward him, hand outstretched.

"Oh! You are very business now, I see. Yes, madam," he said, and gave a bow. Then he cupped her chin in his hand. "So beautiful!"

In the lobby, Abu complimented her, too, and then put her in a cab with the piece of wheeled black luggage she was to carry for him. Later, the luggage tucked under the seat in front of her, Robin relaxed into the recycled air of a jet's shuddering cabin. She had only the word of a virtual stranger that she wasn't smuggling drugs into a Muslim country, but she was headed out of Thailand with two days yet to spare, transformed from a beggared backpacker into a well-off American white woman. As the hum in the cabin increased, she crossed her ankles, set her face. With a breathless gallop and then a leap, the Boeing lifted, tipping her into the fold of her cushioned seat. The metal gleam of Bangkok spread beneath her. Piv was down there somewhere, and a thread in her ear smacked with a soft suction pop as the altitude increased and she left him behind. The loss caused a pang, but she felt good—even the melancholy yearning felt fine. She was a world traveler. Coming and going and leaving behind. She didn't need a fairy godmother, a stalwart father with ample funds; she was moving through the world on her own fuel, taking the first step toward fulfilling the promise she had made to herself in Jim Thompson's study.

During her week with Zella, Robin had spent most of her time tagging along while her patron shopped hard and shrugged off attempts at conversation. "Will you shut up," she'd finally snapped over a market-stall lunch a few days after she'd offered to help Robin. "It's not a job you send in your résumé for. You've got to figure it out yourself." But the next afternoon Zella took Robin to her favorite museum, the Jim Thompson House, and in the taxi ride over she cheerfully provided explication about the American expat who had rekindled the Thai silk industry and amassed an impeccable collection of Southeast Asian art. "You'll love it there," Zella had said. "I do, and you will, too."

She was right. Pushing open the gate to Jim Thompson's walled garden, Robin immediately recognized the place as a personal archetype. Glossy foliage lapped at a teak house whose peaked roofs made lace against the pollution-soft sky. Lotus pads floated on a small pond, and marble statues nestled amid palm fronds. Here in three dimensions—in planed teak and new blossom and carved stone—was Robin's fantasy of somewhere better, somewhere else. She strolled the gardens in a trance of wanting while a breeze stirred the jasmine blossoms that threaded through the undergrowth. Robin speculated that someone as enamored of Thailand as Jim Thompson was must have had a lovely Thai wife, and she imagined herself the daughter of this cross-cultured pairing, a symbol of the best of both worlds, returning now to her ancestral home. She walked up the stone path to the entryway of the house she was supposed to have had.

But inside the house, in her fantasy father's study, amid collections of porcelain and pottery and temple paintings, a Buddha, the most beautiful she had ever seen, derailed her daydream. The statue was similar to one she had bought two days earlier, the single item she had purchased during days of shopping after swallowing her humiliation and asking to borrow an extra two hundred dollars from Zella. Both Buddhas were standing bronze figures, the chins tucked slightly, palms facing forward, eyes limpid. The one at Jim Thompson's was a thirteenth-century antique, and hers wasn't, of course, but it was a wonderful imitation, rich and skilled. A tough green shoot poked through the crust of her habitual, backward-glance fantasizing: she'd acquired the Buddha on her own, coming from the parents that she had, from the dilapidated ranch in a central Florida backwater. She didn't need to imagine being born to Jim Thompson, something that would never be; she could imagine being Jim Thompson herself. The modern, female version.

That's what I'm working toward, Robin reminded herself. The stateless hallways of Subang Airport funneled her into Malaysia, and the air waltzed around her, washing away most of the nervousness and leaving just a soft tickling thrill. Her passport was thunked with a stamp, and she clicked freely past the long low tables where other travelers stood as witnesses to the ransacking of their luggage.

The feeling of freedom didn't last long. Outside customs, as she had been told one would, a man stood holding a small cardboard sign with her name penned in black letters. He wore a white button-down shirt and slightly faded trousers. Robin felt shy and overdressed as she approached him, but she offered her hand forthrightly.

"Hello. I'm Robin Miatta," she said.

He squeezed her fingers quickly in his and bowed from his shoulders, but he did not speak, simply reached for the suitcase's handle. With a gesture of hand and head he indicated she was to follow him. She walked half a pace behind, wishing she could use the bathroom but not daring to request it. The man escorted her to a blue sedan, where he leaned in to speak briefly with the driver in a language Robin assumed was Chinese. He put the suitcase in the trunk, and then he opened the back door for her. She felt passed from man to man as if she herself were the cargo. The door slammed shut.

"Hello," Robin said to the driver, whose thick hair was shaved close on the back of his head. "How are you?" Weaving through the honking airport traffic, he gave only a choked syllable in return, and panic rose in her. Her bladder pressed upon her. Why hadn't she gone to the toilet? Abu had told her that the ride to his client's office would be long, but in the silence and the strangeness, it seemed unending. The car turned off the highway and turned and turned again, always onto a smaller road. Robin felt naked without the suitcase beside her, but what if the suitcase was beside the point, and what she was actually delivering was just herself, a stupid American female? Stu-pid. Stu-pid. Her heart beat that two-syllable rhythm. She looked out the window to try to find her bearings, but the views disoriented her. The mix of market stalls and modern buildings, the splash of billboards and palms were obviously not Thai, but she wasn't familiar enough with Thailand to clearly identify why. Some of the women wore headscarves, she realized slowly. Script was Roman or Chinese.

Finally the car pulled into a parking spot in front of a modest strip mall. Next to a store selling stackable plastic furniture was an office with MUNDAI NUSA EXPORTS written on the window, its door flanked by decorative bushes planted in red pots. The driver cut the car's motor, then he leaped out to open her door. She sent her hands groping to retrieve her backpack before checking herself, remembering that she was pressed and polished and the bearer of a dignified suitcase, which appeared on the asphalt next to her.

"Hello," said the man behind the desk as Robin walked in. "Miss Miatta? I'm Donsum Rong. I trust you had a good trip." He stood and walked toward her. Larger than most Asian men, he had an English accent and was well dressed, with a nicely draped gray shirt and trousers that cut elegantly above his loafers. Robin felt the first thaw of relief— people *did* speak in this country; she *was* here to do business. The desk fluttered with paperwork: thin invoices on spikes; faxes spread, stacked, and clipped together. Maps hung on the wall, and packing crates were stacked up in corners.

"Yes. Thank you. The trip was fine." Should she shake his hand? No, this time she'd wait for cues.

He offered tea, and she asked for the toilet, using the bald British term in light of Mr. Rong's accent and feeling grateful that she was back in a recognizable realm—one where she could read the signposts and make a basic request. Taking tea with Mr. Rong would still be awkward, but at least she would do it without fearing an organ would burst. As she turned to follow his directions to the restroom, he wheeled the suitcase out another door, which emitted a puff of sharp humid stink that made her wonder if that were a toilet, too.

The tea table was so small and low that they sat nearly knee to knee even with it between them. Mr. Rong was vague and soft-spoken, and his eyes occasionally rested on Robin's body but just as often gazed elsewhere in the room: to the fax machine when it started spitting, out the window, into his ivory-hued porcelain cup. They made perfunctory small talk about Kuala Lumpur and Bangkok, and without her own transportation or a home or life to call her own, she could neither sharpen the conversation nor end it. "Oh," she said lamely in response to a platitudinous comment Mr. Rong made about the Malaysian coast. "That sounds nice."

Mr. Rong looked down the vee of her blouse again, and Robin hitched her shoulders, wishing she'd chosen the yellow-collared one she'd also considered in the store. Who cared now that it didn't complement the purple of her jacket as strikingly as the sienna hue she wore?

"It is nice," he answered, and he waited another few beats before finally turning to the business at hand. "Tell Mr. Navaisha thank you for another excellent shipment." Mr. Rong handed her an envelope. "The driver will pick you up Tuesday at ten to take you to the airport. You'll receive our shipment from him. Unless you'd rather I come to get you." He reached across the table to slide his hand up her thigh. Robin stiffened; her armpits pricked with fire.

"No!" she said, standing and stepping backward, slapping down her skirt as if to scare out a bug.

For a moment, the clarity of conflict gave her a brilliant thrill, but Mr. Rong only shrugged indifferently. With bored gallantry he opened his office door for her and put her in the waiting sedan, handing money to the driver.

The next day, Robin went to the Thai embassy to renew her visa. She had forgotten to pack any of her regular clothes, and so she wore her plum suit. It was fine for her walk through the lobby and for catching a cab to the embassy; it was appropriate for her errand, but in the waiting room there she sat next to three backpackers, and without some ethnic clothes to signal camaraderie she felt like she was stuck behind one-way glass. She couldn't remember the last time she had talked with peers, had the typical "where are you going, what's it like there, do you want to go for dinner then" exchange, and she stared at the shaggy British trio hungrily, but they never glanced back.

Chapter 9

When NokRobin goes to Malaysia, she tells me this: "I think I'm going to miss you, Piv. Will you miss me?" She looks cute when she says this. She wants to look that way—little smile, face sideways. At that moment, I know NokRobin wants to make some cuddle, she wants some attention. She asks me: "Are you going to hook up with another girl when I'm gone, Piv? I'm scared I'm going to come back and find you not here. Will you think about me every day?" I tell her yes. Yes I will miss her. Yes I will think about her. I hold her to me and kiss her face. She wears perfume now, from Sogo department store. We buy that together; Abu gives us money. She smells the bottles, sprays them, asks me what do I like. At this time, I don't want to be gone from NokRobin. I like her small body, next to me every night. I like to see how she does her things, everything—cleans herself and smells perfume, talks to people on the street, and how she decides what to buy. And I like that she's sweet and thinks about me, too. Not always talking; sometimes she'll listen very serious. Her heart is generous. So I want to be with her, sure. I want to go with her to Malaysia, to Africa, USA, somewhere else.

But this is some business, and so I cannot at this time, and why do I want to think every day about that one? Why do I want to miss NokRobin, grab for her when she's gone? Better to forget, for now. In one corner of my mind, of course, I do not—we make something together, this business is together. But every day grabbing? No. Only to her I say yes. She wants to hear that—yes, yes—it's the romantic thing.

The day NokRobin leaves, I go to see my friend Chitapon. For four weeks I've been with NokRobin; before that, alone in the North. I carry one rucksack with me, but one other rucksack Chitapon keeps. I have money left from what Abu gives for NokRobin's clothes, but I don't take taxi. With my rucksack I take the bus to Chitapon's soi then hire motorbike to take me down that one. My friend is eating rice in stall across from his apartment building. Chit sees me first and says hello.

I sit with him. He eats kao mun gai, specialty of this stall, and

I order that, too. He tells me that in one month his band play thirteen times. Fallow band. They play some songs by AC/DC, by Pearl Jam, by U2, and some songs they make themselves. Their sound is good. Chit writes some songs in Thai, some in English. His speaking English is not so good, but singing, wow!

Chit asks me where I've been. Why I don't see any of the shows. I tell him only that I've been moving with one farang girl, sweet American one, very pretty, and now she's gone. He tells me he's not sweet anymore with his old girlfriend, Kathy. Chit says she's not beautiful, not pretty. Now he makes something with Wanphen, more beautiful, but Kathy comes every time Fallow band plays, and she pulls at him, wants to talk, sometimes she's yelling. They play tonight, and he says I should come, talk to Kathy in English—he knows I'm like one farang—tell her no, cool down, now he's sweet with Wanphen.

In Chit's apartment he plays new songs on his guitar. For some time I listen, then I look at the things I keep in my red color rucksack there: some shirts, some trousers, one belt buckle from America, shiny, showing the big cowboy hat, and one American book, *A Long Road Home*. One farang girl on Ko Phangan paid to have her hair made into braids, and when she goes home she cuts off one braid and gives it to me. "Remember me," she says. That almost-red braid is in my rucksack, and in my rucksack are tapes: Fallow band, Litobou band, tapes of Sinead O'Connor. I don't have Walkman, but sometimes I can borrow. Sometimes some farang might have speakers for their Walkman, and if I give them the tape, everyone can hear the Thai band play—they might like that. I also keep some photos in this rucksack: English girl on Ko Samet, American lady on that one, pink color of the sun going down, the Australian nurse wearing white uniform in front of one hospital—I ask her to send that one when she goes home, and she did, she remembered to send me—and I have photos of my sister, mother, and father in front of the blue water at Erawan Falls, my grandmother with some flowers near my home. I have many photos. I put them back. Only thing I don't put back in the red rucksack is two shirts and some trousers. These ones I pack in my blue rucksack, and I leave some different shirts and trousers in the red one.

That night I go to Trombone Club to see Fallow band play. I have too many friends there. Some friends are musicians, some still students, some working at restaurant or in shop on Khao San or at MBK Center. I talk to them. Do they go up North? I tell them I have been there with American farang for one month. I talk to Kathy, tell her, "Chitapon says later. Now he is too busy. There are too many other things." The music is loud. I'm talking very loud, but no one can hear me.

The next morning I stay in the bed, smoking cigarette, watching American program on TV. I want to relax like this. Someone knocks on my door. In English, I call out to say the room doesn't need cleaning. Then I remember the maid doesn't speak English, so I call out in Thai. Saisamorn sometimes lets me stay for free in Star Hotel, but the maid does not clean my room every day when I do this. If I want clean room, I pay her myself.

"I had no intention of cleaning your room, my friend."

I jump quick from bed. "Excuse me!" I say, and I put on one T-shirt. I move my hands over my hair to make it smooth, and then I open door. I smile. "Good morning."

Abu tells me he looks for me yesterday. "You seemed to be gone all day, and I have some business to discuss with you. May I come in?"

"Excuse me," I say. "My room is very dirty, very disarray. Please. I think it's more comfortable for you if we talk in the lounge."

Abu smiles. Wow. Too big for this morning. "You just informed us all that your room doesn't need cleaning. I'm sure you were right the first time."

"Okay, I'm sorry," I say. I stand in the door space. "Hello, maid?" I pretend to call down the hall. "I lie, my room is too dirty!" Abu laughs now. He has short sleeves on his shirt and I think I can see thick ropes in his arms under his shiny skin. I step sideways, and he comes through my door.

He sits at the small table by the window. Two chairs are there, and I sit also. The TV still is going; I hear the doctor on that show tell the nurse about the old grandmother's problem.

"I had a long day yesterday," Abu says. "A long, long day." He sighs and shakes his head, his big arms crossed. Then he says nothing.

"Business?" I ask him.

"Ah, yes. Just as well you weren't here. You were enjoying yourself?"

I cross my arms on my chest like Abu. I smile at him—I want one moment to think. What does Abu want to know? What should he not? "I see some friends," I tell him. "My friend Chitapon. I think I tell you about him already. His girlfriend's mother, she's farang, but she divorce the father and marry General Sivara."

"What's her nationality?"

"American."

"American. Of course. It's fine if she's American. But let me ask you something, Piv. Is there any scruple, any bad feeling, about interracial marriages such as this?"

Does Abu want to marry the Thai lady? I never see him with one. No bar girl visits him. I don't think so. But maybe. Maybe there's something I don't see. The Thai woman is very popular with the foreign man. I tell him, "To get married is no problem. It's between two people, what they want to do."

"Ah, Mr. Pivlaierd, you are open-minded, you are an international man, but not all of your countrymen feel that way, I am afraid. In any case, we need your help. We need to involve you in a little business." Abu uncrosses his arms, puts them on table. He does business now, I can see that; he leans close to me. "I'm leaving tomorrow, for a brief side trip. This has been planned. But before I do there's something I need to confirm. I want you to visit Admiral Wattanayakorn for me. Tonight."

I laugh when Abu says this. In Thailand, military man has power. Too much, some say. They do what they want, arrange my country. If they don't like someone to talk loud—*boom!* tear gas—they hit them down. Only the King can tell them please to behave, think of Thai people. Maybe Abu gives him money for something, sure, but it's only me, Pivlaierd from Kanchanaburi Province, how can I make him do something?

"Oh, Admiral Wattanayakorn. Yes. But the admiral is very important. Too important to see me. I think he doesn't have time."

"My friend, it is arranged. He may not want to see you exactly, but he wants to do the business for which you will be sent."

I tell him okay, of course I will go tomorrow. I have to say this. My rucksak is empty, curled on the floor. I already put my clothing into the drawer. NokRobin's backpack stands by mine, but it's bending down, one black color, limp. Her blue dress is inside closet. NokRobin is coming back to this place, and Abu is our something, our spark to make something.

"Good. But Pivlaierd, you will need a suit and a visit to the barber. Or get a pretty beautician to shave you if you'd like, a lady, and ask her to cut your hair."

I laugh. Today I think I'm always laughing. So much it hurts my face, and it's not the sweet thing, not funny. I'm in Star Hotel more than one week now, and I think of other places: the clean room on Ratwithi Road when I was student at Ramkhamhaeng; the wood floor of my grandmother's house in Kanchanaburi. Laughing, I look into Abu's face. I tell him this: "My hair helps me with the ladies." I smile some more. These African men are always smiling about the romantic thing. "Admiral Wattanayakorn is not beautiful. I cannot make my hair to please the man."

"Piv, your spell with the ladies goes deeper than your hair. You can explain to NokRobin your good reasons for changing your appearance. She seems to have a practical perspective."

"No need to explain. The Thai man, he needs to wear the neat hair for business." I press my hair with open hands. It goes smooth to my neck, and I twist it there, too tight. "I do it before. Make some business with hair like this. It's traditional in my country."

Abu leans forward to me; his soft chair squeaks when he does this. He puts his big hand on my leg. I wear some faded Levi's jeans. Their color is almost white now, but there's no hole yet. Abu's hand looks thick and dark on that washed cotton.

"Piv, your hair is fine for a beachfront gigolo. For some slick tout. But if I've understood you correctly, you want to be an international businessman."

I only look at Abu. Okay, yes, is how I move my head, but I say nothing. For four years I do not cut my hair. In the Fallow band, only one singer has hair so long like me. It's not traditional, like I tell Abu. Thai people, my mother, my father, they don't like. But certain ones, certain people—Thai, American, either one, international—they understand this long hair. They think it's beautiful; they think it's the best way to be. Abu takes out money from his pocket. Big pile, folded over. Five hundred, one thousand, five hundred, two thousand. Three thousand baht down on the table, smooth, for me. The same as he gives for NokRobin. If I want, this money could pay for one month of living, no problem.

"You have a day of shopping ahead of you, my friend. A distinguished suit, a distinguished haircut. You meet the admiral at nine o'clock tonight. We'll put you in the car at . . . what do you think is best? How is the traffic at that hour?"

I tell him I will see him at seven thirty.

"You are doing us a favor. It won't go unappreciated." Abu puts his hand on my Levi's one more time. When he's outside the door he says another thing: "And don't forget the shoes and socks. I don't think I've ever seen you in shoes and socks."

Of course I have these. I have shoes and socks; I'm not the peasant. But I will buy new ones anyway, more agreeable to one suit, with Abu's money. I close the door and Abu's gone. I put my cool hair in my face. I wish someone was here now to take the photo of my hair, how long it grows. I light one cigarette and smoke, watching all that time in the mirror my hair and my face.

Three ladies stand around my hair in the beauty parlor. They can't believe it, wow, so much hair. They make small sounds with their mouth, *tssnk*, like my mother makes. They say, how you get so much? All three ladies touch it, hold out my long hair. They say, now we make you look handsome, your girlfriend will like it. One takes sharp scissors and cuts. You'll be handsome! The three ladies laugh together.

You think I'm handsome? I say to these ladies. My girlfriend has left me. Will you be the next one? Two ladies are old, married, I think so. But one is more young. I look at her. She makes her hair curly in the beauty shop, but her skin looks very pretty, pale and smooth. She's tall for the Thai lady, but with the small body it gives her grace. NokRobin taught me this word. *Grace*, she tells me, when we watch some young boy wash in the Pai River. To move pretty and natural, that is some grace. The other ladies push at this graceful one now.

Anchan needs boyfriend, they say. The young one covers her face when the other ladies say this.

I need one suit, for my new hair. Where do you think I should go to get that? I ask them. They say MBK, Atok Market, do I have lot of money? Maybe I can go to Robinson Department Store. They want to know why I buy suit, why I finally get some sense and cut my hair. I tell them business. Some very important business. They're still laughing. My hair is many long black snakes falling to the floor, lying on that floor, and the lady who's cutting steps on those snakes.

Please, I say. I would like to save one piece. The young woman, Anchan, bends down and picks up one of those. She puts it on small table.

For your girlfriend.

No. She's gone. I want one piece for memory, I say.

I don't want to look at the mirror when my hair is falling off, but the young woman and the married one go work with other customers. Now it's quiet around my ears. I hear metal go *snnnt*, each piece of hair falling. Some air is slapping on my neck, little hair pieces scratch in my ear. The barber lady puts some cream into my hair; I feel her fingers close to my skin. She uses the hair dryer—*whoosh*, it's dry so fast. She puts more cream on my dry hair.

So handsome! Much better, she says to me, looking with me in the mirror. My head looks small, but it's still mine. I move, it moves. I look at the side, look at the back. Where my head meets my neck, the hair feels *zzzzz*, soft-rough. Stiff, not moving, but the feeling's not bad.

Oh, so handsome. All three ladies say this—even one customer says it, too.

No, I say. Not true. I stand up to look close in the mirror. I'm so close I feel how cool the mirror is. This is my face, my eyes.

He can't stop looking at himself, they say.

Very good haircut, I say to them. My voice sounds funny, far away from me. I give some money to the lady who cuts. Anchan hands me one long piece, wrapped in some thin white paper, crispy, and tied with string.

Your memory, she says. She looks up at me fast, then looks down.

I have to get some shoes and suit, I tell her, even though she knows this already.

You go now? she asks me. You go today?

Of course, right now. You come with me, help me pick one good suit?

I'm working now. Where do you live?

I do some business in Bangkok. I stay at Star Hotel while I'm here. That big one. Over there.

Where?

I take her to the big window with me. She can see the Star Hotel from there.

What kind of suit will you get? What will it look like?

I say that after shopping, before going to Star Hotel, I'll come back to the beauty shop to show these ladies my new suit, but I'm not looking at Anchan when I say this thing. I look over her shoulder, where another mirror is. I look at myself. Handsome, yes, to many Thai ladies. Now they don't tell me, Why are you looking like this? What your mother say when you look like this? No. My mother will like me now, too, like Anchan, young Thai lady, sweet one, works hard. They all think I'm handsome, but I feel too small. I could get lost. I could sink in the water, and I have no hair to float above me. No hair to tell anyone where I am.

I can't tell Anchan this when I come back to show those ladies my suit, shirt, tie, shoes, sock—all this I wear. Now they really say something about how I look. They say I look like one rich Thai man, and this is very good, the best thing.

Anchan says you live in Star Hotel, the lady who cuts my hair says.

Yes, I tell her. Yes, this is true, but only sometimes. When I do some business sometimes I can stay in Star Hotel.

You take Anchan to see that one. She walks by that every day, but she never goes inside.

It's no problem for me to take Anchan to Star Hotel lounge, so I say okay, why not? It's four o'clock and my business is not until later, and Anchan's work is ended, so we go. It's only few minutes walking, but I feel hotter in my suit than in T-shirt and sandals. We look inside lounge—so cool and dark there, very peaceful, very nice. Two Thai men in there have short hair, like me. But Anchan doesn't want to sit there. She shakes her head no. So I take her to the lobby and buy two Cokes to bring out there. Where are you from? I ask her.

When before this have I sat with the Thai lady? In Bangkok, answer is easy: I have never done this before, not in this way. When I live with my parents in Kanchanaburi I have the Thai girlfriend, sure. The sweetest one is named Mai. First time I make something, it's with her. I am eighteen years old. Wow! I feel lucky at that time. Maybe then I think I marry her. Very sweet. But no, I have to be monk, go in army, go to study—too many adventures are waiting for me. Now she's already married, I think so. And even then, when we were still sweet together, we could never sit like this, drinking Coke in hotel. We never need to tell where we come from, because we meet in Kanchanaburi Province; we know we come from there.

Anchan's from Bangkok. She lives with her family. She's twenty years old and has to beg her family, please, please, let her learn how to work in the beauty shop. She loves this. She's always making something new with her hair, but her family wants her to work somewhere else, some bank or office. I put my hand to feel rough-smooth hairs poking from my head.

Why you grow your hair so long before? she asks me. Why you don't cut for so many years?

I change to English. "Do you speak English?" I ask her.

"*Chan phoot pha-sa Ang-grit nit noi.*" In Thai she says she speaks little bit of English language, so I know she does not.

I talk to her in English anyway. "I do business with farang, and certain kind of ones, they think long hair is beautiful. It's been very good in my business with them. You don't know this," I tell her. "You don't even speak English, what can you know?" Then I speak again in Thai and tell her that different business requires different style. And then I see Abu come from elevator. He sees me, too, and smiles.

"How are you doing, man?" he asks me. He holds out his hand, and I stand to shake it. "I see you're now ready to do some business. Who's your lady friend?"

"She's the lady who makes me look like your businessman," I tell him. "She doesn't speak English."

"We have to get to work soon," he says to me. "Join us in the lounge when you are done with your guest."

Soon after this I tell Anchan it's time for me to discuss some business. I walk with her until after we cross the crowded street between Star Hotel and beauty shop, and then I say good-bye. I tell her I'll see her again, because short hair always needs to be cut.

I feel nervous to see this admiral, sure. Saisamorn's nephew drives me. His car is not too good, but after we pay forty baht to get on the expressway, the air-con comes out, and everything feels easy and cool. The traffic moves, never stopping, and electric signs on top of buildings make lines of light as we pass by. I like this—*swoosh*—it's like some water, and I find pleasure in this driving. I follow that feeling, so I feel calm.

Admiral Wattanayakorn's house is very fine, very rich. Servant opens door for me when I knock on the one in back, and I take my shoes off to go inside. It's not like with sandals, one two, both off, very easy. With these shoes, I have to bend down. The servant takes me to one small room and tells me to sit down. She closes two doors and leaves me in that place. In the corner there is one big vase, very big, stone one— wow, I think that is something old. Maybe from Sukhothai, I think so. One admiral can have great art from Thailand's golden period inside his house. Sure. Maybe that's what I'm looking at now.

I have enough time to think on this, because in this room I'm so alone—no noise, no people. I hear nothing, smell nothing, see nothing. I have never had this in Bangkok. One envelope is in my pocket, I still feel that, but now I don't feel nervous. The quiet room has its own soft sound, and after some time I feel like I am in that sound. I can live in that, and it's nothing. There is no problem there; it's very peaceful. I can meditate. It's good to do every day, but of course many times it's not possible. I can meditate now. It's like I'm nowhere—no fear, no heartbeat; I am away from that.

Then the servant opens those two doors, and I see Admiral Wattanayakorn. I know I must change my face now, close that meditation face. I wai the admiral. He wears glasses in black plastic frame. He doesn't wear one business suit, not one military uniform. He wears one tan shirt, very stiff one, light color. He greets me. I say thank you, thank you for having me in your home. He says I am the guest, thank you. Have I eaten? His eyes don't look at my face.

I take envelope from my jacket pocket and put it beside me on the chair.

March 2 is not possible, he says to me. The date will be March 4. Same flight is okay. Dock N243.

I wai. Admiral Wattanayakorn, I thank you, I say to him.

Admiral Wattanayakorn knows nothing about this, he says. Now he looks at my chin. Today I shave the hairs there. I shave those, but someone else cuts the hair on my head.

Excuse me, I say. I wai again to him.

He knocks one time on the door. Servant opens, and this man— maybe he's not the admiral—shakes my hand and leaves me; he goes deep into his soft house. The servant takes me to the doorway, and I bend down to put back on my new shoes.

Chapter 10

On the flight back to Bangkok, Robin squirmed and tugged at her suit. She had bought some cropped pants and a cap-sleeved shirt in Kuala Lumpur's Chinatown, but they were tucked in her carry-on. Abu hadn't said on the phone who would be picking her up at the airport, and if it were him, Robin knew he'd want her to look professional. If it were Piv . . . Robin wasn't sure which side of her he liked best.

She had tried during her lonely Malaysian days to finger their romance as a touchstone, to get the buffed salt smell of Piv in her nostrils, but he wouldn't function that way. He just remained in the flat back of her mind sitting quietly, watching her. He watched her when she'd bumbled through the meeting with Mr. Rong. Save face, she'd told herself as she staggered away from Mr. Rong's blasé hand on her nylon-coated knee, but that concept was an Asian one she had read about in books and couldn't fully grasp. It popped into her mind because of the Piv-within-her, not her genuine concerns. These ran toward sexual harassment, sexual humiliation, rape.

But if Piv was within her, why couldn't she imagine what he was doing? He sat in her mind, but in the blind spot. Would he hustle other tourists? Would he go home to his family, become what she imagined was the quintessential, family-centered, dutiful Thai? She wasn't sure she had met anyone like that, unless the brothers in Pai counted. Where would Piv sleep if he went home? On a mat on the floor? On a teak bed hung with mosquito netting? On a thin foam mattress with one pink polyester sheet? Her ears clogged as the plane descended, and she heard the world through her own liquid environment. She heard her heart beating. What had her or Piv's future to do with the other's? She only knew she was returning to Bangkok on Thai Air flight 1247, and that in this part of the world, it was 3:00 PM. Abu was more of a fact than Piv was; at least she carried assets for him. She'd held the envelope up to every kind of light offered by her hotel room trying to count the money, determine the currency, confirm the presence of a note, an order form, a report—but to no avail.

Once again, she glided through customs. If anything, the rolling clicks of the case she pulled along gave her confidence. When she exited, nylon straps separated her from the crowds waiting in greeting, and she scanned visages for one to meet hers. If people hadn't been packed so closely, she knew she could have picked out Piv immediately just from his stance, his hair, but her eyes focused instead on a tiny grandma at one end of the crowd. The skin around her temples was pulled tight by her gray and black bun, a printed sarong wrapped around her waist country-style, and she squinted at the emerging passengers with her arms crossed, inquisitive. Then Robin's gaze slid back along the queue and, directly in front of her, met Piv's face. He was smiling, hands in pockets, eyes lit. She felt her own face open even as she noticed his hair. The pang of loss only heightened her glee and relief. She took a step forward, was only a foot distant from him, and she extended her arms. Then she remembered that they weren't supposed to embrace in public. The strap that separated them bumped her just below her waist. They faced each other, full and grinning. She had never seen this posture of his before: a slouch down around pocketed fists. His hands rose to wai her, and her heart leaped at receiving this insider's gesture.

"Welcome to my country," Piv said. Their eyes locked in a hug.

"I feel very happy to be here."

"Please. I can carry for you." He reached his hand out for her luggage. She passed it to him, light without it.

"You cut your hair," she said. They were both still smiling. She reached out to ruffle his shorn mane, but then stopped midair, hand dangling from her wrist—touching this way went against etiquette, too.

"How you like it?" he said. He breezed the top of his own head. "I cut it for you."

"It's different. It looks good. But why for me?"

"For you, I cut my hair. For this business we make now." Robin registered his suit. It was cream colored, loosely cut; it hung well. He had a collarless shirt on, not a tie. His thick hair shone stiffly. She smoothed her own professionally tailored jacket. It felt new again, fresh.

"We're both dressed to make some business," she said.

"Come with me, please. We take taxi." She unclipped the crowd-control strap from its chrome bar. She reclipped it behind her and smiled at him, blushing. They walked to the taxi queue without talking, throwing sidelong glances at each other, fighting to keep the grins from their faces.

"Please," Piv said to Robin in the taxi. "I would like to take one beautiful lady to fine restaurant. Okay with you?"

"Only if you mean that you're going to take me." They let their hands drift to the middle of the cab's blue upholstery and touch there. The short drive into town took over an hour in daylight traffic.

"How was that business?" Piv asked.

Robin painted her trip in broad strokes: The men who met her didn't speak English. Mr. Rong did, but he wasn't very nice. She had forgotten her clothes, but she had gotten another double visa without a hitch. "No one's going to think I'm a drugged-out hippie in this outfit, right?" At Piv's prodding, she described Kuala Lumpur, its Bangkok-like traffic jams, its Bangkok-dwarfing skyscrapers, its general lack of glory.

"Okay, then. We don't go there when we make our adventure. We don't need business there."

"Forget Kuala Lumpur!" Robin cried out, reaching back with both arms to touch the rear window glass. "Foooooorrr-get it!" Then she looked to the taxi driver and looked back at Piv and covered her mouth, which was cramped from smiling.

Her lips kept tilting upward as Piv ushered her into the restaurant, leaned toward her to enthuse about the combination of a certain bitter vegetable with a particular curry, reached under the table to brush her knee while still holding her eyes. "I'm so glad to see you, Piv," she said. "I'm so glad it was you who picked me up and not Abu."

"Abu and those friends left Bangkok yesterday, so of course I come to get you. I'm the lucky one."

"Abu's gone? But I have this shipment for him."

"Russian friend is coming. Russian boss. Abu says that you should give that to him."

"But Abu was going to pay me." Robin pushed away her soup bowl, her water glass, and a small cup of pepper sauce. "Is the Russian guy staying at the Star?" Piv shook his head no. "Well, when's Abu coming back?"

"He's coming soon. He made all the arrangements, no problem. He has more business for us—I told you, I help him—and next time we both go. We make money for our plan together." He leaned toward her, his tongue running along the inside of his cheek. "This is the good one." He dipped his chin at her to emphasize his point and raised his eyebrows slightly. In that gesture Robin could see both his close-cropped, suited business aspect and his long-haired rock-and-roll cool. Her smile flattened under the weight of her desire. She reached for her water glass.

"Do you really want to do something with me? I was wondering on the plane."

"Why you wonder?" They looked at each other for one beat, two. Robin didn't speak. Then Piv half rose from his seat and kissed her on the forehead. "You know Thai people don't kiss like that," he whispered, settling back on his chair. "They don't like to see that. But for you, I do. I tell you already, I want to make something."

"Me too," Robin whispered back. Piv dipped his spoon into the soup. Robin watched him inspect the broth, swallow. "But we need a plan. We need a goal to save for. It'd feel good to save with you. Maybe I'd feel better about this stuff with Abu, then."

He took another spoonful. "Why you feel bad?"

"Why? I mean, come on. There's definitely something creepy going on."

"Abu's good for us now." Piv left his spoon in the soup and took out a money roll from the inside pocket of his jacket. Robin noticed again how new his suit gestures were, how smoothly he performed them. "Now we have this—more than two thousand baht."

"It's a start. But if we're really going to do something, not just mess around, we'll need some serious money—that's only what, like five hundred dollars."

"Sure. We'll get more when Abu comes back. If you want, while we wait for that time, I take you to visit my family."

His family! Piv's invitation dissolved Robin's mental abacus. It'd be challenging—he'd told her they didn't speak English—but it meant he wanted her to know him, was going to let her know him. She'd rise to the challenge. She softly bounced in her seat.

"I want to!" she said. "I want to, I want to!" And this time she was the one who leaned over to kiss.

By 11:00 PM in Star Hotel room 517, the bottom sheet had peeled from the mattress corners. A sliver of street light cut through the top sheet and blanket tangled on the floor. Piv wanted to make love again, but Robin kept her hands on his hips and held him slightly from her. "No." She arched to bite his earlobe, then murmured. "I told you. Not without a condom."

"Shh," he said. "I can't help there's no more. I want to make with you too many times. It's okay. I'll be careful."

Robin twisted from under him. "No," she said. For a moment, they weren't touching. "Aren't you worried about AIDS?" Then she swung her leg over his and put her hand on his smooth chest. His aubergine nipples were small as pennies. "Just go get some more," she whispered. "That store is still open."

"I feel shame. Certain kind of shame, how do you say that?"

"Embarrassment? You feel embarrassed?" She used her open palm to trace wide circles around his pectorals.

"I feel that. Today I already go to that store to get condoms. Same girl might see me there, think, wow, what's he doing. Too much!" He giggled, pulled her on top of him.

Robin began kissing his neck. "It's too much? Okay, then. We'll wait until morning."

"Noooo," Piv said. He adjusted her hips. "Shhh. I'll be careful."

The whole conversation was husky and low. When the phone rang, Robin jerked. Piv scooped her to him with one arm. On the next ring, she wrapped tightly around him and hid her face in his skin. He answered the phone, speaking in Thai, "*Krup.*" He switched to English. With one ear pressed to the sheet and one against Piv, Robin heard his words as if she were listening from inside his body: "Abu told me . . . I have that one . . . Of course . . . Excuse me, but I think now is late . . . No. Okay, I meet you . . . Okay, yes . . . No problem. Sure. Of course." She felt his skin tighten as he reached to hang up the phone, then he curled into her, bringing his knees up so they pressed against her belly.

"Russian one. Volcheck. He wants me to meet him now, at Soi Cowboy bar. To give him the things from Mr. Rong."

"Now?" Robin said. "But you're in bed."

"He says now. We have something that belongs to him. He wants that now." Piv untangled himself, swung his legs off the bed. His face was blank. Robin reached up to touch his hip.

"I'll go with you. Then we can go to the store after." She smiled.

"You cannot. Not this place. It's not for the lady." He went into the shower.

He was dressed and with his hand on the doorknob before she said, "Aren't you going to say good-bye?" He came over and kissed her without diverting his attention back into the room. When he left, she rose and straightened the bed, pulling the rough top sheet over herself, her sticky thighs, as protection against the air-conditioning.

Piv took another shower when he came home at 4:00 AM. He didn't want to talk about his evening. "Shhh," he told Robin when he found her questioning and awake. "You'll see. He says for you to meet him in lounge at noon hour." Piv rolled over and closed his eyes. Robin strained to hear him sleep. He didn't snore; he barely breathed. She wondered if he was faking. She disliked Volcheck already.

Meeting him didn't improve her impression. She had waited in the lounge for twenty minutes, nursing a Coke with lime, before he pushed through the door with a wobbling white woman in tow. He lumbered to Robin's table and sank into a chair with a grunt; the woman minced behind him, waiting until he nudged a chair out with his foot before she sat. "You're the American girl," he said. He flicked his eyes at Robin before looking away. He was chewing on something. His cud, Robin thought. She could hear his breathing. "I want you to take this girl shopping." He had a fringe of pale hair growing from the curve of each ear and hair in other places that shouldn't need shaving, like the bridge of his nose. He patted down his clothing, taking a scarlet-edged handkerchief from his breast pocket and swiping at his brow before tucking the cloth into one inside coat pocket, fishing in the other one, shifting from buttock to buttock to dig in back pockets, then lifting his pelvis to reach into the front of his trousers. He brought out a money clip. "I have only American," he said. He peeled off twenties and they scattered on the table. "You exchange it." After half a year of colored money, the green looked anomalous to Robin, silly.

"She never left Russia before. She has nothing. Get her a few things. And something nice for under. Nadja." He spoke to the woman briefly in Russian. "My girlfriend. What are you called?" he asked Robin.

"Robin. Robin Miatta." Why had she given him her full name?

"Robin." He rolled the word around in his mouth like it was a fruit pit. "Robin. Robin." He switched to Russian. Robin could hear versions of her name speckling his sentences. The woman stuttered it once. She had full makeup on: foundation, blusher, liner, shadow, clumpy mascara. Robin wanted to flake it away with her fingernail, get to the wide prettiness underneath.

"Piv calls me Nok. It's Thai. Do you like that better?" Robin looked at the woman. "Is it easier for you to say Nok?"

Volcheck scowled and brushed the names away with his hand. "You carry the money. You watch her. Bring her back here at five o'clock. I want receipts. And give the money that's left to me. It's not hers."

Robin picked up the twenties and started counting them. Volcheck stood. "How much did I give you?" he asked.

"There's a hundred and twenty here."

He took them from her hand and thumbed them, then added two more from his roll. "That's enough. That's more than enough for her." From his jacket pocket came a small notebook; he muttered in Russian as he wrote.

"And excuse me," said Robin, wrapping the bills around her finger. "But Abu promised to give me something for the errand I just ran for him. You got everything last night. Since he's not here, are you the one handling that?"

Volcheck breathed out hard like a horse, a sound that meant no. "But I'll pay you for today." He let flutter two more twenties then shook his suit back square onto his wide shoulders. Robin envisioned herself leaving the dollars there, walking away, but she slid the money off the table. One bill had stuck to her sweating Coke glass.

Instead of taking Nadja to Siam Square or Silom Road, Robin headed across the river to a district with newer construction. Palmed weeds still grew around the scrubby lots of high-rise apartment buildings, and dogs occasionally ambled in sunshine down the sois. She hoped this might be less overwhelming to the Russian woman, whose wary posture— arms crossed, shoulders hunched, legs sealed together—contrasted with her playful, revealing clothing. The taxi let them out across the street from a shopping center. On the sidewalk, Nadja tugged on her short red skirt with one hand while keeping the other across her chest. Her eyes darted under a stiff brow. Robin had been to this mall before, with Piv, to see an American movie with Thai subtitles. *Forrest Gump* was playing now. Robin had expected to see more farangs in this district because of the theater, but she spotted none on the busy street. "Come on," she said to Nadja. When her words only got a stare, she gestured.

To cross the six-lane road they had to use a pedestrian's flyover half a block up. When she was with Piv, Robin no longer noticed when she was the only foreigner in a room. Walking with Nadja past crowded street-vendor booths, though, she felt self-conscious on the other woman's behalf. They were in a middle-class neighborhood, and in Bangkok people never gawked or shouted *farang, farang* the way kids might deep in the countryside, but Robin suspected a constant stream of covert stares. These didn't alight on her. Nadja, tall anyway, wore wedge-heeled sandals and was quite meaty in her skirt and glimmery top. Robin nudged her and rolled her eyes to commiserate, to help her through. She'd been missing female company. In Turkey, she and a French woman had once traveled together quite companionably for a week using only their limited shared vocabulary and a whole host of eye signals. Language didn't have to be a barrier. But Nadja's eyes just bugged further. Black dust powdered the skin beneath them, specks of mascara or of soot.

"What is it you need to buy?" asked Robin once they were inside. The first display was a bin of tiny, padded, pastel bras that would never fit her charge. "Do you want a shirt?" She plucked at the corner of her own. "Some pants?" She wagged her loose-legged cotton ones. She knew Nadja couldn't understand her, but she had to at least try. "Or more stuff like you already have?" She swept her hand down Nadja's frame. Very polyester, but then Russians weren't known for their fashion. Robin urged her toward the women's department, to let her wander and decide. So much for a bonding shopping trip. Then Nadja touched Robin's elbow and put her hand high on the center of her own chest. She shook her head. "Nyet. No," she said.

"No?" Robin asked. She stared at her face, tried to read something there. "No what?"

Nadja held up one finger and opened her white vinyl clutch purse. The clasp was gold-colored with small blue and green rhinestones. "No." Her eyes on Robin, she stirred her hand in the purse's contents, then offered it over. Robin took it. A cosmetic smell wafted from the satin inside. There was a gummy cosmetic bag, a pink-handled hairbrush, a small flip-stack of photos, a toothbrush in a plastic bag. Robin looked up with a question.

"No, no, no," Nadja said. Her kohl-rimmed eyes were almost a dusky purple. They were glassy, flinting, scared. Was she really Volcheck's girlfriend?

"It's okay." Customers kept streaming in the store, women wearing neat sandals, matching sets, teenagers with platform shoes poking from tight black pants. Robin stepped toward Nadja and took her arm. She could smell the woman's perfume and body heat dissipating into the air-conditioning. Nadja's nipples rose through her blouse and Robin winced for her. She handed the clutch back.

Nadja took it but shook her head urgently. She said something in Russian. She opened the white purse again and pantomimed a sweeping grab. Looking, Robin could see that the pale blue lining was pulled away in one corner. A brighter, centered square with small threads dangling indicated a former pocket.

"You were robbed?" Robin said. "You need a new purse?" They were communicating, but Robin still didn't understand. This was a story she didn't know. She reached under her shirt to her money belt and brought out all the cash she had with her: five hundred baht. She was embarrassed because she'd been sweating and the money smelled like her skin.

"Here," she said. "This isn't that guy's; we don't have to give it back to him. He won't know you have it. At least you can use it to call someone."

Nadja took the baht and tucked it in her blouse, then pressed her purse to her chest.

"Can I help you call someone? Should we go to a phone?" Robin made the gesture of dialing, of holding the receiver to her ear. "Is there someone who can help you? Who should know where you are?"

No answer. But the money seemed to calm her. Robin kept her arm on Nadja's shoulder while they shopped. They looked hard to find big-enough blouses, T-shirts, skirts—all of them meant to be sexy. They spent the equivalent of a hundred and thirty-five dollars, then bought ice cream cones at the food court on the top floor of the store. They licked silently but in a din; dressed-up children were performing lip-synch routines to music that bounced against the skylight and the white floor. The little girls had pink lipstick on, circles of blush, and they were very expressive. Robin watched the miniature, practiced dancing. Then she turned her head to see Nadja staring with blank concern at nothing at all.

"Will you be okay?" Robin asked her. Nadja angled her head to show the frustrated effort she was making at comprehension. The two of them looked at each other, both of their foreheads furrowed, and cheerful pop music clattered around them.

Chapter 11

I don't like this Russian boss, Russian Vol. I make Robin go alone to meet him at noon. I say to tell him I'm asleep, but after she leaves he's coming to my room, pounding on the door. "Open the door," he says. "I pay for your room."

I open the door with no shirt on to show I was sleeping. I smile at him. "Good morning," I say. "We stay late last night. Wow. Excuse me while I take shower. I'll meet you in lounge. Few moments please." But he comes past me and sits in the chair. "Excuse me," I say, but he doesn't leave. Why do I need to be with him too much? Last night I sit with him in Soi Cowboy fuck bar. We don't have conversation, getting to know you, talk about our countries like with Abu. No, nothing like that. Sometimes I talk for him. He tells me to. He speaks good English, but he doesn't like to try with people who don't speak so good like him. He makes me ask mamasan, bar manager, how much for that girl, for one hour if she leaves right now? How much for that one, number sixty-six, for all night? How much business does Soi Cowboy lose because of Naga Entertainment Plaza, do girls cost more there? Mamasan looks at me funny. I tell her please excuse, I don't ask for me, I ask for that one there, that farang.

Some Thai men, they go with prostitutes, sure, this is popular. In every town you can do this. But for me, no, I don't like it. I don't like to pay for the lady. These ladies are poor ones, come from the North, the Northeast, very poor, they have to. I don't have to. Russian Vol makes me ask about this, but I don't want to do anything with them, no. And maybe he doesn't want to, or else it's costing too much, because when we leave that place he doesn't take the Thai lady. Three come after him and touch his arms, say, "Why you don't like me? Why you don't stay?" but he doesn't take them.

Today after I shower I follow Russian Vol to one lounge in another hotel building. We drink in there, and he chews on his straw. Then he says to me, "How much you think you'll need for tomorrow? For your guys in customs?"

I don't know what these words mean, so I smile. I look up at video screen, and I laugh like it's very funny there.

"Hey, dumb shit! For your guys at the airport? What do you usually give them?"

"No problem." I nod to him. "Give them something."

"What the fuck, I thought you had guys. The fucking African told me it was okay we didn't have papers for these because you could get 'em right off the plane." I look at him. His neck is fat. His face is red. I hold my face soft and still. "Do you even know what the fucking Christ I'm talking about?"

Answer to that one: no. Why Abu never told me about this? Why did Abu leave me here? But I can guess something. Maybe tomorrow is March 4. Maybe Vol is yelling about some business with Admiral Wattanayakorn. It's the only thing I have to say.

"Of course I know. Dock N243. Of course I know."

"Fucking black Africans. Christ, what black hole did he pull you out of?" Did I guess wrong? But he's still yelling. "How much, I said! And don't pad it."

Okay, maybe I guess right. Dock N243, and from Vol I know some customs wants money. Too much money, and I'm supposed to give it to them. "Ten thousand baht," I say. I'm supposed to get something coming off that plane.

"Fucking Christ shit," he says. English swear words. He knows too many. "You better not fuck this up."

Star Hotel is better than this Russian Vol hotel. Even in daytime, I see the bar girl working in here. No one's happy. No one's nice, I can see that. American movie on the video screen is spread thin; you cannot see the face, eyes, mouth move, too blurry.

"Please. It's no problem. But you need to tell me flight. The time. How much will arrive." I think I can use Saisamorn's nephew's car. Will it fit inside there?

"It's Royal Jordan flight 617, arriving at 11:20. Dump your girlfriend in the terminal, tell her to call you when it arrives." He makes the stomach noise with his mouth, starts counting thousand baht bills. They're bigger than five hundred baht. They look powerful.

"Excuse. I do not have the mobile phone. Impossible for NokRobin to call."

"They said you're local skill. Worth my money. You're a fucking monkey." He chews on that plastic straw some more. It slices air, up and down. He's too ugly. Of course he must pay for the lady, pay too much. No lady would ever pay for him.

"It's okay. No problem without."

"And leave it wide open? I'll give you my fucking phone for the day."

He gives me his phone. He gives me ten thousand baht, as much as I can think to ask, and he gives without bargaining. I don't know anything about this airport, customs, dock, but I think I know more than him. He needs me to do it. "Okay. And how much money you give me for doing this business?"

Vol takes five hundred baht and smashes it on the table with his thick hand. "This is all your fucking money I have, and you're not worth it. You don't know shit."

"My money? What you mean? No more baht? It's okay. Dollars are for everyone."

After some time of discussion, he says he'll give me one hundred dollars. To me, yesterday, this is big money, enough, but I laugh and say I know the customs, I take big risk, why does he give nothing for this? Three hundred, I tell him. Russian Vol says fucking bullshit no. Fucking black African assholes give him someone with the banana up his ass, fuck that.

Jairong. He has hot heart. Ugly heart. I just smile.

When he wants me to, I hire the taxi driver to go to Star Hotel and get the Russian girlfriend, bring her back. Vol wants pizza food, so I take them to Pan Pan, one pizza restaurant I know. I don't order food. I don't want to eat now—my stomach feels tight, to me this food is no good. When they finish, I can leave them. Nine o'clock at night, and I want to see NokRobin, but first I say, "I do your business tomorrow for three hundred dollars. If not, no problem. I still can stay in Star Hotel. Owner of that place is my friend."

Russian Vol spit on ground. He says one hundred now and two hundred then, when I bring that thing back. Okay, I say. From his pocket he gives me one hundred dollar bill. The most U.S. dollars I ever have of my own, and I see it's nothing to him.

"Where've you been?" That's the first thing NokRobin says to me when I open the door to our room. She's in the bed already. Her voice is not sweet.

"I make some business for us. I make some money. Shh," I say. I take off my shoes and socks and leave them at the door and go to kiss her, to make her sweet.

"Be there at five o'clock," NokRobin makes her voice like the man's to say this. "I had to sit in the bar for two hours with a freaked-out woman who can't speak English. And then some Thai guy comes and just shows her a card and takes her away, doesn't say a word. He could be an ax murderer. She didn't know, she was terrified. Were you with that Volcheck all day? Where were you?" Her words are sharp and fast, and it's hard for me to hear them now. When I'm tired, that's when my mind wants Thai.

"Show me your back," I tell her. "You're too excited. I'll give you massage." She turns over. She's not wearing clothes, but the sheet covers her bottom. I pull up the sheet and touch her hot back through that. I feel tight knots and poking knobs. I want to talk to her like this. To her body with my hands. No English.

"Did Nadja end up with you guys? She's not really his girlfriend, that's for sure. I think she's a prostitute, but maybe she's not even getting paid."

"She's something, sure. Maybe bar girl from his country. But shhh. It's okay. He's not nice one, not smooth, but no problem." I lean to her ear; my body goes all along her back. Her hair smells clean, some still wet. "Tomorrow we do some business. Me and you together. And we make some money. Three hundred dollars. I get this for us."

"Three hundred dollars?" I feel her body fall under my fingers. Too bony, this one. The Thai lady is small, but not too many bones stick out. "What do we have to do?" she asks me. I feel her voice in her body, it shakes soft in there.

I tell her we do nothing. Go to airport. Pick up something from one man who knows that I will come. That's all. Three hundred dollars for nothing, for our plan.

NokRobin is quiet for a while, and I massage her. I go from Thai-style to hot-oil style. I pull down the sheet, use Nivea lotion instead of hot oil. I rub her skin and move things underneath her skin. She relaxes. Maybe we both relax now.

"But three hundred dollars, that's barely a plane ticket somewhere. We'll need a lot more than that." When she talks again it sounds like rain on one empty log. I stop massage then. I shut off the light. We make something, but it's quick, small. After, I watch TV in darkness. Thai show. I want those words to rest my brain.

We pay Saisamorn's nephew to borrow his Mitsubishi, and we leave the Star at eight o'clock in the morning, more than three hours until Royal Jordan plane arrives. We pass weekend market and orchid garden, and I know where we are, to drive is no problem. But when we get to airport, wow, cars go faster. I thought maybe when I am by it I would have one feeling about where to go, but it's too much moving. Ugly Vol is right. I know nothing. Abu is wrong. Why he not tell me? How will I find what I need?

"Doesn't that look like it could be a cargo area, way over there?" NokRobin asks me. But my mouth's too tight to talk. Blue airport bus drives in front of me. White color bus drives on the side. I can see nothing. Everyone goes too fast. I need to go slow, look for some sign, but now the white bus comes close, wants to go past me even though minivan comes up behind. "What an asshole!" NokRobin says. When I can see again, it's just in time. International Terminal. I can drive the car into that lane. Cars slow down again. I stop to let NokRobin out.

Her eyebrows squish, worried. "I thought you wanted me to help you find it before you dropped me off."

"No problem. I can find. Better for you to go in now." I don't tell her it's more peaceful without her. I need to listen to my heart. I need to find my own plan.

My plan is this: I drive away. Away from International Terminal, from expressway, from airport bus. I go on regular road back toward Bangkok. I drive until I see what I want. I don't know it before, but something tells me: one 7-Eleven, parking lot in front.

I stop my car and get out to look. Sky near the earth is white, but sky straight above is light blue, and planes appear there as they lift. Inside, 7-Eleven is shiny like some department store. I choose tamarind sweets to buy; I like the sweet and salty taste. The man who takes my money has thick skin. It's not dark, but it's thick, tough, holes in it. His hair's tough, too. I say to him: Wow. This 7-Eleven is big one. In my district center they have 7-Eleven now, but I don't think it's big like this. Even the ones in Silom area, in Rama IV Road area, they seem small compared to this.

No one is in store at this time. This man begins to talk to me— sure it's big, sure he feels confused at first in airport area, sure he feels lucky when he gets his job three years after being in Bangkok. Before that he worked in toy factory, much more hard job for only one hundred fifty baht each day. He loses that job, but now his pay is better, more like three hundred baht per day. He talks some time, talks past ten o'clock. One lady comes in, wants to buy something. No problem. I move to look at things they sell—toilet paper, deodorant, mosquito coils, toothpaste. When the customer goes, I talk to the man some more. I say: The son of my uncle works near here; he works for airport. He works unloading luggage, and he tells me, hey, you never find your way to my dock. You're from the province, finding anything in the capital city will be too hard for you.

I laugh, then I say this: I want to surprise the child of my uncle. To come to the place where he works. I live in Bangkok and have good job now. Car. I want to surprise him, so then he knows something about the son of his country aunt.

The man says to me: I know someone who used to work there. Maybe he could tell you the way to get to that place.

I reach in my jacket pocket and get Russian Vol's phone. I hold it out to him. Older brother, I say, please, I beg you to try to call and find out.

Back in the car, clock says 10:45. Royal Jordan is coming in thirty-five minutes, but maybe I can find the dock before that time. I follow directions to one small road. The road goes through the row of trees, then follows one long silver fence. On the other side of fence is some dry grass, some cement, very flat. Trying to see through the fence is making me dizzy, and there's nothing behind there. Inside my head I feel I'm falling. I search for too much and there's nothing here.

But then—softly, softly—the cement I thought was flat goes flatter, more flat. And now I can see it, everything: when the cement goes down I see big airplanes coming up to my eyes, flat white buildings black at the bottom with dark openings, cars and trucks like ants moving all around. It's almost eleven o'clock now. The sun is very hot, and what I see is in the distance. I see it shake there, move.

Inside Mitsubishi I feel hot, too; air-condition doesn't matter. I feel hot, but I must do this. Signs say DO NOT ENTER. AUTHORITY VEHICLE ONLY. They say this in English and Thai, but I must drive closer. Where the fence opens and the road turns in, some orange arms reach across the pavement to stop my Mitsubishi, but no guards are there at this time, and these arms won't stop me. At this small entry they're plastic. The friend of the man in 7-Eleven already told me this, and it's true, no problem—when you drive forward the plastic arms bend; they'll let you through.

Then I learn this road is like one river. Like one skinny river, it starts somewhere small and pours into the great sea. Now I'm in the sea of cement, and I can start to see how big the airplanes are. First I feel small. How can I go closer without getting crushed? But then my problem is that in my car I am too big. How can I drive without someone seeing me? There's nowhere to hide, and I need to. Like two white gulls sailing over the water, two hungry cars are coming toward me.

They come from different sides of the docking place, both coming to meet my fat Mitsubishi. I stop the car, and they come close— two white jeeps, luxury ones, thick wheels, and two men in each. I can hear the jeep engines, both running. I can hear metal doors close. Two men walk to my car window. It's the bad dream. They have automatic rifles that I know from the army, and I hate to see this. My fingers hurt and my stomach feels sick. I want to be away, but I roll down window and I wai and I smile. One man jerks his head at me. Tells me like this to get out of my car.

It's like I get hit—*pow*—with hot air when I stand from my car. Hot wind blows my suit against my body, and I can hear the noise from the engines of everything: jeep noise, trucks, airplanes on the ground and moving into sky. One man pushes me with his shoulder, reaches into Mitsubishi to get the car key from there. What can I do if they keep this one? Then that mobile phone sings. It's inside the car, on the seat where I threw it. The man reaches inside there and picks up the phone. Phone beeps again. He looks at the other man, looks at me. He presses the button. "*Krup,*" he says. "*Krup.*" Where is NokRobin now? In my mind I see her hang up the phone. Her face folds, confused. Man puts the phone in his own pocket. I want to take my phone away from that man. I smile.

He says to me: What you doing here? You trespass on airport property, clearly stated by sign. Why don't you stop at that roadblock? I think I should arrest you, take you to chief of airport police.

I still am smiling when I wai and duck my head. His eyes are stony. He holds his gun with two hands, pushes it into my chest. He says again, very angry, short words: Why are you here?

At this moment, I don't know that answer. I can't remember. Excuse me, I say. Engines beat my words. He pushes me again with his gun. Now I remember something. Army training, what I can do in this situation. My arm can come up fast like the bullet behind his gun. In one moment I can kick this man's knee and push my arm down—gun flies down, too. In my mind I see this. But outside my mind is Saisamorn's nephew's car, and this man has the key. The other man writes down number of license. Russian Vol is judging. I think Abu is judging. My head breaks, my fingers hurt, my stomach. But I'm not in the jungle. This is some business. This is the plan. No kicking, not now.

I say: Excuse me. My uncle tells me it's okay to do something here. He says go to dock N243.

Who's your uncle?

If you will permit, I say. I reach into my trouser pocket for the baht bills. Ten one thousands. Folded once, they're almost big as one book. I say: It's arranged already. Please. Dock N243. I think they wait for me.

Gun man keeps his rifle on me. This other man goes to his jeep, gets in. He speaks into small phone that's attached to the radio. Then he comes back from jeep. When he takes the money from my fingers, I smell his cologne. He says: They'll meet him at hangar 12B.

Then that phone sings again. That phone like some child's shoe in the gun man's pocket. I wait one moment, then say: Excuse me. I beg you. Please.

The man holds his hand open for me. Now he smiles. He wants more baht. Phone is singing. I have no more from Russian Vol. I reach into my other pocket, into my own money. There's only some hundred baht notes, but I give this to him. I take the phone. NokRobin's voice comes at me, and it sounds like far away, like international call, from over the ocean. "Five minutes ago, Piv. It landed five minutes ago. Where were you?"

"Okay," I say to her. I turn off the phone.

The gun man tells me: Get in your car, follow me.

I follow him past one plane, and it's as big as the big building. It takes long moments to pass it by. Men in light purple clothing ride machines up to reach into the plane's belly, and they take the suitcases out of there. Everywhere on the ground sit big silver boxes. We drive past these, drive under one long roof and into dark shade. The thick pillars here seem like they're going to hit me. I want to duck while I drive.

When we reach the place where there's no people, no metal boxes, gun man stops his jeep. He rolls down the window and moves his hand to the ground to tell me stay here, then he drives away. Inside my car, engine running, air conditioner, I wonder if that man takes my money and leaves me here, sets me here to be arrested or to be lost, and I will never find my way.

I step out of my car. Some broken cars and trucks and vans stand open; they spill their black mess onto the cement floor. Ugly. Old. No one is here. But I see one thing I like. On one gray pillar, I see picture of Thailand's King. I go to him. I want to talk to him, something like pray. Maybe our King can help me find.

When I go to my King I hear something. Through all the far-off engine noise, I hear one small engine coming close to me. Then I see it—three wheels like a tuk tuk, but these wheels are bigger than that. And on this thing is one man who wears tan color trousers and shirt. He's smoking cigarette. When he pulls up his tuk tuk close to me, all the other noise seems quiet.

He yells to me: What gate? When I tell him, he says: What flight? He nods his head when I say Royal Jordan Airline, flight 617.

He says: Yes. It's arranged. You don't move from here. Then he gets out of his tuk tuk, that engine still running. He comes to stand in front of me. He crosses his arms. He smiles.

We stand like this, then I wai him. I say: Excuse me. I would like to give you the gift, but I met those other ones. I did not expect them.

I show this man my pockets. No thousands. No hundreds. Empty. Only twenty-four baht. I hold this small baht to him. I say: Please. I am young, new to doing this business. Today I learn. Today I make mistakes. Please. Forgive me this moment.

This man smiles. He calls me young brother. Says: Young brother, I do not ask you for money. But this business can be arranged most quickly if I can make one phone call. Do you have phone for me to do this?

Now I see. I reach for that phone. It fits in my hand like someone's fingers would. I give it to him.

He looks at it. What time is it? he says. He looks at me and my watch and smiles. I push the strap, pull it away from the small stick that holds it. It's the watch that one farang girlfriend gives me. Plastic, but this man must be like many people, he loves the style. My wrist feels wet and cool without it.

Open your trunk and wait here.

Then that man gets in tuk tuk and *vroom*, he goes away. His noise get smaller. After he leaves, air smells newer, mixed with the old is fresh lead and gasoline. I open the trunk, and I lean against car door. I don't know what to do now. I am alone. No phone for NokRobin to call me. No watch to see how many minutes pass by.

But one man comes. He drives something like small van, only with open shelves where the walls should be, and these have boxes on them. Brown cardboard boxes like you see in the store, in the P.O., anywhere. His dark blue color shirt has two buttons closed, that's all. He's dark and shiny from too much sun. Not talking, I work with this man to put boxes into trunk. Some don't fit in there. I put these in the backseat of Mitsubishi. Dark man watches when I do this. His van is empty.

I say: This all I have. I give the rest too much. They take everything.

He takes the twenty-four baht. When he reaches for the money, I see his hands are very dirty. Before I turn on the car, I use the key to take dirt from under my fingernails so my hands look clean.

NokRobin is waiting for me where I left her. She's relieved to see me. In the car, when I tell her what happened, she calls me brave soldier. Then she teaches me that word, *relieved*. She says I must feel relieved— and she does, too. And she's proud I'm brave. Don't worry about stupid Vol's phone. Don't worry about money. She has some money with her.

I'm very smart. I did the right thing. She wants me to feel more awake, so she tells me these things. She's sweet, but I still feel tired.

I tell her, "I know what I want to do now with you. I don't want to go to Star Hotel. I want to go and get one drink, to rest there, someplace nice."

She laughs at me. "I've never heard you say you wanted a drink, Piv." She puts her hand on my knee. She wears her hair up on her head with pins, and some pieces come out. She smiles at me, and I see all of her teeth.

Then she turns and leans over to the backseat. Her bottom goes up. Why's she sitting like that? Too many cars, too many buses higher than this car. "What you doing?" I'm too tired to laugh. "Someone can see you."

"I want to see what we're risking our lives for." I hear her slide cardboard. Her feet kick when she does this. "There's no address on them. Just the word *fragile* and the name Prachat Saipradit. Who's that?"

I tug her blue dress. "You want police to stop me because one lady in my car is upside down?" Now she turns to the front again. Hard to drive in too much traffic when she moves like this, takes up the whole car, and this car is heavy now. The trunk's full; I can feel that weight. Other cars go past me. We pass one motorbike twisted all around metal. It's been wrecked. At last NokRobin sits quiet again. She reaches up to put pins back in her hair.

She has money for nice lunch and some drinks, so we go to one place I know. It's on large klong, and you feel that restaurant float on the water, relaxing. I want to feel relieved. I order Singha beer. Today it tastes good. But NokRobin is not ready for relaxing. She's too excited. She turns her head this way, that way. She likes this restaurant on the water, she likes the market we walk through to get here. She points at the fish, the barrel full of snails. She says, "Ooooo, look at that." Then she wants to eat adventure. Order some things that she's never tried, that she thinks farang don't get to eat. Okay, I order turtle soup, morning glory vine, dish with raw pork cut very fine. She tastes soup one time, two times, three times, then pushes it away. She tries the meat. One bite, two bites, eating with her spoon like I show her, but she doesn't like that taste. Then she leans toward me.

"Whatever's in those packages is too hot to go through customs, and we should be making more."

"Three hundred is already more. Better for us not to know what's inside. It's not our business." Turtle soup is not my favorite. For me, the best soup is tom yam, prawn and lemongrass, but farang always eat this, so I order some adventure for NokRobin.

"What do you mean, it's not our business? Of course it is. We're taking risks, and we expect a gain in return. That's what we want, right? That's business."

"It's our business to do what you say, but not to know more. Not at this time."

"Piv, how can we make this worth our while if we don't even know what's going on?"

Bite of turtle feels smooth. When you chew that, it's still smooth. Not too much taste. It tastes like underwater. Why does NokRobin want to know this?

"How can we look in those boxes? They're closed tight. If we do it, Vol will see. Then we have no more business, or maybe some other bad thing will happen."

NokRobin tells me those boxes aren't closed in any special way. She already looked to see this.

She has beer in her Singha bottle. She picks it up, but she doesn't pour beer in her glass. She holds that bottle up to me. "Cheers, Piv. To you and me." We touch our bottles, then drink big sips of beer. When we finish, she looks at me. "Now's our chance. Before we give him those boxes, we have to see."

Chapter 12

Side by side, Piv and Robin walked back up the narrow market lane toward their borrowed car. The air smelled tangy-swampy—they were passing stalls that sold freshwater seafood. Vendors called out to shoppers; they slid scoops of dehydrated shrimp into opaque pink plastic bags, reached into wooden barrels and hooked slick black eels that they rolled into newspaper. Piv stepped into Robin to let a cart of cut fruit go bell-ringing past. The cushion of his suit against her bare arm made her want to wrap her limbs around him right there. She nuzzled her elbow into his. He'd had a stressful day; she'd supply the energy from here. He gave her a small, indulgent smile. When she had even modest heels on, they were almost the same height.

She wanted to stay pressed next to him, but they resumed walking. They moved through to the produce section, where the smells turned garlic-bitten but sweet and ripe. The sunset colors of guavas, papayas, and mangoes popped out of the dominant green. Two monks walked past in perfect harmony with the color scheme, the saffron fabric of their slung bags a shade lighter than that of their robes. Robin shrank so as not to touch them, pleased that, thanks to Piv, she knew to do so.

At the car, Piv opened her door first. She didn't get in. While he walked around to his side, she unlocked the back door and bent over to reach into it.

"What you doing?" he asked her.

She hoisted a box from the floor well and gathered it to her breast, giving a little grunt when she straightened. The package was about two feet long and heavy enough to ache her muscles. She kicked the back door shut and shoved the box in the front seat before squeezing next to it. "Whew," she said. She arched away from the seat to straighten her dress. The box had left a thin triangle of red where it had pressed into her chest. "The big moment. How should we do this?" She looked in the mirror and dabbed at the sweat in the groove of her chin. "Or do you want to drive around to get the air conditioner going?"

He didn't answer, just started the car and pulled into traffic. For a moment, they moved in tandem with a couple on a motorbike, the woman sitting sidesaddle, black pumps dangling from her feet. She carried a yellow shopping bag in her lap. Her eyes met Robin's. Then the car was snarled by congestion. The motorbike moved freely on.

"How much money you have?" Piv asked.

"Six hundred. Why?"

"Give me five. We buy private time." Robin reached into her purse, not sure what he meant but glad he had a plan, that he wasn't just passively following along.

"What do you think's in there?" she said. Piv was monitoring the cars beside him, trying to switch into the next lane. He didn't answer. "I'd bet with you about it, but I have no idea. I mean, drugs I guess, but if it is, can you believe I carried that suitcase into Malaysia? How stupid." Robin hugged herself. "Well, but it turned out all right. And if I was carrying drugs, I guess I'm glad I didn't know it then. Although I should have gotten more money. Not that I'd do it again if it was drugs. Not to Malaysia. God! But I really do think it's something else. I have a feeling. Come on, make a guess, just one thing."

Piv lifted his foot from the brake and the car moved forward another few inches. "Abu said it's not drugs, so I believe. If Vol says that, I don't believe."

"Me too! I don't know why, but I believe Abu. So do you think it might be like he said? African curios? Like old tribal art, or anthropological artifacts?"

"Mmm. Perhaps." He was trying to cut over one more lane.

"Because they have restrictions about taking stuff like that out of the country. Museums are even giving a lot of tribal art back now. You can't just buy the really important pieces in a gallery. But of course it's still in demand." Black market art dealer. This squared with her image of Abu, and she'd heard that thugs like Volcheck had turned Russia's museums into their personal stockrooms. "In Southeast Asia, though?" she murmured, losing the energy to explain her thinking to Piv. "Makonde carvings and Orthodox icons?"

Piv gave a short nod. "Mm." His eyes were on the red meter taxi in front of them.

"Are you listening?" she asked. She hated it when he tuned her out and responded rotely—why didn't he tell her if he didn't understand? But she didn't quiz him further.

Traffic moved more easily when they turned off the main thoroughfare onto a tree-lined road. The air conditioner began to work. Then Piv steered the car into a driveway shaded black as a cave mouth. Robin's body lurched with the quick swerve. She blinked her eyes. That fast, a blue-vested man leaned into Piv's waiting, rolled-down window. The two tossed words between them without moving their lips. Piv's hands on the steering wheel now held a numbered plastic chit. "What's going on?" Robin said. The car rolled with a tidal pull into a marked spot, and instantly heavy curtains closed around three sides of it. In the gloom, Robin sat facing a cinder block wall broken by one metal door.

Piv got out of the car, then leaned back in to pick up the box. "Come on," he said. Robin listened to the thunk of his car door slamming. He turned a key in the metal door, opened it, flicked a switch. Silhouetted by the electric light, he cocked his head at her.

What kind of boyfriend jumped out of the car with no concern for whether or not his companion would follow? Whether or not she knew where they were? "Where are we?" she hissed, suspecting the curtains hid rows of ears. Then she realized she was in the sealed up car. Piv couldn't hear her. She opened the door and put her foot out. "Where are we?" she repeated.

"Shh," he said. He cocked his head again. Not a single piece of his hair moved. He lacquered it now with Robin's gel. The carport's curtains hung from a horseshoe-shaped runner. She panned the vinyl-backed fabric for a crack of daylight, but none showed through. She followed Piv into the building, frowning.

Rough brown carpeting covered the floor and went halfway up the walls; wallpaper with metallic gold swirls finished the trip to the lowered ceiling. Piv set the box down on a round wood-grain table. Robin leaned against the door. She saw her crossed arms reflected in the smoked mirror headboard of the king-sized bed. The clean room smelled musty from being windowless and air-conditioned and too close to the ground. No stilts raising it to the air, no basement carving out space underneath, Robin could sense dirt under her feet. She shot her head forward and goggled her eyes at Piv.

"We don't know what's in this box. Could be anything, but you want to open that on the street? This is better." He picked up a bottle of water from a small tray on the dresser and peeled back the aluminum cap, then poured a glass and brought it to her. She drank, eyes closed, hearing her own squishy gulps. She handed him back the glass. She saw the shadow on his upper lip, the thin baby hairs. He'd never have a full beard. "How do you know you can wrap again so Vol won't know you opened?" he asked.

She felt lonely. She wanted him to touch her. She pressed herself more tightly against the cool door. "We'll pay attention when we open it, then we'll seal it up at the Banglamphu P.O."

He reached for her hand and took three steps backward, pulling her into the room. "Okay?" he said, bending his knees a little to meet her eyes squarely. "You still want to? This place is better?"

She tried to rally, smiled. "You can't learn anything without breaking some eggs," she said. She moved to inspect the package, running her finger along its shiny seam then thumping the box over and over again, memorizing its particulars. He was right. Better to be in a motel room than out in public. Her curiosity returned. She picked at the thick brown tape with her fingernail. "We better peel the tape, not cut it, huh?"

"If you peel, too much box will come off."

"Well, we can't slice it open. What if we do it slow?" She eased one corner of tape away from the box. A skim of cardboard came with it, spreading like a scratchy stain.

"Careful," Piv said.

"Use my knife."

Robin knew Piv loved her Swiss Army knife, its weight and its thickness, its twenty different blades. He'd told her that he'd had one once, the fisherman's version, but a real fisherman had boated him out to Ko Chang, where he was supposed to meet someone on a stormy day when no passenger ferries were making the trip, and Piv had given the knife in gratitude. The person he'd gone to meet hadn't been there, he told Robin when she'd asked. Now she let him carry her knife. He took it from his pocket and nudged her slightly, centering himself in front of the box's seam. Since Robin had loaned the knife to him, he'd had all the blades sharpened. He flattened the second longest one, the thinnest, against the kiss of adhesive and cardboard and lifted the tape slowly, finessing the knife like a violin bow. The separation made a long puckering sound. The tape curled in on itself, revealing its feathered belly, and the top flaps of the box parted to reveal the shine of white plastic sheeting. When Piv was done, he held the tape aloft, a triumphant snake hunter showing his trophy.

Robin pulled back the box's flaps, touching them only on their corrugated ends. The plastic was the same kind her mom had covered windows with during the winter of 1984, when temperatures hit record lows in Palatka and their old oil heater couldn't keep them warm. Layers of the stuff padded the top of the box, but Robin could see the shadowy promise of substance beneath, like a bulky fish poised under the freeze of a pond. She tried not to be too hurried, too greedy, too clumsy. She thought of fingerprints as her fingers searched through the folds and Piv breathed beside her. Then she touched a tighter plastic, the hard resealable joint of an extra-large ziplock bag, one of several. It had heft. She drew it to her, sheeting and balled up newspaper spilling out of the box as she reeled it in.

And there it was: a brown chunk the shape of a bent arm straining against the bag bottom, dirty flakes crumbling off. For a moment, for all she knew, it could have been anything illicit—a huge hunk of hashish, heroin, a bomb-building chemical compound, an art object pilfered from civilization's most ancient ruin. She held the bag by its seal, and the air conditioner reused the silence. She brought the thing closer and spied flecks of black crimson. Her lungs fluttered with hope. A slab of corundum waiting to be polished to ruby?

But no, as she focused she could see that it wasn't rock solid; it was almost fibrous. And it wasn't simply a rough chunk. It arced, narrowed on one end to a smoother point, a giant incisor. The tooth of a prehistoric monster? And then the visual evidence coalesced with some prior knowledge and Robin pictured a rhinoceros charging toward her, bellowing, blood running down its face: she held its horn. "Uh," she breathed. She dropped the bag.

"Careful with that one," Piv said. He picked it up again out of the box, looked into it as if surveying the weather through a window. Robin waited for his reaction, hoping it would guide hers, put her on firm ground. "This thing's not mine. Not mine. But if I have this . . ."

He stared for a moment then shook his head. "I don't know who to sell this to, how much, nothing." He lowered the bag, stroked his chin. "But maybe. Maybe I could find out something. I could ask very careful. I could find out how much they pay for this. Maybe. Sure. Okay?" Piv took Robin's wrist and looked at her watch.

"Who could want that?" Robin said. The brown carpet turned into a rocky downhill under her feet. Piv's indifference chafed Robin. Even if he were being practical, shouldn't he show at least a lip-tightening stoicism?

He smoothed out a piece of plastic and folded it over once, twice, cradled the horn in it. He put the newspaper back in the box, then the wrapped bag, then tucked a second sheet of plastic neatly around, just as it had been. "It's not my specialty, but some farang tell me Chinese people want it for strength of the man."

Robin lay down spread-eagled on the bed. Even if it was leaving the place it belonged, black market art went to collectors who loved it, who'd preserve it, who'd display it under the best conditions. And she had a silly notion that beautiful things placed artfully together created a sort of celestial hum. But rhinos? Just the boxes of horns had weighed down the car so much that the exhaust pipe scraped the pavement going over a bump. Where were the bodies?

"We must go," Piv said.

She could see her reflection divided up among the circular mirrors glued to the ceiling above the bed. Her hair was falling out of its twist. The flesh of her cheek pulled toward the mattress, giving her features a Down's syndromish slant and breadth. "Let me lie still for a minute," she said. "Come on. We're here. Lie down with me." She didn't know whether she'd be embarrassed or excited by making love in a mirrored bed. Probably both. She just knew she'd feel better if they lay naked together.

"We pay for one half hour in this room. That time's over. And Volcheck . . ." Piv folded the peeled tape-snake and put it in the wastebasket. He picked up the gaping box.

"You can rent by the half hour?" One mirror showed only her curled pink hand.

"Many Thai people live with their family; sometimes there's too many people, so it's hard to make something. This room is for private things. Maybe for love. For one half hour, one hour, two hour, sure, something like that."

"It's not just a Thai thing, Piv. We have places like this, too," Robin said. "Husbands go there who want to cheat on their wives. Prostitutes go there."

"For private things. Okay?" He walked over to the bed, sat down with the box on his lap and made to draw Robin up by the arm. "We go now."

"So how did you know about this place? Who have you been here with?" She pulled her arm away from him. She pictured pieces of Piv's golden body filling the circles above her head. She felt queasy. "Mostly Thai girls or farang?"

"Everyone knows. But I don't come here. I never come here before today."

"You don't need to lie to me. I'm not jealous, I just want to know."

"I'm sorry," he said. He widened his eyes. Gave a small, quick smile, a little shake of his head. "I have nothing to tell you. I have not been here before."

"I don't care, Piv. Really. I just want to know what your life was like before now. Who your girlfriends were. What you did. If you didn't come here, then where did you go?" The words bounced dully between her ears, echoes of questions she'd asked before. She was hollow. She lacked the blood or muscle that would let her rise from the bed.

"Nowhere like we go now. Let's go back to there. Let's go to Volcheck so we can go back to Star Hotel, where we can lie down." He flashed his full smile at her, tugged her arm again.

"What did you think would be in those boxes?"

Piv's body deflated in the manner of a sigh. "Before this time, I don't think about that."

"Oh, come on Piv!" He sat slouched on the bed facing the headboard mirror. Robin tried to use a ceiling mirror to spy on his reflection, but she couldn't get the right angle. She gave up. "I don't think I would have gone to Malaysia if I thought it was drugs. I really don't think I would have. But I didn't think it'd be this. It's sort of sad. It's ugly. Don't you think so?"

"No one thinks about this. That's why it's good business. We already make three hundred dollars." Piv stood up. Robin lashed her eyes at him—he had been to this room with other women; he hadn't cared that he might have been setting her up to carry heroin into Malaysia.

He held the box to his hip with one arm. He looked at her impassively. "Before now, I don't know what's in this box. But I know one thing. Volcheck pays too much money. Now he's waiting. Maybe he's called that mobile phone already." He turned and walked to the door. Wedged it open with his shoe. "Now we go," he said to her. He gestured with his head, then stepped out and let the door close.

When she took a shower that night, she didn't shave her legs, not caring that Thai girls probably didn't have sharp stubble, that raspy legs might offend Piv. She was bone weary. At twilight, Volcheck had made her, too, carry boxes up four flights of back stairs to a hotel room. But first, she and Piv cowered under his tirade about where had they been, who the fuck had answered his mobile phone. When he learned what happened to it, he towered over Piv and drew up his arm as if to backhand him. Robin broke into a sweat. Still glowering, Volcheck let his hand drop. "Bastard cocksucking fucker you owe me," he hollered. He kicked at the one box already in the room, the box they had opened, and Robin's heart raced. Her bones and blood and skin hurt. If he hit her, jacked her to the wall . . . With shame she heard herself pleading. Piv had collected fourteen boxes, perhaps fifty rhino horns altogether, and the violent force that had killed a hundred tons of animal was there in the room with them. She began to shake.

But Piv smiled. He apologized once, twice, ducked his head a little. Finally he said, "Excuse me, but I need many people to help me. Impossible without that. I give them what you give me, then I need more. I give my own money. They want more. How I can say no? Excuse me for your mobile phone."

After they moved the boxes, Volcheck insisted they come with him to dinner: hamburgers. The fear remained with Robin—it punched at her lungs, and she had trouble breathing—but it settled enough so that her hatred had room, too. She hadn't eaten ground beef in months, and she felt sick at the second bite; the taste of grease kept rising to her nose. Volcheck ate three burgers. After picking at a back tooth with a finger, he gave Piv the full two hundred dollars owed them without complaint. She wanted to scorn it, but the money fueled her with a moment of confidence. "Where's Nadja?" Robin had asked. She'd seen no sign of her in the hotel room, no sign of much, just a tenty men's shirt hanging on the closet door. "She sleeps," Volcheck said, batting at the air over his plate with the back of his hand, a reflex.

Usually, Robin would pad naked from bathroom to bed, but tonight she wrapped up in a sarong and tucked herself under the sheets before she unpeeled it, dropped it damp to the floor. Piv lay on top of the covers, watching TV, an ashtray balanced on his stomach. The game show host's Thai sounded ugly to Robin, quacking. She shooed at smoke, then curled fetally sideways, her back to Piv. She lay rigid, not wanting to brush up against the day's sharp feelings. But then Piv rose, the bed shifted, and her fears crashed down around her: Volcheck was a killer—he had murdered people, she felt sure.

And he looted animal parts. A lesser crime, of course, but such a savage waste of life reflected on her own chance to be safe, find beauty, find happiness. On her chance and Piv's, too. Robin bristled, ready to flee, ready to pounce if Volcheck thundered up from under the bed with bloody paws extended to bash in their heads.

Piv slipped back into bed, smelling toothpastey. He reached over and stroked her hip, and his attention relaxed her slightly. She thought of the thick, strong three hundred dollars. Maybe Piv knew something she didn't. He leaned closer and nibbled at her shoulder blade. He reached to cup her drooping breast. She intercepted his hand, brought it up to her mouth to kiss, her grip so tight she could feel his knuckles shift.

She whispered into his fingers, "Is it wrong to kill something that's endangered . . . to take that?"

His other arm came out from under him and cradled her buttock, a compromise. Her weight shifted so that she balanced there, was held aloft by his palm.

"Everything you like, it comes from ground. Silver rings, silkworms. And food, too. Things you need, they come from ground. That's normal."

Silver. Silk. "Well, I hope Volcheck doesn't put us in the ground. Or Nadja." She wanted to be like Zella, sipping tea in shops while smiling merchants placed jade objects on the silk square they'd spread in front of her. She was so far from that.

"Shh. It's okay. He has hot heart, but nothing else. He knows nothing." He squeezed her buttock.

"But these are rare animals. Once they're gone, they can never come back."

"Maybe they're still here, but in some different way. One thing cannot stay the same over time. Never. Nothing stays the same like that." He untangled his fingers from hers and reached for her breast again.

"But don't you see? If that can happen to them, it can happen to us—to me. What if it was drugs, and I had gotten arrested in Kuala? I'd be on death row now." She straightened her body and flipped to her stomach.

"Maybe you want to go and live with one monk in the forest temple. Live in the forest and fight for those things. No killing the tree, the monkey, nothing like that. Ajahn Pongsak. He doesn't need money. You know him? He's famous one in Thailand."

"That's not what I mean, Piv."

"He's good man. Some Thai people love him!"

"Well, I'm all for preserving the forest. But that's not what I mean."

"This day is too long. Too long for everybody," he whispered to her shoulder. Then he rolled on his back.

A few moments later, Robin turned her head toward him. He was asleep, one of his hands resting over his heart and the other above his head as if he were taking a vow. She kissed his cheek and his mouth flicked. What vow would he take? Would she? Instead of a promise, she issued a plea: keep us safe from Volcheck.

In her dream she awakened in the backseat of a car and stepped out into a mosquitoey dawn at the tracks' clearing. What she had to do was get to school. She had to follow the train tracks if she was ever going to get to school. But her gait couldn't match the wooden slats of the tracks; her thonged feet fell down into the rocks, her grimy ankles twisted. Mice had died along the rails. Ruffs of purple innards had hardened; flies shot up like geysers when she passed mouse bodies by. The steel tracks glinted weedily straightward. And something vibrated. She lay down and put her ear to the ground and sure enough, something vibrated. She got up and kept walking, because she had to get to school. Thongs slipping, ankles twisting, and the train loomed forward, chugging, quickening, and its whistle rang out and shook her to falling. Her knees cut on rocks. The train's whistle rang out, and the phone was ringing. She was underneath the train's blackness, phone ringing. She had to get to school.

Piv jumped when she jumped; the sound wasn't what woke him.

"Fucking Volcheck," Robin cursed. She hit the mattress and her arm complained at the sudden movement of blood. Before Piv picked up the phone he scratched, yawned.

"*Krup*," he said. "*Krup?* Hello? Hello? . . . Abu! Where you are now?"

Robin heard the low timbre of Abu's voice barely, but the tone of it changed the room. Late night. Love Train. 108 FM coming in from Jacksonville.

"Yes. Okay. That Russian one! I think your country's better. When I do some business for you there?" Piv wiped his hand over his face, dry washing it.

"Okay. Then I come to you in Singapore." His laugh was still sleeping. It came out foggy. He raised himself up and leaned against the headboard.

"NokRobin? She's going to go there? Okay, sure. I'll come, too." His hand stretched across his eyes, fingers and thumb massaging temples.

"Tomorrow's no problem. But if it's only one, then it's my turn." Robin could see his mouth, hung with his brilliant white smile. She wondered if Abu could see it, too. "She's awake. No problem. She's here." The smile faded when he passed the phone to her. He scanned the floor looking for his cigarettes.

"I apologize, Miss Miatta," Abu said. "You will be compensated for the last-minute nature of this favor. Once you're in Singapore, we can discuss amounts."

"In Singapore?"

"A stop in Malaysia first. Do you have a pen?"

Chapter 13

I don't understand this: Why does Abu want NokRobin to meet him in Singapore? Why can't I go? He says she'll find some suitcase waiting for her with Saisamorn tomorrow, at front desk of this hotel. She must show her passport at the airport when she picks up her ticket. Kuala Lumpur's the first stop; she spends one night there, then to Singapore.

I have passport, too. One year ago I get that. I have no trip planned; I get it so I'm ready to take opportunity. When NokRobin gives me the phone again I tell Abu, "I have fresh passport, fresh suit, haircut. Why can't I go to Malaysia and Singapore, too?"

But he wants Miss Miatta. That's what he calls her: Miss Miatta. He says the time for me will come. For this business now he needs me in Thailand. I tell him good-bye, and I hang up the phone. NokRobin lies cold beside me on the bed. Her skin is hard. Small needles stick out from her. Before Abu wakes us, NokRobin doesn't want to give me good night kiss, good night cuddle. Now we have to fall asleep again. Again, no kissing.

When it's morning, then she wants to kiss, be warm, make something. She tells me she doesn't want to make this trip. "I'm scared, Piv. I didn't sleep all night. I don't want to go alone." She kisses me, puts her leg on me, rubs me somewhere so I don't get up to take shower. It's morning, so okay. Easy. We make something. Quick. For one moment, I'm full and sweet with her. But so soon after, she says again, "I'm scared."

Why's she scared? This thing's no problem. No one can smell it, like with some drug. And USA don't care about this animal, so no one looks for that. I already tell NokRobin this. I got three hundred dollars for this good business, and more money's coming, but she's still not happy. She's still too worried and sad. It's five steps from bed to shower. In this room, everything's too close.

"Why you lie down? You must get ready to make this trip," I say to her when I get done from shower. NokRobin tries to show me her eyes. She puts her eyes everywhere in front of my face—when I put my shirt on, when I light my cigarette. She wants me to be happy, to love her. I don't know why. I don't think at this time she loves me. When it's easy for her, she'll leave without me, like the other ones do. She'll leave our plan. Sure.

"Are we still going to take a trip out to see your family, Piv?"

"Sure," I say. From the floor I pick up the travel case she use for her last trip.

"Should you call your parents and tell them we're going to come? Abu says I'll be back in less than a week."

I lift my chin to her. I open the drawer. "What clothes you pack?"

"Or . . . I'm sorry. Do they not have a phone? Do you usually just show up?"

"They have phone. Of course. They don't live on mountain with hill tribe, or under the bridge over Dao Kanong."

"Of course. I'm sorry. I didn't know. I guess it's just I've never seen you call them. I used to have to call my mom every Sunday, or her feelings would get hurt."

When NokRobin gets out of the bed, she has no clothes on. She bends down naked, looking for her sarong. I want to go get suitcase from Saisamorn—ask him who brought that, when'd they bring it—but she's naked, so I can't open the door. I watch her, wait. She complains about the boxes, about some problems with the animals, but Abu chooses her to fly. To get those boxes, to make the deal with Vol, that was the problem. To fly like this, no problem. She tries to wear sarong like the Thai lady, but they never wear it this way, with two ends tied like that. She seems to me like farang now. From this bed now comes the farang smell.

But she looks at me again before I open the door. Her eyes are not blue like the sea at Ko Samui. Not small shined nuts, like the Thai lady. They're the color of plain water under the cloudy sky—not postcard, not special—but they tell me something. They tell me it's not her fault that I don't travel now. She wants me to go with her; it's true. But she can't make that happen.

When she leaves, I feel alone. There are some people at Star Hotel, sure. Farang man and woman sit in the lobby, old ones. Their faces are red. Their necks are red, too. Their skin melts down like bags of custard. I think they're tired of my country. I don't want to know them. I go back to my room.

In my room I try to read one book, *Through a Dark Mirror*, but now I don't remember what happened before, and so I have more difficulty to understand the words. Instead, *Bangkok Post*, easier to read. I see ad for Trombone Club in there, and I call them. Using the phone is expensive to do; it adds to cost of the room, but it's Abu's bill now. I don't care. Trombone Club tells me Fallow band doesn't play tonight. Instead it's RoiSun 5. More like jazz. I heard them before. The sound's not good. I try to call Chit's mobile phone, but he doesn't answer.

I look down and see dirt stains on my suit pants where they come close to the floor. Already I cleaned this suit two times, but there is too much dirt in Bangkok. I need the suit that's darker color, doesn't show dirt. That's what I'll do today, without NokRobin. I'll buy that. To go shopping, I wear my suit pants and one black T-shirt and my shoes and my socks.

I stop first in the beauty shop. It's close, easy to get to—maybe that's why I stop there. Inside it smells like thick sharp soap. Same smell that I remember from when they cut my hair. The air-con is cool, and the big mirrors make it seem more cool. I don't know why I think the mirrors are silver color when inside them I can see all the colors. When I can see me.

They like to see me inside that shop. The married ladies hold scissors in their hands above the customers' heads, and when they see me they smile. They say: Hello, how are you? Last time you come in here, your hair was too long. You like it so much better short that you want us to cut some more already?

The young one, Anchan, she's there, too. She's happy to see me, too. She wears the pink shirt with some small horses across the front part. She wears pink belt, white pants, and pink plastic shoes. I think she likes pink color. Her face is very bright. It looks good to me, smiling. But I don't like her curled hair.

I say to her: You think I need my hair cut more? Your friends say I do. If you think so, please. Please cut it for me.

She shakes her head. She tells me: No. Only small number of days since you cut your hair. You cut on Sunday, I remember. No.

She reaches her finger close to my neck and the piece of hair she sees there. Then she puts both hands to her face. She's all flower pink. She laughs.

I ask her: You work now? If it's possible, please, I would like for you to come with me to buy one suit. I need one new suit. After that, maybe we can eat dinner together.

She has to work until five thirty, but the married ones say to her it's okay, she can go now. No business for her today. She should go.

Traffic is bad. We sit in the meter taxi, and Anchan tells me she wants to buy one Yamaha 120 like her brother's, but she would pick the bright pink color instead of green.

She wants to buy many other things, too. She tells me what in MBK. For me, I get one suit. Light brown one, dirt won't show fast. I get new shirt to go with this. For Anchan, I buy two things for her hair: bows and flowers around the rubber band. Two hundred baht each, wow, but she thinks they're pretty. She puts one in her hair, soft blue one. Then we eat at KFC. She says she likes that taste. We sit by the window in the white restaurant and we eat fry chicken and rice, chocolate custard. Night has come now, but so many lights outside make the sidewalk look very bright. Bright and shiny, like wet rain.

When I see Chit and Wanphen outside the window, I wave and smile. "Chit," I say. Anchan hears this and looks at me, at Chit. His hair is very long. When his band plays, he lets his hair hang down, but now he wears simple rubber band—no bows on that. He doesn't hear me say his name, but he sees me; he looks at me, and Wanphen looks, too. Who is this? They don't know. And then, okay, their faces say yes. They see me now—hello! I think they're very surprised because my hair is short.

In KFC, I ask them if they ate. I give Chit one cigarette. Wanphen doesn't smoke, but she wears Levi's jeans, one black T-shirt saying *Who's the Boss*, and some red and white tennis shoes, maybe old ones from America. She knows how to get the Levi's very cheap. She deals with them, makes some business about that. Her hair is very, very long, and straight. Cool. Pretty. She doesn't want to talk to Anchan. She's polite, but still, I know. Anchan's not cool.

I tell them I make business now. American farang helps me find this one; I get this because I speak English so good. I tell them this business takes me to many countries. To America, sure, I say to Wanphen, but that's in future.

What company? Anchan wants to know.

Is that why you cut your hair? Chit says. He knows me for four years, my first friend in Bangkok. He comes to Kanchanaburi to meet my family. I meet his family in Khorat. He looks at me now. He looks at Anchan. He says: We're going to Sandwich Pub now. Bot's playing with Rhythm Sun, just for tonight, because their bass player cannot. You should come.

So we go. Anchan doesn't want Singha beer, Mekong whiskey, Johnnie Walker, just, please, some Coke. At first I think she's afraid of this pub—crowded and loud with rock and roll—but then maybe she likes it. Ott talks to her, makes her laugh. Chit's old girlfriend, Kathy, talks to her, too. Anchan is surprise that this farang can speak Thai language. She likes to talk to the farang like this.

In Thai, with Anchan listening, Kathy tells me that now Chit comes to visit her in the apartment where last year they lived together. If Kathy says the true thing, he makes something with her there, but he won't stay long after. At Trombone Club, Sandwich, anywhere, he only talks to Wanphen.

Anchan says: You were first wife and now you're minor wife? Very bad way for the man to behave!

Kathy says: I know it! But I still love him. Piv, why is he doing this? I want to be sweet with him again.

I tell her I don't know about this thing. He's sweet with her, but he's with Wanphen now. I don't know why.

I take Anchan home in meter taxi. She lives past the Southern Bus Terminal, and the drive is long. Cost is almost two hundred baht— money keeps falling out of me today. At her home, I tell her yes, I still stay in Star Hotel, but less than one week from now I leave for business. Before then I will see her again. Of course I will. Sure. In the dark corner, where no one can see, I give her one kiss. Fast one—*ssst*. Why not? One kiss is nothing.

At Star Hotel, I have the message from Abu that tells me to call him in Singapore when I get back to my room. The time is already past one o'clock when I get back there.

"How are you, Mr. Pivlaierd? How are you doing, man?" Abu does not sound sleepy. "You must have been out at the parties tonight. Of course. You don't have to tell me. I understand. You deserve some diversion after your hard work yesterday. You conducted yourself smoothly, as I knew you would."

"Thank you," I say. "I think it's okay. In the airport I can be very smooth. So now maybe I can go to Malaysia, Singapore, with my lady friend. I'm lonely when she's away from me." I say that so he'll laugh.

He laughs. "Patience, my friend. We have something big coming up in Florida, in the United States. Wouldn't you rather wait for that?"

His words make my blood feel exciting. "USA. Wow." Of course I can wait, if that's what will come. If he tells me the true thing.

"The National Reptile Breeder's Expo. It takes place in the first week of May. It would be an invaluable experience for you, and we can arrange it so that you have something of your own with which to deal, a commission. We trust you, Piv. This invitation comes because you have our trust."

Why does Abu trust me to go there, United States, but not trust me here? Many Thai people travel to Singapore, Malaysia, it's nothing. In USA, that's where they don't trust the Thai person. They see Thailand and they look for heroin, ganja, drugs. Too many people tell me this. Farang and Thai people both tell me this—everyone who goes there from here—that's how I know.

"But I do have a question for you," Abu says. "What was the word you used for our Russian associate?"

"Excuse?"

"The Thai phrase that so aptly describes Mr. Volcheck?"

"RussianVol? *Jairong*. Hot heart. *Jairong*. I tell you that word?"

"That's it. Yes. He has a hot heart, as we know. So it's best if I have all the facts to intercede on your behalf, if necessary. That is, to intercede on the part of Miss Miatta."

It's like when I read the book. If I know already what's happened, it's easier to understand the English words. But I say it anyway, as if I do not: "Excuse?"

"My question is this: did Miss Miatta tamper with Volcheck's boxes?"

Through my stomach there comes something very cold. Cold, like the mist in Mae Hong Son. "What's it mean, *tamper*? Lift them? She helped to lift them up the hotel stairs. Vol made her."

"Did NokRobin open a box or two, perhaps change the nature of what's inside?"

I want to travel. To fly. To go everywhere. And so I always study the map. I study the map so many times that it stays in my mind. I can see it now. I see Abu in Singapore. I'm in Thailand. In the middle, Malaysia; NokRobin is there.

"No. I don't think so. I'm not with her every minute, all that time. But NokRobin cares about the money; she doesn't care about that box. Why you think she opens that?"

"A business sense. Let's call it a hunch. How's your money holding out?"

"Money? No problem. I buy new suit today. But money, sure. Money's okay."

"Of course. Quite appropriate. I'll reimburse you when I return to Bangkok. It's a business expense. So you're the aspiring business man, and Robin just wants money. You didn't see her opening any boxes. How long was she alone with them?"

"She's alone some small minutes only. I get the gas, some drink, something like that. How can she do something in that small time?" I'm apart from NokRobin. I want to be in the same place, but I'm apart. At this moment, in this situation, maybe it's better for me like that.

"Just a business hunch. But keep an eye on her. Let me know if her motivations change. You maintain at the Star Hotel, Piv, and check in with me once a day. I have my phone with me at all times, so you needn't wait until after midnight to ring."

Chapter 14

The towel beneath her had drooped, and Robin's shoulders slid slick with sweat against the straps of the lounge chair. She looked through her eyelashes at the wash of aquamarine before her, trying to catch the water hovering and rising. Evaporation. Condensation. She wished she could escape into a vapor. Except for the Russians and the Kenyans and her, there were only two other people around the Fortune Dragon Hotel's pool: Asian businessmen in trousers and mercerized polo shirts, both sitting across the deck at a shaded table and working on laptops. Occasionally they tossed a deadpan ogle toward the two young Russian women accompanying Volcheck. Sometimes Robin got caught in the line of fire, exacerbating her sense of being a furred lobster in the sludge-green corner of a grocery store tank: unappetizing but destined to be made a meal of all the same.

She'd left her bathing suit in Bangkok, but the porter who showed up at her room that morning with a note from Abu—*Please join us on the fourth floor deck after noon*—also handed her a one-piece. She'd been summoned. She didn't know why, didn't know how to act once she got there, had pinned herself to her chair like a butterfly, etherized, encased in a black and white design not of her choosing. Next to her, Abu's calves shone. They were the only part of him in the sun; his torso stayed under an umbrella's shade. Jomo's legs were an ashier, hairier black. Then came Volcheck's fat knees—he wasn't reclining, he was sitting upright. His stomach sprang forward out of an unbuttoned shirt; his head was covered with a flapping cap, and Robin could already see a gauze of pink spreading over his blanched thighs. It would serve him right. Piv, on the other hand, could only tan. He'd never burn, never ash. If he were here, she'd bury her face in his tawny glow and take comfort, turn feminine. She didn't dare ask Volcheck where Nadja was this time, but Robin would have preferred her distressed intelligence to the cleavage-brimming fluffery of these two new girls, Irena and Anna. She had tried to share her SPF 15 sunblock with them, had gestured over the men's knees to ask the girls did they want any, and pointed up at the sun. But they had just shaken their heads and caressed more oil into their skin, looking pleased with the sheen.

"I believe it's time for a cocktail," Abu said, breaking the mechanical silence of an air-conditioning unit's hum. "Miss Miatta. Your second day in Singapore and you haven't yet had a Singapore sling. I thought you liked to sample the local flavor." His voice reached out from under his patch of shade and sent her shoulders hiking. She hated that Abu knew anything about her and Piv. "Was I wrong? About your preferences?"

She twisted her silver thumb ring and looked to the deck's corner, where a screen of hanging plants hid the generator and bled kiss-shaped poufs onto the tile floor. Abu allowed no comment she made to go by unexamined for signs of ignorance, arrogance, bias. She had to be careful. "Umm . . . they didn't really originate in Singapore, did they?"

"It's a British drink, actually. The sahibs used to sit on the verandahs and sip them. But in the postcolonial world, you don't have to be an Englishman—or woman of course—to enjoy one of their slings. I'm ordering you one. Or are you saying they're too European?"

"No, that will be fine, thanks," she said. Jomo preferred to have a beer. When Volcheck heard drink orders being taken, he roused Anna and Irena and made everyone repeat what they were having, then translated it to the Russian women, who put on their heels and skimpy wraps and walked shoulder to shoulder into the bar. Robin tried to hide, lowered the tilt of her chair and turned onto her stomach, but Abu continued talking. He described high tea at the Raffles Hotel and other colonial customs he enjoyed. He said he admired British literature—Graham Greene especially, and even Kipling, from an objective standpoint. He peppered Robin with questions until she had to arch her back and cock her head around the edge of the chair to face him, had to admit from this twisted posture that she had never read Greene.

"Never read *The Quiet American*? Oh but you must. And Pivlaierd must, too. I'll get you both a copy."

Carrying a tray of ruby-toned liquids and wet green bottles, Irena bent over to give Volcheck his sling. Robin had to force herself not to gawk at the serving girl, her breasts falling forward, Volcheck's hand sliding up to give her buttock a squeeze. Jomo didn't touch Anna when she handed him his beer, but the way he looked at her, he might as well have. Abu took two drinks off the tray and held Robin's out to her while she turned over to accept it. The Singapore sling was much too sweet. Her mouth puckered and her eyes grew filmy and hot. These people were a bunch of scumbags. Pimps and poachers and whores. She wished for Piv, was angry at him for not being near. Or she wanted to be safe at home, wanted a father who would fly her there. She sipped again. She wanted to get drunk.

A phone rang and Abu and Volcheck both reached for theirs. Abu answered the call sotto voce, in English. Then he switched to another language, his voice a deep lilting hum. What did they speak in Kenya? Swahili? Robin took sips in quick succession. Abu laughed once. When he hung up he spoke to Jomo without switching back to English. He wrote something in the notebook he carried in his breast pocket, then ripped the page out and handed it to Jomo, who rose to go.

Robin inhaled. "I've gotten too much sun," she gushed. She rocked forward to lift from the chair. "I should head in, too."

She felt a weight descend onto her shoulder: Abu's warm hand. "No. Stay out here and keep me company."

"My skin . . ." She pressed her index finger to her shoulder to create a momentary dollop of soured cream on the tough reddish-brown. She watched the pale dot disappear.

"Sit," Volcheck said. He vacated his shaded chaise and walked, punching numbers on his phone, to a table on the other side of the pool.

Robin cringed as she sank down into the seat Volcheck left behind. She gathered her knees to her chest to rescue her toes from the sun. After a moment of silence, Abu breathed deep and patted his palms on his chest, a rich hollow sound. "I usually stay in the Emperor when I'm in Singapore. They know me there, but perhaps I'll switch my regular. What do you think of this place?"

"It's great," Robin said. One of the Russian women let out a two-syllable laugh, and Robin shot a glance her way.

"Don't worry, Miss Miatta. They can't understand a word we say. They're not laughing at you."

"Oh, I . . ." Abu shone a close-lipped smile upon her, catching her struggling against her tangled-up nerves.

"So you think the Fortune Dragon's great. Are you curious about the business that allows me to live half my life with room service?"

Robin blinked. She sipped from the watery dregs of her drink. "You do import-export. That's enough for me." She brought the glass to her lips again, looked over the rim. The sun hung, a lit coin, a thumb's width above the lone skyscraper on the western horizon. So close to the equator, the line between afternoon and nightfall was paper thin, and they had just fallen through it.

Abu turned his gaze from the pool to Robin. He wasn't smiling, but the planes of his face were gentle, relaxed.

"So you can't use the excuse of curiosity to explain why you pry into property that doesn't belong to you?" he said.

The blow of his words hit her backhand, knocking her dizzy though she'd been preparing for it all day. Her throat contracted to supress her jumping stomach. Should she deny innocently—*what property?*—or spit out words of negating indignation—*how dare you suggest . . . ?* As if she could fool him. Her throat spasmed. She threw her hand to her mouth, but it didn't work. She leaned over her chair and gagged up stringy, pinky bile. The Russian women both jerked from their repose to look.

"You must be careful, drinking in the sun." Abu handed her a limp handkerchief and a highball of tepid water. He stepped away to retrieve a Styrofoam starfish float from the deck's railing, then returned to drop it over the sick. It settled with a farty puft. Affecting delicacy, the Russian women gathered their things to leave.

"So, we've gotten that out of the way. And now, Miss Miatta—" He held up his dark-framed pale palm to her. "I'm sure you want to offer the apology that you owe, but really, I insist it's not necessary. Your forthright conversation is all that I ask. You'll give me that?"

"Abu, I'm so—"

He held up his palm again. Raised one eyebrow skeptically, a half-smile on his lips. "Let's start again. You were curious?"

A bird cawed overhead and rose her goose bumps. Robin's throat stung. "I wanted to make sure it wasn't drugs before I carried something for you again," she whispered. The crease where Abu's solid neck gave way to broad shoulders was literally black.

"So you didn't believe my word. Surely you've heard of Pandora's box, Miss Miatta?"

Robin peered at Abu with her eyes big, her heart thumping. The smell of gin and stomach acid was in her nostrils.

"It's none of my business. I'm sorry."

"Relax. I'm not going to pounce. We're just going to talk." He put his elbows out and tented his fingers professorially. "So, you wanted to be sure it wasn't drugs. And what did you think when you realized I'd told you the truth?"

"I was relieved, I guess." She almost felt relieved again, for a moment. The matter to be judged was out in the open, splattered next to her, and all she could do was to wait for the verdict.

"But that's not all, is it?"

"I . . . I don't know. I was . . . confused. I didn't understand."

"What don't you understand?" Abu's lips moved distinctly. The moment of relief passed: he wasn't going to simply let her wait; he was going to make her hang herself. Robin twisted in misery. "Miss Miatta, even if frank conversation is painful to you, I'm sure you agree that given the circumstances, it's not too much for me to ask."

"I didn't know what it was at first, why someone would want it." Robin's voice came out a hoarse croak.

"Really? And you an art historian? A lover of the Orient?"

"An aphrodisiac?"

"You dissapoint me. That's a common Western misconception, but rhino horn has never been used as an aphrodisiac. Very small quantities are used medicinally, but for centuries the horn has been prized for its ornamental value. And now do you feel straightened out? Are all your questions answered?"

"Yes, I . . . I'm glad to know."

"Don't dissemble, Miss Miatta. You're terrible at it anyway. Forthright. I want your true responses."

"Well, it's true that I—there were so many boxes. So many . . . And they're endangered."

She'd given him what he wanted, she could hear that when he spoke. "I could tell you that it's always been the way, in the African bush, to collect what is near to use or to trade. It wouldn't be untrue. And should Western morality interefere with this pattern? But I won't pretend to you that I'm involved in tribute to my forebears. It's only because the animals are endangered that they're worth my attention. The fewer rhinos there are, the more they're prized. And my income supports sixteen people. According to the options open to me, this is a clean trade."

In a Khao San bookstall, Robin had found an outdated volume on endangered animals, and she'd studied the picture of a rhino brought down by poachers. The top half of its head was a chewed pulp. The rest of its body lay untouched; the huge leatherey belly rising to the shoulder of the ranger. Even in the blurry photo, you could see the haze of flies gathered round. The rhino weighed over a ton. A ton—that inconceivable, unattainable mass. I need a ton of things, he makes a ton of money, a ton of prehistoric beast left for flies, vultures, ants that would carry away its flesh, visible mauve bits bobbing in a waved line through savanna grass. A clean trade? But sixteen people was a ton, too, for one person.

"Sixteen, wow," Robin said. If she could flatter Abu with her awe, perhaps he would release her. And she wasn't just dissembling; in part, her deflection was genuine. It had always pained her when her college friends judged situations they didn't understand. She knew you couldn't always count on the world to give you your due, and that what looked like mistakes—having four children when you couldn't afford two, dropping out of school, missing work repeatedly—were often reasonable choices if there was any choice at all. She didn't know anything about familial responsibilities or the realities of sub-Saharan Africa. Her knee-jerk censure shamed her.

But the mass slaughter of endangered animals shamed her as well, and Abu's situation was not her own. She had carried those packages. There was blood on her hands. She'd been desperate the first time, hadn't known what was in them. Did that justify her actions? But what about now, acting knowingly? Having bought some time, shouldn't she be able to find another way to get herself home?

Then the sun slipped behind the lowest stratus cloud, electrifying it into a glory of orange. The whole sky lit up Venus pink, and her questions flared and exploded, became part of the light show. An airplane sliced ribbons above her, and those caught fire, too. And she wanted it. Even trapped, pinned in this isolated hotel, discussing money ripped from the face of an animal, she wanted a piece of that sky.

"Wow?" The word withered in Abu's mouth. "That's your response? Your mind is churning. I'm offering answers. Ask for them now, so you aren't tempted again to sneak and steal." He palmed the phone and let his arm dangle. His legs were pushed out in front of him, crossed at the ankle.

"I don't know," Robin said, trying to find a safe place between his incisiveness and her fear. "I don't know anything about life in Kenya. You're so well educated. Are there not many jobs there? How did you get into this?"

He smiled, pleased. "We have a wonderful educational system but an abysmal unemployment rate in Kenya. I was privileged to get through college—I'll leave off the description of the ridiculous amounts of luck and hard work that entailed. And luck was on my side again, getting me into the military, rising to officer. But the salary was scant. The compensation was the expectation that officers would use their advantages to involve themselves in other profitable pursuits. Drugs, for example. And I can't allow you to think the weakness is only African. You've done your research on endangered species. You can do some on this. Start a campaign. Because it is American men, too. Military men, CIA, operatives posted abroad in Mozambique, Namibia, Nicaragua, El Salvador—they get paid far more than the few hundred we do, yet most of them are involved elbow deep in dirty business." As he spoke he looked at her and gave a soft nod. Robin flared her nostrils.

"Oh, I know. I mean, not exactly, but I've read about stuff like that. It doesn't surprise me." She pressed her finger pads onto her closed eyelids and shook her head.

"I am only trying to ensure, Miss Miatta, that if you pass judgment you do so nonpartisanly."

Abu turned to a waiter entering the pool deck. The server's white shirt reflected more light than anything else around. "A Singapore sling for me. The lady would prefer a ginger ale. And you'll want to send someone up here to clean up her mess." Abu gestured to the ground, the dark stain spreading beneath the starfish float, the smell of vomit mingling with that of flowers and the chemical-infused pool. Robin accepted the humilation.

When the waiter left, she was ready with a question: "If I get caught, as an American am I at greater or lesser risk?"

"Miss Miatta, at least I can assure you on this front. Even the powerful countries, the rich ones who dictate to others, realize that we pose no threat to general welfare." Abu held his drink up to his chin.

The candy-colored beverage looked out of place in his big hand. "The animal trade is second only to the drug trade in terms of profitability, yet it receives only a minuscule fraction of the enforcement money. Even those few who do get caught get sentences far less substantial than do drug traders working with similar worths. And, of course, this is a benefit to me and a benefit to you equally." He sipped.

"It is," Robin said, both relieved and indignant at the news. She looked at Abu, at his wide, ageless face. She looked away. The cloud's belly was pink now, the sky more dusty. The cloud's roof looked to be made from blue smoke.

"But your mind is not at rest."

"No, it is. I . . . ." The temperature had hardly dropped, but suddenly she felt preposterous sitting in a gift of a bathing suit. She reached for her shirt and held it in front of her, but he was still looking, measuring, waiting. "It's just . . . It's not just animals, right? I mean, Nadja."

"Who's Nadja?"

"Anna and Irena. The Russian girls . . ."

"What do I have to do with them?" Abu's tone was no longer professorial; the question was not rhetorical.

"Nothing. I don't know. I . . . ." Robin heard her own cowardice, saw Abu's disgust with it. "But they're part of the trafficking, aren't they?"

"You see why I demand your questions? It's very revealing, how quick you are to involve me in any crime you perceive. I'm indulging my vanity in wanting to set the American mind straight." He lifted his empty sling in cold salute to her, and Robin shivered. "Volcheck is his own operation. For the time being, our interests overlap on a few matters. That's all." He sipped the last drops in his glass. The ice cubes clattered falling back down. "But regardless, here's where you are wrong. You cannot equate a person and a beast. A person chooses. Volcheck doesn't force anything; he offers an opportunity that many are willing to take." Robin saw the bar in Patpong. The one white woman dancing there, the numbers pinned on all the women. She didn't want to talk to Abu about it. He was describing the poverty in Russia, in the Ukraine, in Kenya, his deep voice devoid of the bemused patience that he had used on her before she'd stumbled and accused. She risked an interruption and turned the conversation away from women.

"You're arguing against yourself, then. It's the rhino that doesn't have a choice."

"The rhino can't make a choice. He's lesser. Therefore it doesn't matter. In my eyes, that is God's will. You, however, stole knowledge that upset you and still decided to travel for me again. It's my turn to ask you: why?"

The top bulk of the sky was night blue now, pierced through with a few stars, but the bottom, the part that curved around the earth, still clung to butterfly orange. The low full moon was orange-hued, too. Robin could make out its craters all the way from where she sat in the tiny speck that was Singapore. She remembered being on Ko Tao just a few months ago, charting each sunset and moonrise. No one wore makeup or shoes. She had sat in palmed shade with those nice American guys, those cool Dutch girls. She'd been traveling for months, so she had a store of adventures to share with them, or to play over like movies, private screenings running just for herself. Why, after all that, could she not have gone home? Her money was long gone by then. Why did she feel like she wanted more and more, more Thailand—even if she had to go into deep hock to get it? She had wanted to bottle the sweetness she had found lounging on that island, at peace with the world, at one with the way the earth curves, the sun rises, the tides roll. None of that sounded stupid, there. No wants, no worries. Even money moved slowly. How to learn that? She had thought that Piv could teach her. But then she remembered Zella's rings, the red and golden and blue stones in them. Hadn't she thought Piv connected to that as well?

"I'm here because of money," she said.

"Exactly," he said, the tolerant tone back in his voice. He was looking at the sky. "That's why the Americans are always there. And then you condemn others either for not valuing money as much or for needing it more desperately."

He settled his gaze back on her. She saw again how thick his forearms were, his wrists, his hands.

"I promise that you can trust me," she said. "I won't touch anything of yours again."

Abu sat still with his fingers knit together in his lap. The skin under his fingernails was soft pink, evident even in the gloom. "That's important, Miss Miatta. That's very important for you." Lights came on inside the swimming pool; suddenly the water glowed the soft blue of a gas flame. Absolute dark fell over Singapore. "Your friend Piv, of course, is in a different position than you are. He can afford less ambivalence. As he's told me, he wants to learn a trade that will allow him to travel. And he is practical. He understands the benefits. How would he put it? 'This is one good one.' Yes. I think that's exactly how he'd say it. This is one good one for us all."

A shock went through Robin. The Thai inflections from Abu's mouth sounded almost mocking. Piv's voice was the medium she had been swimming in for over a month, but she hadn't heard it in four days. Abu stood from his chair, tapped each foot so that his shorts straightened. "Supper?" he said.

"You've talked to Piv." She gripped the rounded plastic arms of her chair.

"Every day. I need to keep my eyes in Bangkok open."

Robin's empty stomach clenched once again.

"Oh. How's he doing?" She saw that one aspect of the quandary remained unexhumed even after her and Abu's moral deliberations. How *had* Abu found out about her snooping? How did he know to press her about her ambivalence? She buckled with a nostalgia for Piv that was like a fierce pain, but she knew she couldn't tell him about this conversation with Abu. She'd wait and see if he tipped his hand.

Chapter 15

How many ladies I been with? Why does number matter? I don't know the answer to that one. How many farang ladies I been with for some time, more than one week? Easy to know that: before NokRobin, five. First one, American girl, Susan, from Rocky Mountains. Then one Swiss girl who tries to teach me German. She says Rocky Mountains are number two, Alps are better, but she can speak English, and so most times we speak that. Then one Canadian girl, one Australian girl, and one Australian nurse. These all say they'll never forget me, that I am too sweet, I am too handsome—beautiful for the man, that's one word they teach me—and sometimes they say they love me, sure. These ladies are sweet, too. Pretty, of course. But I know these farangs feel holiday love. In happy days, not working, everything's cheap for them, sun shining, it's easy to love someone. Any hard thing, or when the holiday ends, that love goes away, like the wave at Hua Hin goes away from the shore. Maybe it leaves some white shell, some seaweed, some broken crab, something, but this all goes away soon, too.

I wait in the airport for NokRobin's plane that flies from Singapore. When she comes, I watch how she carries her bag. Her arm bends to carry that heavy thing; the bag bends her over. She walks with short steps, too fast. She wears her blue dress, not the business one, and it's like blue sky over her sandy skin; her nose is like the soft pink sun. Her face is crooked, looking for me. I watch her face. When she finds me, I see something. Her eyebrows, forehead, lift up and crease. Her mouth twists because she's close and far. Her shiny eyes ask me ten thousand questions. For that moment, she doesn't move. Then everything falls down—her crease, questions, twisting—now there's only one thing: shiny eyes that need me in them. Not for happiness, this is some different thing. I know she loves me. She works now, not vacation. She's not even happy on this day, not smiling. Now I know. It's okay that I don't make trip already. USA will come. She loves me in this other way.

"Who are you?" she says when she walks up to me. "Who are you?" She makes this joke.

When she's close to me and smiling, I can see she has some pain from love feeling. This American farang, maybe she never feels this way already. Thai people wonder: Why do these farangs come alone to our country? Why do they sit alone in restaurants, go alone on train, alone to see something? But I already ask too many farangs, so I know. They say it's good to be this way—the word to say it: independent. They say, Why wait for someone else to travel with them? Maybe they'll see something more if no one's with them. Maybe then no one will annoy their nerves, make them move too fast or slow. So I know, for NokRobin, who travels alone for so many months, moving when she wants to, it hurts her now when love makes it more hard to go. But it's okay for her. I love her, too. We stand, our toes close to touching.

"Your nose is bright, wow. Like pink sun. You go to beach in Singapore?" I say this soft. I tap her nose. I look one way, other way, smile. Then, quick, I kiss her there.

"The hotel where we stayed had a pool. I brought you a postcard of it. You'd like it there." NokRobin's mouth smells like orange juice. When she talks, her lips kiss each other. I take the heavy bag from her.

"I like every hotel if you're with me," I tell her. We go outside to get in taxi queue, and when we walk, we're very close, very soft, like between her shoulder and my shoulder is some easy-to-break thing.

But with NokRobin it cannot be Thai style; we must be international. When we stand in queue, she says, "Piv, I know this isn't right to do here, but I'd feel better. Please. Before we get in the taxi, can we please hug?"

Many people are around us, but I put the heavy bag down. I open my arms to take her in. I smell airplane on her clothes. I smell sky. I feel her body all along me, more soft on top, her bones growing when she breathes. I think maybe the people look at us when we make this cuddle, twist up their face. But it's okay. No problem. Smell from NokRobin's hot body takes over smell of the airplane. Soon I think she takes me home.

However, at this time I don't tell NokRobin that Abu has one plan to take us to United States. Why don't I tell her this? She wants to go back to Star Hotel right now. No restaurant. It's Saturday and we pass by weekend market, and she loves that place, but she doesn't want to go there. She doesn't want to have cocktail in Star Hotel lounge. She wants to lie in bed. So we lie together. We make some cuddle, we make something. After that, we lay on top of the covers without our clothes. NokRobin likes to do this. She's not shy, like the Thai lady. But when I ask her to tell me about Singapore—What's it like there? How much money did she get? When's Abu coming back? What Abu say?—she acts shy. She rolls up like the small centipede, tries to cover her body with the sheet. Now, very sudden, I remember, I wonder. Is some trouble concerning the box why she acts this way? Maybe Abu said something? I put my hand on her. Very soft, I move my hand on her skin.

"Why you don't like Singapore?" I say into her hair.

"How do you know I didn't like it? Did Abu tell you?" Her body closes tight. I move my hand, soft, to open her heart so she won't leave.

"I don't know if you like it. Please. I cannot go. I never leave Thailand. Share trip with me."

NokRobin rolls on her back. The sheet falls off her body, but she pulls it up again.

"There's not much to share. I had to be with them all the time. And Volcheck's such a scumbag. He had two girls with him, from Russia. They were barely wearing any clothes. I know they're prostitutes." She looks at me. Hard eyes. "Prostitutes? You know, bar girls?" she says. She want something from me, but I don't have it fast enough. "Don't you care? I guess living in Bangkok makes you used to it."

Four days speaking Thai, English words don't come fast now. It takes some time to find. "No," I whisper. "I'm sorry. I never go to bar girl like that. I don't like that. No."

NokRobin's face changes. Her eyes get soft, I see them. Now she can't find words to say, even though we speak her language.

I move my hand, put it on her shoulder, put my other hand on her other shoulder. "I'm sorry you're alone there," I tell her.

She rolls to me and I take her. I hug her. Something passes through my mind, but no. She's afraid of Abu. She doesn't like Abu. Why would she tell him about those boxes? No. The way he knows is not like that.

"It would have been better if you were with me."

NokRobin and me press together. We have dry, smooth skin like powder is on us. Only powder, no clothes. We lie quiet. In the hallway of the Star Hotel, someone closes the door. NokRobin moves her head to look at me. Her eyes are almost green. More dark green now than I have ever seen them. "I feel like a bad person," she says.

"No. Not bad. You're very good person." Her head fits between my shoulder and my collarbone. "Very good person. I love this good person." I tell her this many times. Maybe one hundred times.

She tells me sweet things, too. While she does, she presses onto me, onto me, onto me. I feel her hair from down there. I think we'll make something again. I get ready. And we do. It's nice, the way we do it. Better than the first time. It's full of peace. I think she feels better. But for now I wait. I wait to tell her about the big business in the USA with Abu.

Next day, I still want to wait to tell her about USA, but I think it's good time to tell her about one other plan, idea I have that I know will make her happy. I choose the right place to tell her this. We go to Phra Athit Road and eat lunch, then we take river taxi to Tha Chang Pier. I hire one long-tail boat for us there. Only us, no other tourists, and the driver will take us along the river and klongs for two hours.

As soon as the motor starts, NokRobin feels exciting. She smiles, and where the driver can't see, she holds tight onto my arm. She likes to see my city go by. Everything's there for her. Wat Phra Kaew, Grand Palace, Wat Pho. Apartment houses of rich ones with balconies and gardens on rooftops. Small houses of poor ones with no windows, no walls, cooking outside. We go down the Chao Phraya and then into Klong Phadung Krungkasem. People are outside with their buckets, washing themselves, washing their clothes. Klong water is black and shiny on top, like the hard wings of some beetle. People have small restaurants along there, small stores, all outside. NokRobin wears the white Udon shirt that she got in Pai, and the wind presses that loose shirt close to her body, and her tan neck is long. This ride goes by very smooth for us, nice.

From Klong Phadung Krungkasem we go to Klong Saensaep. I tell the driver to go this way. There's wats on both sides of the klong— red and gold roof above the green trees—and NokRobin thinks they're beautiful. Then we go underneath expressway, and it's dark for some moments, and she doesn't like that. Then there's more people's houses, and then the house connected to my idea. I ask the driver, please, stop the motor for some moments.

"Look," I say to NokRobin. "Jim Thompson's house." I know she loves this one. She goes there with her friend, and she always wants to go again because she loves it so much. She thinks Jim Thompson is number one guy; she wants to be like him.

She makes happy sound now when she knows that she sees his house. "Oh!" That's all she says. With the motor stopped the klong seems quiet, even though in Jim Thompson's garden someone is using the saw to cut wood. The driver smokes one cigarette, and I can smell the smoke mix up with the sweet and rotten klong.

"This is the way he planned for people to see it," NokRobin says after some time of looking. "From the klong. And wasn't he right! It's so much better, seeing it this way. Look how it twinkles."

Twinkles, I don't know that. But the red house is very pretty. Shape is tall and small like NokRobin's body, little measure wider on bottom than top, and the roof in the Thai-style. I like to see that.

"Now we're somewhere beautiful, so I can tell you my plan for our business," I say to her. She looks at me and smiles.

"I thought we had a plan."

"I thought of something better. Something like Jim Thompson. I don't know why I don't think of this already." I light one cigarette and blow. I stretch my legs in front of me, make the boat rock some small amount. NokRobin looks at me very close. She wants to know what I say. I can feel her waiting. When the boat gets calm again I ask her. "What is the thing you love to buy? The thing you love to look at? What you want to sell?"

"I don't know. All different things. You know I love that Buddha. But we can't afford to sell anything like that."

"You study art at university," I say to her. "You like art things, nice crafts. It's no problem for you to get ideas about Thai style, what you think farang will like, and you can draw pictures. It's easy to get them to make it for you here, whatever you want. Just like Jim Thompson. And if you order many, price is small."

"What are you talking about? I don't understand."

"Jewelry. Silver jewelry. That's what you love. You show the factory how to make some good design, something special. It's cheap to make that here. Then we take that to your country, to another rich country, and we sell it for five times, six times the money we pay."

Very slow, NokRobin makes her funny face—happy, like the baby clown. "A jewelry designer." She whispers that. "You're saying I could be a jewelry designer? Ha!" She laughs one time. She likes my plan. She likes me today.

"You can draw some pictures of ideas, then I'll talk to the factory. I know some friends who already do something like that. They'll help us. Okay? You like this plan?"

"I love the plan." NokRobin puts her feet on the seat of the boat and holds on to her knees. "I'd love to do it. I love that you think I can be a jewelry designer. But how much would this cost? Wouldn't we need thousands of dollars?"

"Thousands of baht, yes, but dollars . . ." I shrug my shoulder. "Not so many. And money is coming. I think so."

NokRobin smiles at me the biggest smile she gives all day. "So I come up with a line of silver jewelry, and you get the pieces made cheaply right here, and we sell them together?" Sometimes her face is not beautiful. Farang face, hot and sandy. But her big smile, happy eyes, make her look beautiful right now to me.

"Yes," I tell her. "That's my idea for us. That's my plan."

We don't talk when driver starts the motor and turns back down the klong to Chao Phraya. The motor runs, and the air is smooth, and we see everything again, but we don't say many words. Only one time NokRobin speaks. She asks me for the army knife. She uses the small blade on that to cut the long white string that falls out from the bottom of her shirt. After she gives knife to me again, she puts the string on my head. She makes the shape of one circle on top of my short hair. I don't know where she learns about the Thai wedding ceremony—that the most honorable guest puts white string on the head of the man and the woman when they marry—maybe from studying something about Jim Thompson she learns about that. But when she puts that string, I think even more that her feeling for me is not just for today. That she will stay with me. That we're attached and will move together, over the world.

Chapter 16

For three days, Robin and Piv visited the sites of Bangkok. They went to Wat Pho, the national museum, the royal barges, the major residencies—King Rama V's and Jim Thompson's again, coming at it overland this time—and Robin followed the tours and quizzed Piv and jotted notes and made drawings in the thick, square book she had begun to carry with her, the paper handmade in Nepal. She'd taken several studio art courses as part of her major, and she'd been quick with a sketch in her first few years out in the real world, but that had fallen off when she'd gotten into cars. It felt right to be doing it again—something fast she was good at, something pretty and purposeful and loose.

"See," she said to Piv on the fourth day, using her pencil to put the last few touches on the page in her lap. They were sitting on the sala steps at Wat Suthat. The glossy marble floor of the wat's courtyard and the gold leaf and whitewash of the buildings amplified the midday glare, so even in the shade, Robin wore sunglasses. She'd been looking back and forth between her paper and a lotus rising on a poker-straight stem from a large porcelain bowl. Now she handed Piv her sketchpad.

Piv tilted the book; he tilted his head. He traced one swooping line with his tea-colored finger. "Very good one. Beautiful," he said. Robin blushed and chewed her lip. She had drawn a necklace of four long links, two of which curled up at the ends into rootlike gestures. Twined together, they made a stem that would rise from the lowest point of the necklace up a wearer's clavicle, where it blossomed. It was her favorite thing she'd drawn so far, the first time she'd felt her efforts might justify Piv's praise. He touched his sandal to hers. "Farangs never see one like this. That's why they'll buy it. Special. Like you."

Robin smiled at him. He smiled at her. She leaned back on her arms and softly joggled her knees. The edge of a cloud rippled over the sun, and the water of the lotus pool sparkled. Orange robes, hung on ropes tied between the sala's white pillars, fluttered in front of a standing gold Buddha. Inside the bot, monks chanted prayers that were being broadcast over loudspeakers hung underneath the eaves, but there was no one in sight; Robin and Piv were alone, and the throat-stinging hassle and racket of Bangkok seemed millions of miles away.

Robin took back her book from Piv and folded it closed. Without speaking, in unison, they stood and walked to the bot. Robin approached with assurance—she now knew that it was okay to climb the stairs still shod, to enter the shade of the portico; that she could wait to slip out of her sandals until just before stepping over the raised threshold that led to the interior. Walking lightly, the marble floors cool on her bare feet, she went to look at the murals that covered the walls so that Piv could go privately to the heart of the room and kneel before the Buddha statue she'd read about in her book: it was from fourteenth century Sukhothai. Her attention was split between the dusky fantabulous paintings and the sight of Piv, his head bowed slightly, his pressed hands raised, the crest of his top lip silhouetted in the dim light, curved more gracefully than anything she could draw. But he had asked her to draw, and her sketches—her ideas, her sensibilities, her eye and her taste—were really going to be made into actual things. Her heart bloomed with happiness.

When they left the wat, they faced another minor landmark, Sao Ching-Cha, the Giant Swing. It looked like a shiny red utility tower, except that its two poles were joined at the top with carved screens instead of metal bars holding wires and circuits. All of the tour books described the annual ceremony that used to take place here: men swung in high arcs and tried to grab a bag of gold attached to a tall bamboo pole. But only some of the books mentioned that many people died trying to reach the treasure. Now traffic careened unconcernedly around the swing—cars, trucks, buses, tuk tuks, motorcycles that revved and darted alarmingly. Robin and Piv waited for the infinitesimal break in the flow that would allow them to cross the road. They were on their way to meet a friend of Piv's, who Piv had been told could help them with the logistics of getting silver things made cheaply. When, where, how much, by whom—and where would they get the money? A familiar carbon-monoxide ache crept up from Robin's throat and into her temples. A vision of a rhino galloped by. She took a deep breath and stepped with blind faith into the path of an Isuzu minivan, hoping the driver would slow enough to let her cross.

They'd already met with several of Piv's friends and acquaintances that week, Thai guys who supposedly had connections to factories. Robin couldn't tell who Piv knew well and who he didn't. The men all had an easy air of familiarity with one another and with the bartender at Jimmie's Rasta Bar. The conversation might start out with an exchange or two in English—"Hey man, where you been? You eat yet?"—but inevitably it would slip into Thai. Piv would buy rounds of Singha or Coke, and Robin would sit half-smiling and ignored, and eventually she'd start craning her neck, looking around. The backpackers she'd partied with on the islands appeared to be long gone, but there was always another crop with bad jewelry on, and she'd scope out their ubiquitous hoop earrings decorated with crosshatch and silver spheres in order to fuel her confidence in the necessity of her own designs.

Today started off little different, except that they met at the Joy Luck Club, an arty café on Phra Athit Road that was more of a Thai hangout than the backpacker-oriented Rasta Bar, and except for the fact that when Robin tuned out the conversation between Piv and Bong— the friend of a friend—and began to look around, this time she did see someone she knew coming in through the door.

"Zella!" she exclaimed. Piv and Bong looked at her. "Zella! Hey!"

Her fairy godmother! It was unmistakably Zella, her voluminous curls swirling around her head like a cloud, her extremities spangled in gem-studded silver and gold. The woman slung a bright tapestry bag over the back of a chair and tossed a quilted pouch onto a table. What great timing! Zella'd know how to get this silver thing going. Robin was moving toward her before noticing Zella's companion. He had copper skin and dark eyes, and with his heavy silver chains and a red shirt open at the neck, he matched Zella in drama; he was even looking at Robin in the same way, like she was a mildly curious stranger.

"I'm Robin. Remember? We hung out together in Bangkok a couple months back . . ." Robin's expectation of a gushing reunion dissipated. "You loaned me money."

"Sure," Zella breathed. "Sure. Sit down. Meet Guy."

Robin sat. There was a pulse of silence, an almost imperceptible exchange of glances between Zella and her date.

"How was India?" Robin asked, because she had to say something.

"India? Oh, it's always the same, isn't it?"

"Where'd you go after Delhi?"

"Delhi? I haven't been there in years. No, we've been up to Laos."

The waitress came, and Robin tried to regroup. Zella *had* been headed to Delhi, hadn't she? In one fit of pique, hadn't she made a big deal about getting there late? Then she heard Guy speak to the server in Thai. He was Thai, and she hadn't even known it! He was a size or two bigger than Piv, but still—Zella was a *we* with a Thai guy. Robin felt a confused blush at the similarity of her own situation. Might it somehow look as if she'd been copying?

Zella took a peanut from the small bowl that the waitress had left on the table, and Robin noticed that the slim, pointy fingernails she had envied were now unmanicured and crested with slivers of dirt.

"Laos. Cool. It's still pretty rough there, right?"

"Oh, Laos's divine. It's like the sleepy, sleepy, Wild West. Isn't it darling?" she said to Guy.

"Wild," he said.

Was he really Thai? With his thick black hair and a slightly beaked nose, he could have been Mayan, Peruvian, Montnaguard. Robin could also see that Zella's nails weren't the only thing about her that looked worn. And yet the sunburst of lines sketched around her eyes, the cracks in her lips tinted with that morning's coral lipstick, the faded cast of her black cotton garment—it all served to embellish her appearance; it gave her an elegant patina. Of course she'd been in Laos, where the hoards weren't yet but would be soon. Robin felt convinced that in Zella she was previewing the next season's look.

"So what'd you send back to the studio from up there?"

"Well, not much, really. The mail, you know. But here's something." She unzipped the pouch on the table and took out a bundle of soiled turquoise fabric, which she unwrapped with leathery fingers to reveal a blackened opium pipe. "The real deal. I've got a friend who knows a buyer for this chain of head shops. They'll love these."

Head shops? What about Alexander McQueen? Robin eyed the long, thin opium pipe, but didn't reach to take it. It might be the real deal, but she had seen so many fake ones piled on the factory-made blankets at tourist-trap market stalls that she had no interest. Zella set the pipe down and flipped a few other squares of fabric from her pouch: teal, fuchsia, scarlet, burnt orange, shot through with complex silk embroidery.

"They do some goooooorgeous things with fabrics," Zella said, drawing out the word like she was reclining into it. "But they've already butchered a lot of the old pieces. They make the scraps into these little bags."

Robin picked one up. It gave off a sweet, musky smell at the touch, the organic prototype for the manufactured scent wafting from a magazine subscription card. This was all Zella brought back? At least both sides were antique; it wasn't backed with some cheap poly print, like most of the ones in Chiang Mai. She unzipped it, saw a passport inside. "Nice," she ventured, tipping the booklet half out of the bag, hoping for a distraction from the paucity of Zella's find. "Perfect place to keep this. Do you mind?" Passport sharing was a regular traveler's card game, but Zella had never offered hers in the time they spent together. Now she just shrugged.

The photo was recent: Zella was as tan in the picture as she was here in person, with the same smattering of gray in her mane. But Robin was surprised at the names.

"Gazelle Ester Raboniwitz-Johnson," she recited. "Where'd you get all those?"

Zella's eyes narrowed. "*Now* I remember you," she said. She slid her elbow forward on the table and dropped her chin in her palm. "You're the one with all the questions. 'How do you dooooo this for a living? What designers do you know? I don't have any money left, will you give me some moooore?'"

Robin recoiled, hurt and shamed. She'd never asked for money. She'd never asked after any names Zella hadn't dropped—falsely, it was starting to seem. Robin looked over at Piv, who was rubbing the inside of his cheek with his tongue as he listened to Bong.

"Johnson's my husband's name," Zella said, her tone suddenly blandly congenial. "When we got hyphenated we made our tribe names our legal first names, too. His was Bear. We were Rainbow Tribe kids. You know how it is." No, Robin didn't know how that was. She didn't know if Zella was putting her on. When they'd shared a room, Zella wore Prada sandals, not Berkinstocks. "But that was ages ago, obviously. So then I became Zella."

Robin couldn't see far enough under the table to tell what shoes Zella was wearing today. Why did she even care? But another question popped out. "You were married?"

Zella split a peanut between her thumb and forefinger. "He sends me a check whenever I ask. I guess that's married."

Guy said something to Zella in Thai—did he live off the rich bear's proceeds, too?—and Zella replied in kind. Robin felt a prick of sadness and of jealousy. They could speak together in two languages.

Zella turned to Robin, but spoke as if still addressing Guy. "No, she doesn't need that," she said. "She needs to keep her money. She's a baby. A different generation. She should stay here where they're making it safe for her, where they're nationalizing the hill tribes, where they're giving the trek guides a lecture and a license. They're even setting up roadblocks on the way to Phangan. That's the way it's going now." Zella took a deep breath and lolled her head on her neck while she kept her eyes on Robin, viewing her from different sleepy angles as if intuiting an antique's real age, its secret depths. Robin remembered that look. It was one of the things that had enamored her of Zella, but now that she was its object, she bristled.

"It's time to go away, darling," Zella said to her. She gestured gracefully with her wrist and palm. "Don't ask me any more questions. Don't ask me what I do for a living. You'd better figure something out for yourself. You'd better go away."

Robin took a last peek at Guy. The open shirt and the chain on his broad chest made him look piratey. Without saying good-bye to either Zella or him, she stood and went back to her table.

Piv and Bong had decided to go directly from the Joy Luck Club to the factory, leaving Robin to finish the day's itinerary on her own. She'd planned to visit the student galleries at Silpakorn University, but there wasn't much to see there, and she spent most of the next few hours sitting at a picnic table within the walled campus, waiting until it was time to meet Piv in the nearby park. She nursed a giant Slurpee from the 7-Eleven and watched the students cluster and disperse. Some of the young women still dressed as schoolgirls in white blouses with Peter Pan collars, others wore platform sandals and flared black pants with tight print shirts. They all ignored her. Even if Gazelle Ester Raboniwitz-Johnson was a stoner and not a design scout, Robin still envied her: she could speak in Thai to Guy. Probably that was why secrets and silences existed between

Robin and Piv, because there was a whole world of language that she couldn't enter with him. She kept her sketchbook open, but she couldn't concentrate on her jewelry ideas or the details of Bangkok. She doodled faces idly, generic cartoon visages that gradually became more specific: her own face, then Abu's, then Piv's.

He appeared at the agreed-upon spot almost on time, and he brought with him a rented mat and plastic bags of still-warm fish cakes and fried oysters, the sauces packaged separately, in miniature. They spread the mat on the grass and ate their greasy dinner while he told her about the factory salesman—a friend of Bong's uncle, a very nice guy. The cost of a gram of silver remained the same—about six baht—but the cost of workmanship went down as the numbers went up. Piv had some rough estimates. Neither Robin nor Piv had any idea about how much Robin's design might weigh, but at least Piv was familiar with the metric system. He guessed that it would be around fifty grams— that sounded like a lot—and they used Robin's sketchpad to do some calculations. With the sky deepening to evening, and the lit, gold spires of the Grand Palace reaching into the velvety blue, the numbers sounded magical. They lay on their backs in private reflection, but Robin didn't feel that the silence postponed their mutual understanding this time; she felt like they were very close. The remaining twinges of Zella-envy blew away. The last of the day's kites were being flown overhead. One advertised an outdated Batman movie, one boasted stars and stripes: red, white, and blue.

"That flag's for you. It flies for your country," Piv said.

Robin fiddled with the straw in her plastic bag of Coke, trying to make it stand in a perfect vertical. "Piv, I haven't told you this, but I'm not even sure it will be news to you."

"Oh no, it falls!" Piv said. He reached out to straighten the toppling straw. Once it was upright again, he kept his finger on it. "Tell me some news." His eyes danced.

Robin paused a beat. Should she? Yes.

"Abu knows. He knows we know about the rhino horn."

Piv turned his face away from Robin's, keeping his finger on the straw. He looked over his shoulder at the child holding the spool of the America kite. The boy ran a few steps, then fell down. When Piv's face came back it was hung with a sheepish smile.

"Oh no," he repeated. His tone hadn't changed. In an exaggerated gesture he hit his hand to his head. The straw slumped down. "Maybe we're in trouble now."

Robin searched his face. "I hope not. I don't think so. Abu didn't like me sneaking, but he didn't really seem to mind."

"With Abu, sure. It's no problem. But how does he know this? You tell him?"

"He just knew. Believe me, I've been wondering how." She took an extra breath. "But it really doesn't matter, Piv. I don't care how he knows. He explained what it was like for him at home, in Kenya, but I still feel confused. I mean, they're endangered. They're disappearing from the face of the earth—" She stopped herself. She hadn't meant to bring up the animals.

"What he say?" Piv asked.

"He said it's pretty safe. That it's not like drugs."

"No. Did he say, Why did you do this with Piv, cut open this box? Did he say, I know you did this, now tell to me, how did you do it? And then did you say, Piv takes me to the hotel room where we cut open this box?"

"He didn't ask for specifics. I don't even think we talked about you." Robin sat up, tried to face Piv. He leaned back on his hands. He turned his head away from Robin, away from the little boy, to the spires of the Grand Palace. He sucked his teeth. Robin could see the muscles in his face work, the muscles in his throat. This must be his anger, she thought, but why? She was the one who'd been put on the spot. She was the one trying to be honest. She heard her own voice from a place far away.

"Actually, Piv, he was so unconcerned about you that I wondered if you told him we opened the box, if you two had already had a conversation. But then I decided it didn't matter. I trusted you anyway." The way the streetlight hit his profile, Robin could see the rough texture of the edge of Piv's skin. For the first time she thought he looked unclean. That he needed to scrub harder. She had wanted him to volunteer information, but she couldn't stop herself from pushing: "But maybe you didn't even need to snoop around," she said. "Maybe you knew all along what Abu was doing, and now you're worried that he thinks you told me." She gave a rough laugh. "I could have assured him you didn't. You played that well."

Piv glowered at her; his eyebrows sunk into hurt angles.

"I did not know," he whisper-hissed. "I learned with you. You want to cut that open, I take you there. I didn't want to, but I learned with you."

He looked away again. Robin's chest went achey. She didn't know anyone else in Bangkok. She needed to know him. He was her only friend.

"I'm just trying to tell you it doesn't matter that much what Abu thinks happened."

"It matters. I think so. What if he asks me? If he tries to find out in this way if I lie, if he can trust me?"

If they had been alone, she would have wrapped her arms around his humped shoulders. "You can say whatever you want, Piv. I didn't tell him anything. But he's not going to ask you. He does trust you. I can tell." Even without her arms around him, she felt his skin ripple like a horse's shaking flies off.

"Sure. Okay. No problem." He grinned at her. "You love me," he said.

Robin had to bite her mouth to keep herself from smiling. "Sure. Okay. You want me to? No problem," she said. She pushed his shoulder. He nudged her shoulder back, then straddled her hips and pushed her all the way down, pinning her arms onto the woven straw mat.

"Yeah, sure. You love me." He smirked, raised his eyebrows suggestively. Then he flopped off her and lay facedown on the mat, his lips still upturned and his eyes closed as he snuggled into the ground.

When it was completely dark they folded the mat and returned it, Piv pocketing the deposit of twenty-five baht. The busy market set up at the edge of the park confused Robin. In the crush of the crowd, textured conversations rising, electric lanterns throwing long shadows in the new dark, she grabbed for Piv. As she cupped his wrist, she saw she wasn't the only one reaching for him. A Thai woman's palm brushed under his other elbow. Just a quick sweep, then the hand was gone, but Robin saw it, and the woman was still standing, smiling. Piv stopped. The woman jabbered brightly into his face in Thai. She giggled into her hand. Her prettiness stuck Robin like a burr, but she had no style. When she turned her head to gesture to her girlfriend, Robin eyed the garish hair decoration she wore. The girlfriend was the first to see Robin. Glances flew between the three women like paddled chrome balls, all expressions shifting—Robin's rose high, haughty, the other two faces turned down—until the sets of eyes all landed on Piv. He hadn't met the woman's chatter with a single smile, and he didn't smile now. He barely nodded. Cool. But he did say something to the duo. *Farang*, Robin heard. A few more sentences. *United States*. If only force of will could make her understand what they were saying. Then Piv nodded again, and the two women melted away as she and Piv pushed through the crowd.

"Who was that?" she asked when they paused on a quiet corner.

He shrugged. "One girl. She works where they cut my hair. She doesn't speak anything. Only speaks Thai."

Chapter 17

For some days when NokRobin gets back from Singapore, we're alone. No one calls. We do what we want to, we plan our private business. But this is our business also: After five days, six days, something like that, Abu calls from Africa. Vol calls from somewhere, too. Phone rings sometimes in morning, sometimes in night. Many times when we're asleep. "Fucking Volcheck. Fucking Vol." NokRobin always says that, even when she's not awake. But it's no problem. Sure. Time is different where they are. Abu calls and tells me to do something: Go to Thai Farmers Bank, pick up money that comes on the wire. Borrow one car again, drive to Wattanayakorn's house and make some arrangement there. Go to Soi Cowboy, find this other man and get some elephant horn and tiger skin from him. Wrap these in the special way and take them to the airport, to the dock—nothing goes through customs. They'll fly to Delhi. From there they go to someplace I never heard: Kazakhstan. Then Vol picks them up and takes them to United States, where they want them, where I'll go soon—that's what Abu says.

NokRobin says, "But I thought people in Thailand loved elephants. Doesn't it make your heart break? Don't you love elephants?"

I tell her that since logging ban, there's no work for elephants to do. Some can carry tourists, but still there's too many. They're not allowed to work in Bangkok anymore, and not all can live very comfortable in the zoo.

"So it's save the trees and kill the elephants?"

I tell her that where this man gets horns, I don't know. Maybe that elephant is already dead. Maybe still living, and horns are cut off without hurting the rest.

We have this talk in the daytime, and I can't talk long, I have to go. I should not be late to meet this man. Sometimes when I'm gone, NokRobin stays inside the room and draws her pictures. This time she says she'll go to the zoo. But when I come home with enough money for the first necklaces we ask factory to make, she's very happy.

Next day, we have to go to the airport together. This time not to drop off—better for me to do that alone. This time we're picking something up, live turtles. Now it's easy for me to go to the airport. The road is busy, but no problem, and I don't have to use Vol's phone, I have my own. I leave NokRobin where the people get on, and when she calls my number, I know what to do. Three men—three thousand, two thousand, one thousand baht—and I get three blue plastic boxes with cuts on the side. It's very quick. But only two boxes fit in the trunk, unfortunate for me. One box must fit in backseat. When NokRobin gets into the car, we can hear them. Live turtles. They make that noise: *sssss, tttpt*. Scratch and hiss. They're not dead. We know. So when we're on the road, why does she want to? Why do we need to see this?

"If my credit cards have taught me anything, it's that you might as well face things," NokRobin says. "Abu knows we know about this; it's not like we're sneaking, so let's just see what kind of turtle is worth all this money."

She always want to do this. When I drive, she always want to turn around and make trouble.

"Please, sit. There are some police. You want them to see? Very expensive trouble to get in. Please."

"Where are they?" She sits straight and looks for police. She tries to be good, sits on her hands—but she still talks. "They probably wouldn't care about these turtles anyway. That's the point. No one does. People can just get away with it."

"They care about the turtles if that's what can make us give money to them."

"Listen," NokRobin says. She whispers. "God, they're really clattering around in there. You think they've been like that the whole flight? They're angry." She presses the button to make the window go down. She wants to make the strong smell leave, but it's too hot outside, too noisy. She presses window back up. No wind and you can hear the turtles again. "I don't see any cops. I have to look, Piv."

She tries to fit through two front seats. She's too big, gets stuck between. The car is still, stopped in traffic, but she makes it move. Then, pow, she gets through the seats. She's in the back. Now I'm like one taxi driver; she sits far away from me. I can move the car forward one small amount, so I step on the gas. She looks out the window, one hand on the box.

"I can feel them moving," she says.

For one moment, she's calm. Maybe she's sad, but she rests; she's quiet. Then she gets too busy. She opens the silver buckles that keep the box closed. She pushes the plastic cover back; it blocks the back window and makes the light turn blue.

"Ugh!" NokRobin puts her hand on mouth to stop this soft scream. Then she says, "Oh my god, they're poking at each other's eyes. Piv, look, it's awful."

Should NokRobin look at turtles in this car? She should not, I don't think so. I already told her, too many people, too many police, too many dollars for each one. And she can't stay calm. She's too excited to do smooth business. She thinks what's right, what's wrong, what's it mean about her life.

But I hear these turtles—*sssss*, clack, clack, clack. Very expensive ones, from some island near to Africa, and they've already been to many countries; they're special. Sure, I want to see that. I show NokRobin. Please, study how: how to look, know something, and still be calm.

Traffic goes slow. Stop, go, gas, brake. I move my mirror, very small motion. Six rows of car in front of me. In back of me, in the mirror, turtle shells are the only thing I see. Black melons slide together and go clack, yellow patterns like stars, like batik, something like that. I don't change my face. Then I see one brown leg, waving. Small claws like bear or tiger has. Then it pokes out its long neck—this is one head. Mr. Turtle!

His face is yellow on the bottom, green on top. He has black and shiny eyes. It's true, he's angry. He looks at me, and he doesn't like to see that. He opens his mouth and makes the sound. I can hear it now. It's not *sssss*, more like *hhhheeeee*. Other turtle's foot comes up; Mr. Turtle's head goes down. Shells all move—clack, clack, clack. NokRobin puts her eye in the mirror, too. It catches me there. We look in the same place, the mirror, and we see each other. I don't see her lips; I only see her one eye. Gray-green turtle eye. She speaks soft.

"I just wish you'd admit that some things are wrong. You confuse me." Then her eye goes back to the turtles. "Oh, they keep stepping on each other!" she says.

She reaches her hand—too quick—in there to stop one, to try to push the top turtle away. They all cry loud now—*hhhhheee*—sounds like some spirits are in this car! NokRobin jerks her hand away. Then she puts her hand back in, tries to move the top turtle again. But he doesn't like that. From his bottom side comes his red spray. I see it in the mirror.

"Ew," NokRobin says. The road opens in front of me. I press the gas, go forward. The smell is bad—sharp, painful. That turtle smell fights in my nose.

Why did you look in there? I want to say. I say nothing. I press the windows open. All four windows come down. Maybe NokRobin will yell soon, always some problems about the animals, so I want the wind to blow loud. I don't want to hear. I move the mirror so I don't have to see.

I leave her at Star Hotel, and I drive those turtles by myself to one man named Kobjitti, who works for Abu. Better this way. Abu says it's better if she doesn't know anything, if she never sees anyone but me. I go to Trombone Club after I'm done with Kobjitti, and there's Chit, Wanphen, Tick, even Anchan, hair-cutter, who comes there with Kathy—I didn't know before that they have been friends since the time I introduced them. Everyone there is polite. Everyone there is laughing. Everyone there is happy I came, and they say they want to see me more.

NokRobin is still awake when I come home from taking Anchan and Kathy home, but she doesn't come to touch me; she doesn't ask me where I've been. She's on the bed, leaning against that wall with her knees up and one small book open between her legs. Her hair's up, too. She looks small and lonely there, clean. She tells me Volcheck called to yell more. He wants to know why did I turn my phone off. Abu called to ask how did our business go. She keeps talking very calm—it's some new voice for NokRobin.

"I asked Abu something: 'Didn't you promise us a honeymoon?' Because he did. And I don't want to fight with you, Piv. Let's go away somewhere together where Volcheck can't call. Abu said it's okay, there's nothing else you have to do right now."

I take one cigarette and sit down on the chair. Most times she stands and hugs me immediate after I come in the door. No hug makes me feel light now. Too light. We look at each other while I'm smoking. Then I get up and go to her.

"Where you want to go?" I say the words into her hair. "What you want to see in my country? We have money now. Phuket, Ko Samui, stay in nice bungalow there. Air condition. Swimming pool."

She stops our hug to look at me so serious. "I thought you were going to take me home, to meet your family. Don't you want to do that anymore?"

"Sure, I want to," I tell her. "I want to take you to my home. Meet my mother, father, sure." We hug again, but now we lie down. I can put my legs on hers. "But we can go somewhere else, too. For some honeymoon. Hua Hin's close to my home. We can stay in nice hotel there."

"Oh, I know where I want to go! I want to go back to Pai. We had such a good time when we were there. It's so pretty and calm. Can we? Can we go to Pai?"

"Okay," I tell her. Pai is far to go for only few days, but I feel her body when she says this word. I feel it makes her happy. "Okay. We'll have one honeymoon there."

In Pai, NokRobin wants to sleep at Riverside Lodge, the dirty place that we stayed last time, but I say no. I tell her that for honeymoon, I want to sleep at the new resort. They don't finish building it at that time, but still you can stay, and for cheap price. The rooms are good for NokRobin, good for me. Two big doors open up so you can see hills, you can see fields, but there are screens, there's air-con if you want that. The big teak bed has mosquito netting, but this is for decoration, to make tourists feel like it's very mystery, that's why NokRobin thinks it's here. There are no bugs inside our room, and the sheets are very clean—you can smell them. This resort is our home for three days. No other guests share it, only one family of workers who live there while they build. Their daughter cleans our room if we want that. Me and NokRobin are peaceful together, romantic, no more problems. When we make love together, I feel exciting. She's one bird, and even on top of her, I feel us lift. I think about USA, one business there, one Thai-American child. These things I think about when we make something at this very sweet time.

Chapter 18

No first-class buses routed through Pai, so at dawn Robin and Piv climbed on the third-class one. The paved road through this part of the mountains had been laid about twenty years ago, but the rough state of it made it seem biblical, an archaeological find, and the bus staggered and slowed with every gear shift. The marigold and jasmine strung from the rearview mirror jerked so rapidly they looked like hummingbird wings. Rumor was that a bigger, four-lane highway was going through—that was one of the things the Pai Resort was banking on. Looking over the road's edge at sharply angled jungle, Robin wondered where they would put the extra asphalt. What part of the mountain would they blast away? She mourned it, but was relieved when they switched to a deluxe coach in Chiang Mai.

They arrived in Kanchanaburi Town after nightfall, and there caught one more transport, a lonely songthaew. The moon was just a sliver. Robin knew Piv's family lived outside the provincial capital, but she hadn't expected the ride there to be so absolutely black. Next to her, she could feel Piv rolling supplely with the truck's lurches. To him, this route was like breathing. He didn't need to see, but she missed the moon's glow.

At their stop, she welcomed the electric light emanating from a row of homes. She bounded out of the truck onto a crunch of gravel curb and waited while Piv went to the driver to pay. She was surprised at the dwellings. No porch lights burned, but the glow of the lit picture windows indicated a row of two-story town houses with white shutters and broad garage doors. Because of the blackness, the songthaew's puttering, the soft hills, Piv's vagueness, the taste of bugs, Robin had half anticipated she was heading toward a bamboo farmhouse with pigs living underneath. The truck drove away, its departing ruckus accentuating the night's quiet. Suddenly, she was down-deep scared. Piv slung their pack onto his shoulder and headed for the door, but she hung back. He stopped. Turned. Pecked her mouth dryly.

"Okay," he said, giving her wrist a tug. "Come on."

Two steps closer, Robin saw what kept these houses from being unchecked American suburban subdivision homes: the shutters looked aluminum, but the walls were unfinished cinder block.

Following Piv, she stepped out of her shoes at the threshold. The screen door opened directly into a living room focused around a color TV. Robin lagged at the door frame, and Piv strode in. He waied quickly, then caught the backpack slipping down his shoulder. A round-faced girl, her cheeks circled in white paste, beamed up at him from her seat on the floor. From a chair, a dry curl of a man bobbed his head happily, his bottom jaw flapping. Piv's mother just scowled. She held a square of glittering white tapestry and gestured with it up the stairs that bordered the small room.

With Piv up the stairs, gazes fell on Robin. She had memorized some basic Thai phrases for the occasion, but they were frozen just above her reach. The sister's smile softened, and her gaze turned down shyly, perhaps embarrassed to have been caught in a beauty routine. The father still nodded happily and beckoned her into the room. The mother went back to her sewing, her elbow avoiding the tin of pearly sequins balanced on the flat arm of her chair. Then all eyes drifted back to the TV set.

There was nothing else to do or say. No one offered her a seat. Robin felt her bones were going to break by the time Piv descended the stairs.

"Sit here," he told her, pointing to a hard yellow couch. "This one is for visitors." He made her a cup of instant coffee from the water pot and fixings set out on a black metal tray.

"They know I'm like farang. I like hot coffee. That's why they have this," he said.

He took his own cup and squatted down on the mat with his sister. He slurped his drink. He picked up a sequined square from his sister's pile and spoke to her, then turned to Robin. "My mother teaches her how to make this. Very beautiful. One man in Kanchanaburi town buys these things, sells them to U.S., where you live. I told my sister that you live there."

Robin smiled again at the sister. "Beautiful," she said. "*Très jolie*," her freshman-year French drills kicking in under the linguistic stress.

The Thai word bubbled up as well: "*Suay.*" The sister's face registered only appeasing befuddlement. Robin must have gotten the tones wrong. She tried again. "Beautiful. *Suay.*"

Piv laughed. "The way you say that means bad luck," he told Robin. "*Suay* means bad luck. You want to say *su-ay*. Rising tone. *Su-ay.*" Robin tuned her ears to pick up his different inflection, but she heard nothing she could understand. She tried again anyway—"*Suay*"—and was rewarded with a shy and pitying glance from Piv's sister.

"Maybe my mother can show you how to make one," Piv said.

"Sure," Robin said, both of her hands gripping the coffee mug, her legs crossed at the knee and again at the feet.

Piv turned to his mother. His grin was blinding. Robin realized that for all the charm he'd turned on her—and she sometimes felt subsumed by it, choked up, suspicious—she'd never gotten a smile this big. His mother's skin was butter-smooth, butterscotch, pulled over cheekbones as high and regal as Piv's, but her hair, twisted into a bun, had finger-wide streaks of gray. And her mouth was hard and fixed, plump lips ironed into a purse. It killed the beauty she surely must have had. With infinitesimal movements, she signaled negative to everything Piv said. He didn't bother to translate. Still smiling, punctuating with short laughs, he offered other questions, presumably farang-neutral—Robin took personally her hostess's freeze—until the knife-mouth softened into a recognizable prototype for Piv's. All the while she jabbed sequins onto a piece of muslin.

The TV on, the family all sitting—one member swallowing bile— the prim house, decent, a crown of achievement but without any room for grace: it reminded Robin of Palatka. She pictured her own mother. She's still pretty, Robin told herself, the perennial consolation implying that something might yet happen for her, but behind that banner slogan lurked the faded tints and frown lines that accosted Robin on her last visit home. She would have liked to imagine that her mother would be generous in welcoming Piv into the house, but with a sinking heart she saw the likely stare of fear, incomprehension. And she heard a command spoken when she was fourteen; she still felt the shame: "Don't dance with them anymore, honey. I know it's only dancing, but you can't let them think dating's okay." Robin had occasionally bristled at some farangs' attitudes toward Piv—they treated him as irrelevant, uncomprehending, a hustler, a tout—but in his own country he always had the upper hand. He would be the farang, the foreigner, at home. She'd never thought of that. Palatka was so far away.

But she and Piv had both come far; they'd both gotten out. No wonder they had drawn together. They wanted more: space and motion, possibility and beauty. A wider range of everything than was offered to their mothers, whose potential was cut off by kids, by cruel or unreliable or ineffectual men, by lack of funds; who were stuck. Without knowing anything else about Piv's mom, Robin knew that much.

The family didn't have a hot shower, but Piv insisted on heating water for Robin to bathe. She stood in a clean, tiled room and washed Thai-style, sluicing the warmth over her with a bucket, soaping up, then rinsing off. Afterward, she self-consciously balled up all her stray hairs from the drain on the floor and opened the window to push them out. The Turkish-style toilet had no flush, and there wasn't a waste basket. Piv had given her one of his sister's sarongs to wear. The two ends had been seamed together to make a loose tube, which wrapped around much more neatly than the open-ended cloth that Robin owned. She stepped gingerly out into the kitchen. Piv was waiting for her, but the fluorescent living room light was turned off. Everyone else had gone to bed. Was there another bathroom? No. She blushed with the embarrassment of taking too long and blushed again, protesting in whispers, when he insisted that of course they would share his bed. No one expected them not to.

The huge bed, with a six foot teak headboard, nearly filled the room. A metal stand with a mirror above it sat in one corner. The white cinder block wall was bare.

"Was this your room when you were growing up?" Robin asked. She sat on the bed with the day's clothes in her lap, scanning for signs of adolescence or childhood: trophies or schoolbooks or one favorite toy. Nothing. Piv took her bundle from her.

"We moved here when I was seventeen years. We feel lucky to have this house. This one is good. New."

He took off his jeans and T-shirt and folded them on top of the backpack, then turned off the light and came to bed in his bikini underwear.

"Does it feel weird for you to be back here?" Robin whispered.

"Hmmm? What do you say?" Piv squirmed deeper into the bed. "It feels good to be in my home."

"But does your mom feel angry because you're gone so much, because you live in Bangkok?"

"No. She's not angry. I do business. When they're old, I'll help them. Sure. They know that."

The answer didn't sit right. The day's sensations rolled through Robin: the shake of the first bus, the long roll of the second, the clenched anxiety she had felt since they'd reached this home. She tried to relax. Piv's breathing grew regular.

"Piv," she whispered. "Piv." She poked him. "Hey, I don't think your mom likes me."

His hand grazed her hip. "She likes you. Sure. Because you're *suay*. *Suay*. Very pretty." He tilted his face and nuzzled into her hair.

At least it's only one more night. Then we're due back in Bangkok, Robin thought. But that promise wasn't enough to relax her. She was awake to hear the chickens cackle and to see the gray light of sunrise suffuse the room.

She must have dozed finally, because when she woke later in the morning, Piv was gone. She lay for a while waiting for him to return from the bathroom or kitchen and gather her up. She strained to hear his voice amid the downstairs activity. She looked at her watch. Twenty after ten. Resentment ticked in. Didn't he know how awkward she felt? That she needed his help? She rose and swiftly dressed. Her most likely Thai-girl outfit had been tried yesterday. She put on silk harem pants and a scoop-neck T-shirt and made the bed, then sat on it to give him a few more minutes to redeem himself, to save her. Those minutes ticked by. She sighed and stood. She needed to pee, badly, but she still wanted to postpone going down. She checked her hair in the mirror.

She was finger-combing the tangles out when the door flew open. She jumped to look and saw Piv's mom. Wearing a flowered shirt and matching lavender pants, she held a short-handled broom and aggressively swept the joint where the floor met the wall. Robin stood stock still and smiled.

"*Sa-wat-dee kha*," she murmured—it was the only Thai greeting she knew, and she wasn't even sure it was appropriate now. The older woman, moving into the room, just scowled at the floor she was attacking. Robin stepped sideways, but the space she occupied, between the end of the bed and the back wall, was very small. As the bamboo broom swept closer, Robin side stepped until the only option left was to collapse back onto the mattress, her knees over the footboard, her weight on her hands. Piv's mother swept beneath her dangling feet. She wasn't using a dustpan. Her overt hostility dissolved Robin's shyness.

"Where's Piv?" she asked. Surely a mother must recognize her son's name. Her voice grew loud. "Where's Piv? Piv!"

Finally the woman stopped her sweeping and looked up, her face drawn with disappointment and full of contempt. She had a scattering of birthmarks by her left eye. Staring at Robin, she flicked her wrist twice at the window.

So he had gone? Or did the gesture mean that they'd all be better off if Robin were the one to leave?

Piv's mother swept her way out of the room and closed the door with a thud.

She must have sent Piv on some errand, made him go. He'd be right back. Summoning bravery, Robin went downstairs. She went to the bathroom. When she came out, Piv's father gestured to the tea tray. He'd poured her a mug of hot water. She put a tea bag in it, not Piv's instant coffee, and perched again on the yellow couch, to wait for a very long half hour before a motorbike rolled into the driveway.

Piv came in with a joyful gait, with a happy face, with a bag of fruit.

"You sleep this morning, wow!" he said.

"Where've you been?" Robin asked. But he was already talking to his mother, holding up fruits Robin had never seen before—some brown and bulbous, some hairy. Grudgingly, his mother accepted a rust-colored pod from him, sniffed the skin, nodded, then took the bag.

"I told her tonight I'll take her to restaurant, very good one, in town."

"Piv, I've just been waiting here. I've been up over an hour. Where have you been?"

"I rode the motorbike into town. I told you my father has that. You'll go, too. Today we'll go ride."

"You couldn't have waited?"

"I needed to use the international phone to call Abu. Better to call in the morning our time. I told him that I bring you to see my family. He says sure, it's no problem if we stay here two more days."

"What if I don't want to stay here?"

"Okay. No problem. Today only, I will show you Bridge over River Kwai, very famous one. We'll go on the motorbike and you can see."

But alongside the banks of the slow-moving river, Piv proved quietly intractable. They sat watching a boy on an elephant caress his beast as he waited for tourists who might pay for a ride, and Robin had to ask several times about bus schedules before Piv replied.

"It's better to stay more days, not leave so soon," he said.

He brushed aside Robin's claims of maternal hostility. His mother was just busy. She'd warm to Robin when she had more time.

"Please," Piv said. "We stay together. This is my family."

Robin went back to picking at the ground with a stick. She let a curtain of hair fall over her face, blocking her view of the two tourists who were being loaded onto the elephant's back. Piv twisted around and put his head on her lap and looked up at her. "Please," he said again.

He promised her daytimes of tourist fun. He'd take her to see a cave temple; he'd take her to a waterfall. A party boat floated down the river, music trailing behind it, and he told her that the two of them could spend an evening on one. By the end of the afternoon, Robin acquiesced, a pit of dread still lodged in her stomach but her mood softened by the flecks of sun coming in through the trees.

Because his parents had declined the invitation to a restaurant dinner, Piv brought home take-out food. On the motorbike, they'd wedged the bag between Robin's front and Piv's back. The five of them ate in a circle on the living room floor, Piv serving Robin out of the bowls placed family-style, describing the different foods to her, then turning back to the Thai conversation. It was his juggling act, but even living it vicariously, Robin felt exhausted.

Still, once they were tucked in bed, lights off, he began caressing her.

"No. I don't want to in your mom's house," she whispered.

"Shhh," he said. "No problem."

He continued with his touching, soft but sure. Her body responded. I could be in the pits of hell, she thought. In the midst of a big sale, and if it were him, I'd still want to, I can't help it.

Trapped all evening in an unwelcoming house, Robin found solace in their joined skin. He ripped a condom packet open. She fit to him, relaxed.

But at the first creak of the bed, it was Piv who froze. Abruptly, he sat upright. He yanked the pillow from under her head and threw it on the ground, along with his own.

"Too noisy," he said. "Floor better."

"What?"

"Shh." He spread a blanket out, gestured for her to slide off the bed. Confused, self-conscious of her nudity, she did so, but once on the floor she remained sitting, her brows knit and mouth half open, until he eased her back onto the pillows with his chest and shoulders. It was so dark.

"Okay?" he whispered.

"Yeah," she said, because she'd never answered otherwise when they lay naked together.

With some effort he pressed into her again, and she went along, trying to regain that space, the warmth, the rhythm. The window shutters were open, but there was no moon or street glow. With her hands obligingly on his shoulders, she felt how little there was of him: bone, muscle, skin, nothing extra. His face was against her neck. It seemed to take so long this time, and the blanket and pillows shifted so her backbone rocked on hard floor. Piv's lips found hers, but for the first time they seemed sloppy and artless. Her mind was elsewhere until she felt him straining, approaching his climax, and then she wished him on. She tried to help, but only because she wished it over.

Afterward, he lay very still. His heartbeat thumped against her. It galloped, cantered, trotted, finally walked. He pulled his head back. Because there was no light in the room, nothing reflected from his eyes.

"My wife," he whispered. He kissed her.

She kissed back but felt herself retreat from her skin.

Why had he spoken then, she later wondered. She had otherwise taken so much pleasure in their lovemaking, couldn't he tell when she had taken none at all?

They were squeezed into the two feet of space between the bed and the wall. He slipped under her so that it was his body that pressed against the floor. Hers was half on top of him, scooped close by his arm.

"I want you be my wife," he said. She felt him watch her.

What to do? If there had been more room for noise, she might have chuckled and made a joke, but the thick silence, the secret proximity, forestalled this. And she couldn't hedge with a vague romantic declaration. Awash in this strangeness, as alone in her life as she ever had been, she didn't know what love meant. She couldn't say anything.

"Okay?" he said. "You marry me?"

He kept massaging the base of her neck with the hand that held her to him. When she didn't answer, he asked again. "Okay?"

"I never thought about it, Piv. I never thought of getting married."

She hadn't, really. At least not very specifically, which surprised her. Especially considering what she'd done for money. She'd stolen things, misled, rushed people, hounded, wheedled. She'd borrowed far past what she had, which led directly to now—erranding for gangsters, trafficking in dying species. All this, until she didn't know herself, and she'd never thought of marrying rich? Not even when she'd dated guys born into money or pulling down big bonuses? No. She'd had contempt for their cushions even as she'd laid in them. The alienation this contradiction inspired combined with the doctrine of independence implied in the lives of artists she'd most admired took quid pro quo marriage off the table. But smelling Piv's fruity breath infuse the nook where they lay, Robin's stomach sank. At the least, a husband should not be a deficit.

"Don't think about it. Be. Be my wife."

"But why? We'll have our business. We can travel anywhere we want, come and go. You won't need papers. We don't need to be married."

Piv sat up. She felt the loss immediately. He lowered his head toward her.

"I've been with many woman. Too many. When I make something with you, I never feel like that before. This is not for the papers. This is not because you're from U-S-A." He punctuated the three initials sarcastically.

Robin reached out for him, fumbling in confusion about his urgency and hers. Her hand landed on his knee, but he stood and it fell off.

"We haven't even known each other for two whole months. Let's talk about this later," she said. Her voice was pleading.

She pushed herself into a sitting position, but he stepped over her. He picked up his sister's wadded sarong and tied it around his waist with one hand. In the other hand he held their knotted, spent condom. He left the room, closing the door softly behind him.

The next day they went to the Erawan waterfalls. Piv was polite, charming. He flirted. But that was all. He wouldn't say a nonjoking word about what had transpired. His mother forgot to scowl at Robin, but she never smiled. The third day they took a first-class bus back to Bangkok.

Chapter 19

One day after I return from my home in Kanchanaburi, Abu returns to Star Hotel. Jomo, Yoke, they're still in Kenya, and Abu misses his friends, I think so, because he always wants me with him now. He says he wants to teach me something about this business.

When we make business, no, NokRobin's not there. When it's time to relax, sure, sometimes she comes with us. We eat at Thai restaurants—Abu can eat food that's spicy hot. We drink in lounges—not always at Star Hotel, sometimes Red Elephant Bar, Brown Sugar Bar, or the pub in Indra Regent. And we go to see one concert. Abu wants to hear Buddy Guy, blues guitar player from United States, so he buys three tickets. Very expensive. One ticket costs more than one thousand baht. NokRobin buys some special clothes to wear when we go there. She wears one small black skirt, one small shiny shirt. Wow. Sure, I can still think this. We still make something. Sometimes in morning, sometimes in night, but more than one time? No. Now it's never like that. Now I'm never that hungry. And if I don't see her every day? No problem. Maybe it's better. I leave in morning and don't come back until late. She stays awake to wait for me, and I think she wants to talk to me, but she can see that I don't want to, so no. Maybe we make something, but we both stay quiet. At this time, it's more important for me to talk to Abu, not to feel sad about NokRobin. More future.

Me and Abu go to see Kobjitti. When I go alone to see him at Sweetie's Basket, I wait outside. I tell the boy at the door to go get him. But with Abu, we go inside. It's two o'clock in afternoon, but some farangs drink in there already. They look at Thai women. These ones dance, look sleepy, wear bikini. If they don't dance, they sit with the farang man who buys them milk so he can touch them.

"Hello, hello," Kobjitti says when he sees us. Before, I talk to him in Thai. The way he talks now, I can hear that he doesn't speak good English. "Welcome. Welcome. Please. Sit. Drink. You drink."

Abu asks for Johnnie Walker but for me, just one Coke.

Hurry up, get these drinks, make this man comfortable! Mr. Kobjitti says in Thai to one girl. He brings over one chair for himself, and he sits down.

When the girl comes back she stands behind us. She puts her hands on shoulders of Abu and starts massage. Western kind, not Thai-style. Her face doesn't move. Her red paint nails are like small plastic jewelries on the yellow shoulders of his shirt.

"My man tells me you've taken good care. It's appreciated," Abu says to Kobjitti.

Kobjitti smiles. It takes too long, but then he understands. "Yes. Thank you. Thank you."

"And now let's see this round of cargo." His drink is finished already. Kobjitti and me don't finish our Cokes, but we all stand up and walk away. Bar girl is left to find someone else.

We go to one building in the alley off Soi 23. Abu's like one giant. Very strong. Too big in that hallway, too big in that small room that's smelling like animals. Room has two beds—one with toy bears and pigs on it—one small dresser, and one big cage made from wire. Cage is bigger than the bed. Inside there is where the turtles live. They look dusty, but some move around. I bend to count them. Twenty-four turtles should be inside there. Abu doesn't wait for me to count. He opens wire door and reaches in their house. He picks one up. Mr Turtle yells— *hhhheeee*. His mouth opens wider than his whole head.

"Ah, they still have that fighting spirit," Abu says. He holds the turtle out to me. "Feel the weight of this." Whenever Abu says something, Kobjitti smiles and laughs. I don't want to, but I take that turtle.

It's heavy, wow. I use two hands to hold the shell. It feels like turtle tries to swim.

"Each shell is its own original, which is of course what attracts the collectors. I have a Japanese dealer coming this week. What do you guess he'll pay? Once we exchange the yen, it will be a little under nine thousand U.S. for each one."

At that moment, the door to the room opens. Very pale woman puts her head inside the door, and we can hear some ladies laughing too loud.

Get out of here! Kobjitti yells at them. The door slams shut. "Sorry," Kobjitti says. "Sorry. Sorry." He smiles.

Abu takes turtle from me and with some thick pencil puts one red dot on turtle's back. Then that turtle goes inside the cage again. Abu's hand goes, too. He picks another turtle and looks at him—his belly, his shell. Then another turtle, and again, again. On some turtles he puts red dot.

"Tell Kobjitti that we'll stop by the bar tomorrow evening at nine o'clock. The marked cargo should be in a carrying case somewhere on the premises."

Abu closes the cage and goes to wash his hands in these ladies' bathroom. When he's finished, I'm excited to wash my hands, too. The floor in the bathroom is cement, not tile. Only one small towel in there, and it's already dirty, already wet; it smells like moldy bathroom. I don't want to use it, but I do. It's better to have clean hands, dry hands. When we go back out to the hallway, the pale-skin lady waits there with one friend. They still laugh, and they say something about how big is the Negro man. When we walk by, Kobjitti tells them to be quiet.

Abu takes me to some hotel near Soi Cowboy that I've never seen before. He says he wants to use their business center, and they will let him get and send fax for small price, and he wants to have one cocktail, and they have the relaxing lounge on the first floor. I wait for him in the lounge when he's in the business center. I sit alone while his ice cubes melt in Johnnie Walker.

When he comes back, he holds some paper. "The world is shrinking, my friend. As a Kenyan man, I can sit here with you in Bangkok and get a call from Cologne. This customer wants a rare lizard found only in the Philippines, when it's found at all. If all goes well, he and I will meet for coffee in Orlando, and that lizard will change hands, for a price that is more and more standardized. Look at this." Abu hands me what he holds. Long line of numbers goes down the right side of both pages. Next to every number is some word in English, then in something like German, then in some letters like I never see before.

"What's this?" I say.

"It's a standardized price sheet."

"No, this letter, this language. What's this one?"

"That's Russian." Abu picks up his Johnnie Walker and says words over his glass before tasting. "The Americans and the Russians.

With all the changes that have occurred since I was your age, they're still both much too influential in countries like yours and like mine." To make the toast, he lifts his eyebrows at me instead of lifts his glass.

I look at the paper again and read the English words. They can buy everything they want to. Dead things: tiger bone, parts of elephant, rhino, and many things I don't know. Alive things: kinds of snake, kinds of lizard, tortoise, frog, kinds of bug. I ask Abu, "These numbers, what money are they for?"

"Dollars, of course." Five thousand dollars for one dead bug. Wow. That's too crazy. Who wants to do that? It's because those ones are hard to find. If it's easy to find, instead of paying then they smash that bug. I think so. "But it's time to meet your Robin. I'll be needing her services again soon; it won't do to let her languish."

I don't like to hear this: *your Robin*. Abu throws some money down to pay for our drinks. I think I see two purple bills and one red— eleven hundred baht. When I was one student, I lived on this amount for one week, maybe two weeks, sure. To see it now makes me feel something very strong: I want to be away from this. I want to eat supper with Chitapon, sitting on his floor. After that I want to sit, relax, talk in Thai, listen to Chit play some songs on the guitar.

"Oh, I forget something. I'm too stupid," I say to Abu. I hit my hand to my forehead. "I'm too stupid, now it's not possible for me to go."

But when I explain to Abu that I forgot I have one appointment, he says, sure, it's still possible for me to go to meet my friend, and he gives me some money to spend when I do that. He tells me not to worry about NokRobin. He'll take her to her meal. He'll ask her for her service. He'll even show her papers that will make her calm down about those animals. He tells me to go with my friend, and he'll take care of it all.

Chitapon's not at his home, so I buy khao moo daeng from the vendor in front of his building, and I sit down to eat that. Vendor feels sad for me because I eat alone. She brings some food for herself, and she sits down to talk to me. She tells me two more hours, then she'll pack up her cart and go home. Not to her home near Udon Thani, no, to her home in Bangkok, just one tent where she lives with her husband and keeps her cart at night. They'll go back to Udon Thani for harvest season. They have house there, she tells me, some land for farming, but money is not enough to always stay there.

I tell this vendor thank you for eating with me, for talking to me, that her khao moo daeng is very good, then I say good-bye. I take meter taxi to Trombone Club, but Chit's not there. Another friend tells me why not. Tonight Fallow band plays at Sandwich Pub. Okay, no problem. I get in one tuk tuk and take another ride.

When Chitapon sees me there, he smiles. He leaves the people he's talking to so he can come and talk to me. He asks me did I eat already. He asks me how's my business.

I tell him business is good, that the man I work for takes me to see Buddy Guy. In my suit pocket I have half of this ticket, and I show Chit that.

Buddy Guy! he says. He pretends to play guitar like him. Then Wanphen comes to see me. She asks me the same questions Chit already does: Did I eat? How I been? I look so business, how's my business?

Business is good, I say again. Then I say something else: In two weeks I go to Florida, to United States.

Wanphen gets the Levi's she sells from some Thai person who lives in the USA, but she's never been there. "You go to USA? You get big *E* Levi's!" She laughs because she sounds funny in English. Then she talks again in Thai: If you find me those, and they're not my size, we'll sell them and we'll split the money, okay? She laughs again. She's very exciting.

I tell her, Levi's, sure. I'll get you those. They're very cheap over there. No problem.

No, she says. The ones I want are special. You can't buy those new. You have to find them. Old ones. Old ones. Big *E*.

Sure, I tell her. I don't understand, but I say, Okay, I'll buy for you.

She jumps up and down, because she wants me to know something. She says: The tag, it has to say big *E*, not little *e*. Big *E* on the back pocket.

She turns around. She watches my face over her shoulder when she touches the pocket of her jeans. Her hair is almost down to her pocket. She's very pretty, with her own kind of style, and I think Chit is lucky she wants to be with him.

She says: On here. You read English, right? You know the letter *e*? You understand?

Okay, I say. Sure, sure. But let me see.

I pretend to bend down to look at her pocket. Wanphen turns around and steps away from me. She laughs again.

I think you read English, but you can read it in the United States. You don't have to read on me! Your girlfriend will get angry.

What girlfriend? I say. NokRobin's face comes in my mind and hurts my head.

Your girlfriend. I see her over there.

I look in the corner where some farangs are, but NokRobin's not with them. What girlfriend? I say to Wanphen again, but then I see Anchan. She sees me, too.

Is not! I say, but Anchan's already coming.

She wears orange color jacket to match her orange color trousers. Fallow band starts to play and their guitar sounds mean and good. Anchan doesn't look good like Wanphen, doesn't look like rock and roll. I buy her one Coke, and then I say, Excuse me, I see someone I must talk to. Good-bye. I go to stand in front of the stage with Wanphen.

When Fallow band takes break, Kathy comes there, too. Because I can speak English to her, and because she used to be sweet with Chit, she thinks she's my friend, but I don't want to talk to her now. She's always pushing something. Tonight she pushes about me and Anchan.

"She says you're blowing her off, Piv. Did you really break up with her to go out with some farang?"

Anchan stands by the door when Kathy says this. I see her look at me. I think she'd be ashamed if she knows what Kathy says now—too pushy. Too farang.

"No. I didn't break apart. How can I break apart when we don't make something together?" I say.

"You didn't take her out? You didn't give her this?" Kathy shows me the blue hair decoration. Anchan still stands by door. Her hair hangs down now, too curly. She looks at me, looks sad, no smile. I never could guess that she would act this way. I thought she was shy, polite. "You're her first real boyfriend. You really hurt her feelings."

"Excuse me," I say. "I was never her boyfriend. No. Why you think that?" I don't want to touch that blue decoration. Fallow band goes onstage to play again. I wanted to talk more to Chit and Guy, but now it's too late. Anchan watches me. I don't smile. Her face gets more sad. Then she opens the door, and she leaves Sandwich Pub. Good.

"Oh, great, Piv," Kathy says. "I'm finally getting her out to the clubs, and you make her cry within an hour."

"I don't make her!" I say. Kathy puts this blue thing in my hand and walks to the door to follow Anchan.

Wanphen laughs at me now. She doesn't need to understand English. She knows what Kathy says to me, I think so.

I tell Wanphen: Those times you saw me with Anchan, those are the only times I meet her!

Wanphen thinks this is too funny. She likes to see Kathy get too hot and lose face. I hold blue decoration out for her. I make this joke: You want this decoration? To go with big *E* Levi's?

She tells me I have to wear that until I find my girlfriend again. That because my hair is short now, I have to wear the decoration like one bracelet. She puts it on me. Wow. It's ugly, but I keep it on to make this joke with Wanphen.

When I go in room 517, I feel surprise. It smells something like Sandwich Bar in there—air-con and Singha beer and Khrong Tip. And it's dark. TV light is the only light, but no sound comes from that. I see one fire dot, the spark from cigarette.

"Hi," NokRobin says. I can tell from the fire dot that she's sitting at the table. I want to see her face. I turn on the light.

"I feel surprise," I tell her. "I never see you smoke, so I think you're one robber." I laugh. I wish she'd laugh, too.

"Can you turn off the light?" she says. "It hurts my eyes."

I turn this off. "I'm sorry that I have one appointment and cannot meet you."

"I'm sure Abu already told you everything, anyway, right?"

"No. I don't know. What he tell you?"

"He gave me some bullshit about these being free-range rhino horns, and he offered me five hundred dollars to take them to fucking Singapore." Why she's so angry? Does she see that hair decoration on my wrist when I turn on the light? If she thinks there's another girl, will she feel jealous? Want to keep me? Or will that close the door forever? Better not to have the risk. I put my hands behind me so she cannot see.

"Supposedly there was some authorization by the Zimbabwe conservation department to dehorn the black rhinos that live on one of the reserves," she says. "Then no one will have a reason to kill them. I guess the horns are meant to go to some government department, but *phh*—" She makes sound like she spits. "So much for that."

No, she's not jealous. I take the decoration off and put it in my back pocket. She's mad about these animals, something about that. She only cares about them.

"And when I balked at doing more of this rhino stuff, he told me something even more interesting. That the next stop on his little world tour is Florida. Orlando. He's offering me a ticket home."

"Florida, USA? Wow."

NokRobin stands up and turns on the light near the bed. Now my eyes hurt. I put my hand to my face.

"Like you didn't already know!" NokRobin says. "Like you didn't know he's flying you over there, too!" She sounds so angry; her words hurt like that light, they hit my headache. "When were you going to tell me, Piv? Huh?"

"Shh. I tell you. I always tell you what I know. Why you angry?"

"I'm not angry! I'm hurt. I'm confused. You don't tell me anything. Even less than before. Maybe you're the one who's angry at me—I'm not even sure. Are you? Why can't we talk about what you asked me in Kanchanaburi? About what's going on?"

"It's no problem for you now. You get free ticket home."

"But it's a problem for me and you, Piv. We need to talk about this. What about our plan? Why don't you believe me when I tell you I want to be with you?"

I take my hand away from my face, and I look at NokRobin. She wears white color underwear and one white singlet, that's all, not very many clothes. But around her neck she wears that silver necklace that we made together and I picked up at the factory yesterday. It looks strong, shines nice. It makes me happy and sad to see it there.

"Shh, okay. I believe you. No problem." I step to her and touch our necklace. Happy and sad both.

"I'm sorry about what I said at your mom's house. When you brought up marriage, I just didn't—"

"Shhhh," I tell her. I don't want to hear her say why she won't be my wife. Words about that hurt me. I make her stand, and I kiss her lips so she won't say them. Her lips taste good to me, and I kiss them again and again and again. I still want to make something with her. I shouldn't want to, but I can't help it. I hold her and I kiss her and I want to make our plans and our love grow together again.

But then her lips stop kissing. They stay by mine, but now they talk into my mouth: "Piv, please tell me the truth. What did Abu say? Are the rhinos really still alive somewhere or not?"

I tell her that Abu says nothing about that. That I don't know. I want to kiss again, to stop her talking about the animals more, but even when our lips get busy, I can feel that she is gone from where we are. She's with the animals, and she's flying to Singapore.

Chapter 20

Everything looks the same, Robin thought as she checked her styled hair in one of the Star lobby's mirrored columns. She and Piv were waiting inside the hotel while the manager's nephew got the Mitsubishi, and she wanted the reassurance of what had become familiar: the hair-sprayed sheen of her dress-up-and-fly mode, the straight pink lines and reflective surfaces of the Star. She turned to smile and blink her eyes at Piv in a last-minute effort to retrieve him from the far-off reaches he had climbed to, but he seemed impervious, and her stomach looped in sets of figure eights. When she stepped outside to meet the car pulling up at the curb, beads of sweat rose from the skin in the hollows under her eyes, from the webbing between her fingers. It was almost April, the hottest month of the year in Bangkok, but as usual, Robin saw no visible signs of perspiration on Piv as he ushered her into the gray interior of the car. She smoothed the seat of her silk suit while he loaded the wheeled black bag packed by Abu.

When the nephew began forcing his way into the stream of traffic, she kissed her fingers and pressed them to the car's window, but Piv had already turned from her and was glancing over one shoulder at the intersection. The way the sun hit, his profile was outlined in a golden glow. The image filled her with an emotion too big for her body; her ribs felt like a bivalve cracked open, its morsel scraped out. His refulgent lips, his flat nose, his delicate posture, his hair. His stiff hair. *That* didn't look the same as it did the first time she left. She craned around to watch him pull open the door of the Star Hotel. She wanted to pound on the window, to shout to him not to give up, to keep on loving her. She fingered her neck, where a silver lotus rose to the dip of her throat. She was wearing the necklace they had made together—it didn't complement the tailored lines of the suit, but she wanted the ballast of it, the reminder of her larger reasons, her solid goals: designing jewelry and import-export with Piv. She recited the plan again to herself: First they'd go north—the market for their jewelry would be better in New

York, and she wouldn't mind crashing with friends if it were for an exotic reason. Then they'd hop over to California—Asian-influenced stuff was big on the Pacific Coast, and flights back to Thailand would be cheaper from there. She'd wait to pay off the creditors until after she'd earned enough profit to invest in some stones and had found enough really good contacts to make more expensive designs worthwhile. And then, maybe then—if he still wanted to and they were getting along great, if they knew each other truly and could really communicate—she and Piv could talk seriously about getting married.

She touched her necklace again. Since coming back from his parents', she'd polished the plan alone. Piv had been only polite and distant—even, with a couple of torrid but silent exceptions, during sex. If only he would let his guard down and open up to her, or at least listen to her try to open up to him. He'd surprised her with the marriage question, so she hadn't handled it right. No one should decide about marriage after only two months; that's what her mother and father had done, the hick and the carpetbagger—and look how that turned out. The point about her and Piv was that they were different. She wanted to explain that to him. She wished that she could go back in time so she could be cajoling him into happy postponement right now. But the car rocked forward to the airport—past Chatuchak Park, past a small shantytown roofed in green plastic, past a mall built to look like an antebellum mansion except for the neon Cartier sign on top.

"Hello. Did you have a pleasant flight?"

Robin looked up from the circling black luggage belt. The man who spoke to her was wearing a gray suit. He was Asian-complected, but his English was stateless. He didn't look at Robin; he kept his gaze on the plastic tongues dangling from the mouth of the conveyor.

"Yes," Robin said, startled. "Fine." It wasn't impossible that he was American and recognized her as a compatriot.

"Where did you come from today?" His hands were clasped behind his back, and his face was so relaxed it seemed to float. Robin dismissed the idea that they shared a nationality. Something about the man's contained fluidity, something about his gold Rolex—or was it a knockoff?—pegged him as indelibly Southeast Asian.

"Bangkok."

She and the man looked together at the jerking belt. An aluminum trunk emerged, the rubber tongues draped momentarily over it. A crowd of waiting passengers rustled to readiness.

"Oh," he said. "Are you traveling for pleasure?"

Robin started. This was a question travelers answered at immigration, not one they traded in waiting-room chit-chat. She shrugged irritably. No other luggage emerged from the chute. The stickered trunk chugged forward, solitary; no one rose to claim it.

"Business, then?"

"Why do you ask? Where have you come from?" She strived for a tone of cheery curiosity.

"Oh," he said. "The luggage for your flight will be released to another bay, bay number seven." He stepped aside to give her room to pass. "Have a nice stay in Singapore."

She whittled her way to the edge of bay seven's moving belt. Despite the air-conditioning, she could feel herself begin to sweat again. Silk wasn't absorbent. There were no windows in this wing of the airport, just vistas of putty-colored carpeting and white walls. And there was no smoking; Robin reminded herself that she couldn't even chew gum here, in public Singapore, and the thought made her stickier. She was uncomfortable in her professional shoes; her feet wanted to spread into sandals.

A suitcase came through onto the belt. After a moment's pause, there came another: a bright yellow hard-sider with an identifying blue ribbon tied to its handle. Robin pressed her shins up against the belt's rail and looked toward the new luggage coming into view.

"Hello," said a man just to her right. He was imitating her posture. "Where have you traveled from today?" His sentence structure was impeccable, but he spoke as if through a mouth full of marbles.

Robin turned to look at him. Another sepia-toned man in a platinum gray suit. "Bangkok," she said, because to protest the question would seem unnecessarily churlish.

"Oh yes?" he said, still bending forward for the best view of luggage. "Business or pleasure?"

Robin forced herself to smile. "You're not the first person to ask me that today."

He straightened and turned to her. The two stood on guard. Robin offered no information. From the corner of her eye she saw a two-wheel black case pass by on the belt. Then she saw another one, a similar model. She wanted to snatch a bag and stride away, but without stooping over to read the tags, she couldn't know which one was hers.

"Have you been to Singapore before?" he asked.

"Why are you asking me?" She tried to make her voice teatime light.

"It is just conversation." With long fingers, the man reached into his jacket and flapped open a wallet to reveal a gold and blue seal. A roving customs officer. "I greet passengers. How long have you been in Bangkok before coming here?"

"Greet them? You mean by asking questions?" The important thing was to be calm. Why was her own shrill voice filling her ears? Waves of heat crashed over her head.

"What's your occupation?" the man asked.

"I already told them that at immigration. Excuse me, I see my luggage over there," Robin said. She stepped away from the man too fast; her carry-on tote bumped against him, and she jostled another suited person in her rush to get away.

On the other side of the luggage wheel, she paced behind the wall of passengers, hiking her sagging tote straps higher on her shoulder, twiddling her rings. It'd been stupid to bolt from that man. She needed to act normal. She needed to act normal, because something was wrong. Something was going to go wrong, and the best thing she could do would be to leave the suitcase circling in the airport and walk cleanly away without drawing attention to herself.

Shut up, she told herself. You're paranoid.

But her suspicions kept pulsing. She scanned the crowds. They were on to her, on to something. She should leave empty-handed. Without the case that Abu packed for her she was as innocent as if she'd never done anything, never known a thing. She just had to bend over and—snip—with a flick of her army knife cut off the identifying luggage tag. The idea filled her with a rush. Home free, on her own, she'd disappear into Singapore and away from smugglers. The crowd was thinning. Best to do it now, before her bag was the only one left. She slipped her hand inside her purse to search for the reassuring fold of blades. Her knuckles bumped against a lipstick tube and the fluffy rough of balled Kleenex. And then she remembered: Piv had her knife. If she wanted to do this, she'd have to get down on her knees and rip the tag off with her teeth.

Stop it, Robin thought again. Stop it, stop it, you're being overly dramatic. Look, there's the customs guy talking to that chubby wife with a bad perm. He's asking her the same questions he was asking you. You aren't carrying drugs. This isn't TV. Pick up the bag. It's a simple task. Two days from now you'll be in Bangkok with Piv. Hold on for two weeks and you'll be heading home together, with something to show for your nine months away.

By now the luggage wheel was almost empty. Robin walked to the conveyor belt and slung her case to the ground. She slid out its thin metal handle. She carefully put her declarations form in between the pages of her passport. Then she joined the customs line behind a family who had a cart piled six feet high with leather-edged suitcases and cardboard electronics boxes. The queue moved slowly toward the officials who pointed travelers through one of two detectors, giving Robin enough time to will herself into a numbness that chilled away her heat. The men had red ribbons around their flat-topped hats and sat unsmiling on high stools. They eyed the form of the well-stocked family in front of Robin before giving them a quick nod.

"Where are you coming from," they asked Robin in English, looking down at the answer in her passport, not at her. "How long were you there? What were you doing there? You've been in Singapore before? For how long?"

A hum rose inside her. They should be just shuffling her along, not asking questions. She moved her lips, but she couldn't hear her own replies. Finally the man gestured for her to go. She stepped away into a tunnel of wind, a rushing of temperatures, hot and cold whooshes of relief.

But no. A pincered hand gripped her elbow.

"Excuse me. You were asked to step over there." The man who held her was dressed in green.

Two more olive-clad men, these ones with smoky plastic gloves on, stood behind a low, wide table, waiting for her.

"I'm sorry," Robin said. "I didn't mean to. I just didn't hear." But she strained away from the hand on her arm. If it hadn't held her, she would have been running away.

They started the search with her purse, then her tote, and as she stood there, forced to watch, her reactions played out on a split screen. On one side: indignation. Who was this man, this foreign man, sniffing her Nivea and feeling the seams of her cotton bikinis, the cups of her grayed white bra, tossing aside what she wore next to her skin? In this enactment, she was genuinely put out, offended. How could she— well-educated, well-shod, white, clean—be subjected to this invasion of privacy? The customs agent flipped through the pages of her journal, then held the covers and shook the book upside down. A postcard of Sukhothai fell out, the pretty ticket to Wat Pho that she'd been saving. She had half a mind to call a supervisor and protest.

But in the other half of her mind, on the other side of the screen, her desperate hope was that the supervisor would not be called. She cowered, humiliated. Feeling herself drenched with guilt and deserving of punishment, she still sent begging eyes to yank pity, boredom, lust— whatever it would take—from the agent so that he would turn her loose before cracking into the black case. It didn't work. The customs official gestured for Robin to repack her tote, and her hands dutifully folded slippery rayon and recapped jars while he inspected the outer compartments of the suitcase. Inside Robin's mind, her abject half tore at the flesh of her impervious one—she pounded, slashed, and trampled her, but the beating had little effect. The rigid denial of the supercilious American girl broke down, but the flame of entitlement that allowed her to see herself as an exception continued to burn: I deserved better. If this is what I had to do, so be it.

The officer had opened the suitcase and was pulling out a stream of women's clothing: a red lined skirt, a bone silk blouse, a natty blazer, which was balled up. He unrolled the blazer and dipped his hands into its pockets. Abu must have packed all this, but why? For a moment, Robin's mind emptied. She was baffled. She knew nothing. There was no fight to be had. Maybe the last months existed only in hallucination, and some other life—a real one—would present itself as soon as she blinked. Then the officer reached in farther and drew out an oversized ziplock bag. He held it in front of his face just as Robin once had. There were the horns: two earthy curves spooning; two massive, stacked apostrophes that had previously signified ownership. It's nothing, Robin thought, steeling herself. She supposed she could feign surprise, but the effort seemed impossible. It's nothing, she wanted to tell the man who opened the bag, sniffed, then set it on his opposite palm and lifted to test its weight. His face didn't change as he rubbed the horns through the plastic, sniffed again, then reached in to scratch the surface. The tip of his plastic glove came out tipped with dirt.

"What's this?" he said to her.

"Nothing," Robin said. Nothing nothing nothing. Rhino horns. If only he would show a glimmer of interest in her, a ghost of a smile or even the erotics of wielding his power. There was still time for him to let her go. But his face was blank as he took a walkie-talkie from his belt and spoke into it.

Profanities ran through Robin's mind, directed first at the man standing before her, but easily attacking Abu, too, and Volcheck, and the men in suits who had spoken to her earlier, and the woman at Don Muang Airport who had made her check the suitcase even though it was carry-on size, and soon the curses ricocheted and struck everyone she recently knew—fuck, fuck, fuck—fuck Piv for his cool beauty, fuck Zella for being lying and mean, fuck Yhan and his smiling German wife in Pai for the siren call of their happiness. Fuck.

The man set the horns down on the Formica table and continued through the suitcase, pulling out another set of horns as well as more women's dress garments before a pair of men in creased khaki—the demanded/dreaded supervisors; not just one of them, but two—walked up and spoke to the searcher in Chinese. The horns passed between them until a single man ended up with both bags. He looked at Robin for the first time.

"Horn of rhinoceros. On the international list of endangered animals. According to international agreement and the law of Singapore, it is forbidden to carry this across our border. You break the law. You are in our custody."

Three pairs of eyes glanced off her. She felt obliterated, buried, scarcely present. When questioned, she responded; her voice small, her self receding. This was not her drama after all, she sensed early on in the inquisition. She barely mattered. She said that she had been given the suitcase, that she hadn't known what was in it. She said she was coming to Singapore from Bangkok, that she was American. But if she had hoped her nationality would suggest that their treatment of her might have consequence, her passport revealed her as backpacker flotsam: France for a month, then Italy, Greece, Turkey, where she had walked from

Europe into Asia and flown on to India, then to Nepal, moving always at a snail's pace until the recent flurry of short hops from and back to Bangkok. She had to answer to it all.

She was escorted to a holding room, a pen of blind white walls marked with a high expanse of silver one-way window, where she repeated her statements for a revolving cast of tight-lipped men. Between interrogations, she sat alone in the cold room for long stretches. She was locked in, but not bound in any way. She was free to pace, but she didn't touch the plastic-cased horns that sat on the brown table in front of her as a testament to brute greed, the unavoidable sum of her guilt. Two hours passed, then three. She was quizzed by several teams of interchangeable men. They wanted to know how much money she had gotten for carrying the horns. Did she have the money now? They took the cash she did have and counted the big bright bills before putting them in an envelope. What was she supposed to do in Singapore? What else had she carried? All this was asked in inflectionless English. They talked among themselves more animatedly. Once, a man shorter and slighter than she was picked up both bags of horns and let them fall back down on the table with a crack. She jumped in her seat, then took her twitching hands from atop the table and sat on them.

"When did you see the suitcase for the first time?" he asked her. She couldn't take her eyes off the horns. Her face crumbled.

The man repeated his question, and when he didn't get an answer, he grabbed one of the horns from the bag and thrust it toward her face. She jerked back, horrified; her chair screeched.

"When was the first time you saw the suitcase?"

"This morning," Robin said, bringing her hand to her nose and sniffling. Anticipating the questions that had previously followed this one, trying to be good, she carried on. "I didn't know what was in it. They gave it to me at the hotel."

But the man seemed not to listen. He and his companion headed toward the door and shut it behind them, leaving her alone again for another long hour. The fluorescent lights sizzled. It was 9:00 PM. Would the next time she slept be in a Singaporean jail? She conflated everything she'd ever heard about Southeast Asian prisons and punishment into one horrible lump and fell into a sort of trance, imagining herself sustained on a diet of worm-speckled rice and caned until her body went into shock. Would her father come visit, or would he disown her once the twinkle of her potential was gone? Would this be the news that would break her mother's back? Robin felt a wail swelling in her chest. Then the door's steel handle crashed against the wall as two broad-shouldered white men followed two Singaporeans into the room.

One of the Caucasians wore dark blue trousers, the other one wore a mustache and khakis. Their jackets were open, their shirts unbuttoned at the collar. They didn't wear ties. They loped into the room, and when they sat down their knees spread wide in their roomy pants. They leaned over the table each in succession and said, "How ya doing, Robin," while grabbing her hand and giving it a quick shake. The khaki man said, "Believe it or not, we're from the U.S. Fish and Wildlife Service. Bet you didn't expect to find us here, huh? You thought we stayed over there in Yellowstone." He grinned. Robin gave him a single weak chuckle. Then the blue guy—"I'm Ray. This's Robert"—raked his fingers through his longish forelock, rubbed his tanned, lined forehead, and said, "Now, what's a girl like you trucking with rhino horns for? Did you need a little cash? Is that how you got yourself into this mess?"

A hand-in-the-cookie-jar chagrin spread through Robin, and one half of her mouth lifted in a smile. It'd been so long since she'd been with normal, true-blue Americans. Even if she was on the other side of the law, she knew she could talk to these men, explain, and they'd understand at least her words, her idioms, her inflections. They might lock her up, but they wouldn't let her molder in a dungeon. Ray's long blue legs stretched themselves out under the table.

"Yeah, you got it. That's how." With their encouragement, she told about Piv, not mentioning his name or nationality—just, "I hooked up with some guy"—and she talked about how she didn't want to leave Thailand once she met him, but had to in order to renew her visa. She told about how she lacked the means to buy tickets. She said that she had met men who offered to pay for her flight if she'd only carry a suitcase for them. Then she said that all she wanted now was to go home, and that the men had promised her a ticket there, and that's why she kept carrying the bags, even though she suspected it was something very wrong. Her temples beat as her eyes filled up with tears. She thought that maybe she should let herself cry.

Ray sighed. "We've seen it before. You kids go traipsing around the world and get yourselves in trouble. Eventually you have to come home," he said.

"That's what my dad told me," Robin answered, picturing a different sort of dad.

She didn't disclose anything about her overdrawn, overdue credit cards or her hungry desire for jewelry, and beauty, and pride, and Piv. She didn't explain how if she'd been willing to let go of these things, she would have been safely home long before. But that was okay. They accepted the edited version; her motives weren't important.

"Maybe we'd like to, but we can't just let you go, you know. First off, we're only talking to you thanks to the courtesy of these guys here." Robert nodded toward the Singaporean men who were standing near the door. "There are international laws against what you're doing. I've spent years trying to get countries together on enforcing those laws. Otherwise, the world'd be stripped naked quicker than it's already going." Robert lowered his head to look her in the eye. Even in this sterilized, triple-sealed holding tank, he exuded an outdoorsy aura.

She said that she understood the direness of the environmental situation. In a hurt voice, she claimed that she never would have carried those bags if she had known what was in them. She wished this with a depth of feeling that made it almost true, but Piv's voice tugged at her: You think it's something you buy in some store? "What's going to happen to me?" she asked.

"That depends." Ray ran his fingers through his hair again, sweeping back the burnished lock that kept falling sheepishly over one eye. "One thing, you're going to have to tell us the names of those men."

It was a relief, really. "The main guy's Volcheck. He's Russian. At least that's what he said." She felt lighter after she said his name; he was so clearly noxious. But the two men kept looking at her as if she hadn't spoken. Ray cracked his knuckles. "And he had friends," she added.

"Who?"

"Africans. From Kenya. Jomo. Yoke." She paused, surprised at herself for hesitating. "Abu." Oh, that was why she didn't want to say it: Abu's name was the garment covering Piv's. One more word and she'd be pushing Piv stripped and stumbling into this white inquisition room. But she wouldn't do that. She wouldn't. And besides, he didn't have anything to do with this. Not really. She blinked at the men. They blinked back, and for one horrible second she thought they were going to ask her to continue.

"You know last names?"

She exhaled. "No, they never told me."

Robert leaned into his fists. "Volcheck Smirnova, Abu Navaisha, Jomo Mwenguo. How does that sound?"

Robin's mouth dropped. She needed the earth to stop turning so that she could catch up.

But the moments kept ticking. Two sets of men were watching her. Ray took her passport from his inside jacket pocket. Robin wanted to reach for it—the ticket to a place whose laws she understood—but she trapped her reaching hand again under her thigh.

"How do you know who they are?" she asked in a whisper.

Ray leafed through her passport, tilting back in his chair. Then he let the front two chair legs fall back to the floor with a klunk.

"Robin, you look like a nice girl. You probably went to college, keep in touch with your parents. Just thought you'd see the world before settling down and getting to work, am I right? But what you've been doing is conspiring with international gangsters. Now, you wouldn't do that at home, would you? Why do you think it's okay to do it when you're here?" He stopped talking and shook his big head in disappointment.

Robert squinted at her, still tilting and ducking his head to see right into her eyes. "These guys are rough stuff. They're running a million a year, maybe more, in animal products and this's just a little sideline for most of them. A lot of our info we get from the FBI. Of course we know who they are. These guys are part of a ring responsible for killing off or displacing more species than any other single entity, and our job is to save those animals. We've got files on all of those bastards this big." Robert made a C shape with his hand and held it in the air definitively.

The wildlife agents knew a shocking amount. They were aware of the few things that Robin was cognizant of—the names of certain clients, of Mr. Rong, the conference coming up in Orlando—but their disclosure also filled gaps in her knowledge and revealed the lies she'd chosen to believe: Abu wasn't even really Kenyan; he was a Tanzanian. Animals were often accepted as payment for drugs. Animals were used as a cover and stuffed with heroin. There had been a recent massacre on a Zimbabwean reserve, an inside job, with twenty rhinos gunned down over two days as if hundreds of thousands of dollars of fences and surveillance and guards didn't even exist. Robert rubbed his eyes with his hand when he spoke of this, and the sight moved Robin. So she wasn't ridiculous for taking animals personally, as Piv sometimes made her feel.

"I'm sorry," she said. "I'm so sorry. I didn't know." Tears came into her eyes again. "But if you know everything, if it's against the law, why don't you stop them?"

Robert stood up. He put his hands in his pockets; his trousers were so baggy it looked like there was room for several hands more.

"You probably do think it's that easy, don't you?" He stopped walking and turned to her. "Besides, how would you have made your little pin money, then, huh?"

Robin looked at her foot, at the two wormy purple veins bulging above the pinch of leather upper.

"Robin," Ray said, "I know you want to go home and get yourself on the right track. You don't want to deal with any trials or fines or lawyers' fees, and you don't want to be looking at incarceration overseas. So listen, these guys have given the go-ahead—they'll let you walk out of here today and eventually get yourself home free if you're willing to work with us on getting details about the Orlando gig."

Trial. Fine. Fees. Incarceration. The words hit with the impact of an auto crash. Her skull jerked forward and back. "Of course. But I told you everything I know."

"We need to know more. And you have to make it your business to find out."

Robin fluttered her eyes and bobbled her head. She felt an oceanic sway: the fear and poignancy and dismay rolled out on a riptide, while a sense of unfeeling unreality rushed headlong in. She was being blackmailed into double agency. She had a sudden urge to laugh—it was that cinematically cliched and over the top, that impossible. But then that urge turned seaward, too, and she was bobbing in an exhaustion so deep that drowning seemed preferable to struggling against the current. She had never wanted to kill herself, but she wanted now not to be alive.

Chapter 21

One day after NokRobin leaves, Volcheck comes. He brings the new girlfriend, and they don't stay at Star Hotel, no, but Abu and me still spend too much time with them. Abu takes me to their lounge, Ploy Fun Lounge, not nice one. Inside, I see some electronic games, some blinking lights. Volcheck sees me and says, "What the fucking shit's he doing here?"

Abu says, "Easy man, Mr. Pivlaierd is here to help us." He puts his hand on my shoulder.

Volcheck makes noise with his nose like some water buffalo. He waves at me to say okay, I can sit down. I don't like that Russian Vol, no way. But I act smooth. I smile, sit down, act like I want to. Like I should say thank you very much to Mr. Fucking Shit who lets me sit there.

One African man, one Russian man who's too ugly, one girl that doesn't speak anything—what do they say to each other? Without Yoke, Jomo, more polite people, this meeting's not for fun. It's for business, sure. So I listen. Abu and Volcheck say half words, very quick. Sometimes, no one speaks. Four people, no one says anything. Vol chews on drink straw. Abu presses on calculator. He shows Vol those numbers, and Vol moves his big head, makes one sound. Not English, not Russian, no language, just animal sound, I think so. He pushes his hand on table and stands up. Abu stands, too.

"We'll just be a moment, my friend. Take care of the lady," he tells me.

I look at the girlfriend. "Hello," I say. "Would you like anything?"

"Hello fine thank you," she says, but she doesn't understand even one English word, I can hear that from the way she talks. She just learns to say these sounds; to her they have no meaning. She drinks all her Mekong Coke already, so I take one fresh ice cube from the bucket at our table and put it in her glass. I pour from small bottle of Mekong, then from small bottle of Coke. This lady's big everywhere. Big on top, too big for her shirt. She's not pretty, but I know ugly Vol only gets her because he pays. Even if they're not pretty, no girl wants to be with him for free.

Some minutes later, maybe twenty minutes, Abu and Vol come back. We go to restaurant where the food is as ugly as that Russian. Big meat in one piece. They give you knife, and you have to cut. This is one farang thing I don't like. Vol points his fork to the ceiling. Big piece of meat on that. He eats from his fork. He talks while he chews.

"Where the fuck they get this beef?"

After eating I wish we would go to Star Hotel lounge, because then it's no problem for me to say, Excuse me, I'm too tired, I must say good night now. But no. Unfortunate that not my fate. Abu says now we go see Kobjitti at Sweetie's Basket. I don't like to go to Sweetie's Basket, and I really really don't like to go there with the woman. I try to excuse me from this trip. I smile, rub my eyes, rub my stomach. "This big food makes me too sleepy," I say. But Abu doesn't let me, so we all get in one taxi, and I tell the driver where to go.

When we're there, I feel embarrass for everyone, everyone in that place. When Kobjitti comes to our table, I feel almost glad to see this dirty man, because maybe now we can leave to visit those turtles. Kobjitti stands and smiles, and Abu takes his hand and squeezes that one. He doesn't shake; I know the difference, this is one squeeze. Abu's hand looks black, not brown, in this disco light, and I see Kobjitti's fingers crush together, bend, silly. His fingers don't know what to do. Then Abu lets go. He leans and says something to Russian Vol. Music's too loud, I don't hear; I don't know what he says. Kobjitti's skin looks purple, the color of some flower on the day when there's no bright sun. Disco lights flash, and his skin goes purple, yellow, purple, yellow. His skin does this and his white shirt.

Vol says something to Kobjitti and points with his elbow to his Russian lady. She sits there. I don't know what she sees. Her eyes turn purple, yellow—that's all. Vol says something again, yelling this time, but it's so loud that I still can't understand his words. I only know he swears. Kobjitti wais. Vol's words are heavy on him, but way he bends his head, holds his body, I know Abu is the one who makes him afraid.

I get up to go to the toilet, and Abu says something like: where you go man, stay here. But I act like I don't hear him speak. Inside the toilet, the wall is made from small black tiles. One farang man—blond hair, red color skin, red eyes—sits on the floor and leans his face against that tile. His mouth is loose. He doesn't move from the time I come in there to the time I leave. I walk past him and walk out the door of Sweetie's Basket. There's so many lights on Soi Cowboy that it's bright like daytime instead of night.

I buy food from street vendor—egg yolk that they make sweet—and I lean on one wall to eat this. Sweetie's Basket has only one shop front, but other clubs on this street take up two or three or four shop fronts. These big ones are the new ones, owned by Thai police or by German people. Bar girls are asking people to come inside their club and some Thai boys doing this, too. These boys all wear white shirts and black waistcoats. They speak English. They say, "Welcome inside please sir. Beautiful sexy girls for you." Now maybe they speak only small amount, but if they're smart, they'll learn more. This job gives them opportunity. When I finish my egg, I go inside Sweetie's Basket again. It's not nice here—but opportunity, that's why we come.

Abu smiles very big, his teeth white-purple, that's the only thing I see. He pushes Singha across the table to me, says that he orders my favorite when I go outside to breathe.

"We go see turtles now?" I ask him.

He laughs. He shows with his hand where the ladies dance on one shelf with big mirror behind them. "All this, and you want to see turtles?"

I look at the shelf one time fast, but then, wow, I look again. I see Vol's Russian lady! She's not wearing any clothes—no tight shirt, nothing. Just her underpants. Her feet stand still, but her middle part moves. She's not looking at anything. I sat with her already in Ploy Fun Lounge, when she has clothes on. I don't want to see her like this.

But, I don't know why, I look again. I have seen many farang woman, sure. I make something with them, and they don't wear clothes when I do that, of course. And on Ko Samet, Ko Phangan, many girls take off their shirt on the beach. They don't wear the top part of their bathing suit, and even if I don't want to, I have to see that. But I have never seen one as big on top as this Russian lady. I don't like it. I like someone more small, with the Thai-style body. But I can't stop looking.

One song keeps playing too loud. I think I never heard this one before. At first, I cannot understand the words, but I try hard to listen. Slowly the words come clear. They sing, *Do it funny lady*. Then the guitar makes the same sound as those words: *Do it funny lady*. Again and again this repeats—the voice and then the guitar singing back—and I think of NokRobin. Way she talks, way she moves her face, way she laughs, that's funny. She's my funny lady—the words in the song are strong—but that doesn't mean she stays with me. I listen hard to the music. Soon I can separate everything out: guitar part, bass part, drum, words. Maybe I can teach this to Fallow band. Outside Sweetie's Basket, if Fallow plays this song, it will make good rock and roll.

Do it funny lady: those words are in my head when Abu picks up my Singha bottle and bumps it down on the table. He puts his other hand and his mouth close to my ear. "How does that sound to you, Mr. Pivlaierd?" His voice so close it's like one long stick poking hard into my brain.

I look at him. That song's finished. Disco song plays now, no more rock and roll. Abu turns from me and speaks to Vol, loud: "I give him what he's been asking for, and he looks at me like it's nothing."

Vol lifts his big shoulders and makes sound with his lip like one horse, then turns back to look at the shelf where the ladies dance.

"What?" To talk here is like yelling. I smile. "What you give to me?"

"You're going to go to the Philippines, my friend. I have an errand there for you. Isn't that what you wanted? Aren't you the young man who wants to see the world?"

Abu laughs and puts his hand on my shoulder and shakes it. It's hard to hear in this place, hard to know for sure that it's true, that Abu says it's my turn now, my chance to go. I smile slow.

"It's my turn now?" I say.

"It's your turn to do some work, man. And I'll schedule you a couple days of sight-seeing as well, to oblige your interest in foreign cultures." Abu nods toward the Russian lady and laughs, even though she's not the funny one. "Let's talk more over a nightcap at our regular," he says to me.

Star Hotel lounge is quiet—at this time me and Abu are the only customers—but the Sweetie's Basket noise is still in my ears, like some rock concert very far in the distance. Sometimes when I hear this distant noise, after seeing Fallow band, Buddy Guy, Ax Zone, I feel lonely because the fun thing is done, the music in the distance is only some ghost. But this night when I hear it, I think maybe I will get close and closer to that music. Soon I can attend it; soon I can hear it, all the different parts.

Abu tells me the schedule. Tomorrow NokRobin comes back. He says I can have my lady friend for three nights if I want that. Then I fly to Philippines alone. She cannot come with me, because Abu thinks she might not be cool about my business there, which is to get many snakes and one small lizard, live ones, and carry those on the plane.

"Sure," I say. "Okay. While I'm in Philippines, it's NokRobin's turn to wait in Bangkok, like I do now."

"Ah, but perhaps we should consider whether it's worth keeping her waiting. I've got others scheduled to meet me in the U.S. Why should we risk her, when she continues to fan her delicate sensibilities?"

I know Abu is the reason NokRobin is still in my country, so I laugh very polite when he says he does not need the one it took me so long to find. I make my head low. I answer the first thing I think, very quiet: "We dream together."

"Time to wake up, Pivlaierd. She's one of those Americans who brag that they tread softly through the world then become bullies once on their own shores."

I don't understand all the words that he says. I laugh. "No," I say. "I don't think so."

"I didn't figure you as a one-woman man." Abu takes whiskey ice cube into his mouth so it makes the lump in his cheek like someone hit him there, but he still smiles so relaxed, his eyes lazy. You can hit him, but he knows he's the one who can cause the most hurt. "This is reality, friend, and your instinct better be right."

Chapter 22

Robin's eyes hadn't yet adjusted to the algae-hued green of the Star's lounge when she walked into Abu's voice as if into a spider web: "What would you like to eat, Miss Miatta, now that you've returned to the spicy choices of Bangkok?" Her heart knocked silly as a punching bag at the sound, and she grasped Piv's elbow for support.

In Singapore, Robin had been numbed with dread. She'd been so crushed and empty that she could scarcely summon the energy to rise from bed and pour herself a cup of tea let alone feel anything so passionate as fear. But once she made it through Bangkok's customs and saw Piv standing there, suited up and smiling with both his lips and his eyes, some feeling lit inside herself; a crescent of hope kindled in her chest. Within minutes her skin was consumed in a fire of pinpricks, like glass popping and shattering inside her brain. A little hope, a little love, a desire for something, for life—that's what made her feel terror instead of collapsing into a stunned, dead heap of it.

"Miss Miatta," Abu demanded. She stammered a greeting, demurred choosing the restaurant, and so they went to a German place on Sukumvit Road, Otto's Black Forest, where even the heavy air-conditioning could not erase the dissonance of eating leaden food on a tropical night, and where the delicate half bow of their lederhosened waiter only added to the nightmarish quality of Robin's past few days. It took all her composure to sit straight in the wooden booth and order sauerkraut salad. Next to her, Piv sat slurping a bowl of chicken soup and asking Abu questions about Singapore. Abu turned the questions to Robin, inquired whether she was aware of her own country's impatience with Singapore's markedly Eastern recipe for success, how she herself felt about it, and whether she had discussed the issue with her contact, Mr. Yeo.

"How do you know Mr. Yeo?" She felt like she had flopped a wet fish on the table—something that obvious, repulsive, and dead, stinking of her treachery. But Abu answered benignly: they had met at a reptile conference five or so years back; Mr. Yeo was an exporter who had a variety of needs to fill. That wasn't close to the kind of information the federal guys had set her loose to collect, and her brain teemed as if with skittering ants, frantic for relayable details about the Orlando gig, but her attention kept getting drawn to Piv.

She had no choice about Abu; she'd give the Wildlife guys all the information she could come up with on him and Volcheck—poachers, both. But what about Piv, unnamed by the Americans and unfingered by her, and unguilty, as far as she knew, of blood or violence, of anything other than having a dream and limited circumstances and an accommodating morality and a plan? And an electric presence. Even in this fug of boiled pork she thrilled to him. She so wanted him. She wanted him at least to be safe. But if he went to Orlando, he'd almost certainly be busted whether or not she breathed a word about him to Robert and Ray. And what about her own safety? If she didn't warn Robert and Ray about Piv, and he got caught anyway, wouldn't she have to answer for her silence? It would be infinitely better for them both if he never got on the plane.

But Piv was dying to go to the U.S. The only way to keep him off a plane to Florida was to tell him in no uncertain terms that she had been apprehended by the U.S. Fish and Wildlife Service—not a very menacing-sounding agency she realized—and that they knew all about Abu's business and, with her coerced help, they were going to close in on it. She'd have to use easy words like arrest, force, prison, police, jail, and she'd have to repeat herself and make sure he was telling the truth when he said he understood each term, because sometimes he pretended comprehension, she knew that, and she knew he would resist the fact that his international business opportunity was going to end in a sting. What she didn't know was exactly where his loyalties lay.

"Really?" Piv was saying now, subverting her attempt to thwart another of Abu's American poli-sci lessons. "Really the U.S. was against ASEAN?" He smiled and blinked, offering the animation of his naive shock like a gift, playing the straight man to Abu.

"The *Bangkok Post* has covered this as well as anyone, my friend. Certainly better than the *Herald*. They want to withhold IMF money from Indonesia if they follow the Singaporean model."

"Ah, but American model is better, I think so. More fashion, cool music, home of rock and roll." His smile shifted from a minstrel's grin into a sly loungey beam.

They went from the restaurant to a katoey floor show at the Asia Hotel, where Robin slipped away to use a pay phone. She dialed the number she'd been given, had been told to memorize. "Nothing," she told the American man that answered in monosyllables. "I've been with them all evening. I've been trying to get them to, but they haven't said anything about next week."

"You're going to have to fax us everyone's itinerary. And we need to know exactly how many are coming and what exactly they're bringing in."

"They won't tell me. They aren't saying anything."

"Try harder. You've got to insinuate yourself. Do what it takes."

Outside, the sky was as overfull as she was; it was starless, moonless, stuffed with bruised dense smog. She and Piv exchanged only a smattering of short sentences when they finally closed room 517's door behind them. Then they were on the bed, the room thick with their customary darkness, parting folds and creases to emit the humid silk that cocooned them away from the worlds they wore with their clothing. When the borders of their bodies dissolved, Robin gasped in a little wave of joy, but it crashed against the bund of fear around her heart. She exhaled a sob, and then they wouldn't stop coming.

"What?" Piv whispered, still inside her. "What?" A touch of impatience. He softened and fell out.

If she told him, and he told Abu, what then? The Zimbabwean massacre and the hacked flesh of the rhino and the violence that hovered around Volcheck like a swarm.

Piv stroked her back dutifully.

"Why are we always with Abu? I don't want to see them. I just got back. You like him more than me. Why can't it just be us alone?" She curled tightly to Piv, pressed her forehead to his chest and snuffled into her hand.

"Shh. Shh," he whispered, and for a while that was all. Then, "Remember when you had that problem with your visa? Because of Abu that problem's gone. I like him because he lets me stay with you." He tried to lower his head to kiss her, but she didn't want her wet, sticky face to meet his. He massaged the knots of her spine instead.

"Tomorrow day Abu already plan we go to floating market all together. Please, he buys us tickets to your country. Better for us if we go, and you show you like him, too. Then tomorrow night, anything you want, only me and you."

She kissed Piv's pecs, stuffed her tears into dry hiccups. Eventually said, "Okay. You're right. Okay."

They didn't tell Abu about their date. Instead, at Piv's insistence, Robin peeled off the piece of tape that held closed a bag of Piv's favorite thick yellow cookies and used the adhesive to affix a folded note to the door of their room. In the elevator on the way down to the lobby, they held hands. Robin wore a long, fringed skirt and a faded T-shirt—her backpacker clothes—and Piv had on worn Levi's and a Pong T-shirt; he was dressed like a cool Thai guy. She'd asked that they go to Khao San, and in the collegiate din there she hoped she'd be able to tell him, if not everything—she couldn't risk everything—then at least something. She hoped she'd be able to feel where his heart was.

But they dropped hands as the elevator reached the ground floor, and when the doors parted, she saw Abu leaning back into the rose-colored easy chair in the center of the lobby. He lifted his hand to them and smiled wide.

"You look comfortable, my friends. Ready for your evening cocktail?"

Robin knotted her hand in the strap of her hill tribe bag. Piv laughed.

"We're going to Jimmie's Rasta Bar. You know that one? NokRobin says she wants to go there."

"A rasta bar? Imported from the brothers in Jamaica, eh? That's a culture that travels well. Have you been to Jamaica, Miss Miatta?" Without touching her, through only the adjustment of air currents, Piv steered Robin toward the chair. "So you're going to listen to Mr. Bob Marley tonight," Abu said as they got nearer. "No, woman, no cry," he chanted. Then he chuckled. "Go on along. I don't want to interfere with the romantics. You only have a couple of days together."

Chapter 23

Before I have this business with Abu, I used to go to Jimmie's Rasta Bar as the good place to hear music and meet the farang ladies. Satit knows me; if no farang buys for me, sometimes he gives me my Coke for free. But tonight I want Singha. NokRobin wants Singha, too. He gets those for us and then he asks me something in Thai: Can NokRobin speak our language? I say no. She tries to say something, but she only speaks English language. Then he says NokRobin's nice, she's pretty, he knows her from when I bring her here before, but why does he hear from Kathy that I have Thai girlfriend now?

I think Kathy confuses me with Chit, I say. We both laugh at that one. Since the time when Chitapon forgets Kathy to make something with Wanphen, Kathy tells everyone from the Trombone Club that Thai people are prejudice against farangs. She says this is wrong, like the people from her country who feel prejudice about blacks. She says the only difference is Thai people always think farangs have money; American people never think that about the blacks.

I'm not prejudice, I say to Satit. I tell him I like black Africans. I still like my farang lady.

When NokRobin hears this word *farang* she looks at me like I hurt her. She hears this word, and she thinks I say something bad about people like her.

"I tell him I like the farang lady," I say. I smile at her and Satit smiles—he speaks good English, of course, to have this business.

I talk in Thai again: What's some new music? He tells me about one band called Asia Dub Foundation. Very international. These people from India who live now in England, where they get the Jamaican influence in their music. Maybe he'll play that later tonight, after the customers are already coming. Jimmie's Rasta Bar is behind Khao San Road on one small soi. It's all outside, on one square of cement behind the short building; the buildings on each side of it are longer. Overhead, Satit built the bamboo and thatch roof, so farangs feel like they're on

Ko Samui or Ko Phangan, even if they have to wait in Bangkok for some visa, some shopping, or to get ready to leave our country. But if you're on one island, even in hot season, breeze from the water can make you feel cool. In Bangkok, between two buildings, you cannot get that. Tonight, there's only two farangs in Jimmie's Rasta Bar. When it's so hot, the backpackers want to go to the air-con disco, I think so. I feel bad for Satit because he cannot have place with air-con, and so he loses business.

"I'm sorry I speak in Thai to my friend who owns this bar," I say when Satit goes to some new customers. "Now I speak in English to you, okay?"

NokRobin gives me strong look. Her face is greasy tonight; colored lights from the thatch roof shine on there. I tell her that in hot season she should put powder on her body, to keep her body cool, but she doesn't do this. She thinks the white powder looks ugly. She looks down and touches the places on the table where the colored lights make spots, one pink and one green. With her finger she connects them together. When she looks at me again, her face is more soft. Then she asks me something.

"What did Abu mean, we only have a couple of days together? We go to Orlando on the fifteenth; that's not for over a week."

"Oh! I don't tell you?" I slap my hand on my forehead. "In three days I go to Philippines. I travel, alone, to make some business for Abu."

"What? No, you didn't tell me!"

Now she knows that I can go somewhere, too. Her face looks something like surprise, afraid. When she has to go to Singapore, Malaysia, she says she doesn't want to do that, but now she can see that to be left is what feels worse. She moves her leg too hard and the table shakes.

"Shh. Calm down," I tell her. "I have to get certain kind of animal. Live one, I think so, very special. At this time it's not possible for you to come with me. But it's no problem. You stay here with Abu, and we meet again in United States." I tell NokRobin I'm like one traveler now. Philippines, Hong Kong, USA. "I'm like you were. I don't know when I'll come back to my country."

I light one Krong Thip and lean back on my small chair. I move very slow, smooth, relax. I try to show NokRobin how to be peaceful, but she doesn't follow me. She moves too fast again. This time when the table shakes, one bottle of Singha falls onto cement floor—crack!—and breaks into three brown pieces. The beer makes foam at our feet. The smell of beer is in my nose. Anyone can smell that, sharp, like bread that grows mold in wet heat. I think NokRobin might feel embarrassed she makes this mess, this smell—but no. She doesn't care about that.

"What do you mean you don't know? Are you staying over there? You mean you aren't flying to Orlando with us on the fifteenth?"

I say nothing, because Satit comes now to clean that broken bottle. I feel embarrassed for NokRobin. Maybe she starts to feel that, too. "I'm sorry Jimmie," she says. She moves to get down on the ground with him to help; she holds big, brown glass pieces in each hand, but he tells her please, let him clean, it's no problem. He takes glass from her.

When he leaves, I'm surprised to see that NokRobin's not too ashamed to stop talking. Beer smell keeps coming from cement, but Satit brings her another Singha, and she speaks as loud as before. She says it again, like crash never happened: "You're not going to be on the flight from here to Orlando?"

I explain to her about that thing. How she, Abu, Volcheck, fly from Bangkok to Hong Kong, and I meet them there. Then we go to Orlando. We go together, but we act like we don't know each other. Sure.

She holds on to the table when I say this. She doesn't want that table to shake anymore, but she still moves too strong. She leans over and gets too close to me.

"But maybe it's better if you don't go on that flight. What if there's a problem, Piv? What we're doing is illegal, you know. What happens if we get caught?"

Her face is hot. Khao San Road is not my choice anymore. Why did I let NokRobin say where we go? It's better if I take her to some nightclub with air-condition, where loud music will cover any shouting.

"Please. Speak quiet. Why you want someone to hear?" I tell her.

"You don't understand. No. No. You might get caught. You should stay here."

I whisper to tell her we won't get caught. This is not some big crime. Why does she worry about that? "Please." I tell her.

Now she bounces when she talks to me, something like the baby would do. "You're Thai, Piv. At U.S. customs, Thailand is going to equal drugs. You'll probably get stopped. You'll get searched, and they'll find whatever you have. You shouldn't do this." Her face screws tight, like you would do to some lid from one jar. "You should stay away. You shouldn't go."

I make my eyes very cool when I look at her. I freeze her now, so she cannot speak. She cannot yell anymore, cannot bounce around. For some moments, I enjoy this silence. I can hear laughs from some other table. I can hear Bob Marley. Singha bottles clink. Tuk tuk starts to move. But NokRobin is frozen. She waits for me. When I want to, I talk to her again.

"Oh, now you say I should not." I speak like one American. If it's ugly, I don't care, I still say it. "You don't want me to go to Philippines. You don't want me to go to USA. You use me for one guide when you travel my country, but you want to go to your home alone."

I think NokRobin sees some ghost when she looks at me now. She says nothing. Then she says too much, too fast.

"No, that's not it! I want you to go. I want to be with you. I love you!" She reaches her hand across table to touch me, but I am too far. She looks silly, her arm one rope that she cannot throw to good purpose. But her voice gets quiet. "I'm just worried you'll get caught," she says. "That we'll both get caught. We need to work together, to make a plan, just in case."

I nod at her, sure. She cannot keep me from her country, but one plan is no problem.

Five farangs sit together at another table. They have been in my country for some time, at least one month on an island, I think so, because they are brown almost like Thai people. On their wrist they wear the friendship bracelets you can buy for fifteen or twenty baht on the touristic beach. Now these bracelets fade because of the sea and sun. One lady sitting there wears very short skirt. Her legs are long and brown, and she has friendship bracelets around her ankle, and I can see her like she's on Diamond Beach, lying close to the blue water, one small bathing suit on, putting oil on her skin so it shines.

"Listen, Piv. This is important. We need a signal, so if there's trouble the other person will know to get rid of any incriminating stuff—incriminating means illegal, anything to do with animals or whatever. Understand?"

NokRobin is scared because I can leave without her. That's the reason she wants to make me feel scared, too. "Listen to me," she says.

"Do you want to end up in jail?" I know what she's wondering: will I guide her in my country if I can go to any country, always go somewhere new? Maybe it's true that she loved me. Maybe she wants to keep me outside her country because if I go there she thinks I can find the girl with more money, with some good credit cards. She wants to keep me, but not to be my wife.

At that other table, brown farang lady moves very slow, crosses her legs. Her skirt is too short, wow! She's very pretty lady.

"Piv! Look, if you see the police, if you know there's risk, rub the top of your head, okay? If I know something bad is going to happen, I'll rub the top of my head. Piv?" NokRobin moves so much I have to look. She rubs her head like she's stirring something, and her hair rises in the air. She looks too foolish.

I'm already far away, but I try to go farther. I turn my cheek to her. "Why you want to touch my head? Thai people don't like that!" I smile to show I'm cool.

"I'm not going to touch your head. If there's trouble, I'll touch my own head. Do you understand?"

She always asks do I understand something. I study English, I study farang. Of course I understand. For me, it will be no problem in her country, because I can stay cool; I can give my attention, and I can work hard. NokRobin thinks that because she cannot, no one can.

That short skirt woman makes something with one farang guy at that table, I think so. Way that he looks at her, way that he touches her, I think maybe they meet each other on that island and now they come here, Bangkok. It's the first place they come together. He tries to touch her down there. Then they kiss. They move their faces, use their tongues, very ugly. Maybe they're drunk, try to make something right here. Sure, some farangs do this. Some nights, Satit find condoms in the toilet.

NokRobin looks at me, those colored lights still in her eye. How many times have I looked at her? Maybe one thousand times. Maybe ten thousand times. It's not true what Kathy thinks, that Thai people are prejudice. Many Thai people marry farangs. They can be happy, if they pick the right one, if they try to know the other culture, sure. But most important to be happy is to know the other person. To look ten million times.

"I want us to be together in the States." NokRobin's whisper is like one finger touching my ear. I think she knows that she looks foolish when she rubs her head, but she doesn't care. Her face looks sweet now. Not beautiful, not smooth, but sweet, cute, like some little sister who worries.

"Do you like Abu more than you like me?" she asks very soft.

I move more close to the table. I touch under her chin. "Why you ask that question?" I say to her. "Abu's not the pretty farang lady."

NokRobin gives me one very small smile. Her eyes are shiny. From the lights, from sweat, or maybe from some feeling. "He's the pretty African man, don't you think so?" she says.

"Not my specialty."

"Your specialty is farang girls, right?"

"This farang girl." I touch the bone on her face. "You."

"What about that girl with the short skirt over there?"

"At this time, my specialty is you."

We smile small smiles at each other. On the table, our hands move close; they almost touch.

"You'll travel, Piv. You deserve it. But let's find a safer way for you to go."

"Shh. I'll be careful."

At that moment, I can smell garbage, tuk tuk fumes, lead in air, beer foam, and too many kinds of food scents; I notice all the smells of Bangkok. I live in the capital city, so I feel used to this. Sometimes I can forget that I smell it, but sometimes I remember very strong, like now. I think about somewhere else, the mountains near my home, and I think about one small white flower that grows there. Some years ago, when I visit my home, I meet one farang biologist who tells me that the flower belongs to the rose family, and it doesn't grow anywhere else around this whole world. He has to come to Kanchanaburi to see it. When I visit after that, I always go to the mountain and look for this flower. First time I find, I pick it and bring it home to my mother, but other times after that, to see it is enough. When I find that one, I feel very lucky.

When NokRobin comes to Kanchanaburi, I want to show her, but we don't find that flower. Maybe it's the wrong time of year; it doesn't come in the dry season. Or maybe we're not lucky. Maybe she will never see it now. We will never get married. Okay, that's no problem. Maybe it's not true what she says, that she wants to be together in the United States. Instead, she might not want one Thai boyfriend in her own country. *Mai pen rai*. Love is like everything, it can change. But maybe we will be like the farangs say, "just friends." She knows something about me. She knows my dream. I know something about her, her worries. Across the world, maybe we can still remember this. Even without our bodies, without our romantic thing, even if we cannot help each other, if we're not together, perhaps we still have one small flower we have both been lucky to see.

Chapter 24

Robin hadn't watched Piv walk out of the room. Instead, she had lain flat in bed and listened to the door's automatic bolt slide back into its groove. She tracked the faint sound of the elevator rising in its shaft, opening its doors, and falling down toward the lobby—Abu and Piv going off together without her—then she got up to lock the door from inside. Last night after coming home from the bar, Piv had undressed her with the tender precision of a jeweler, then devoted his lips and hands to her body for over an hour. Twitchy with tentative surrender, she worried over how to convince him to leave Abu without endangering herself until her body detached, and she was scarcely aware when Piv gave up on the lovemaking and lay docilely in her arms.

But she had gone to sleep with a plan. Now she picked up the orange and gold enamel box that sat on the dresser and brought it into bed with her. They called it their cash box, but the bluntness of the title was softened by the rounded edges and a slightly domed top that gave it the air of a tubby Rajasthanian Santa. They had the equivalent of almost three thousand dollars inside in a mix of Thai and American currency, but they owed fifteen thousand baht for the bracelets still at the factory. That left about twenty-four hundred dollars.

Twenty-four hundred bucks. How pathetic. She'd seen people order half that amount from the *J. Crew* catalog without changing out of their pajamas, and she had been willing to do almost anything for it, as if it were a princely sum whose interest she could live on for the rest of her life. She stood and walked back to the dresser. In the top drawer lay a purple silk pouch that bulged with the hard edges of jewelry. Six hundred dollars worth of necklaces took up surprisingly little space. Robin loosened the pouch's drawstring and clattered the pieces onto the cream-colored pressboard. She saw a jumble of gleam already losing its luster; the low-grade silver would tarnish soon if no one wore it, and in the sallow light of day, the jewelry looked to her like silly hippie stuff, the product of a mind addled by too many months of backpacker aesthetic.

She picked up a necklace and held the clasp closed at her nape, looked into the mirror hung above the bureau. The five long lengths of chain weren't falling right; she couldn't quite get the lotus piece centered. And she herself looked terrible. No matter what else, she had always assumed her youth and passable prettiness, but now one eye was narrowed and twitched and both had circles under them. Her tan looked smudged on. Her breasts hung skimpy and limp.

She put on a T-shirt, then bagged the jewelry and set it and the cash box on Piv's pillow. She wanted it to catch his eye as soon as he walked in. She didn't want an extra moment to pass without him knowing what she had decided: She would save him. She would give him everything, the money and the silver, and tell him to go to the Philippines on Abu's dime and to disappear. Maybe he'd be able to sell the jewelry. Hopefully he'd still want to come to the United States; she'd suggest they meet in New York or Chicago, somewhere up north, far from the scene of the crime. Piv was the last chance she had to do something remotely honorable. She had to accept responsibility. After all, everything he owned could fit in two canvas bags; to him twenty-four hundred dollars *was* a lot. He'd never been given opportunities that she had chosen to blow: getting her degree, traveling the world.

But then her need for exoneration rose up: Don't stop making excuses for yourself only to make them for Piv. He might love you in bed, but who introduced you to Abu?

Who introduced you to Abu? She'd asked Piv the same question early on. "Oh, I know him for some time now. He's my friend. Sure." That's what he'd answered. A non-answer. She'd gotten used to those, from him. She sat still on top of the rumpled sheets, all the questions she had posed and Piv had evaded wrapping thick as rope around her. Where had he lived before he met her? What had he done to make a living? The aspects of his life he had allowed her to glimpse only left her with more confusion. Robin remembered dancing away as his mother jabbed a wide broom closer and closer to her feet; she remembered tumbling onto Piv's big, hard bed to get away. His mom hated her, but Piv had denied and denied it. Why? And then there was now: what was he talking about with Abu?

Robin slung her feet to the carpet. She walked around the room touching the few things that Piv hadn't yet packed: the Walkman she had gotten him, the hair gel. The travel case he'd carry tomorrow lay open on the floor, and inside it, the worn paperback he'd been reading since the day she met him rested on top of his carefully folded extra suit. She bent down to see what else he was taking to America. Two T-shirts, one dress shirt, a few cassettes, a pair of dark socks, and a handful of candy-colored bikini underwear. His skinny backpack was propped next to the suitcase, strapped up and ready to be dropped off at his friend's house on the way to the airport. Robin lowered herself into a crouch and unzipped the side pocket of the pack; a small wicker ball fell out. She'd never seen it before, never seen Piv play a sport, never heard him speak of one, yet this was one of the things he'd chosen to keep near him. I don't know him, she reminded herself. She picked up the ball and cupped it in her palm with an embarrassed reverence; it was a mystery as small and sad and tender as a movie star's sock.

She unzipped another pocket. What was she looking for? If he were an American boyfriend, she'd be snooping for a note or journal entry, some words that were private and therefore true. Of course, if she found something like that of Piv's, she wouldn't be able to read it anyway; it would be in Thai. She puzzled over that for a moment, multiplied the difficulty of expressing oneself in a second language by the additional hurdle of using a whole new set of linguistic symbols. Her fingers quit searching and sank idly into the unzipped pocket, as if she were a riverside laundress stealing a moment to daydream, hands finally still under the water's cool. Did Piv think in the Thai alphabet or in the Roman one? Did people think in letters at all? Although Robin had a few Thai phrases now, the script itself was indecipherable to her, all humps and bubbles and sassy kicks. Perhaps Piv meant to be clear with her. Perhaps his elusiveness was an inadvertent product of their cultural divide.

Her thighs ached from crouching, and she caught herself holding her weight at her hips rather than letting it sink toward the ground as Piv had taught her to do when she'd wondered how people in the villages could hold the pose for so long. She forced herself to relax her limbs down, and her hand dipped farther into the backpack's pocket. Her knuckles grazed something crushable and scratchy, and her fingers became her own again, reaching and grasping. She withdrew an object from the bag, raised her hand to eye level. She held a lace-edged blue bow and flowers attached to an elastic. Expecting a tender keepsake of Piv's, her mind went blank. This was no piece to the puzzle, no part of him. But slowly she realized that was exactly the point—the frilly hair decoration belonged to someone else, not to Piv. Certainly not to Robin, whose taste didn't run to this kind of feminine glitz. It belonged to another woman. A woman. A girl. Someone Piv cared enough about to want this piece of her near.

Robin fell back from the crouch onto her bottom. She stared at the blue pouf in her palm; she lifted it to her nose and sniffed. Inhaling the intimate perfumey grease of scalp was like walking full force into a clear glass wall. Momentum stopped with a full-bodied slam. Embarrassment mixed with intense physical pain. Piv was using her. This shred of a thing both clarified and confirmed her great fear: she was one of many, manipulated; of use but not beloved. When the phone started braying incessantly, it was only an echo of the siren in her head.

Then the phone went quiet, and humiliations rained down in quick, articulated succession: She was an orgasm-addled naïf who'd fall for anybody who'd do her, anyone with a tight belly and pidgin phrasing. She was the kind of stupid, easy Western girl who gave others a bad name. No wonder she hadn't talked to any women in weeks. They must be shying away from her like they would a bad smell. No wonder Piv's mother had displayed disgust. And Piv. Robin recalled instances of his icy remove, a certain curl to his lip.

But also . . . those lips soft and parted, reaching for hers again and again. The thousand kisses reflected in his eyes.

But those were lies in his eyes. Because did he look like that at the other woman, too? Did he bring her home? He did. He did. Other *women*. The Thai home just a tool of his trade.

The phone drilled into the room again, and Robin flailed an arm up to the nightstand and swatted the handset off the base. Other women, another woman. A female voice emanated from the toppled phone. Was that an American hello? No. It was Thai, *ka*. The voice rang out clearly now: *Ka? Ka?* Of course. The blue-hairpiece lady was Thai. Robin could assume that much. Farangs were necessary, easy, but when Piv could choose he'd want someone tipped in gold jewelry who never spoke too loudly or said the wrong thing. The Thai pair was probably together now, at the love motel Piv had taken Robin to once upon a time, where they had opened that box and the whole gory nightmare began. He was at that love motel with his beloved—no animal parts, just those two—and their matched bodies were reflecting off every mirrored surface.

But no. No. The film of their lovemaking flapped to a close, leaving a lit, blank screen. The phone's dial tone pulsed through the room.

There were always animal parts, now. Everywhere. At this moment, Piv really was with Abu. *He cheated on me!* It was a realization as painful in a den of smugglers as in a high school cafeteria or a college bar, and she stifled a sob. Never mind your hurt feelings, she told herself. You're in danger. *He used me!* No, stop it. Stop it! Abu and Robert and Ray and Volcheck. She had to keep her attention there.

She started to cry.

Chapter 25

I fly on planes before today, sure. First time is four years ago, when I fly from Bangkok to Phuket with one American lady who wants to get to the beach fast. But this is my first time to fly like this: the plane I'm on now is leaving my country; I am alone; I fly over the South China Sea. And I'm happy now to travel alone, not with the farang lady. The way NokRobin acted before I left, to be apart is good for her, good for me. If she doesn't like me anymore, if she doesn't want to make something anymore, okay, then we should do what's comfortable.

Yesterday when I came back from Oriental Bar, NokRobin looks very white. Her tan seems gone and her mouth looks small. She looks sick. When I ask how she feels, she says yes, she's sick, her stomach is sick. She gets up and goes to bathroom, and she walks bent over. The door shuts loud. I think she feels embarrassed.

Sometimes farangs get sick when they come to my country. Thai food is different, very hot, and there is different kind of germ, different kind of taste. So sure. Maybe the stomach doesn't like it. Even when some farang is here for long time this can happen again, like one surprise. Since I've known NokRobin, I already see this happen to her. And when she's sick, even when she's still weak, still hurting, sometimes she likes to make cuddle, make love, so her body feels good again. After long time, NokRobin comes out from bathroom and she lies on the bed and I go beside her. But no. She doesn't want this. She pushes me away. She curls up like one hot snake.

"It's my stomach," she says. She goes in the bathroom again.

"How are we going to divide the jewelry and the money," she says when she comes out. Her eyes are pink like sunset. "I suppose you want half."

We never talk before about half. We talk more about one whole, about the whole thing we build together. But if she wants to talk about half, it's no problem. I shrug.

"Half that jewelry still at factory," I say.

"Well, take the necklaces then, but you should leave me an extra thirteen hundred baht so I can pick up the bracelets if I want to. Otherwise it's not fair." I look at her. She stands by the bed. Her face is white, sick, like some ghost, bad. She takes off her fisherman trousers, but she leaves on her dirty T-shirt when she gets back in bed. She pulls sheet around her head. From underneath there she says one more thing: "But leave me a couple necklaces, at least. So I can see them."

That's the last thing she says to me until today, when she says she's sorry, she's too sick to go to the airport, too sick even to go down to the lobby and see me in the taxi. I tell her I will take only half the necklaces. She can take the rest; they'll all be together again in her country. "Okay," she says. "Good-bye. Good luck." She says this like she's dead to me. She gives me kiss, but it's dead. When I see her on the airplane to her country, we must act like we don't know each other. And when we're in her country, I don't know for sure, but I think she plans for us to stay like this—dead to each other; not friends but strangers, necklaces apart. Bodies apart. She's one more farang lady who wants to fly to the next place by herself.

But this time is different. This time, I don't get left with only five hundred baht, six hundred baht that someone gives me. This time, I have half of what we make together. In my bag, sixty necklaces. In my wallet, twenty-seven hundred baht that mixes with eight thousand dollars from Abu. When the plane lands in Manila, I make my mind blank. I concentrate on that. Immigration, customs, new airplane, no problem. I don't think about the bad things, and so they stay away.

In Cebu City, I take taxi to Casa Magellan, one hotel where Abu already reserved the room for me. Next to the stairs I see one picture of Jesus, one of Mary, and there are some purple flowers around there— not orchids; these are flowers I've never seen. In room 26, I take off my clothes and step into the bathroom, into the warm shower, and the airplane smell leaves from my hair, from my skin, and floats into the air. The shower works good, warm and clean, and when I'm done I feel clean, too. I put one white towel around me, then I lie on the bed.

Abu tells me that this hotel has international phone, and he tells me calls to make: call the number he gives me to find out where to buy the gun, call the number to see where I go to pick up snakes, call the number to talk about Gray's lizard, call him. I think I should pick up my arms so I can dial the phone, but I can't move them from their place on the hard, green bed. Too tired. I'm in Cebu City, Philippines, all alone, and I wonder something: maybe the Philippine girl likes the man from Thailand. I don't want to meet bar girl, prostitute, nothing like that, but maybe I can meet one girl that knows about the rock and roll club, the good restaurant, something special, sure. She speaks English and I speak English, too, and she lies with me on this bed, and she wants to make something. She wants to be with me. She'll feel very sad when I have to leave. On that day, she'll go with me to the airport, and I'll give her money to take taxi back to her home. I give her money, but that's not why she's with me, no. She likes me. She has the dream that we can make some future.

I still feel tired, but now I can move my body again, and I roll on my side and put the clean white pillow in my arms. I want to pretend everything is calm now, and I have ten thousand dollars, and here in my hotel room I sleep with my wife.

Abu calls deep into the night. He doesn't ask about the gun; he doesn't ask about the lizard, who did I call, why did I not call him. He ask something else: "Your bird felt the need to sneak out of the hotel at midnight, my friend, and *sneak* is not too strong a word. Do you still feel so sentimental about her accompanying us to the U.S.?"

"Sorry, I sleepy. What's it mean, *sense it me too?*" But even in my sleep I know this: reason why Abu likes me is because I'm good with the ladies. He tells that to me first time we ever speak. NokRobin's dead eye gives me too many other problems to worry about—not just my heart and my body, also with Abu.

"It means I thought she was the one being led from between her legs, but perhaps it's you." Now he talks ugly like that fucking Vol.

"She goes to call her parents, sure. Middle of the day where they are. She always tell me that she want me to meet her mother and father like she meet mine, to show them this Thai guy she loves. She says when they see us, see her so happy, maybe they can find some amount of money to give us." I laugh so he knows I have no worry.

"I think the reptiles are a better bet, man, although admittedly you'll need more than your fine skin and quaint phrasing in my line." I don't understand all his words, but I hear that Abu believes again that the ladies like me, that NokRobin loves me. I need him to think this even when it's not true.

Chapter 26

Robin had been in bed for fifteen hours when the phone woke her up at 4:00 PM. Abu, Volcheck, Piv's girlfriend? She let it jangle. She didn't want to know. But: "Are you really trying?" Robert had sneered at her last night when she'd made her check-in with nothing new to say. "Are you telling me they're turning you away? Because you're an attractive young woman, and I find that hard to believe." Oh, God. She let the phone ring again, tried to hunker back down into unconsciousness. But Robert's voice was still there: "You better get over your delicate stomach," he'd threatened. "We're not going to waste Singapore's goodwill on someone who doesn't give back in return." She reached her arm to the phone. Too late. She answered to a dial tone.

She propped herself up, and the bedding shifted, releasing air that was heavy and stale. Piv's backpack was gone. Piv's suitcase was gone. His cologne and his wallet from atop the dresser, half the money he and Robin had earned together, half of their hundred and twenty necklaces—gone. She felt an echo in her chest. Piv.

Stop it, she told herself. Robert. Abu.

Her empty stomach clenched itself more tightly and grumbled. She hadn't eaten yesterday, had thrown up the little she'd consumed the day before. Feeling ridiculous for not feeding herself, for half hoping that she could get out of this mess by perishing of starvation, she stood and let her spinning head settle before walking to the minibar by the door. In rooms with regular housekeeping service, a maid checked the inventory in the dorm-sized refrigerators each day and added the price of any missing items to the bill before restocking, but Piv and Robin didn't receive this attention. They'd drank all the water, Singha, Kostner, Coke, and Orange Crush, eaten the Kit Kats and chili peanuts and Nestlé bars, and nothing had been billed, nothing replaced. Now there were only some packets of shrimp crackers and a small vial of lychee drink left. Robin ripped open the bag of crackers and tongued a white wafer. It turned gummy in her mouth, fishy and starchy. Sustenance. She ate another one, pulled off the plastic tab on the lychee juice. When the phone rang again, she took a deep breath and answered.

"So hey, lady!" It was a smoky woman's voice. "Finally you answer. Yesterday it sounded like you were throwing the phone."

Robin's mouth went dry. Was this Piv's girlfriend? Was Piv's girlfriend American?

"Who is this?"

"Who is this? It's Gazelle Ester Raboniwitz." There was a pause. "You don't remember? It's Zella, that's who."

"Zella?" No, it couldn't be. Zella couldn't have found her here. Her heart gave a tentative, engine's-on stutter.

"Your fairy godmother." A fine layer of sarcasm dusted the words, but when she said she was in the lobby and wanted to come up right away, Robin agreed.

Her appearance still sucked in Robin's eyeballs: her hair, her polished stones, her thin flitting wrists stacked with four inches of metal. She walked around the room, casing it, and drew light toward her. But her eyes weren't reflecting anything. And the sunbursts of lines crowning her cheekbones were duplicated in the skin at the bend of her elbows. And was that a mottled tan there, or dirt? Was that a crusted scab? Was grease not pomade clotting the hair around her hairline?

Zella parted the plastic-lined curtains and looked out at Lan Luang Road. The chedi rising from the Golden Mount at Wat Sraket was just visible through the smog. "What's it cost you here a night?" she asked.

Robin was embarrassed that she didn't know. She made something up. "Twelve hundred baht."

Zella let the curtains drop and continued her trip around the room. At the dresser she straightened one of the necklaces that Piv had left after he'd counted out exactly sixty. When she picked it up and hooked it on, Robin found herself holding her breath, anxious to hear the appraisal.

"I haven't been seeing this. Where'd you find it?" Zella stood adjusting the links in the mirror, arranging her face to make it photo-ready. "But there's not enough centered weight pulling down to make it hang right." She tensed and released her shoulders and the links settled back asymmetrically against the skin of her throat. "Where'd you say you picked it up?"

"We had them made."

Zella turned away from the mirror. She caught Robin's eye and then rescanned the room's surfaces. "Really? Who's we?"

"I designed it. This Thai guy dealt with the factory."

"They're good at that, aren't they? So then, where is he?"

"Where's Guy?"

Zella laughed. "Touché." Then the countenance she had smoothed a moment ago in the mirror pinched back toward a point between her brows. She studied Robin—studied her eyes, mouth, her ratio of fat to muscle to bone. "That's why I'm here," she said. "I need that money you owe me."

"What?"

"Yeah. Actually, I thought you'd offer it when you came running over to see me last time, but I didn't want to say anything. It's just now I really need it. I think it was more like five hundred bucks, but we can call it four."

"I paid you. Don't you remember? My cards got sorted, and I got a cash advance, and I paid you the day before we split up. Fourteen thousand baht, and you'd only given me twelve."

"No. You didn't."

Robin stood with her mouth open. Silence. Zella gave a tight smile. Their eyes remained locked, and Robin picked up the packet of crackers from the table and started eating them, crunching down twice on each puffed disk before putting the next in her mouth. Sustenance. Sustenance. She could make sense of this if she wasn't so hungry.

"No, you didn't." Zella repeated, putting on another necklace. "You were up shit's creek, and I bailed you out. Hey, I didn't mind. You reminded me of myself when I was young, just trying to stay on that crazy highway." She finished adjusting the second necklace and looked at Robin in the mirror. "Of course it's not as crazy now, and here you are, shelling out twelve hundred a night while I'm in some dive on Khao San. It's time for you to pay up. You owe me, and I need to get back up to Laos."

"I don't owe you. I did pay."

"Hey, didn't I buy you that Buddha?" Zella turned and pointed to the statue on the high dresser. A *puang malai* still hung around the Buddha's neck where Piv had placed it, the jasmine blossoms shriveled and brown. Zella walked over and crushed one of the flowers between her fingers until the petals dissolved into oil. "What else did I buy you? I know you wanted some of everything I had."

"You loaned me the money. *I* bought the Buddha. I paid you back."

Zella took two swift steps toward the bed and bent sideways to reach between the mattress and box spring, searching efficiently, professionally, knowing that's where backpackers often kept their money belts.

"Hey!" Robin cried, when Zella pulled out the gamy, ugly belt. A handful of receipts fluttered to the floor. Zella slid the passport out and sliced it toward Robin like a Frisbee, moved toward the door while counting some red and purple bills. "That's mine!" Robin yelled. She jerked herself between Zella and the exit. The bones of their forearms crashed together. She breathed Zella's hair into her mouth. She pushed the heel of her hand into the side of Zella's head, felt the deep halo of frizz press up against hard scalp.

"You owe me four hundred bucks," Zella hissed. A foot kicked her shin, a knee shoved her thigh aside. Robin grunted. She clawed for the necklaces around Zella's neck. The door was half open now; the hotter air of the hall washed over her. Her force was pushing Zella out rather than pulling the money back in. Then her arm was caught by the door. She howled.

"I was your fucking fairy godmother, there when you needed me." Zella said from the hallway. She pulled more tightly on the door handle, one eye and faded coral lipstick visible through the vise that trapped Robin's arm. "You're just too fucking spoiled to repay the favor." She released her hold on the door slightly so that Robin could yank her purpling limb from it. Then Zella slammed the door shut. Robin chained it and bolted it and took the lychee drink, still slightly cold, and rolled it over the bruise on her arm. She was shaking, but she felt a coin of pride that Zella had made off with so little and was left with a bloody scratch on her throat.

Fuck Thailand. Fuck everyone. She had to do what she could to get herself home.

She found Abu easily, in the lounge. He was sitting alone, facing the door to the lobby, a bottle of Johnnie Walker and the ice service at his elbow, but nothing else, no papers or books, on the polished stone of the table.

"Ah Miss Miatta. When did you begin to feel better?"

"Just this afternoon." She took a seat. "I think I might be ready to eat something. May I join you for supper?" She tried cocking her head and smiling, flirting. I need to be like Piv, she thought, swallowing down the lump. I need to employ charm to my ends.

"You're ready for a night on the town with us, eh? But I was waiting for you today. I had hoped we could go to Jim Thompson's house. Beautiful place, and Piv said it's your favorite. I wanted to see it through your eyes. You do know Thompson was a CIA agent, don't you? He made a show of adopting Thai culture, or at least the aesthetic, but he was part of the American campaign to win hearts and minds by any means possible."

"No, I—I didn't know that. But I do love his house." She wanted a glass in her hand, something to cling to, and she sensed the bartender waiting for a signal to bring one, but Abu ignored him. "Um, what's the plan for Wednesday, before the flight?" She tried batting her eyes. "Could we go then?"

"I must admit that I'm not certain how the level of involvement in Thailand compares to that in my own country or in Central America, but I should think it would have been even greater here, due to the proximity of what your country calls the era's major conflict."

Abu's incisive gaze squashed her flat, reflected an ignorant and charmless American. "I didn't know," she muttered. But she needed to be like Zella, to exude a confidence that would allow her to appear to be what she was not. She inhaled, sat tall again, gestured to the bar for a glass. "I know more about his collections. There's a great collection of ivory at his house. Will there be anything at the convention you think he would have liked?"

"Of course you didn't know. You didn't care to know. But when it comes to my business, you're curious about all the little details." The bartender approached, but Abu raised his hand to avert him. "You seem nervous. Pivlaierd mentioned that you were anxious on his behalf, worried about his safety as he enters your country. I want to put your mind at ease, with regard to that. Piv comports himself beautifully. Merely being a national of Thailand is not the black mark that it used to be."

"I am worried about him. I want him to be careful, that's all."

"No, *you're* the one I'm worried about. A young woman away from her country for much too long, coming in from a hot spot. Almost inevitably, you could be pulled aside."

Robin stutter-blinked again—a reflex this time, not batting—a last-ditch backward paddle out of dangerous waters.

"What will you do if they open a case you're carrying for me—the case with contents of such interest to you?"

"I, oh—" What did she say? What could she say? "But they won't. But they . . . I don't look like a backpacker anymore."

"What you look like is a perfect candidate for a controlled delivery." He reached under the table to her thigh and grabbed a fistful of her flesh. "Even knowing that I'd hunt you down and find you—and that is precisely what I'm telling you: I'd hunt you down and find you—a white American like yourself, fat with false innocence, meeting your own again, you'd forget it. You'd do whatever they tell you. Maybe you're already doing it now."

"Abu, no. What?" She gasped the words, her breath gone from sucking up the pain of his grip.

"No. You'd betray me while looking me straight in the eye. And you'd betray your Thai lover just as quickly. Go to Jim Thompson's house whenever you like, and study from your master. You won't be flying for me."

She struggled to breathe. "Abu, no, I—" Gulp. "Abu, no, I won't. I wouldn't. I believe you. I know. And I love Piv." She believed herself passionately, choked up with the truth of it, but she saw Robert, too. What would she tell him? What would they do to her? Abu stood and left Robin sitting alone across from his smudged glass. His hands were reaching in his wallet, plucking bills for the bartender, but Robin's quadriceps still stung from his clench when he walked out of the lounge.

Chapter 27

When I'm in Bangkok with Abu, he took me to Pastuer Institute Snake Farm, where they keep some snakes to make medicine. He took me to Siam Farm, the big animal dealer in my country, where they sell legal and illegal animals both. He made me pick up snakes and look at their color, feel their bellies, feel their muscles, feel how they move, so I'll know which ones are healthy. So I'll know which ones are pregnant. Those are the best. He made me study pictures of Gray's monitor lizard and of the kind of coral snake and pit viper that are only in Philippines, and so very special. He told me that when I meet the dealers, I must act like I have knowledge. I must show I know about these animals, so dealers don't try to trick me. So they trust me. He told me the story of one American lady, newspaper reporter, who wanted to uncover some animal dealers in Jakarta. She tried to talk to these dealers like she's one customer, collector, but they understood that to buy something was not her goal. At night they followed her until she walked in the darkness. Then they held her down on the dark road, and they drove the car over her legs many times and smashed them. True story. She went back to the United States with one wheelchair. She didn't try to talk to those dealers again. Abu told me how to act, what to do, what to say, so no one will think I'm like this lady, sneak something around. And he told me where to buy gun, because the dealers will have gun, and the thieves will have gun, and if I get something too special, maybe someone will try to take it from me.

So first day I wake up in Philippines, I get the piece of paper out and dial the phone number. Someone answers with the word I don't know. "Hello," I say. I feel embarrassed. My words don't come even though in my dream I practice for this moment. One good thing is this: no one can see me. After too long, I can speak. "My friend Abu tells me to call you. He says you can help me buy something."

"Something? Sure, we can help you buy something." Heh, heh, heh. I hear this rough laugh. Where does this voice come from? From what person? What place? They laugh at me there.

"Excuse me. Perhaps something like one small weapon." First the gun, then the animal. First the gun, because after that, it's over. I don't have to think about it again.

"Okay," he says. "Sure." And he tells me where to go.

I walk toward the market to find the taxi, but even before the market, on the streets they sell everything. Teenage boys wear dirty towels wrapped around their heads; they sell newspapers. One old lady sells small statues made only from sea shells. One small girl, dirty face, dirty dress, sells flowers from buckets. Her eyes look sad. Maybe if I buy some flowers and smile, she'll smile, too—but no, at this time it's better if I don't carry flowers, if my face doesn't smile. To make this business, I should look tough. Many people on the street are selling food, and when I think about one gun, the smell makes my stomach hurt. Maybe I should not buy it. I think for me the gun might be bad luck. I stop walking. Across the street from where I am, one store sells stereos. Some song I know blasts out from there. What song is it? I try to hear. When I listen, my thinking's pure. Then I know: the Macarena. Very popular. Dance music is not my favorite, but it makes me feel good to hear that song. Like this music, I travel over the world. I can move strong, to strange places, and not be afraid. No, it's no problem to me. I am not afraid to make this business, to buy one gun that Abu thinks I should have. I walk up to one guy who leans on taxicab while he eats some white pudding with the spoon.

"Excuse me," I say to the taxi driver in English. I show him the address. "How much you charge to take me here, wait for me while I do business, bring me back?"

The smooth road turns into the rough road. The big buildings turn into small. The roofs go from tile to tin. I see some chickens now, and dirt on the ground. Some children around food cart look at this taxi when it drives past. Where do we go? No one knows. Not even the driver knows. He stops the car and takes my paper with the address written down and asks some man. They speak their language. They wave their arms. Another man comes to join them. Dark skin, with his shirt all the way open. They hand the driver one small glass. He drinks from that, then gets back in the car.

"Okay," he says to me. He presses the gas, and the car kicks back stones. The radio keeps playing American songs I've never heard before. Finally the taxi stops in front of one small store, open to the street. I lean out window to speak to the boys sitting there, but they don't talk to me. One runs over the dirt to the house behind the store, and he comes back with one man who says his name's Carlito.

This guy smells drunk. He holds one brown bottle in his hand. He raises his bottle and drinks some beer. "You know the African, *di ba*? Are you Pinoy? No? Thailand? Okay, I must be on the tourist list now. Ha! You could be Pinoy, though. You could be if you were." He laughs again. Heh, heh, heh. Now I think he laughs because he thinks he makes some joke. Because he's drunk. "Sure, sure, I can help you." He pretends to box with those boys. They laugh and hit him. "Not out here. Come with me."

Wow! It's hot in that house. Fan blows, but it's still too hot. The TV plays American program, and two ladies watch that. The young one holds the small baby and waves purple fan. The old one sits, chews watermelon seeds. I see black shells on the floor. I see ants crawling up the leg of the table to a Crush bottle there. Carlito says something to the ladies and they leave, then he pours beer from his bottle for him and for me. He lifts his glass.

"Ahoy," he says, then he drinks.

"*Chok dee*," I tell him. He likes that. He laughs. He says it, too, then asks me what it means.

"Something like good luck." I lift my glass again. "*Chok dee*." He hits mine with his.

His beer is gone now. He goes to the bed against one wall and bends down on his knees. From under there he brings out one wood box. Yellow paint is peeling off, but I can read the letters: Bumble Bee Diaper Cream.

That box holds guns. He unwraps four from old, gray cloth and picks up each to show me. He wants me to pick them up, too. I do. I try to study. I look at each one very close. Three black. One silver. Some made of metal, one of plastic. Some small marks on all of those. Someone already carried them. Someone already shoot. I pick one up, the little black one. It's small but heavy. Small and heavy both.

Carlito reaches in the diaper box and takes out something. "Go ahead and load it." It's one box of bullets. He puts them on the table and pushes them to me.

I hand him the gun. "Please," I say. I stand up. I feel ants are inside my shoe. They're biting my foot.

"What are you, *bakla*? Heh, heh, heh. You need a lesson, *di ba*? This is how you do it." He takes the clip out and puts in some bullets. "See?" Then he shakes them out just to put them back in. He says it again: "See?" He thinks I don't know how to do that, but it's not true. No. In the army I use AK-47, I use service .45. And I don't think this plastic gun is so different from that one. Sure, I can do this. But in the army, loading the gun and shooting is something I do too much. Why do I want to do that again?

Carlito spins the gun on his finger and smiles at me. Then he points the gun at one lady's magazine picture. "Oh, Baby Fuentes, why'd you fuck around on me?" He pretends to shoot that picture. "Boom!" Then he laughs. "Come on," he says. He wants to leave the house.

Outside, the light hurts my eyes, but my nose feels better. Today maybe it's thirty degrees, but it feels like mountain air after I am inside that house.

Pow!

He shoots that! He shoots that gun into the air! Dogs start barking. Why did he shoot that?

"Baaaaaby Fuentes!" Carlito shouts. He laughs too loud. More dogs start barking. My ears are still ringing from that sound. The two boys run out from their store. They laugh and jump. They push each other into dirt.

"Go on, go on. Try the Glock." He holds out the gun. He wants me to shoot it.

"Oh," I tell him. "Very good. Sure. But I don't want the police to come."

"Why would they come here? Come on. For *chok dee*, come on."

He puts the gun handle into my hand. It's warm. From some distance, another gun goes off. Pow! More dogs barking! In the street below the house, more people come. Some guys, children, ladies.

"Go ahead. Come on. See how it feels."

Did Abu do this? When does Abu shoot his gun? I feel confused. It's hot like the jungle. Dark like the jungle. A bug is biting my ankle; someone is coming; Carlito should quit talking, shhh! I put my arm up and pull on the trigger, then—boom! Boom boom boom boom! I shoot my arm off. My arm flies back. The gun falls down.

Everyone's laughing. Sure, I laugh, too. But no. No thank you. I don't want to try again, try another one. No more beer. No.

"This gun is good," I say. "Wow. Sure. Like the army. I'll think about it. I'll come back tomorrow. *Kawp-koon krup.* Thank you. *Sa-wat-dee krup.* Okay. Okay. But for now, good-bye."

I get in the taxi. The street is full of too many people watching, but when the driver starts that car, those people move enough for us to pull away.

"If you want a revolver, I know where you could go," the driver says to me.

I don't answer. I feel too much disgust. Because of ants, watermelon shells, Abu, jungle, and me, too. Disgust. How come I forgot about how quick it shoots, the power when you shoot it? I remember too much—how come I forgot about that? My arm hurts where it meets my shoulder. Where my rifle used to go.

Then I look on the dashboard, and I see something. One gold statue of Mary, important woman to the Christian religion. This statue's small face looks something like NokRobin's, sure. When NokRobin comes out from shower, sometimes she wears the towel over her head like that, like Mary wears. Clean towel only, never dirty. She lays it over her head and pushes it behind her shoulders, like long cotton hair. That makes her head look sweet, her chin look sharp as one point. Her eyes at that time are always open very wide. Like Mary, sure.

When I ask NokRobin what she believes she says no, she doesn't have Christian faith. That religion's not for her. She likes the Buddha better, even though she doesn't understand anything about that. But NokRobin, Mary, Lord Buddha, at this moment, in my mind they're all together. I can feel them with me now. It's very clear. I should do what's comfortable. None of them want me to make something with the gun.

I don't feel nervous when I go to meet these animal dealers. I go see one dealer. I go see number two dealer. They don't have Gray's monitor lizard like they promised, but everything's smooth, many snakes, other lizards. No problem. And I don't feel nervous when I go to see dealer number three, even though there are too many men around that place—four or five. They have black fingernails and they stand around one shiny gun. They laugh and point. But why should I feel afraid? If I buy the Glock from Carlito, does that give me knowledge? No. I don't need the gun to make them trust me. I have Abu's name, and I have the truth: I come to buy, not to uncover something. I don't trick you, so please, don't trick me. Don't try to tell me that you show me Gray's monitor lizard when what you show me is water monitor, very common one.

I try to be polite when dealer number three does this. He hands me water monitor and he says it's Gray's. I say nothing. I put that lizard back down in its bucket, pull the screen over the top of that. I walk away from him and look. To me, this place doesn't seem secret. It's in some village that's close to Cebu City. It's on one paved road. Palm frond roof overhead, so it's shady. No walls, so anyone can come there and the wind can blow through. When I walk away from the lizard, some lady come and buy turtles. She wears plastic sandals and one faded T-shirt that says something in English: Miami Heat. She's some country lady, that's all. These turtles aren't special. They're just for eating, for turtle soup.

To get to the snakes I came to see, I have to follow the dealer away from his market. We walk short distance down one dirt path to the wood building that looks soft and sad from seeing too much rain. He pulls three big baskets from underneath there. When you look into that, snake bodies are all you can see. They're moving, twisting, but slowly. That picture is always the same but always different, like the sea. Like some black and yellow sea. The dealer reaches inside the basket with one long hook and brings out the single snake. I grab it like Abu showed me, my thumb behind his head so he doesn't bite. I grab quickly, with one motion, like this is every day. My face is blank. No fear. No disgust. With my hand behind his head and my hand holding his body's middle, I feel his snake strength, like some cool leather whip. I feel his tail. It scratches my arm like some dry ghost. I look at his gold eyes, his red mouth, his black tongue. I look at his belly, the color of one banana. He's skinny as three fingers, longer than my arm. "How many do you have?" I say. The dealer says fifty. I take time looking. I choose ones I want—most colorful, most alive—put them in another basket.

Sometimes in Thailand, you see the guy who wears the cobra around his neck. Some young guys might do this, because the kids will come around then, the girls might—they'll want to touch it; they'll think he's cool. Sometimes you see the man in the park who wants to get healthy, who wants to get strong. He'll drink the blood from one cobra.

And in the United States, someone will pay maybe one thousand dollars for this snake that I buy now for two thousand pesos. To all these people, I'm thinking the same thing: why? The snake is dirty, not beautiful, not friendly. It's nothing I want to be.

The profit, that's the only thing I want. And when I get that, I'll turn it into something better. Something silver, something gold, with my partner, NokRobin. She's the one to do this with. If I don't do this business then she'll love me again, sure. She'll love it when I have money. Maybe I can get five thousand, six thousand dollars for selling these snakes. And I can grow my hair again; she'll like that, too. And then I won't come back to this dealer who takes my money—sixty thousand pesos for the snakes—and tries to lie again.

"Oh, I almost forgot," I tell him. "I'm looking for something. Very hard to find. Gray's monitor lizard. Bright green. Maybe you can help me find this?" I give him the chance to save his face, but no. He insults me. He shows me water monitor again, says it's Gray's. "Okay," I say. But I don't touch that when he holds it out to me. I look away from that dirt-colored thing.

I already told the other dealers that I'll call them in the morning to see if they have found Gray's lizard in the night, but I don't think this will happen. One Gray's monitor lizard can be worth twenty thousand dollars. You can dream about that money, but even for Abu, it's not as easy as you think.

Chapter 28

"Offer to do a body cavity."

"It doesn't matter. I told you, he doesn't trust me. He's worried about a controlled delivery. What's a controlled delivery?"

"That's why I told you to offer the body cavity. Just offer whatever you have to. Whatever they want."

"Just, please. He hates me. I can't do anything for him. You know the itinerary. What does it matter if I'm on the flight?"

"You get in his bedroom—"

"He'll kill me. He'll literally kill me."

"You stay by his side and tell us exactly what they say and where they are—and you get on that plane, or I'll personally deliver you back to Singapore."

Leaving her standing in the doorway of his hotel room, Abu let Robin beg. Let her stumble over the offer of her body's holes. "If you're worried about a controlled delivery, can't I carry something inside of me? Isn't there something I can do for you?" She reached her hand to his chest. She let her phlegmy words hang publicly in the echoey hush of the hallway. Abu shifted his eyes to acknowledge the maid who passed by, transforming her servant's invisibility with the power of witness. He spoke so she would hear him address Robin in a tone that needed no translation.

"I take it this means you've overcome your moral ambivalence about the animals. How gratifying. But I don't want you. Jomo might have, and Piv, but . . ." His left eyebrow lifted, his right eye squinted and locked hers. "I never understood it. The one before you was much nicer."

No. No. No. Robin sank down at the threshold, arms falling between her legs. Her rib cage felt cracked open—the wound to her pride, her self, her heart. She needed to go before Abu kicked her, but she couldn't rise, couldn't catch her breath.

Abu stepped to relax his shoulder against the doorframe. One of his polished black oxfords was inches from Robin's sandaled foot, the top of her bent head was level with the creased drape of his pants' knee. "Why don't you buy your own ticket home?"

Robin agitated her head no. She prayed to disappear into the floor, to shrivel into a sand crab and scuttle away.

"I've certainly thrown enough money your way."

She covered her face with her hands. "We spent it. And I maxed out my credit cards and had to pay a lot to them," she mumbled.

"Were you aware that Kenya pays twenty-five percent of its GNP to service its foreign debt? And that's low by African standards." Abu nudged Robin's cheek with his knee. "Your country loaned tens of millions to Zaire during the Cold War with full knowledge that it was going straight into Mobutu's bank accounts. Now you're holding the people of Zaire accountable. Did you know that?"

"No." If she stood up, she'd be too close to him, her breath at his throat.

"As an employee, you're worthless to me. Ten to one you'll be stopped, and a full body search isn't out of the question. You have no fortitude. But you're a young white female, not Tanzanian, not Nigerian. You're a decent business risk." Without the lift of his usual amusement, his face looked older, flat and hard. "Here's the deal I'll make with you," he said. "I'll let you keep your ticket, and within a week of your arrival you pay me back double the cost, or I sell the debt to Volcheck." He crunched his hard leather heel onto the top of her foot; she snapped her head up and yelped. "Are we clear? Eighteen hundred dollars to me, or you're dancing wherever our Russian friend sends you until the debt and any expenses incurred are repaid."

The splattered lights of a disco ball. The *thump thump thump* of dance music on tawdry docudrama shows, on Patpong. But she'd be on the plane. Robert and Ray would catch Abu, lock him up, lock up Volcheck before they could ever hold her accountable. Right? Robin cried out again, and Abu lifted his foot. "I don't have a choice. Whatever you say."

"Stand up," he said. "As you wished, you'll spend the evening with us. I want you at dinner when I tell Volcheck about this arrangement."

Abu and Volcheck had arranged to meet two Thai men at Papaya Garden. One of them, Dang, had a square jaw and well-shined wire-rimmed glasses, but the other one was slightly unkempt, with pocks in his face and limited English. "She had a Thai boyfriend," Abu told the men. "The two of them spoke English together, of course, as well as the language of love, but I think he also taught her a little of your language." He turned to Robin. "Won't you say something to our guests?"

Robin shook her head. "Oh, I can't." She stood in front of an underlit fish tank of giant prawns. Their antennae tapped at the glass.

"Ah, the typical American. Speaks nothing but English, won't even try. But come now. Surely after all this time, and your love of this country—your love of its inhabitants . . . " He paused to chuckle. Robin smiled wanly. "Say something," he demanded.

"*Phasaa thai mai dai*," Robin said to the men. I can't speak Thai.

Dang smiled and nodded indulgently, but the other man didn't encourage her or seem amused.

The conversation at the table was intermittent. Speaking English, the different accents traded names of species, categories of paperwork, surnames from a half dozen languages. Robin tried to remember details to toss like meat to the FWS that evening, but her mind was full of static, waiting for Abu to offer her for sale like a snake, like a lizard, like an animal's appendage torn from its heart-beating rest. He never did, and immediately after the meal, he excused himself abruptly. Feeling Volcheck's eyes suck onto her like leeches, Robin asked to leave the table as well. There were vases of orchids by the sinks in the bathrooms, and she took a long inhale as she touched each purple-white blossom. But the flowers didn't offer an escape route; eventually she had to return to her seat. Abu's was still empty; Volcheck rotated his massive frame around on his chair to watch her walk through the room. He moved his mouth in seeming response to the Thai men, and then his tongue resumed working his teeth to extract the last fibers of food from the cracks. Robin tugged her skirt down and crossed her arms across her chest. She tried to keep her eyes focused on some point in the far distance as she settled back into her chair. Pig, she thought. I hate you.

Volcheck shrugged. "Too skinny," he said to Dang, using his pinkie to dislodge something his tongue hadn't pried from his molars. Then he took a deep sniff. "What you get for her?"

Dang looked away. He muttered a translation under his breath. The other man muttered something back. She caught some numbers: *sam roi ha-sip baht, see roi baht*; three hundred and fifty; four hundred baht, a query.

Pig! But her stomach went cold. Eighteen hundred dollars. She'd tried to smudge the FWS into just a bad dream, but now she needed them.

"Where's Abu?" she demanded. She gripped the table.

"Gone," Volcheck said. "We go too. Get up."

"No. I'm staying here. I'll get back by myself." If they tried to force her, she'd scream. She felt a cry nudge into her throat and crouch there, waiting. She'd let it pounce if they touched her. She would. Blood drummed through her.

Volcheck lumbered to his feet. "Get up."

"No!"

He shrugged and gave an accompanying squirm of the mouth. He wadded some hundred baht notes and threw them onto the table toward her plate of half-eaten food.

The Thai pair took their leave from her and the trio filed out. There was a black stutter as they pushed through the door. Robin slumped alone at the table. The adrenaline drained from her, and her shoulders and elbows and wrists began to ache. She became aware of the spectacle she must be making of herself—a shrill, deserted farang woman crumpled like a stained napkin with the debris of a meal. A waiter hovered near, not sure of the protocol. She looked at him and then at her watch.

"Is there an international telephone nearby?" she asked him. She tried to think of the Thai word. "International *tho-ra-sap*?"

By the time she got up to the brightly lit twenty-four-hour phone center, she was desperate to find someone who cared whether or not she was okay, someone who could share her blame. It was 11:00 AM in Philadelphia. Her father worked at home. She'd call collect. He'd better be there.

"Princess! Baby! Don't you stay out of contact like this again. Why haven't you called?"

It was the indication of concern she'd been hoping for; she lit right in: "I haven't called because I was really in trouble when I spoke to you last time, and you let me down."

"Aw, sweetheart. Aw, Robin. I've been goddamn worried about you since the last time. You know there's nothing I'd rather do than give you what you ask for, but I swear, I'm in a real jam."

The familiarity of his rote made her despondent but righteous. She *was* alone. No *wonder* she had gotten into trouble. She let the accusation lay dead on the line.

"Come on now, Robin. You know when I have it it's yours. Who gave you free reign with the credit card that summer at Macy's? Who took you to Disney World as many times as you wanted when there was no place in the world where you'd rather go? And then who finally managed to instill some taste in you and took you to—"

Ah yes, her father: erratic provider of upper-middle-class perks, child support shirker, and exaggerator extraordinaire. It was true that he could be outrageously generous and had fine taste. The summer after Robin starting taking band he gave her a sterling silver flute. But meanwhile, her mom had lost her job and had been unable to pay the electric bill, and they'd kept their block cheese in a five-gallon cooler filled with gas station ice. Between the two parents they might have been able to provide a modest, safe circumstance, but no. She cut off his monologue.

"It's your fault!"

There was a heartbeat of silence. Then her father's voice, reasonable and low: "I realize that, Robin. And what I'm telling you is I'm paying the price. I'd already consolidated once. I had no choice but to go to court to get the creditors off my back. How do you think it made me feel to have to tell you I couldn't help my favorite girl?"

Courts. Help. What if she ended up needing that eighteen hundred? But mostly . . . she was someone's favorite girl. It gave her a moment's rest. "Are you talking about bankruptcy, Dad?"

"Robbie, yeah. But I've got a job going now, and hey, while I'm thinking of it, did you ever bump into that Smith girl I told you about? Margaret Wheeler's daughter, in Taiwan?"

"I'm in Bangkok, Daddy. Thailand, not Taiwan."

"I know, sweetheart. But if you do happen to, don't mention anything about this, okay? And if you could not mention it to any of your college pals either, because I think Margaret's colleague sent his daughter to Skidmore, too."

"For God's sake, Dad." Robin's voice spiked raggedly. "I'm in trouble. Real trouble. You don't know the things I've had to do." She started crying. Sobbed. "You don't know," she hollered through a wall of tears and mucous. For long seconds the phone line sloshed with her body's liquids and grief.

"Sweetheart? Sweetheart, shhh. Calm down. I know you're far away now, but don't you worry. We're going to get you home. Between your mom and me . . . Baby, I'm embarrassed about my situation, but I've got this equipment here, state of the art. I've got it worked out so—listen, Robbie, what kind of trouble? Can you say?" She broke into a fresh wave of crying. "Shhh. It's okay. Whatever you need. I'll sell some things and then a ticket will be on its way."

Robin subsided into rhythmic sniffs. Ashamed of her outburst, she still felt soothed by the reaction it had evoked.

"It's too late, Dad. I'm already coming home."

"You've already got a ticket? That's great! That's great, sweetheart. Whatever it is, it's going to be better once you're home." The robust confidence in his voice made him sound small, dwarfed by his brave willingness to sell his equipment, diminished by his gratitude that he wouldn't have to. And she understood. She understood.

"I had a Thai boyfriend." Robin said it without thinking. Another tear ran down her cheek, silently this time. Forget Thailand, Kenya, the Philippines, the jungles and savannas and life's woes. She was a teenager from Palatka awed by Philadelphia, turning to her father after she'd placed her bets on a guy who'd broken her heart for the very first time.

"Don't tell me. He did something to you. Princess, what is it? This guy, is he . . . ? Were you protecting yourself?"

"No. We were careful." The one area in which she could make this claim.

"When are you coming home?"

"I'm leaving tomorrow. I land in Orlando the day after that. Then we'll see. I don't know." Oh, to be a love-maimed teenager. Oh, to be simply dealing with a bankrupt father and herself headed that way. But she felt fortified. However small she was, she existed. She needed someone to know.

"What time do you arrive, sweetheart? What's the flight number? I'm going to try to be there. I'm going to make sure your mom is."

"No, Dad. Don't. I mean it. And don't tell Mom. But listen, if I don't call within a couple days, you better come looking." How to say it so he'd hear it, without alarming him? She tried to chuckle. "I'm kidding. But just in case, write down this name: Abu Navaisha. I've been staying at the Star Hotel, 286-6732. The code for the country is 66. The code for Bangkok is 2. I'm in Bangkok, Dad. That's Thailand. Remember." She gave one more wry laugh. "Margaret Wheeler's daughter's not here."

Chapter 29

Nothing's so easy as you think.

Okay, this sounds like the simple thing to do. Abu tells me to put the snakes in nylon stockings then wrap those to my ankles so no one at the airport knows where to look. Directions to do it: Put one snake in there. Spin that stocking leg around and the snake spins, too, into one ball. Now quick, make the nylon tight around him. Tie the knot. Then put another snake in there. Spin. Tie knot. Sure. Sounds simple.

But I start this job at 1:00 AM. When the sun came up at 6:30, I finally had twenty-three snakes in. It took me that many hours because the snakes don't like it. They want to fight. And I'm one person. Think about this. From the dealers, I have twenty-four snakes in three different cloth bags. Each bag has something like seven or ten snakes. How can I get only one snake out? I can't reach in my hand. Those snakes will bite me! I have to ask in lobby, to one sleepy guy, at 1:00 AM: "Excuse me, young brother. I need to hang something in the bathroom. Please. The clothes hangers in my closet won't move from there."

The thick clothes hanger he gave me is good for picking up heavy snakes, but it's not good for bending. I need to change its shape, but I can't do this with my hands, so I use the bathroom door to squeeze it. It takes me many tries. I squeeze; the hanger flies free to hit me in the chest. I squeeze the door on it again; the hanger falls down and bangs—*clack!*—on the tile floor. After some time, finally the hanger changes to be skinny and long. When the maids at Casa Magellan see this, to them they will see the mystery. Saisamorn finds funny things like this many days at the Star Hotel. Sometimes he would ask me: What reason did those old American tourists have to cut one big square hole in the middle of the sheet? What is the reason that the Cambodian man took the soap dish from the bathroom wall and screwed it into the wood above the bed? Maybe I have the answer now. Maybe it's something about the turtle or the bird or the snake. Or something else about money. You cannot always guess the strange thing you will have to do for that.

It's after 2:00 AM when I open the packs of nylon stockings. Wow! These are very short and skinny. They don't look like ladies' legs at all. But you know something? It's not too hard to put the leg in that small hole, because the leg wants to be there. Snakes don't want to. They won't help you. I push my arm down where the lady's foot is supposed to go and spread my fingers to stretch there. Then I do the same for stockings number two. I put the second pair inside the first one, make it double, because these stockings always rip. Everybody knows that. Then I take these double stockings to the bathroom and close the door.

I hold the stretched stocking in one hand. In the other hand, I hold the hanger. I open one bag and use hanger to hook one snake. This one is the habu, green pit viper. I lift my arm and out he comes, not so big but feeling heavy because the way I hold him on the hanger.

And don't forget these snakes are moving. I hook him by the belly only, but his head moves through the air and wraps his body around the hanger. Now he twists around there tight. His whole body moves like water. It moves something like one line of ants—when you look quickly it seems still, but it's getting closer all the time. This snake is getting closer to my hand that holds the metal hanger. He's moving farther from the stocking in my other hand. His mouth is open. I see his teeth there. Why didn't I think of this? How can I grab behind his head when I'm holding something with both hands? I drop the stocking so I can take his head, but too late! He strikes out for my other arm.

Crash! I drop that hanger on the floor.

He's too quick! That snake is like one dancer, moving sideways to the door. His head goes under. Stop! I put my foot down on his bright lime body. I press down harder when I feel him try to move. I want to crush him. But one thousand dollars is too much to lose.

Now I have one snake under my shoe. Twenty-three snakes in bags. Zero snakes packed up like balls.

Very careful, I pull this snake backward. I bend down and use my hand to pull, my foot to make him stay. I feel him fighting. He wraps around my wrist and squeezes. At the end, he makes his jaws big. I can't pull his head under the door. I have to open that to slide him out. My foot's on his neck, but maybe he can still turn and bite.

No. I'm the quick one now. My thumb is on his head. I got him. I put my fist into the stocking. The whole snake is covered with nylon.

I did it! But I have to get my hand out. With my other hand, I grab his head from outside the stocking, then I let go with my hand that's inside. But that doesn't mean he lets go of me! His one-meter body's wrapped around my arm as tight as one bandage. I roll my wrist. Slowly, slowly I can get free. I pull out my hand. And when I swing that stocking around and around, Abu's right. That snake get scared. He curls into the ball. I tie him very tight in there, and I feel relief.

After that, some snakes go in there easy. Some snakes, very, very hard. And one escapes. One mangrove snake, larger and more dangerous than habu. Five o'clock in the morning. He disappears too fast; his golden belly moves like spilling water. I don't want to look. I don't want to chase. Casa Magellan, I give you the expensive pet. For me, I don't leave for my plane for three more hours, but I don't close my eyes even though they've been open all morning, all night. I think maybe that pet snake wants revenge for his friends. Maybe he'll bite me if I close my eyes and lie in bed.

I use NokRobin's Swiss Army knife to cut the double stockings at their vee so the legs aren't connected anymore. I put those two legs, heavy like dirt, like stones, like metal, on the bed while I shower. In the nylons, the yellow and green of the snakes looks the same as dirt. I don't know why, but the shower feels like sand; it doesn't feel like it's getting me clean. I soap myself once, twice, three times. I don't know when my next shower will be. I shave and put on cologne and comb my hair.

Then, before I put my trousers on, I make ankle bracelets out of the snake-stuffed stockings. I try to think that the snake balls are like big, brown pearls when I wrap three rows of them above each foot. I wrap them like Abu told me, high enough so when I sit and my trousers lift, no one can see. The empty waist part of each stocking I pull tight. I tie that piece around the first knot, so that the bracelets stay still. I use some silver tape to stick them to my leg, so they don't fall down. I put on my suit trousers and to test, I walk in front of the mirror. I raise my knees high like if I have to climb stairs. I sit in front of the mirror. I cross my legs and lean like I have to reach to get my Coke from the waitress. I light one cigarette and watch myself smoke in the Casa Magellan hotel in Cebu City. No matter what I do, no one can know those bracelets are on me, but I wish I could take them off and go into the shower again. I try to think that they're jewels—like topaz, like emerald—but no, my thinking can't make those bracelets beautiful to me.

Chapter 30

It was just after dawn, but Robin was already packing for the afternoon flight when Abu rapped on the door and pushed into the room. His eyes jumped from corner to covered surface and lighted on her flopped-open backpack on the floor by the bed. He pulled it up and began frisking it, unzipping pouches with hard yanks and running his hand along the edges. "You're not to pack a single thing that could raise an eyebrow, do you understand? I don't want you in a position where you have to be explaining." He eyed the Buddha on its perch and pinged its shoulder with his index finger. The bronze range dolefully. "You can't take this."

"But I have the papers." Robin had felt so knowing when she insisted upon the permit from the vendor as part of the purchase price.

"The papers are probably fake." He turned the bed, rummaged the cultural prizes Robin had laid out there: sarongs, statuettes. "No," he said, tossing on the floor an antique tapestry, a lacquerware bowl, a framed temple painting whose brittle glass cracked from the fall. He emptied the sack holding the lotus necklaces and the one with the hundred odd bracelets she'd picked up at the factory the day before, and he rooted through the silver with a two-fingered poke. "Looks like goods to be sold for a profit. You can't take these." His eyes met Robin's for the first time since coming into the room. She shriveled. How could she hate him so much and still be diminished by his contempt?

"But they're worth money. Maybe you could take some toward—"

Abu picked up a necklace out of the pile. He looked at it casually, then tossed it onto the mound of clothes on the bed. "They're not worth much. If you're really that attached, you'll have to take your chances with the post."

When he left, Robin tentatively surveyed her belongings. The slew made her queasy, like smelling tequila for the first time after a disastrous night out. But there was the same kind of irresistible pull, too. The hair of the dog. The mass of bracelets and necklaces were the one solid thing she had to show for her whole miserable mess. What if she didn't pack the jewelry all together, but stowed individual pieces here and there?

She got up to examine the bag before stopping herself. For God's sake. What was she thinking? Wasn't she running a great enough risk? She slapped her own face in reprimand. A doughy sound filled the room when her open palm contacted cheek. She did it once more. Her jaw slid sideways under the impact. But she couldn't deny that the bracelets had turned out well. She put one on and let her arm fall to her side. Like the necklaces, the bracelets consisted of five primary pieces, but these were cylindrical, the ends of each molded to resemble a tight bud and joined to the next with an additional small round link. Piv hadn't seen them yet. She wondered if he'd notice this one on her wrist, if he'd be the least bit interested in the tangible result of all their planning. She felt a twinge in her chest, closed her eyes, and smelled the musky hot wax and cold grass smell of the Black Canyon restaurant in Pai, where, tipsy on Mekong, she had first connected Piv to her dream of making money from beauty. Then the tequila gag reflex kicked in again, and Robin's guts wrenched. Her cheek still stung from her slap.

This *stuff*. This poisonous, low-down, corrupting *stuff*. She began shoving things into the room's wastebasket: spirit money and paper lanterns and saffron candles that she'd picked up for pennies in local markets and once held as keys to Asia's mystery, antiques or skillful imitations that she'd believed would slake her longing for all the beauty back home that she couldn't afford. Soon the plastic container overflowed with debris from eight months of yearning and delusion.

But it didn't feel right. She looked at the crumpled luster of the tapestry in the wastebasket, and the sight made her hands itch. She wanted to smooth the nubbly weave. It wasn't the silk's fault that covetousness had sickened her. It wasn't the silver's fault she'd paid for it with spoilage. The maids would likely rescue the worthwhile things, anyway. Why make them dig through the trash? Robin went downstairs and, with effort, explained to Saisamorn that she wanted a cardboard box. She packed it with her extraneous clothes and souvenir bounty and placed the jewelry she'd designed carefully on top. Then she wandered the halls until she found the maid she thought the prettiest, the one with eyebrows as fine as watercolor brushstrokes. She was sweeping a room's tile threshold with a whisk. Robin pressed through the girl's smiling confusion until the box was in her hands, the broom dangling there, too. "Please," Robin had said, "I want you to have it."

Back in room 517, there wasn't much left. When Abu came back to inspect her flaccid pack, he found only two necklaces, three bracelets, and one monkey statue along with the bare essentials. He insisted Robin follow him out the door, but even with him looming, she paused at the threshold. The well-used bed, the smog-smudged view of cement towers and golden stupas. Something bumped and thudded in her brain. She looked at the Buddha one last time, and, bringing her hands together awkwardly, still trying to hold onto her purse and her pack, she waied.

In a second-from-the-aisle seat, midway down a 757's vast center row, Robin watched as the TV screen on the seat back in front of her showed an animated picture of the flight path: she was leaving Bangkok, leaving Thailand, flying over Cambodia, Laos, Vietnam. When the plane began its descent into Manila, she became sick with a new wave of panic. The air in the cabin heated and thickened within moments of the grounding. Passengers terminating in the Philippines stooped and fumbled, impatiently shifted. Her hand delivered fingernails to her mouth in a gesture she hadn't made since college. Piv would be boarding. Piv. The mule she knew about, the man she had lived beside. Slivers of nail curled and scratched at the back of her throat. The departing procession drained away glumly. Flight attendants worked to freshen the cabin, but the oxygen supply seemed half what it should have been. For thirteen hours she'd have to share this paltry supply of air with him. She started panting. Finally, almost an hour after landing, a rustle of new passengers drifted down the aisle.

Of course, there was a chance she wouldn't see him even now. It was a jumbo jet. She could hear the shuffle and clunk of people and things rows ahead of her, passengers settling into place whom she might never glimpse. Piv could be one of them. Or he might have ditched them all, both her and Abu. More clever than both of them and perhaps now off toward the sunset with his lady of the blue ribbons. If there was a lady of the blue ribbons . . . Robin's muscles clenched, waiting. She gave a quick prayer that he had gone so that she wouldn't have to answer for his presence to the Wildlife guys, so that she wouldn't have to answer to herself for the leaping in her chest.

But then. Coming down the aisle. On her side. There he was. Gut-deep shock.

Piv was so beautiful. Of course, she'd always understood this, recognized the fact. But here was the surprise: She knew his face well. Calm. Controlled. But not inscrutable. No, not blank. She could read confusion there. She could see exhaustion. He'd been struggling.

He met her eyes.

An undeniable light went on in his own. His mouth lightened visibly. Piv. He saw her, and he looked brighter, beyond beautiful. More than that fact—he glowed for her. Or not *for*, but *because of*. With. With her he was an east-beach dawn, a west-beach sunset. She felt her own eyes warm with hope and relief and something more. Piv. Yes, Piv. Only three rows from her, now only two. He cast his eyes down; her attention was drawn to a tiny flutter at his waist. It was his index finger, lifting to tap twice on her aisle's outer handrest as if wanting to reach across the seat separating them and touch her. He was about to step past her. She looked up and blatantly, hopefully smiled.

He turned his face away. His visage still a sunset but his eyes somewhere else.

Heart-crushing. Heart-hardening. She'd been mistaken.

Or maybe not. Abu and Volcheck might have been watching, and Piv followed orders. Not to speak until out of customs, these were their instructions.

But a sign? Surely they could exchange one last sign? Another meeting of the eyes or the swap of a smile?

His lips pursed fastidiously. So stern and negating. Like hard plums. Or a kiss. Was he looking at her over his far shoulder, even as he turned away? Or was he searching the seats for the blue lady, or for another seduced, addled mule? It was totally within his power, she knew, to round up a half dozen farangs who wanted, needed, were simply willing to take a small risk for a ticket or a story or some cash. Or for him. There was an obvious backpacker right over there. What was she carrying? The line surged forward again. Piv kept walking. Robin didn't dare turn her head to see where he went. She remained buckled to her seat all through the boarding.

When the plane reached cruising altitude, Robin got up and walked toward the bathrooms, scanning each row of seats on her way there and back. She saw Volcheck, but that was all. Where was Piv? If he'd see her, glow again, slide up to her, or slip her a note, she'd tell him. She'd tell him as clearly as she could that when the plane set down he had to walk empty-handed away from Abu. So where was he?

Robin squirmed in her seat for seven hours, rising to wander the plane every couple. Her body grew sore from craning, from twisting, and she never saw Piv. He must not have wanted her to. As with everything, she'd been mistaken. About his glance, about his dusky finger tapping, about him. Over Alaska, she finally slipped into a half-doze. When she closed her eyes, she saw sweet plums, salted plums, pecans, policemen. Oh, Piv. Was it all you thought it'd be? Up in the air for countless hours, speeding over the world, halfway toward outer space, backward through time? She saw a citrus souvenir shop and a bag of gold swinging from a utility pole fixed on the side of I-95.

Chapter 31

NokRobin always says she likes my country—she loves my country, loves to be in Thailand. One time I ask her: "What don't you like about USA?" Her answer was very simple: Disney World. But that's only one place. She doesn't have to go there. I think she means something more. So, because it's NokRobin, I can ask again. Very direct.

"*You* know," she says to me. "They think they're making something fun, but instead they're making everything boring and the same, and it's all about money anyway. They charge this huge admission, and what you're paying for is to have exactly the same experience as everybody else. And not just Disney World. Everything's too expensive, especially compared to here."

She went to Disney World too many times when she's small, sure. She grew up around there. She goes maybe six or eight or ten times— Epcot Center, too—so many she says she doesn't remember. Because of that, no, I don't think she wants to go with me to that place. But maybe I'll go anyway. Disney World is famous, very big, very important. I understand it's not the artistic place, but I want to see where so many people from the whole world want to go.

I asked NokRobin another question: what does she like about her country? She says she likes that it's big. You can go many different places. If you want to be hot, you can go somewhere. If you want to be cold, sure. If you want to be very dry, very wet, anything, there's someplace in the United States for you. And she likes that so many different races of people live there. She says they're not always fair to everybody, which is bad, but they try to get better about that. People try to live together. Also, many different people means possibilities for very good food.

NokRobin says that even where it's hot in her country, it's not as hot as the hot season in Bangkok or Philippines. But I sit on that plane for thirteen hours—I don't even get up one time because I'm afraid those snake bracelets will fall if I walk around—and when I finally step out into the USA, first thing I think is the air feels the same as the place that I left. I walk down the tunnel that's wet and hot. On the wall, pictures of Disney World, Busch Gardens, Sea World, pictures of America. Then I'm inside air-conditioning. Dry and white and very big, bright place, but I can still smell the things that grow when it's wet and warm. I don't love this, but it makes it feel like my home. Maybe this is okay, because I'm wearing the bracelets and it's better for me at this time to be calm, not think of the new things. It's better not to think of my emotions, to let them pass me like some clouds. I need to attend to each moment, to be inside it, so I can be with whatever happens now. Because right next to the hot growth, I smell something else. Maybe you think it's impossible, but it's not impossible to me once I empty my mind. I smell NokRobin, even though I don't see her. I smell her sweating, then burning. I can smell that she knows something that makes her afraid.

Then my eyes find her body. Abu tells me not to look at NokRobin during this trip, and when I saw her yesterday on the plane, very nice, very pretty, and she's happy to see me, I wanted to look, but I turned away. That felt good. Not looking is business between us, and her smile says to me that maybe we will make some romance together again. I can be patient when I think that.

But now when I look I see something different. Two very business people stand close to NokRobin. One farang man, one farang woman. Both of them wear some kind of blue suit. All three face the tunnel that connects to the runway.

I don't know how, but I know: these people in blue suits didn't get off some plane. NokRobin's eyes look worried. They don't look at me. Deep in my heart, I know: at that moment, romance is gone.

Then it's like magic. I see more of those people. Not all in blue suits, but I can see who's not tired from one very long trip. Maybe six people. I see more. Maybe twelve. It's like I wear the special glasses. I see them move fast. They move outward. Like someone dropped one stone in the middle of fish.

Now Russian Vol comes from the tunnel into this big room. I think I see NokRobin's chin move, her eyes get small. I see some fish swim by her, toward Vol.

Then NokRobin sees me. Everything's very clear for me in this moment. No feeling, only truth. Because her eyes are not blue, before this time I never think they're like the sea. This is wrong thinking. Now I see correctly. They're not like the sea in my country—soft, peaceful, blue—they're like some ocean that I have only seen pictures of. They're like the rainy, rocky sea. Gray-brown and crashing. Waves trying to escape from that place. Dangerous. Trouble. She brings those with her. Why didn't I understand before? Those fish that stand by NokRobin want to know what she's looking at, so they follow her eyes to me.

But she turns away now. She looks at someone else. Then she brings her hand up and rubs and rubs her head. She makes that sign. Very fast, so no one can follow, she looks one more time at me. Like the ghost who's been awakened from the stream.

Who is NokRobin? She's only secrets from me. She rubs her head and tells me to get rid of those animals, but this is too late. Before she does this, I already see everything. I already see her gray and cold. I already look for the place to get these bracelets off me.

I look for the toilet and I see nothing. I walk quickly now, but not too alarming. I'm very calm. I look for some closet, some cave, something in this big, white place. The fish are everywhere, but nothing will happen. These clouds are passing. They're not reality to me. NokRobin's eyes made my emotions start crashing, crashing like the ocean, like the sea, but I don't feel that. I only watch it happen.

I see some door. It has silver handle. That's all I need. One door. Toilet. Something. Privacy.

On that door the sign is small and says in English only: PRIVATE. CUSTODIAN. This is for me. I turn the handle. Locked. Again I try. Again. Locked. Locked. The other door I go to is the same.

I'm coming closer to lines of people. Passport line or search-you line? I don't know. I can't remember which came first in Philippines. Above my head are signs. Pictures of luggage, passport, bus, car, sure, but the arrow says one thing for all: go straight. Maybe this time I should break the rules. If I could ask Abu, he would tell me. I don't see him. I look around. No fish too close to me. Maybe it's very simple for me to enter United States. Maybe no one will look at my legs. Maybe this is my destiny, to be safe. I stop to breathe and make my heart go slow.

Then I hear something, like the movement of kicked chickens. Very quick. Then I hear something else: one shout. My back gets stiff. Then I'm like everyone—I turn to look.

It's Russian Vol! Two men hold his arms back, but he leans forward. His stomach pulls him toward the floor. Then Vol jerks up like the rusty saw. One man is coming closer; Vol jerks back . . . He spit on him! He spit on him! Another shout. Russian Vol yells something. He makes this! Too much trouble!

Everyone moves quickly. The fish run back toward Vol—the fish are on him!—other people curl up and move away. I move away. I hate that Russian Vol. I hate him. I want him away from me. He yells again and hurts my skin. His yell sends something electric deep inside of me.

No animals. No snakes. They must leave. I can't take these into USA. I hate them. They're heavy. They're poison. They have to come off. But where? Nowhere to hide in this big, white room.

Okay. Here's something. Silver carts against the wall. They're pushed together. I think if I get behind them, no one can see me.

They're too close to the wall. I try to move them, but they're connected all together. They're too strong. I can't get behind. I try to get under. Volcheck's yell comes after me again. I hear that. It hurts me. Below the cradle part of the cart in front is some small space. No walls on that, but no one will look here. No yell can come. I climb over the bar that attaches to all four wheels. I'm all alone. No one will see.

It's very crowded under here, but I can still move. I reach inside my suit pocket. I feel the Swiss Army knife. When I crouch down like this, my trousers rise high over my shoes. Still, my trousers cover the snake bracelets. I reach up and feel that. In the jungle, if the poison snake bites you, you use knife to cut out the place from your skin. When I want bracelet off, I put my knife up my trouser. I cut off that stocking. It feels very thick and the blade doesn't move, so I make my hand more strong. Outside the cart, feet pound around me. Feet pound around me, and I still hear Vol. That bracelet doesn't fall off quick enough, so I cut there again and again. Many times. All the knots I tie yesterday, I cut those. All those snakes I got in there, I want them gone. I feel something wet. Maybe I cut myself. I feel something cold, maybe snake blood. But still it's not coming off. I have to do this. Get this bracelet behind me. No animals. No snakes. No Vol. But it's not coming off.

Then I remember: tape! I reach my hand higher and pull that tape from my leg. I pull and cut. That pain is nothing. And then okay. Okay, I got it! I hold the bracelet. Snakes and stocking, it's separate from me. I throw that like it's burning. I throw that bracelet from the row of carts like it's one grenade. Away from me before explosion.

Blood on my hand. I don't know where that comes from. I reach inside my other trouser leg. I start to use my knife again. Please. I cut you out. Please. Be gone.

Chapter 32

Robin would indicate which passengers she knew. The USFWS would keep an eye on them. The immigration officers would discretely pull the suspects aside. That was the plan. But from the moment she stepped off the plane into Robert's hungry gaze, Robin knew it was going to go wrong.

The Wildlife law enforcement agents were shadowing too closely. When Volcheck stopped walking to consider a drinking fountain, the flat-bellied, broad-shouldered agent following behind kept moving until the toe of his shoe grazed Volcheck's heel. Volcheck glowered. Instead of apologizing, the agent bristled, offended. Volcheck took a few more steps then stopped to adjust his trousers. The agent bumped him again, this time in the elbow.

"You fuck," Volcheck said. He gave the man a shove.

They were on him like sharks. Two men pinned his arms. Volcheck hollered. The football player flashed his credentials. Volcheck pulled back and spit. His profanities echoed through the corridor. Security guards ran over—clubs, chains, radios clanking—and Volcheck used his bulk like a crowbar. He rocked and he kicked.

An alarm went off. Inside her head or outside, Robin didn't know. She had one thought, one emotion: get out.

Robert and his partner leaned toward the scuffle. Robin dropped her bag. She crossed her arms at her navel and bent over, covering as much of her body as she could. She scuttled. Keeping close against the wall, she half walked, half ran, her back hunched in a curve. The only place to go was toward customs. In the painful tensed lock of her limbs she still clutched her purse. Her money. Her passport. Her way to get out.

Then, slithering at her, a surrealist painting come to life: gold and black scrawl against industrial gray, a bad dream . . . the tempter, the devil . . . Jesus, what was that? A snake. And, God, then another. This one bent and disfigured, electric green. Pulsing forward with jerks, body ending with a frayed gray pulp. A mutilated serpent. A mangled piece of legless squirm. Coming from where? Robin followed its trail backward, to a row of hard silver carts. American supermarket-style. Clean chrome, not a jungle. But, Jesus. Red blood on the gray. Red blood on beige trousers. Red blood on the hands of a contorted Piv. Another snake streamed from him. The tail of a snake lay by his shoe. Snake pieces, and his arm sawing, hacking. Raw power Robin had never seen him use.

She slowed in horror. Went limp with blood-struck awe. But still moved forward, drawn there.

Robin felt a hand on her wrist, her shoulder blades meeting, her chest thrust up. A single clawed grip secured both her arms.

"Hold on." One man's voice blanketed the inside of her ear.

Two men and a woman surrounded the silver cart. Crouching. Low down. Guns drawn.

She had to save herself. Save herself. She couldn't holler stop.

Chapter 33

When I see them come at me, I think one thing: I wish I sent that money to my parents. Almost two thousand dollars I have of my own now, but I kept that for NokRobin. I kept that for myself. I give nothing to my mother. Now I feel ashamed. I feel too ashamed. I should never come here. Never go to Philippines. I want this to be over, to start again. I want to go back to my home. *Yak glap meuang Thai.*

Strong legs stand above me. Maybe I say that to them. I feel my mouth moving. But if I say that, I speak only in Thai. I'm too sad now. Too ashamed. Too afraid. They point guns. They want the knife, and I give them that, sure. Why do I want that? It's nothing to me now. That money is nothing to me. And I say nothing. For talking, for thinking, at that moment my English is gone.

Chapter 34

After spending a handful of hours in an airport security lounge, Robin was transported in the back of a white minivan to a holding facility on the industrial fringe of Orlando's flat sprawl. When her escort told her to hand her purse over to the clerk who stood behind a waxy check-in window framed in smudged handprints, Robin realized she was in custody.

"But I haven't been charged with anything. No one's read me my rights," she protested.

Just cause, innocent until proven guilty, free speech—she'd heard these touted as cornerstones of democracy, but she'd never connected legal principles to her own concept of freedom: the possibility of transformation via the right school, the right products, the open road. She hadn't known that U.S. Customs could detain anyone without offering a reason, and even if she had known, she wouldn't have understood the implications; she'd not been interested in Thailand's stance on civil liberties. At 10:00 PM, the lights of the windowless room she was locked in blinked and dimmed, but they never went dark. She stretched horizontally on one of the benches molded to the floor, rested her head on her crossed arms. One elbow jutted meanly into the fiberglass, and her temple ached where it rested on her wrist. She tried to sleep, but her consciousness jittered around like a bagged goldfish in a terror of wordless loss and stupid confusion.

In the morning, she was at the drinking fountain trying to freshen her mouth when a metallic scrape broke the fluorescent hum. "Robin Miatta?" said a young man in a uniform the green of corroded rust. He held the door open with his shoulders. "Come with me."

All that day and into the next she was taken out of the room periodically. When called, she'd straighten her skirt and press down her hair and put her swollen feet back into her pumps. She was never restrained; a light grip on her elbow guided her through the scuffed, chalky corridors. Once she glimpsed a flash of a penitentiary orange jumpsuit. Once Robert stormed past, leaning hysterically into his cell phone as if he had a bee in his ear: "What do they mean, they don't have a record? They had a record in January!" When she met with him in one of the featureless interrogation rooms that reminded her of the deal carrels at Lowell's Nissans, he was so distracted he barely saw her. When she met with Ray, a secretary poked her head in the door and told him he had a fax from Nairobi. "What about Marseilles?" he asked. "Jesus Christ." Then he disappeared. Robin pointed out Abu through a two-way mirror on three separate occasions, but no one seemed to care about her testimony or ID. She didn't get it. If they couldn't be bothered about a couple rhino horns, a handful of turtles that crossed borders other than their own, what had Robert and Ray been doing in Singapore, anyway? She had no one to ask.

On the third night, two sari-clad mothers and four children smelling of citrus were incarcerated with her. Robin left them the six benches and lay on the floor, so exhausted she slept in the powder of tamped dirt and shoe leather. An escort woke her the next day to take her on her rounds. The room spun when she stood, and her legs nearly buckled. The families were gone, but curry still wafted. She wondered if her father had contacted anyone yet, how long she could legally be kept from a phone or a shower.

This time, two officers she'd never seen waited in the examination room, both with swarthy shadows over their jaws. After a volley of greetings, one of them pressed a button by the two-way mirror to reveal a motley, mixed-gendered line-up: a Caucasian man with long red stubble and a *Tintin Goes to Saigon* T-shirt on; a neatly bearded Arab in a pinstriped dress shirt; a light-skinned black man with a loosened tie and a twisted mouth; and Piv. A battered, tousled Piv. Still wearing the trousers with black blood at their hems. Robin hadn't seen or heard of him since the incident. Heat shot through her veins.

But no, it couldn't be him. The way he sat with his knees pressed together. The way his shoulders sloped toward each other. The dull cast in his eyes. It wasn't him. A raw bloody place inside her rubbed open and throbbed. Where was he? What had she done?

The men allowed her a moment of silence. Then the questions began, a machine-gun spray of American words.

"Recognize anyone?"

"No." The fact that her voice worked, that it came with such ease, surprised her.

"No one? Take your time. Some of these guys were on your flight. Not even a maybe?"

"I'm sorry. No."

"Not even the one on the left? He's the one who made the big mess."

"Oh. Yeah. Well, I recognize him from that. From the other day."

"We saw you looking at him."

"I couldn't help it. Of course I looked." She had looked and rubbed her head, but that hadn't been enough, had only made it worse. She hadn't told him.

"Pretty gross, wasn't it? Pretty pathological. What's his deal? Was he in on it, too?"

"I don't know."

"Does the Kenyan know him?"

"I don't know."

"We're talking about planning and abetting terrorism. You *need* to know. You want to be responsible for that, to stay here and take the heat?"

She paused at the top of her breath. Then exhaled. "Of course not," she murmured. "I've told you already about Abu. Where's he?"

"I doubt it's a coincidence—that guy with the snakes, you tied up with the reptiles, too. Tell us. What's his story? What's the story with this guy and the Kenyan?"

"I'm sorry. I wish I could tell you. I really do. But I don't know."

Piv slid his eyes from his shoes toward the edge of the room he was in, and his eyebrows—those calligraphic gestures—drew toward a point, formed the outline of a steeply pitched roof. Three weary creases cut into his forehead. Then, in apparent response to command, he looked straight at the mirror with hurt, numbed dismay. After some moments, the window went black, but a rotating cast of characters came in the room to knock on her brain, the voices sometimes menacing, sometimes cajoling, sometimes weary. *"Does he . . . ?" "Do you . . . ?" "What about . . . ?"* She said it every time they asked her: *I don't know.*

It was less subterfuge than the agonized wail of a woman scorned: *I don't know why he did it. I don't know why he left me. I don't know if he loved me even a little.* But his beautiful face, wilted and battered. She had done that. They had done that. They said his name again and again: Pivlaierd Sreshthaputra. What did it mean, who did it signify? "When did you meet him?" they asked. "Is he the one who approached you?" He'd never told her how he spelled his last name. The despairing plea of a woman driven mad from being kept at bay: *I don't know*.

"Fucking cunt!" The swarthy examiner who looked Mediterranean slammed his hands on the table and strode out of the room.

"Sorry. We're just frustrated that you aren't able to help us." A few more questions and his partner left, too. She sat alone in front of the darkened five-by-eight window, her own smeared reflection an agonized specter in the black glass.

It was nearly two hours later before they came at her next, this time bearing fries and a hamburger, the smell of American franchise filling the room as the curtain went up on the same lineup—Piv now leaning his head back against the white wall. His eyes were shut. Even through the glass and despite a piercing headache, Robin recognized the ink black line of his fused lashes, the ochre hills of his lids. She'd studied them so often when she thought he was asleep. Sometimes he would smile when he sensed her looking.

"I'm going to ask you again. Please point out Pivlaierd Sreshthaputra."

"You guys already told me. He's there, the one in the suit."

Her fingertips pulsed with the memory of the flick of his eyes beneath his soft skin.

"Okay, so you can identify the subject. Why did he let loose those snakes on Wednesday?"

"I'm sorry, I—do you want me to make something up? There's just no way I could even possibly have any idea."

Her head pounded. She was nauseated and trembling. But a steel beam of fact swung into view: what she really didn't know was anything about the blue hairpiece, anything at all about that, one way or another. The humiliation of having let the pomaded thing dictate her actions made her feel sick. The space between her and Piv had been so magnetic. Night after night, afternoon upon morning, simply glancing hands on the street or in a cab, they'd dizzied themselves from the polar sway, the energy drawn from one to another and back again. What did it matter if he'd never cried with her, if he'd never spoken his last name, if he perhaps rented a room by the occasional hour with someone else? Whatever rules of conduct he had brought to their coupling, she saw now that he had recognized their rare treasure. What would have happened if when he'd asked her to marry him, she'd laughed and given at least a joking okay? But here they were instead, imprisoned, imperiled, separated by the thick glass of betrayal. The assault of her full accountability smashed into her. She quit responding to the men at all, except to grimly shake her head no.

When they roused her at 3:00 AM for another round, her vision was blurred at the periphery, host to floating sunspots. She couldn't feel her limbs, stumbled into the hallway walls. They had stacked all the chairs from the interrogation room, forcing Robin to stand as Robert and one other man and a woman whipped their questions, yelled profanities, leaned over to whisper insinuations. The one thing she heard was: "He must've fucked you good," hissed in a stage whisper. Her stomach went cold at that. She almost cried No! Please let it be no! You don't understand! Her right hip buckled, and she flopped toward the floor, caught herself with a jerk.

Then, "Here's your boyfriend," the woman said. She pressed the switch again, and this time Piv stood alone on display. He was looking straight toward her with cloudy-glass eyes. He was all she could see. Half conscious, head pulsing, he was all that she knew. She knew him. She knew him. She felt sunlight shoot up her spine. They could do what they would with her. They could imprison her, fine her, flog her—she wouldn't care. Even if it meant Abu would hack at rhino horns unimpeded for years. Even if it meant she'd never sit down again, never leave this room. If given twelve million dollars right now, she'd pay it for the strength not to betray him.

"Come on, Robin. Say the word, and we'll let you go home. What's this guy got to do with Abu?"

It was on the tip of her tongue to vow *I'll never tell*.

"Maybe this will jog your memory: fifty-one days at the Star Hotel? We've got the fucking records, girl! Stop lying! We've got the fucking records!"

She stumbled backward to the stacked chairs and buried her face in her arms on the seat of the top one. It smelled of rubbed pennies and graphite, the odor of a stultifying high school classroom in the hick backwater from which she would never be far enough away. "What records?" Robin said to the chair. "I don't know what you're talking about. Why do you keep picking on me? I don't *know*. I don't know I don't know I don't know." The heat of her breath intensified the dirty alloy smell. Condensation beaded on the beige plastic seat.

The next day, eighty-odd hours after they had detained her, they booked her for abetting the transportation of a hazardous substance. Two days later, her mother posted bail, and Robin was released to her to await sentencing.

Chapter 35

You want to know all about that jail? If you do, sure, I'll tell you. I'll tell you at night. During the day, there are many things to do here for the tourist. You can trek to see hill tribes or maybe rent motorbikes and go to see the waterfalls or go to visit Pai—I can get you the trek guide's name, the motorbike rental, directions to all the good places, to the delicious restaurants, no problem. But at night, not so many things to do. In the dark, we're far from Pai, and anyway, there are no movie theaters in that small mountain town. I'm sorry, but no Hollywood movies play there or Thai movies either. There's no discotheque. Not yet. They plan to, but they don't build that yet. I'm sorry. Please stay one more night at this resort anyway. It's my job to make you happy, make sure you don't get bored, don't leave this place for some big city, Chiang Mai or Bangkok. Even Mae Hong Son has the discotheque and bar girls. Pai will, soon, sure, but not tonight. If you want, I can tell you who to talk to about the opium, how to get that adventure. But if that's not comfortable for you, no problem. You can stay inside here, listen to the night sounds through the screens. You can stay here where it's not too hot, not too cold, and I can tell you the very sad, very exciting, very dangerous romantic story about me.

You're farang, like NokRobin, so you probably want to hear that, right? You probably want to hear about the bad things, the sad things in my life. With the army in the jungle. What it's like in that American jail for six months. How it feels to be deported, forbid to enter again the place where you dreamed to go. How shamed I made my parents feel. You probably want to know who I feel angry toward, who do I hate. Sure, you don't care who it is, or what—even if it's your government—you only want me to tell you; you want to know about my sadness, shame, anger. Then you can think you know me better—me, your tourist guide at Pai Mountain Resort. Then you can think you understand me, understand something about Thailand. Then when you go home, you can say: Oh yeah, Thailand. Our tourist guide told us all about that. We were up there where they grow opium, where they still make heroin. Really wild. Oh, but there's some shame, they're chopping down the forest, burning down the jungle. It's environmental mess. And the economy! This young man, he has so little. Sends all his money to his family. No wonder they always try to cheat the tourist. Got to watch out for that over there. You can say, Oh, it's so sad.

So sure, no problem. It would be better if I could put it out of my mind. The past is gone, and forget about that. But for the moment, no, I don't forget, so I can tell you. Maybe NokRobin remains in my mind because I have to be around farangs to make some money for living. Some of them are polite, very nice. Some of them are angry, rude, ugly. Some, nothing. Nothing at all. Pale, puffed with fat and money, blank. And some farang women are cute, pretty, sure. Sometimes they want to make something with me as part of their vacation, and on occasion I do, but for one night only. Only for release. The way their skin looks naked, the way they show themselves like that so easy, the way they smell—it's the same as before: bad and good. Bad and good both. But for romance, for marriage, I want to be with Thai now.

Still, I study you. I study farang to find the answer to things I keep wondering.

Okay, I understand NokRobin loves the animals. We all love something. Animals are something, too. Maybe she helped the fish catch me, because she thought that if she saved the animals, something good would happen to herself. *Tham dii, dai dii; tham chua, dai chua.* Maybe she wanted that more than to help me.

But I'm the person. We slept together, ate together, made something together—the three most important parts of living. She would not marry, but don't you think she love me at least some small amount? More likely thing is this: she didn't want to help the fish to catch us. Maybe they found out something about her, made her tell them. When I remember about it now—she was always so nervous, so upset about something. Sure. Okay. They made her. My heart feels better for one thump when I think this.

But next thump, I wonder again. I wonder again, and it hurts me, because I ask: What did NokRobin think of me, this person she trusted with her body, if she couldn't tell me the truth—even when it wouldn't hurt the animals, wouldn't hurt anybody, would save my pride and dream? When I look at farang, I'm always asking: Do you know? Do you know?

So I tell you about something that makes me feel ashamed. Now do you like me better? Sure. If you're bored tonight, far away from home, and want to listen to someone speak English, but in the Thai style, I can tell you. Listen to me. In some ways you can say this is my job now: you want to know, and I can tell you almost anything.

Chapter 36

Robin stepped out over the threshold, the screen door slapping shut behind her with a quick, sharp *poing*. While she was growing up, the door remained gaping open, shifting lazily with the breeze and letting bugs in if you didn't give it a backward shove, but someone had fixed the spring, and now the slab of metal and mesh was stingy with what it let pass. Robin supposed the coil would loosen in time, though, and in another few years a perfect equilibrium would at last be reached: A door that pushed open easy to the pressure of a human hand, closed slow and gentle, but firm, tongue giving way to groove with an affirmative click. A poignant countryish symbol of lemonade and lazy days. Maybe she'd have paid off her debts and vamoosed from Palatka by then, to start anew somewhere else—this time for real, for good, for something true—but she couldn't be sure. With the fines and the fees and the credit and school, she owed close to sixty thousand dollars. It'd take a while. Maybe she didn't even care how long. She was safe at home, the men who would have indentured her fled or deported. She felt muffled with a soft new patience.

Dear Piv . . . she wrote in her mind. *Dear Piv, I'm so so . . .*

The weather helped. The air this early evening held a perfect balance of warmth and cool she didn't have to wait years for, and it lulled her to peace. No air conditioner needed, but no more than a thin blanket or two at night, either. More like a mountain summer than November in north central Florida. She hugged a zippered sweatshirt around herself and stepped with bare feet into the yard. The tough grass was chilly between her toes, but the dirt retained the afternoon's warmth, although all that was left of daytime was half a thumbprint of sun and a smudge of orange along the west horizon. In the east, the sky's blue deepened to velvet. She could begin by describing it to him. She dragged the lawn chair from under the willow and set it in the middle of the yard so she could sit and watch the shadows blur and widen, the orange wash distill into a crimson thread and then disappear.

Dear Piv . . . She'd started the letter ten thousand times. A line, a half a line, that was as far as she got, and then she'd be quivering before him, ashamed and hopeful, her eyes wide and her mouth open. He'd be watching her impassively, and no sound would come out.

Weather and shifts of light were two of the things she had missed most during ninety days in jail. Weather, light, and quiet—and right now, with her mom still at work and her niece, Tiffany, with her own mother, all she could hear were cicadas and the distant traffic from Route 17 and the muffled cries of the baby two doors down. She had to appreciate this—weather, light, and quiet—a perfect gift for an eve of reflection: she was starting a new job tomorrow. Yes, at a lot, but in Jacksonville, worth the hour commute because the money would be better. Not to mention that she'd had no choice. It had taken her over a month to get a single interview. She had thought that having worked in New Jersey would be a boon to getting employment here, that she'd have her pick of dealerships—but no. Never mind. It didn't matter. She'd been lucky; she'd gotten a job, a legitimate job. She didn't need everyone to want to hire her. As long as one place did, she'd be fine. She was lucky.

Seeing a flash of rainbow in the yard near the driveway, Robin pushed herself up from the chair. At the last minute, Tiffany must have abandoned her mascot xylophone before going off. Robin began bending to pick it up, but then she straightened, cocked her head. A slanted ray of sunlight infused the red and orange bars, just those two, and made them glow. The grass rose almost as high as the thick wooden body of the thing, and she liked how it looked, the bright multi-hued notes framed by the textured green, a few yellow willow leaves stuck among the blades like dashed brushstrokes. She liked how it looked, and instead of picking it up, she lay on the ground beside it, her body cupped around the arrangement, protecting. The hard nub of a mole tunnel bumped at her hip. She felt the rivet from her jeans press into her flesh. Gratitude stole through her, a sweetness. Tomorrow she started a job.

Dear Piv, I'm going to be selling cars again, and if you wouldn't mind seeing me, maybe I could save up to buy a ticket . . .

She rolled on her stomach and spread her arms. The low end of the xylophone grazed her right shoulder. She closed her eyes and extended her lips to kiss its edge, then nuzzled her face toward the ground and inhaled. The dry autumn had left the grass brittle and odorless, but the earth had a wormy, fecund aroma. It smelled so particular and familiar that she could taste the clayey, sandy grit in her mouth, feel it between her teeth as she had when she was a dirt-eating toddler and again as an elementary school know-it-all—she'd returned to her babyish habit defiantly after learning in class that if worms didn't eat soil, oxygen and water and sunshine couldn't get through.

"You're not a worm. You're a little girl," her mom had said when she caught her, and she'd slapped Robin's hands and washed her mouth out with soap.

Robin pictured the worms beneath her, munching and wiggling their way down deep, making growth possible. She turned her head and opened her eyes. As she stared into the grass, minutia became visible even in the thickening gloom: an ant carrying a pink speck of bubble gum though the spiky green jungle, a pale wisp of a spider perched midblade, the gossamer wing of a maimed flyer lying, deserted, next to the mean dot of a flea. In Thailand—in India, China, Singapore, Sumatra—the sun would be perched on the first edge of a day, the same old tired sun she was losing tonight, but yet somehow new. Had he woken yet? Was it warming him?

Dear Piv, I'm so sorry I didn't tell you in time about what was going to happen, but at least I never told them about you. Please believe me. They tried to make me, but they couldn't. I know it was too late to help you, but can you forgive me? Do you still dream of traveling, because maybe I could . . . but where would she send it? She didn't know his address. She didn't even know how to spell his last name.

With her arms spread, she could almost feel the curve of the great, round, blue and green globe she was spinning on. She should get up now. She should get up before her mother came home and worried that her unusual posture meant she was still depressed, or that something more had gone wrong. But she could feel the gravity that kept her holding on, that pressed her flat to the earth as she made her embrace.

Acknowledgments

This book wouldn't exist if not for the help of some kind people and for a string of fortuitous circumstances that stretch back to the beginning of my adult life. For instance, what luck that my first employer out of college, First Publishing, would begin to implode soon after I joined their staff. They eventually bribed the few employees who hadn't quit or been laid off to stay until the bitter end by offering us five thousand dollars if we did, which, even after taxes, was more money than I'd ever seen in one sum. I knew I wanted to take the windfall and travel with it, but I wouldn't have thought of going to Southeast Asia if not for a conversation with Barry Cassilly over dim sum. In Thailand, much of the perspective I gained on Bangkok beyond Khao San Road was thanks to my friend Jillana Enteen, who was working there and who graciously hosted me in her one-room apartment whenever I came through town. *Currency* is not autobiographical, but I did get in scrapes while backpacking, and the worst one occurred after Jillana had returned to the States. I'm not sure what I would have done if Tuk from the Bangkok Center Guest House hadn't come to my aid in the last weeks of my trip. Wherever he is, I cannot thank him enough. Back in Chicago, I eventually entered the University of Illinois Program for Writers, where I started the experiment in voice that became this novel and stumbled on to an article in the *New York Times Magazine*—"The Looting and Smuggling and Fencing and Hoarding of Impossibly Precious, Feathered, and Scaly Wild Things" by Donovan Webster—that introduced me to the world of animal smuggling and helped me find my plot. Also, I met Gina Frangello. She, along with Cecelia Downs, Laura Ruby, and Karen Schreck, read this novel many times and improved it with their comments and suggestions. They coached me through rounds of agents, rejection letters, and near-misses. And years later, Gina asked to read the manuscript again, with an eye toward publishing it. I am very grateful to her, Stacy Bierlein, Dan Wickett, and Steve Gillis for the opportunity. I'm also grateful to Amy Davis and The Writer's Workspace in Chicago for providing me with a quiet place to make the last round of edits. Before that, the Ragdale Foundation and the Norcroft Writing Retreat gave me time and space to write. And I'd like to say thank you to my husband, Mark DeBernardi, who traveled with me when I made a research trip to Thailand, and who has kept the home fires burning when I traveled back in my mind.

MORGAN STREET
INTERNATIONAL
NOVEL SERIES

Inspired by the award-winning anthology, *A Stranger Among Us: Stories of Cross Cultural Collision and Connection*, the Morgan Street International Novel Series celebrates literary novels set outside the United States by writers from any nation. These works explore issues of race, identity, and political affairs through the lens of human relationships. Characterized by vibrant, compulsively readable storytelling, the Morgan Street International Novel Series will appeal to global citizens and armchair travelers as well as students of international literature and cultural studies. For more information about the series and other forthcoming titles from Other Voices Books, please visit www.ovbooks.com.